V. ASTAFIEV

The Horse With the Pink Mane

D1260000

VICTOR ASTAFIEV
The Horse
With the Pink Mane

ВИКТОР АСТАФЬЕВ
Конь
с розовой гривой

Progress Publishers

Moscow

Translated from the Russian
Illustrated by Boris Markevich

A $\dfrac{70302-314}{014(01)-78}$ 137-78

CONTENTS

6   Sergei Mitrofanovich *Translated by Robert Daglish*

38   The Hands of a Wife *Translated by Robert Daglish*

56   A Troubled Dream *Translated by Robert Daglish*

78   The Siberian *Translated by Robert Daglish*

100   A Siberian Polonaise *Translated by Robert Daglish*

118   The Horse with the Pink Mane *Translated by Robert Daglish*

136   Granny's Day *Translated by Robert Daglish*

168   Autumn Sorrows and Joys *Translated by Robert Daglish*

184   On a Far Northern Peak *Translated by Robert Daglish*

195   Capercaillie *Translated by Robert Daglish*

198   Shepherd and Shepherdess.
       A Modern Pastoral
       Translated by Natasha Johnstone and Hilda Perham

326   Afterword

SERGEI MITROFANOVICH

To the memory of the
Great Russian singer,
Alexander Pirogov

The leaves were falling in town as well. Green leaves from the poplars, yellow from the lindens. The light linden leaves were swirling about the streets and pavements, but those of the poplars lay in still circles at the foot of the trees where they had fallen.

As he made his way down the street Sergei Mitrofanovich began to feel conscious of the noise his wooden leg was making in the sound-filled and yet, at the same time, hushed city. He walked slowly, trying to put the leg down on the leaves, but the tapping persisted as loud as ever.

Every autumn he was summoned from the little logging settlement where he lived to appear before a panel of medical experts, and every year the feeling of resentment ate a little deeper into his soul. This year it had reached such a point that Sergei Mitrofanovich, who had been putting up with all these quite unnecessary medical examinations since 1944, had finally asked:

"Hasn't it grown again yet? "

The doctor raised his head and gave him a displeased look.
"What did you say? "

Goaded on in a way he had never been before by this accumulated bitterness, Sergei Mitrofanovich repeated, louder:

"Hasn't the leg grown again yet, I said."

The nurse, who had been filling in cards at the next desk, looked round and fixed a suspicious eye on Sergei Mitrofanovich, impressing on him by her whole appearance that this was a place where people kept quiet, and that if he, a war-disabled out-patient, had taken it into his head to get violent because he had been drinking or for any other reason, she was going to pick up the telephone and dial 02. The militia was in no mood for half-measures these days. "They'll soon put you in your place, my man. So you'd better behave yourself," she seemed to say. But noticing that the disabled veteran had lowered his head at once and did not know where to look or what to do with his shaking hands, the nurse cast a victorious glance round the barn-like consulting room.

"You can get dressed," said the doctor. He removed his

glasses and started polishing the lenses with the hem of his gown.

Sergei Mitrofanovich's clothes and wooden leg lay in a heap in one corner of the room. As he hopped away between the desks, like a soldier running the gauntlet, the empty leg of his underpants lashed the chair legs and the strip of carpet between them. His body felt unbalanced without its usual counterweight and he was afraid of lurching over on to one of the desks, upsetting someone's inkwell and spoiling someone's white coat or polished desk-top.

He reached the corner safely, however, flopped down on to a chair and looked round the room. The members of the panel were busy with their own affairs. They were a hard-boiled lot, he realised. No one had watched his precarious progress between the desks. The doctor who had been last to examine him was scribbling something on a form.

Sergei Mitrofanovich dressed, strapped on his wooden leg and returned to the desk. The doctor was still writing. He stopped for a second, nodded to a chair and actually moved it towards the disabled man with his foot. But Sergei Mitrofanovich did not feel like sitting down. He waited patiently. What he would have liked most would have been to go out and have a smoke.

He stood thinking that as the years went by he was seeing fewer and fewer familiar faces among the men who appeared before the panel. They were dying off but the system was still as rigid as ever. He himself hadn't so long to go now, and how many days had he wasted on such examinations, on applying for various forms and certificates, waiting in queues....

The doctor put a full-stop, blotted what he had written with a sheet of children's light-blue blotting paper, and raised his eyes.

"Why don't you sit down?" he said, and added in a confidential, apologetic tone: "All this form-filling, you know."

Sergei Mitrofanovich took the certificate, folded it in four and put it away in his wallet, awkwardly holding under his arm the new cap he had bought specially for his visit to town. Having disposed of the certificate, he put the cap on, but at once pulled it off again, hurriedly, and made a respectful little bow.

The doctor gave him a gap-toothed smile in return and spread his arms, as much as to say, "What can I do about it? It's the regulations! "

Sergei Mitrofanovich smiled back with forced sympathy, sighed, and walked out of the room, thankful that it was all over till next autumn.

Next autumn always seemed a long way off.

In the street he decided to have a smoke. He pulled out a cigarette, lighted it and started reproaching himself: "Once you had spoken up, you should have gone through with it. Regulations! If you, and someone else, and someone else besides, would only get together and put in a word in the right quarter, they'd soon change them regulations. They're not carved on tablets of stone, are they? And anyway, people can move mountains nowadays."

On the way to the station he called at a shop and bought three peaches in a plastic bag, then went into a help-yourself cafe, collected two portions of sausages and a glass of fruit custard from the counter, and sat down at a table that had no cloth on it but was perfectly smooth and clean and was covered with a pattern of thin light stripes.

At the same table sat a girl with long, straggly hair, who was also eating sausages and at the same time reading a thick book that seemed to be full of ruled lines, triangles and signs, and letters that were not from the Russian alphabet. She did not stop reading even while she was smearing mustard on her sausages, cutting them up with her knife and fork and washing them down with sips of tea from a glass, all of which she did without knocking over anything on the table. "She must be cute! " Sergei Mitrofanovich thought. There were small striped lanterns hanging from the ceiling. The walls were light-blue and they, too, were covered in stripes going this way and that, and the flimsy curtains were also striped. The whole café was wrapped in a kind of light-blue twilight. A breeze stirred the curtains, stirring the smell of cooking with them.

What a pretty little place!

"Enjoy your lunch, lass," he said as he rose to leave.

She tore herself away from her book and stared at him distractedly.

"Oh.... Thanks! I mean.... Thanks! " And as an after-thought: "Good luck to you! " and again she dug her nose into the book, scraping at the now empty plate with her fork.

The café door was narrow and made entirely of glass. Two young fellows in identical, unseasonably light jackets opened it and made way for Sergei Mitrofanovich. But this only flus-tered him and in his haste he forgot to say thank you.

Out in the street the linden leaves were still whirling about. Cars glided past uncommunicatively. Trolleybuses with their windows still open as in summer went bobbing gently by. Children were going home from school, their uniforms still autumn fresh.

Sergei Mitrofanovich stumped wearily into the booking hall of the station, bought a ticket and settled down on a massive bench to wait for his train.

A crowd of boys and girls poured out of a suburban train that had just come in. They were all wearing trousers, and their jackets, of some foreign make, were all alike, and what with their hair being cut short, it was not so easy to tell the boys from the girls. Some of them had perhaps a dozen mushrooms in their baskets, others even less. But they were all carrying armfuls of rowan branches and they all had dark, bird-cherry stains round their mouths. They made straight for the ice-cream stall.

Should he buy an ice-cream, too? Or, maybe, have a drink? But Sergei Mitrofanovich was afraid of ice-cream because of the sore-throats he was always getting.

"That's the war, that is, still taking it out of you," his wife would say. As always, at the thought of his wife, he felt his heart soften a little and, having made sure that no one was looking, groped in his jacket pocket. Panya always loved a present, whatever it was. And this time it was peaches! She had never tried them in her life. "Aren't they wonderful! " she would say. "They must have come from over the sea? ! " Then she would put them away, and, later, make him eat them.

The station was becoming more crowded. A group of shaven-headed recruits led by an elderly army captain, with an escort of girls, marched in and occupied the free benches. There was not enough room for all of them and Sergei Mitrofanovich moved to the end of his bench to make more space.

Three of the lads dumped their things on the bench — a thin little ruck-sack, a laced-up sports bag and a bag with straps, rather like a German field-bag but not so handy and all plastered with bright little pictures.

Of the three who had settled themselves beside Sergei Mitrofanovich one looked as if he were carved out of cedar-wood and was wearing a woollen track-suit. The second was as round and bright as the yolk of an egg separated from the white; he kept tossing his head and reaching up as though he missed his forelock. The third was not very tall and had a big head; he seemed to be one of the quiet sort. He was wearing a grey windbreaker, to which there clung a curly-headed girl in a thin pink blouse and a short skirt with a split at the side.

The first young man, so it turned out later, was called Volodya. He had a guitar and seemed to be cock of the walk among the lads. There was a girl with him, too, a well-fed lass, in light-blue slacks and a thick sweater that came half way down her thighs. It had a wide neck, like a horse-collar, and her hair hung down on to this collar in smooth bleached tresses. Everyone called the second boy, the ginger one, Yeska, though he insisted that his name was Yevsei. He had four girls with him, all to himself. One of them, judging by her colouring, was his sister, and the rest must have been her girlfriends. Yeska's sister was referred to as "transistor", probably because she chattered so much. Sergei Mitrofanovich had no difficulty in discovering the third boy's name, for the curly-headed girl in the pink blouse kept repeating all the time, with or without cause, "Slavik! ... Slavik! "

Among these lads, all apparently from the same block of flats or, perhaps, from the same college, there was one young fellow who seemed to have drifted into their company by chance. He was wearing a checked cap and a collarless shirt fastened at the neck by a single brass stud, and he also had a raspberry-coloured scarf, one end of which dangled down his back. His face was shifty, his eyes sharp and intelligent, and Sergei Mitrofanovich spotted him at once as one of those artful dodgers without which, for some reason, no group of Russians is ever complete.

The captain, having marched his squad to the station, kept himself to himself on one of the far benches, from which he could see everything and himself remain unnoticed.

Not many parents had come to the station and they hung about in corners in a lost fashion, quietly wiping away their tears. The lads were not very drunk but made a lot of noise and showed off their independence.

"Just been called up? " Sergei Mitrofanovich asked, to make sure.

"That's us! Raw recruits! " Yeska-Yevsei replied for all present, and waved to his friend with the guitar: "Volodya, come on — let's have a song! "

Volodya struck all the strings at once and both boys and girls roared out:

> The Black Cat's a clumsy lout!
> And life's just one big roundabout!
> But Blackie's luck is always out! ...

And voices picked up the tune raggedly all over the hall:

> But Blackie's luck is always out! ...

Sergei Mitrofanovich shook his head. "Young devils! " he thought.

Only Slavik and his girl did not sing. Slavik grinned sheepishly and the girl snuggled up to him under his windbreaker.

The parents — rather ironically, to be sure — joined in the song about the black cat, and no one sobbed out that plaintive farewell song *The Last Short Day Is Nigh.* There were no accordions. The women did not wail, as they had used to before the war, nor did the recruits rend their shirts and threaten to smash any enemy to smithereens.

From the "Cat" the youngsters went on to an altogether stupid sort of ditty. Volodya strummed away zealously on the guitar and the boys and girls hopped from one foot to the other.

Chick-chick, cha-cha-cha!
Chick-chick, cha-cha-cha!

The words didn't mean a thing and there seemed to be no music either, but everyone enjoyed it. They laughed and shouted and jerked about, and even Volodya's girl tapped one shoe against the other and, when that flashing, glassy hair of hers dropped like a screen over her eyes, she would toss it back impatiently over her shoulder.

The captain had spread a newspaper on his lap and was eating tomatoes and bread, making no attempt to intervene. He raised no objection either when the lads produced some vodka and started drinking straight from the bottle. The first to try it, of course, was the fellow in the checked cap. He was the only one who knew how to drink from a bottle; the others mostly played the fool, making terrible faces and merely shaking up the contents. Yeska-Yevsei took a swig and at once made a dash for the station's capacious rubbish bin, and tears ran from Slavik's eyes at his first gulp. This made him angry and he shoved the bottle into his girl-friend's hands.

"Here! " (The girl gazed at him with puppy-like devotion, unable to understand what was expected of her). "Here! " Slavik pressed the bottle on her with blind persistence.

"Oh, Slavik! ... You know I can't drink without a glass," she stammered.

"The lady requires a glass! " Yeska-Yevsei reappeared, wiping the tears from his face, which had suddenly turned rather grey. "Come on, there! " he shouted an order to the lad in the checked cap.

The latter darted obediently over to Yeska-Yevsei's shoulder-bag, fished out a white plastic carton with a picture of a rosy-cheeked woman on the lid. Surely, that face on the label for Viola cheese looked like someone, or someone looked like her, Sergei Mitrofanovich thought, glancing round, and almost at once his eyes lighted on Volodya's girl—she was the one!

"Eat the cheese! " Yeska-Yevsei commanded, "and give the container to the lady! Since she simply cannot...."

Since she simply cannot drink without a glass! the others chanted. It seemed they didn't mind what they sang or how they sang it.

Volodya strummed away on the guitar but with rather forced enjoyment, and, though he pretended to ignore his girl-friend, his eyes roved in search of her, putting on an expression of blank indifference as soon as they met hers.

"Very tasty! " the outsider in the checked cap bawled, sucking cheese off his finger, and added a dirty word.

"Hi, you! " Slavik turned on him sharply.

"Slavik! Slavik! " the girl beat on his chest with her fists, and he turned away, noticing that the captain was looking in their direction with a frown.

Meanwhile the carton was being passed round.

Volodya drank half the contents and bit a piece off a chocolate that Yeska's fiery-red sister had slipped into his hand. Then he held out the carton under his girl-friend's nose.

"You know I can't drink vodka," she said, frowning disdainfully.

Volodya stood holding the carton at arm's length. His cheekbones were hardening and his straight black brows were contracting over the bridge of his nose.

"Seriously, Volodya, darling.... Word of honour! "

But he wouldn't budge and the girl took the carton between two musical fingers.

"Really, you are.... It'll make me ill."

Volodya supplied no reaction whatever to these words. The girl poured the vodka angrily into her painted mouth. The other girls clapped. Volodya pushed the rest of the chocolate into her open mouth, roughly, like a gag, and strummed ferociously on his guitar.

"Looks as if your affairs are in a bad way, my lad," Sergei Mitrofanovich was thinking, when someone tugged at his sleeve. It was Slavik's girl. She was offering him the carton.

"Please, drink to our boys.... And ... and for everything! " She buried her face in her hands and fell, stem-broken, on her Slavik's chest.

He took her under his windbreaker and, forgetting himself, began to soothe and rock her.

"Ah, you little wag-tail! " Sergei Mitrofanovich murmured to himself. He rose from the bench, pulled off his cap and dropped it on the seat.

Volodya muffled the strings of the guitar. Yeska-Yevsei, looking quite squiffy by now, put his arms round his sister and all her girl-friends in one huge embrace. He was the kind who made friends with everyone, but not close friends. The time would come when some iron-fisted woman would get hold of Yeska-Yevsei and run him for the rest of his life, fully believing that she had saved him from waywardness and destruction.

"Well, young people..." Sergei Mitrofanovich began, and cleared his throat. "Well, now.... Here's to the kiddies not being afraid of thunder! How's that? " And with an effort he drank the vodka from the carton, in which white rags of cheese were still floating. He even affected a grunt of pleasure, evoking great enthusiasm on the part of that artful one in the cap.

"That's the stuff! That's a soldier for you! " he exclaimed, and in a confidential, man-to-man way nodded at the wooden leg: "Where did they chop your leg off? "

"At the war, boys, at the war," Sergei Mitrofanovich replied.

He preferred not to talk about how and where his leg had been blown off, and so he was glad to hear a voice on the loudspeaker announcing that his train was in. The subject of his leg was dropped automatically.

The captain rose from his distant bench and ordered his party to follow him.

"Come on, Dad, you string along with us! " Yeska-Yevsei shouted. "We're going to have fun! " he added, clowning and putting on a country accent. "It'll be fathers and sons! As contemporary literature asserts, no conflict exists between the two...."

"Educated young brats!" Sergei Mitrofanovich reflected. "Plenty of patter! Our old Ukrainian sergeant-major couldn't have handled 'em. They'd have had him in fits with their humour alone...."

> *Dearly recall,*
> *Await him through all,*
> *The soldier who's gone to war...*

They were singing properly now, without any clowning, these boys and girls that he was limping after. They all had their arms round one another, except Volodya's girl, who walked along by herself, swinging the laced sports bag, and Sergei Mitrofanovich sensed that if only decency would allow it, she would gladly have left out this last stage of the leave-taking and said her good-byes as soon as possible.

Volodya punched away at his guitar and didn't give her a single glance.

Sergei Mitrofanovich spotted a kiosk on the platform and stumped towards it on his wooden leg.

"Where are you off to?" Yeska-Yevsei called after him, and his new acquaintances stopped.

Sergei Mitrofanovich made signs that he would be coming in a moment.

At the kiosk he bought two bottles of foreign Vermouth. There was no other wine except Champagne and he refused to spend money on that stuff.

He climbed up into the carriage. What with the smoke, the hubbub and the laughter, he was a little taken aback, but the sight of the captain had a reassuring effect. He was seated near the carriage samovar, thumbing through a newspaper, again with a full view of the carriage.

"Army friendships last well," shaven-headed young men were barking at each other in the corridor, as they clinked glasses.

"Yes, but a bit too long sometimes!"

"What, kissing again! Too short the night, eh?"

And they struck up that poignant old favourite:

> *Too short the night,*
> *The clouds are sleeping...*

"You don't know what army life's like yet, boys!" Sergei

Mitrofanovich thought to himself with a chuckle. "You don't know anything yet. Wait till you get there! The captain's just giving you a bit of leeway to start with. But he'll put the screws on out there! Tighten them up properly, he will! "

The old front-line song had stirred up memories and he was in a hurry to join his young acquaintances, so as not to get depressed.

"Volodya! Yeska! Slavik! Where are you? " Sergei Mitrofanovich paused and listened as if he were in a forest.

"We're here! " came a voice from behind a seat partition half way along the carriage.

Sergei Mitrofanovich squeezed his way along the tightly packed corridor. "So, here you are."

"Yes, we're here," Volodya responded. His mood had worsened and he was no longer hiding the fact from anyone.

"Well, young soldiers! This is from me, to send you off with! " Sergei Mitrofanovich plonked the bottles down on the compartment table.

"Why did you spend so much money? " they all protested at once, except for that one outsider, who had, of course, already captured the window seat for himself, topped himself up with a few more drinks and now had his cap right over his eyes and his scarf on the peg over his head, asserting that this place was his and his alone.

"That's the idea! " he approved Sergei Mitrofanovich's action, and grabbed a bottle. "Now we'll open her up! "

"Who's got the corkscrew? " Yeska's sister cried above the din.

"What do you need a corkscrew for? You're living in the past! " The artful fellow winked at her and, like a squirrel stripping a nut, ripped off the gold paper with his teeth and pushed the cork into the bottle with his finger.

Well pleased with himself, he surveyed the company and again winked at Yeska's sister. He was making up to that girl, but she was keeping away from him and not troubling much to hide her distaste. And when at last he did manage to get an arm round her, she snubbed him with a sharp:

"Keep your dirty paws off me! "

He took his arm away but seemed to attach no importance to what she had said. As though by accident he would touch her knee, or even higher, and soon she moved away from him to another seat.

The loudspeaker on the platform announced: "Train No. 54 will depart in five minutes. Passengers are requested...."

Sergei Mitrofanovich and the lad in the cap were pushed aside by boys and girls as they jumped up. Yeska-Yevsei hugged his sister and her girl-friends. They were crying and laughing at the same time. So was Yeska. The girl in the pink blouse clung on to Slavik like grim death and looked as if she would never let go. Big, babyish tears rolled down her already tear-stained face and left grey marks on her blouse. Her eyes were made up in Japanese style and all the colour was running.

"Don't howl, kid! " Slavik mumbled, and shook her by the shoulders to bring her to her senses. "You promised you wouldn't cry...."

"Boo-hoo.... All right, I won't.... Boo-hoo...."

"That's the stuff! " the lad in the cap exclaimed with a hoot of laughter. He was now isolated from the rest of the company. "Aha, what's she been up to ... getting wet, ain't she? "

But Sergei Mitrofanovich was not listening to him. He was watching Volodya and his girl, and he felt sorry for Volodya.

"Well, do your service, Volodya. Guard the Motherland...." She pecked Volodya's cheek with her painted lips and stood there, not knowing what else to do. She kept tossing her bleached hair back fretfully.

With his arm resting on the upper bunk, Volodya stared morosely out of the window and said nothing.

"Write me a letter if you feel like it, Volodya," she said, and turned to the crowded corridor. "What a noise! ... And they all reek of hooch! "

"Enough! " Volodya snapped. He turned her round and steered her out of the carriage, shouting over his shoulder: "Enough! Come on, chaps! "

The boys and their girls moved towards the exit, all except Slavik's girl. She suddenly sat down on one on the seats.

"I won't go! "

"What's this? Why? " Slavik swooped on her like a hawk. "Disgrace me, would you? "

"All right, I will...."

"Got a bun in the oven, she has! That's for sure! You'll have a little soldier-boy waiting for you when you come back, Slavik! " the artful dodger commented, wriggling in his seat. "Or a little soldier-girl! "

Sergei Mitrofanovich put his hand on the girl's drooping shoulder. "Go along, dear, go along. Say good-bye properly. Or else you'll cry all those precious minutes away, and then regret it afterwards."

Slavik glanced gratefully at Sergei Mitrofanovich, and piloted the girl out of the carriage, holding her as if she were sick.

"It's always the same. At all times, always the same," Sergei Mitrofanovich thought sadly, chin in hand. "Partings and tears, partings and tears...."

"What about a drink while the cats are gone? " the lad in the cap suggested. He was depressed by his isolation, and rubbed his hands as if he felt chilly.

"When we drink, we'll all drink together."

The train started. Slavik charged in, scrambled on to the little table and forced his big head between the narrow sliding panes of the window.

The train was getting up speed and, just as in times past, the girls and women and mothers were running after it, and the fathers and grandfathers were waving on the platform; but the train moved faster and faster. Yeska's sister hurried after it with her red hair flying and shouted something as she ran. Volodya's young lady took a few steps beside the carriage and halted, waving her hand smoothly, like a swan's wing.

Slavik's girl kept up the chase longer than anyone. Her tight short skirt hampered her and she staggered as she tried to catch Slavik's outstretched hand.

"You'll fall! You'll fall, I tell you! " Slavik shouted from the window.

The train rumbled over the points, swung round a curve and the girl flew out of sight, like a pink-breasted bird.

Slavik hung out of the window like a sack, his arms dangling outside and his head thumping against the thick wooden frame.

The boys sat in their seats, subdued and quite different from what they had been on the platform. None of them spoke. Even the lad in the cap had fallen silent and stopped wriggling.

The steward appeared and started sweeping up and grumbling. Tobacco smoke floated out of the windows. The carriage wheels counted the ribs of the bridge as the train crossed the river. The wooden houses of the suburbs stretched along the line, gradually melting away among the woods and groves. The train ran on without jerks or whistles, at the same steady speed, as though it were flying low over the earth, its business-like clickerty-clack putting its passengers in the mood for a long journey.

"Slavik! Slavik! " Yeska-Yevsei remonstrated, tugging at his friend's trousers. "Are you going to stay like that till we get there? "

Slavik manoeuvred himself back through the window, squeezed into a corner and pulled his windbreaker over his head.

Sergei Mitrofanovich bestirred himself, picked up one of the bottles and, looking round for the empty cheese carton, said:

"Why are you all so down in the mouth? You're not going to your deaths, are you? To war? Come on, let's have a drink. We'll talk and have a song, maybe. I don't know your 'Black Cat', but I'll sing you my favourite."

"Well, why not? " Yeska-Yevsei also made a move and pulled the windbreaker off Slavik's ear. "Here, you, what about it? Volodya! Boys! Someone's made us an offer. And he's an old chap, you know...."

Sergei Mitrofanovich looked at Slavik and gave a sigh. "Never mind, boy. It'll all pass. It's not the troubles behind you that matter, it's the ones ahead."

"Let him be for a while," he said to Yeska-Yevsei and, having found the now cracked and crumpled cheese carton, added, louder: "May you have a good sergeant-major."

"Wait a minute! " It was Volodya, who had just come out of his trance. "We've got mugs and spoons, things to eat— we've got everything. We were just showing off at the station." He gave a dry, sober little laugh. "Let's do the thing properly."

Now they drank and talked in a normal, human fashion. The experience of parting had made them more straight-forward and accessible.

"I want some, too! " Slavik shouted. Spilling the wine and choking, he gulped it back, threw the carton aside angrily and again pulled the windbreaker over his ear.

The lads again started asking about the missing leg. Appreciating their friendliness, Sergei Mitrofanovich began to recount how his battery had faced a sudden tank attack in a forest, before they had had time to prepare for action. The forest was tall, Carpathian pine, and the trees in the firing area had to be felled during the battle. Two gun-crews were detailed to do the felling, while the other two swung the howitzers into position. The observation post on the edge of the forest kept hurrying them on, but the pines were thick and there were only two saws and four axes altogether. They worked stripped to the waist, sweating despite the cold, while a stream of threats and curses came over the line from the observation post.

The curses ended in a howl: "Tanks very close! They'll crush us! Open fire! "

It was impossible to open fire without felling another five or so of the pines in front of the guns. But in war the impossible often had to be made possible.

They opened rapid fire.

A shell from the gun commanded by Sergei Mitrofanovich hit a tree, the gun-crew perished under the short-tailed howitzer, which had been overturned by the explosion, and their commander, who had been standing a little further back, was flung into the air.

He woke up in hospital with one leg missing, stone deaf and speechless.

"And that was the end of the war for me, lads."

"Well, what do you know! And we thought—" Yeska-Yevsei began.

Slavik poked his nose out from under the windbreaker and stared at Sergei Mitrofanovich. His tear-swollen eyes had sunk deep into their sockets and his head seemed even bigger than before.

"You thought I lost it blocking an enemy firing slit, eh? "

"What about your wife? Did she take it all right? " Volodya asked. "After you were wounded, I mean."

"Of course, she did. Came to the hospital to fetch me. All in proper style." Sergei Mitrofanovich glanced keenly at Volodya.

It had never occurred to him then or since that Panya might have rejected him. And in hospital he had not heard of anything of the kind either. Even the "samovars"—the men who had lost both arms and legs—had never talked in that vein. Maybe they had kept their thoughts to themselves?

"A woman, our Russian woman, can't leave a disabled husband in the lurch. She may leave a healthy one, she can have a fling while her husband's away, but she can't leave a cripple or an orphan! Never! Our women have their hearts in the right place, and always will have! And you, young men, you mustn't think badly of them. That one of yours," he turned to Slavik, "she'd go through hellfire for you."

"Let me kiss you! " Slavik wept drunkenly and squeezed in beside Sergei Mitrofanovich, who felt an impulse to stroke the boy's head but didn't dare.

"Well, lads," he mumbled huskily. "What about a song? What do you say, chief? " he asked, addressing Volodya. "There aren't any babies in the carriage, are there? "

"No, we've got nearly all the carriage to ourselves," the recruits clamoured. "Come on, Dad, let's hear you! "

By the lads' voices and smiles Sergei Mitrofanovich guessed that they thought he was very drunk and were expecting him to come out with some real corn like "Oh, rowan-tree, my lovely rowan-tree," or "A machine-gunner I was born and a machine-gunner I shall die! "

He glanced at them out of the corner of his eye and smiled faintly to himself, then began to sing softly in a deep, sonorous voice that he hadn't lost as song-leader for his company in the reserve regiment, despite the frosts:

> *When fair is the day,*
> *Or gloomy the night...*

The grins vanished at once. Confusion and a new attentiveness appeared on the lads' faces. Just as intimately, as though absorbed in some discourse, Sergei Mitrofanovich went on:

> *Always of you*
> *Are my thoughts*
> *And my dreams...*

At this point he half-closed his eyes and, instead of throwing his head back, sat with his hands folded over his knees, leaning slightly forward and swaying with the movement of the train, and then, very softly, on some inward note, checking the cry that was about to burst from his breast, he concluded the opening bars:

> *Who will caress you?*
> *Comfort and love you?*
> *Call you his darling, his own? ...*

From his voice, untainted either by drunken peasant sava gery or drilled sophistication, one could tell his character, the gentleness and cordiality of his nature. He revealed his whole self because there was no dross in him, no darkness, no hidden corners. Listening to Sergei Mitrofanovich, a man was no longer alone, he felt the need for brotherhood, he wanted people to love him, and to love them in return.

The man sitting before the lads was no longer a cripple with a wooden leg, dressed in an old-fashioned jacket and blue high-necked shirt. The baldness, the greying temples, the wrinkles that were so out of keeping with his youthful face, his scarred and blackened hands had faded into the background.

Before them was a young, gallant gun commander with a row of medals on his chest.

And he himself, as soon as he began to sing that song, which he had heard once on a record and now sang in his own way and with many of his own words, also saw himself back in the family of his gun-crew, young, healthy, with a thick forelock, respected not only for his singing and his easy-going nature.

The lads who had listened to Sergei Mitrofanovich in such surprise were also thinking to themselves that with his voice and skill he could have been singing somewhere else. But no one throws their talents away as readily as the Russians. How many of our Russian nightingales have bawled their voices to shreds on a coachman's seat, with the army on the march, in drunken orgies, or in the solitude of the taiga? How many voices have been lost in our Russian wilderness? Who knows?

...Clickerty-clack went the wheels. Sergei Mitrofanovich had finished his song and was still sitting in the same position, with his wooden leg stretched out under the table, and his hands, so unlike his voice with their nicks and scars, still resting between his knees. His face now was a little paler, the stubble was showing under his lower lip and his eyes were far away.

"That was something," Yeska-Yevsei murmured, and shook his head as if to throw back an unruly lock of hair. Red-heads are usually curly.

Noticing that artful fellow in the cap was about to chip into the conversation and knowing in advance what he would say ("We used to have a bloke in camp who could do a marvellous croon about love and parting"), Sergei Mitrofanovich looked out of the window and slapped his knees.

"Well, boys, I'm getting near my stop." He smiled shyly. "The songs and the talk made the journey pass quicker. Let's say good-bye." As he rose to go, he felt something weighing down his pocket. "Why, I've got another bottle here! Can't you use it? I don't want any more."

"We don't need it. We've got plenty," Slavik said, staying his hand. "We've got money and drink. Take it home with you."

"Well, it's up to you. All I wanted...."

"No, thanks," Volodya supported Slavik. "Remember us to your wife. She must be the right kind of woman."

"You don't need to tell me that," Sergei Mitrofanovich replied simply and, to put the lads at ease, added: "We've got a chap who works in the steaming shed and he's always bragging, 'What a man I am! Here I am, living with my fifth wife, and never gave one of them cause to complain'."

The lads laughed and followed Sergei Mitrofanovich down the corridor. At the door they lighted up and smoked. The brakes went on with a screech and the train stopped at a small station with tall misty firs towering all round it. There were even fir-trees growing in the station square. An old piebald horse, tethered by a long rope, was grazing near one of them.

Sergei Mitrofanovich lowered himself carefully from the carriage step and steadied himself on the greasy trampled ground, through which the rock showed in places. The train, as though this was the moment it had been waiting for, moved off almost at once. Sergei Mitrofanovich raised his cap.

"May you serve in peace, lads! "

They were grouped closely behind the steward, watching him. The train picked up speed and the locomotive thudded away into the dense firs beyond the station. Then the carriages, too, drummed over the points and soon only the current collector was visible above the trees, striking blue sparks from the damp overhead wires. When the last carriage had disappeared and all was quiet, Sergei Mitrofanovich repeated:

"May you serve in peace, lads! "

That was how those young servicemen would remember him—standing on his wooden leg, his bare head streaked with grey, his long jacket weighed down by the bottle in one pocket, and behind him, a little station called Fir Halt.

Nothing went past that might give him a lift and Sergei Mitrofanovich had to limp the whole four familiar but long kilometres by himself.

Fir Halt dropped away behind him, and the firs too. They formed a wall round the station and beyond them were clearings and wasteland, where even the snow fences were made of lopped firs and the ground under them was dark and damp.

In the autumn of 1945 the new timber had just been springing up on the clearings and everywhere there were marshy clearings dotted with red cranberries and cowberries. Here and there stood hay ricks of various sizes with sagging backs, like aged horses.

It had been a better autumn than this. The sky had been wider, the distant horizons had been gleaming in sunshine and a shimmering envelope of what seemed like a spring mist covered the earth.

Or perhaps everything had seemed smarter and brighter because he was on his way home from hospital, from the war. Every blade of grass, every bush, every bird, every beetle and ant had been a joy to him. After lying in bed for a year, deprived of memory, hearing and the power of speech, he could not see too much of the world that had just revealed itself to him again. His hearing was still bad, he could not recognise some things, and his speech was halting. If Panya had not been warned about it by the doctors, she would have thought he was mad.

He would catch sight of the creeping thistles on the fringe of a wood, then notice the hawkweed, the goat's beard, the nipplewort and the stick-tights and would be upset because he could not remember their names. They all had yellowish flowers and apparently his memory, as it then was, could not distinguish between them.

"Dandelion! Dandelion! " he suddenly shouted delightedly, and plunged into the thickets on his crutches. He got tangled and fell over and, lying on his belly, picked the scraggy flower and started smelling it.

"So you know a fall dandelion when you see one, do you?" Panya confirmed as she cleared the cobwebs off his face. He could not feel cobwebs yet and was still oblivious of smell.

He stopped beside a rowan-tree and stood staring at it, trying to make out what had happened to it. The stems were there, but no berries.

"The birds have pecked them out," Panya explained.

"Ah, the birds! " he said, beaming happily. "The wid— woodcocks? "

"The woodcocks and the thrushes. All birds like berries. You know that! "

"Ye-yes."

"You don't know anything any more! " Panya murmured
sadly to herself, remembering her last talk with the head
doctor. He had explained patiently and at great length how
to look after the sick man, what he could eat and drink and
how he should rest, and all the time he had looked at Panya
as though he were weighing her up. He had inquired casually
about their children. And she had replied in confusion that
they had not had time to do anything about children before
the war. "But why worry? We're still young...." "What a
pity! " the doctor had said, avoiding her glance, and after
that they had somehow not been able to say much more to
each other.

Only on the road from the station to the settlement had
she grasped the full import of his words, their cruel truth.

But Sergei gave her no time for grief and reflection. When
they came to a stream he attacked the bird-cherry, grabbing
it in handfuls.

"It's sw-sweet! "

"It's been standing a long time. Of course, it's sweet! "

He had stared at her fixedly. Only a little while ago, not
more than three months, had he begun to taste sweetness. Up
to then he had not been able to distinguish it from sourness
or bitterness. Panya had no idea what that meant. He began
to look ill and Panya realised that his shell-shocked brain was
tired, and began to urge him on. Once more, but without
much persistence he pointed out to her the wild hops twined
round the bird-cherry.

"It was a hot summer," she explained wearily.

"That's why there are no cones. They're all stem and leaf
this year. Hops need moisture."

He hung limply on his crutches and she regretted that she
had let him have his way and not ordered a cart. They frequently sat down to rest by the haystacks. He would take the
hay in his hands, squeeze it and smell it, and new life would
appear in his eyes. Apparently he could catch the smell of
hay.

The math was fresh and green on the mown patches. The
rattle-boxes displayed their faded blossoms and here and
there a pale-pink knob of late clover was to be seen. The sky,

bleached at the edges, was still and clear. Its ghostly stillness promised frosts.

As they drew near the settlement Segrei stopped asking questions and heaved himself along desperately, though he often had to stop.

The settlement with its fringe of bare vegetable patches looked naked and forlorn amid the grandeur of the forest. The houses had blackened with age and there were not many left. The young forest was creeping up to their walls. The settlement was overgrown and half-deserted. There was no noise, no bustling life. Not even the sound of children. Only the chug-chug of the power generator in the background and the smoke rising from the charred workshop chimney asserted that the settlement was still alive and working.

"M-m-mum? " Sergei stammered, turning to Panya.

"Mum must have stared her eyes out by now, watching for you. Let me give you a hand up the hill. Come on, dear! "

She took her husband's crutches, and practically carried him up the hill, but at the top she gave the crutches back and they walked down the street side by side in the proper manner.

"Our darling boy! " Panya's mother burst into a wail as she saw them. "What have they done to you, those German butchers! "

She loved her son-in-law as much as her daughter, and showed her affection for him more. Now he stood before her, thin and pale from lying in a stuffy ward for so long, like a sprouting potato from the cellar.

"Are you going to stand and look at each other for ever? " Panya snapped.

The old woman kissed her son-in-law with faded lips and complained as she helped him up the steps:

"She's been giving me an awful time, she has, the witch. Now at least you're back home." And her lips quivered.

"Stop pestering my soldier, will you! " Panya protested with her usual domestic condescension, surveying her mother and husband, who had once again formed the unspoken alliance they had maintained before the war.

Whenever he had to walk from Fir Halt to the settlement

alone, Sergei Mitrofanovich would relive his return from the war.

The spruce, the firs and newly sown pine and larch, having waited their time, were now beginning to rear their dark shapes above the leaf-bearing timber. The lindens were pushing their way up to beat the conifers, twisting their branches, bending their black trunks, but not yielding an inch.

There were not so many ricks in the clearings because the trees were encroaching now on the mowing patches. But the bogland was a different matter. The trees there had wilted and died before their roots could take a proper hold.

The late mushrooms on the hill slopes had been singed by the morning frosts and their tops were leaning over. The frost-nipped bird-cherry and rowan were shedding their berries into the tiny forest lakes.

Some time they would start felling again round Fir Halt, but meanwhile they were only chopping down the old birch groves. Before the war no one ever cut down birches. When the conifers had been felled, they had switched over to producing bast and plywood.

Sergei Mitrofanovich was a saw-sharpener, and Panya was in the wet shop, where the birch stumps were soaked in hot water, then rolled out like paper, the hard cores being thrown out for firewood.

Sergei Mitrofanovich turned off the road on to a path and followed the bank of the little river Karavaika. At one time the grayling had bred there, but the loggers had polluted the water so badly that the river had died. It was clogged with rotting logs, stumps and workshop waste. The bridges had sunk and were overgrown with grass, and the only creatures that could flourish here were grass snakes.

The path wound up from the river to the allotments, from which the potatoes had already been harvested. Music was coming from a loudspeaker mounted on the club building. Sergei Mitrofanovich stopped to listen. The song was not Russian. At first he thought it was a woman singing. When he reached the allotments he realised it was a boy, and that boy was singing as no boy had ever sung before.

He imagined the boy singer seated on the bank of a river,

tossing stones into the water and thinking and talking to himself of what he saw and thought, and for all their childish simplicity those thoughts would reveal a very deep and ancient sorrow.

The boy was imitating his elders. But even in his imitation there was unfeigned sincerity, a childish trust in his own pure and unsmirched world.

"I wonder what country you're from, sonny? " Sergei Mitrofanovich murmured. He tried hard to make out the words but it was no use, and still he felt worried about the boy. He felt sure something terrible was going to happen to him, that he would call down some disaster on himself, and Sergei Mitrofanovich tried to breathe as quietly as possible, so as not to miss the moment when he could help.

Sergei Mitrofanovich did not know that it was already too late to help. The boy had grown up and vanished like some outmoded trinket on the junkheap of the pop-music market. Fame had burst into his life like a lightning flash, and died away for ever in the brief memory of the public.

The club radio began to talk, but Sergei Mitrofanovich still stood with his elbow resting on the wicker fence, and for some reason felt sad and guilty towards this boy singer, and towards the lads who had gone off to serve in strange parts, far from home.

Because Sergei Mitrofanovich had no children of his own he felt that all children somehow belonged to him, and he was always anxious about them. Probably this was because while he was at the front he had assured himself that this war was going to be the last, and that his mutilation and suffering would also be the last.

They had been unable to do what they had dreamed of. He had failed, and so had the father of that boy with the golden voice. They had all failed. War lurked like the hot embers in a stove and its fires were always breaking out now in one place, now in another.

And this was what troubled him all the time. This was why he felt guilty towards the young. Once he had heard a worthy old man speaking on the radio. The things he had said! The young people nowadays, they had no appreciation of any-

thing, no respect for their elders, they had forgotten all that
had been done for them, all that had been built....

But what did he want, this old codger? Did he want them,
too, to run about half naked? Not have enough to eat,
enough sleep? Did he want them to feed the lice and bugs in
overcrowded barracks? Why did he make out it was he who
had given the young all the good things, and all the bad had
dropped on them out of the sky? And why did he speak of
the children in this way, as if they did not belong to us at
all?

Sergei Mitrofanovich had got so worked up that he actually spat at the loudspeaker and switched it off.

"It's only too easy to scold and poke fun at the young
generation," he thought. "We feed them, so they have no
right to argue. Run them down, then. And later they will run
down their children. And so it will go on and on, with no
beginning or end. But if only we could grow up enough
ourselves to make the kids respect us for something else but
the food we give them. That would be the thing! Even a
she-wolf feeds her young, and sometimes sacrifices her life
for them. And the cubs lick her face for that. But is that
what we want? Our faces licked? Then why keep telling the
young about pride and self-respect? We teach them one thing
and then crush it out of them ourselves! ..."

Panya had come home from work and was waiting for her
husband. She had not been considered beautiful in her youth.
Dark-skinned, with high cheek-bones, and hands that had
early grown accustomed to toil, she had looked mature even
before she married. But the years had gone by and her
popular girl-friends had faded and lost their charms in the
humdrum of family life, while time had scarcely touched her.
Her eyes were not quite so bright now. They were a little
softer and more intent, and her face was not so round; her
cheeks had sunk and showed up her steep unwomanly forehead with that double line across it which, despite all feminine ideas of beauty, suited her well. With her tireless capaci-
ty for work and for taking life as it came, she now roused the
envy of her more querulous friends.

"It'd be a different story if she'd had a houseful of children and not such a wet rag for a husband."

But she never quarrelled with them or argued about her life. It would have upset her husband, and she could not enjoy something that distressed him. She knew very well that all the good that was in them had come from each other, and that they had tried to overcome the bad together.

Her mother was pottering about on the vegetable patch, pulling the radishes, beet and carrots, and clattering her pail with displeasure. There were eight flats in the house, and each family had about a third of an acre for vegetables near it. By constantly working on the allotment Panya's mother sought to prove that she was earning her keep.

"I do believe you're a bit drunk?" Panya asked, meeting her husband at the top of the steps.

"I am, a bit," he responded guiltily, and went into the kitchen before Panya. "I ran into some recruits, so I...."

"And what of it? You can have a drink if you like. I've nothing against that."

"They gave you their regards. All of them did," Sergei Mitrofanovich interrupted. "And this is for you." He handed her the plastic packet. "And this is for all of us." He placed the handsome bottle on the table.

"Why, they're as nappy as mice! Can you really eat them?"

"You're a mouse yourself!" Sergei Mitrofanovich replied with a smile. "Call mother. No, wait, I'll call her myself." Suddenly his head drooped, and he added, "I don't feel so good today."

"Mitrofanich! What's the matter?" Panya darted up to him, lifted his chin and looked into his eyes. "Stirred it all up again, have they? Yes, they have." Then it all came out in a rush: "Now just you listen to me. Don't go for that check-up any more. You always come back like a wet rag. Don't go any more. Please! Do we need the money all that much?"

"It's not that," Sergei Mitrofanovich replied with a sigh and, opening the door a little, shouted, "Mother!" And louder, again, "Mum!"

"What is it now? " the old woman responded grumpily, and rattled her pail to make it known that she was a busy person and not to be disturbed.

"Come inside."

Panya's mother had once been a sociable sort and not averse to a drink at any time, but now she made herself out to be a model of self-denial. The sight of the bottle on the table set her off grumbling again.

"For what fine occasion is this? Have they given you the second category? "

"No, left me in the third."

"In the third! They'll grant you the second in the next world, I expect."

"Sit down and stop grumbling."

"Do you think I have much time for sitting down? Who will dig the vegetables? "

"How many vegetables have you got out there anyway! Four radishes and a dozen carrots! " Panya said. "Sit down, do! You've been invited."

The old woman rattled the stopper of the wash-hand-can, sat down sideways at the table and picked up the bottle with its colourful label.

"How they've plastered the bottle, eh! Cost a pretty penny, I bet? "

"Not all that much," Panya retorted, as if to justify her husband's spendthrift conduct.

"Very tasty! " Panya's mother declared after drinking a glass in genteel fashion, and Sergei Mitrofanovich remembered the lad in the cap licking the cheese off his finger. "Why are you being so stingy? " the old woman snapped at Panya. "We've got some pickled gooseberries somewhere, and some cucumbers. We've got everything! " she declared, striking herself proudly on the chest, and darted off to the cellar.

After her second glass she said, "I'll be eating you out of house and home," and went out, leaving husband and wife alone.

Sergei Mitrofanovich was sitting in the front corner, leaning his head back against the wall with his eyes closed. His wooden leg had been wiped clean and was drying on the ledge of the Russian stove, and his leg and body felt much easier without it.

Having cleared the table, Panya sat down beside her husband and put her arms round him.

"Why don't you sing something? You don't sing much nowadays."

"Listen! " Sergei Mitrofanovich opened his eyes, and somewhere in their depths Panya spotted a gleam of pain. "You know, I don't think I've ever told you I love you, have I? "

Panya gave a start and looked quite frightened for a moment.

"Whatever is the matter? Why? "

"Yes, you can live all your life and never do the thing that really matters."

"Don't frighten me like this! "

He groped for her and drew her close. The back of his wife's head seemed as helpless as a child's under his palm. She settled down under his arm and kept her face hidden, as though she was embarrassed.

After a while she stroked his face fondly. Her palm was calloused and snagged his unshaven cheeks. "Nappy," he remembered the word she had used. Panya snuggled down on to his shoulder.

"My dearest! My own darling! You want everyone to be happy, but how can it be done? "

"We're getting old, you and I," he murmured, feeling the knobbles of her backbone.

"Go on! "

"Yes, we are," he insisted gently and, easing away from her, said, "Pour me just one more and we'll drink to all of us, old 'uns." Then he suddenly changed his mind. "No, let others drink to us, if they think of it. And we'll drink to the boys. They're still on their way, I expect, now."

Panya rose quickly and filled the glasses to the brim and, when they had drunk, gave him a smacking kiss on the lips, then covered her face with her kerchief.

"Hark at them! " came the old woman's grumbling voice from the passage. "Won't they ever have enough kissing and cuddling! If they had a pack of children, they wouldn't have time for so much necking."

Sergei Mitrofanovich's lids quivered and a helpless expression suddenly appeared on his haggard, unshaven face with its tuft of stubble under the lower lip. The old woman had hit where it hurt most.

"Must you always let your long tongue wag! " Panya wanted to retort. "It's all very well to have children while they're young, but then you have to break your heart parting with them." But over the years she had learned when to speak and when to hold her peace.

"Don't take any notice of her! Why don't you sing instead? Perhaps it'll make you feel better."

Sergei Mitrofanovich sat for a while with one hand clutching his face and then began to sing, very softly, as though to himself:

> *Like a passing nightingale*
> *Our youth has flown by...*

Panya listened and listened, and then had to cram her kerchief into her mouth. She didn't know why she was crying, and at that moment she loved her Sergei so much that had he told her she must go out and die for him she would have gone out then and there and died fearlessly, with a bitter happiness in her heart.

With her hands still pressed to her mouth and barely able to see him through her tears, Panya lamented to herself, "Oh, Mitrofanovich! Oh, my one-legged soldier! It looks as if you'll never get over the war till your dying day. Where's your memory wandering now, I wonder? They've ploughed up the trenches and the cornfields are growing over them, but you're still there, still there...."

"And sing that other one. The one about you and me."

"Ah, that one. All right, let's have the one about us."

> *When fair is the day*
> *Or gloomy the night...*

And once again Sergei Mitrofanovich saw before him those shaven-headed boys, and that girl with her tear-swollen face running after the train. His song now was for them, too.

The old women seated on the wooden coping in front of the house listened and sniffed. Panya's mother was plaintively relating for the umpteenth time:

"They invited him to join the men's chorus, but he wasn't having any, the silly muggins."

"Well, look at it this way, dear. If they was all to be taken on in the choirs and choruses, who would there be to do the farming and fighting?"

"That's just where you're wrong, Ankudinovna. Anyone can farm and fight. But talent is given by God. And why is it given? It's given to be used."

"Everyone has some talent, but no provision is made for it."

"Well, I had a talent for bearing children."

"There's plenty of that kind of talent about and to spare."

"Quiet, women, listen."

But the old women had missed the song with their chatter. They waited for a while and yawned a while and then, some making the sign of the cross, and others, without more ado, went off to their homes.

Night closed in on the settlement. Frosty air drifted up the dells from the lowland by the river, and soon the grass was covered with hoar-frost. The vegetable patches, the math on the mowings, the roofs of the houses, all began to turn white. The forests stood motionless and the last leaves on them grew numb.

In the morning the forest would swell with rustling and ringing, but as yet a dark sky with bright, needlesharp stars would float over the settlement. Only in autumn are there such mature, well-formed stars.

There was tranquility on earth. Everyone was asleep. And somewhere, in a foreign land there lay a gun-crew, many gun-crews, that would sleep for ever. Heavy with its burden of metal and blood, the earth had meekly accepted the jagged shell-splinters and muffled the sounds of battle, but in the body of the old soldier the war lived on, and he would feel it there always.

* * *

THE HANDS OF A WIFE

For Manya, my true
friend and companion
in life

He pushed on up the mountainside in front of me and the slippery stones sank deep into the moss under his boots. Sheltered from the sun by swishing sedges, and crackling chervil and black currant branches, the whole slope was oozing silently with hidden streams and streamlets. Bird-cherry, willows and alders linked their crowns over this mass of undergrowth, muffling the faint, chick-like voices of the springs. Birds fluttered in their branches, mice scuttled away instantly among the roots, and owls with staring eyes hid from the daylight that blinded them. This was a place where bird and beast lived, multiplied, searched for food, drank from the streams, hunted one another and, therefore, pursued a stealthy existence. To sing, the birds went elsewhere, higher up the mountain, where they had an earlier view of the sunrise and a later one of the sunset. When they sang there, they were seldom attacked.

I could see only Stepan Tvorogov's back, now disappearing among the bushes, now reappearing in the open. His unusually well-developed shoulder muscles bulged under his faded shirt. He walked leaning slightly forward, his right shoulder a little more so than his left. He was very springy and compact, and he trod firmly, putting his whole foot on the ground. He had to be good at staying on his feet because he had no hands.

He did fall sometimes, but always on his elbows or on his side; that was what the jutting right shoulder was for. He fell lightly, without any fuss, quickly sprang up again and strode on.

I had difficulty in keeping up with him, grabbing at bushes, at the sedges and anything else I could reach. I cut my hands on the sedges, which hissed underfoot like a nest of snakes, and, thinking that Stepan had deliberately chosen this accursed slope to show me how agile he was in the taiga, I swore under my breath.

Eventually he turned round and asked sympathetically if I was tired and, without waiting for a reply, suggested, "Let's have a sit-down, then."

I seated myself by a spring that, having pecked its way out of the slope, spun round in a small hole under the moss before darting away like a lizard into the thick grass, where it soon discovered another spring and, cooing joyfully, leapt to meet it from a steep-sided boulder. The hole where the spring had been born was lined with thick-grained sand that had been washed white. An ant was floundering there. To it the hole must have seemed a huge sea torn by the elements. It had resigned itself to its fate and only now and then stirred an arm or leg in an attempt to gain a hold somewhere.

"He's drunk himself dizzy," Stepan said, smiling.

He picked up a twig with his hook and dipped it in the hole. The ant got a grip somehow, climbed on to it with difficulty, sat there for a while, then hurried away into the grass as though it had suddenly remembered its wife and family. Stepan threw the twig away and concealed his stumps between his knees. I had noticed that he always did this when seated. His face was thoughtful. It had few lines on it but those it had were all somehow fundamental, as though they had settled there not merely by the whim of nature, as though they were not just wrinkles but boundaries marking certain far from trivial events in this man's life. The whitish eyelashes that are common among the people of the Northern Urals curtained his half-closed eyes but I could still feel the stern searching glance he had directed at me.

I drank from the spring and smoked. Stepan seemed to be dozing, but perhaps he was merely allowing me time for a rest. His gun lay beside him and a cartridge belt hung across his chest, well up under his chin. He drew cartridges from it with his teeth and inserted them in the breech of his gun, also with his teeth. He pressed the trigger with an iron hook that was strapped to the stump of his right arm. This was a device he had puzzled over for a whole year, until he saw it one day on the door of his own cottage. To mow grass he pushed one stump into a metal tube fixed to the scythe in place of a handle and fastened the other in a rawhide thong. It had taken him nearly two years to devise that. He had not been so long mastering the axe—about six months. He used a long-handled axe with a butt for the shoulder and a thong near the blade. Now he could do his own carpentry. He had built his own log cabin, his own hayricks, he did all his hunting and trapping himself, he had made skis for his son and had even carved the weather-cock on his roof, so that it would be as good as the one on the house of the boy next door. One new year's eve a railwayman who happened to be staying with them had started pawing Stepan's wife Nadya. Stepan had thrashed him. Thrashed him himself. They had only just managed to save the railwayman, and he did not come to stay with them any more.

Stepan's hands had been blown off by dynamite in the pit. He had been nineteen at the time. There was no mine in the settlement nowadays. The seams had given out and the settlement had become derelict and deserted. There were only a few houses left—the forest warden's, the cottages belonging to the workers at a small state farm, and the one that belonged to hunter Stepan Tvorogov, ex-miner.

I had questioned Stepan about all this already. But I still felt there was a gap somewhere that prevented me from writing my article, although I had strict instructions to bring back a feature on this handless hero, who was the best hunter in the district.

"You've left it too late," his wife Nadya had told me with kindly sympathy. "You ought to have come in spring. Stepan took in a treble quota of furs then, but we're not setting up any records just now. I'm busy at home and Stepan will have his own affairs to attend to till the winter season comes round."

"The man's got his orders," Stepan had said sternly. "It doesn't matter much to his chief whether we're setting any records or not right now. Produce the goods, and that's that. We'll just have to tell him all about ourselves and maybe he'll have some ideas." And after a pause, he sympathised too, "You've got a tough job on, you have! What can you write about us? Now then, Mother, show him all our family photographs. Perhaps he'll find something there."

I now knew the whole history of the Tvorogov family. I knew what a terrible blow it had been to his mother and how long it had taken her to get over it. Stepan was her only son. Her "man" had been reported missing in the last war. But somewhere there was still that gap.

"Did you make me take you out hunting to see how I

shoot without the use of my hands? " Stepan interrupted my reflections.

"Yes. Well, not really," I replied somewhat confusedly. "I just wanted to be out in the Urals taiga and have a look at things."

Stepan frowned. "Have a look at things? "

He bent his head, and with his lips pulled out the grouse lure that was tied with thread to his lapel. He whistled with it and almost at once a cock grouse responded challengingly and flapped into the air. Stepan's eyes lighted up and he gave me a wink. "He'll be over in a minute! There're crowds of 'em around here."

Stepan imitated the cry once again and the bird flew down from a fir-tree, settled quite near us on a springy willow branch and swung to and fro, looking round aggressively as much as to say, "Who's this asking for a fight? "

Stepan picked him off, unhurriedly blew through the barrel of his gun, reloaded it, collected the bird and walked on with no further comment.

When we had reached the top of the mountain, he halted and said quietly: "Have a look at this, if that's what you wanted."

I looked. Mountains and forests stretched before me as far as my gaze would reach; slumbering mountains, forests hushed in the meditation of autumn. The face of the taiga, furrowed with paths, roads and power lines, bore the vivid flush of imminent decay. The streams wound hither and thither, drawing their yellow nooses round the mountains and distant forests, and it was as though the very nerves of the earth were exposed in those gorges, gullies and dales. The whole scene was majestically calm. The forests knew of the great sleep that was to come, and the rustle of falling leaves had already begun to lull them with whispers of autumn rain, of deep snow, and of the spring that must be long and patiently awaited because every living thing on earth, and forests, too, live in eternal expectation of spring and joy. Enchanted by the sad music of autumn, the forests were shedding their attire, dropping leaves into the bright streams and draping their mirrors, so as not to see there the reflections of their unsheltered nakedness.

The earth was putting on its coat of leaves in readiness for winter. Its sounds were muted and all that could be heard was the rustle of leaves and murmur of streams replenished by heavy dews, frosts and frequent but not as yet persistent rains.

But the mountain on which we stood seemed to live a life apart from the rest of the forest. Its trees had been felled about ten years ago and its slopes were dotted with rotting stumps, mouldy on top and with decayed mushrooms clustering round their sides. Young lime, rowan and birch wood had sprung up densely round these stumps. They had already overgrown the shoots of raspberry and willow herb, marched into the mowing patches, joined up with one another and were playfully, without sorrow, scattering their yellow, purple and orange leaves. The slim rowan saplings already had their first crop, their first three or four handfuls of berries, and were showing them off to everyone with a trustful swagger. But even as I watched, a great whirling flock of thrushes descended on the rowans, uttering loud businesslike cries as they pecked the large berries and fluttered from tree to tree, and soon the rowan-trees had no berries. They stood there in dismay. And then the tomtits perched in them and began their soothing twitter that seemed to say, "This is only what you were born for, little rowans, to feed birds with your berries."

"Well, what have you decided? " Stepan asked me unexpectedly.

I shrugged and watched the soaring flock of thrushes.

"I don't know," I confessed. "I shall find it hard to write about you. I doubt if I'll produce anything."

"Of course, you won't," Stepan assured me, also watching the birds. "What can you write about me? That I'm a cripple who doesn't go begging but earns his living himself? That came from my mother, that did. We'd never been ones for sponging on other folk. We had always worked to keep ourselves." He paused for a while, turned towards me, eyed me closely and, having apparently reached some conclusion, asked gently, "Will you mind if I criticise you a bit? They say criticism's our guiding light, don't they? "

"Why should I mind? Treat me as a friend."

"All right, then. Well, this is the fourth day you've been living with us, just quietly finding out what's what. And you stick around me all the time. But what am I? " He looked at himself, at his boots, his cartridge belt, his gun. The only thing he didn't look at was his stumps. "It's Nadya you ought to have been keeping your eye on. Her hands! They're the main thing. She has only two, like anyone else. But what hands they are! Still, what's the use of talking. I've said they're the main thing." He moved over towards me confidentially. "How can you write about them? How? But if you don't write about the main thing, there's no sense in wasting paper. Isn't that so? All I can say for myself is that I love her. Sometimes I think I'll get drunk and tell her so. But I never manage to get it out. Now, if you could only write about that, about all the wonderful things I sometimes say about her in my own mind. The kind of things people sing about in songs. Otherwise I don't reckon you'll get very far." He mused for a while and his face became kindly and rather simple. "Yes, it's a problem, that is, how to speak out everything that's in your heart. You can't find the right words, they're all so feeble and pale somehow. Still, to hell with them. Sometimes a thing's clear enough without words. You know what? " Again he looked at me, as though weighing me up. "Come with me. I'll show you something. Not for any special reason, just as man to man...."

A power line ran down to the settlement. The bony, long-legged pylons had pushed aside the timber and undergrowth. The ground had been trenched under them and between them stood ponderous hay-ricks. Their sagging backs were coated with fallen leaves that lay there like dying embers of a fire, and, as these burned out, the ricks grew darker and towered grim and solitary amid the green aftermath.

At one spot the broad cutting of the power line was crossed by a little stream hiding among the peaty hummocks and under the rotting creepers. It was a timid, voiceless stream, but it carried fresh water. And so it attracted all kinds of small growth, and one crooked bird-cherry bush had crept out of the forest darkness into the cutting in its wake.

The inspector of the cutting had for some reason neglected to chop it down. Perhaps he had been hoping to enjoy himself on its berries if there was a good yield that year, or for some other reason.

Stepan stopped by this bird-cherry bush that had taken just one timid step out of the taiga and surveyed it from foot to crown, but not as he had surveyed me. He seemed to caress the bush with the gentle warmth of his glance. I had never seen anyone smile at a bush, and certainly not a mere bird-cherry, so I, too, glanced at it with interest. There was nothing special about it. Just one of the kind that people sing and write verses about, and sometimes strip off its branches till they nearly kill it.

The brown-stemmed berries, all glistening with juice, peeped out from among its foliage like birds' eyes. The leaves were already speckled with rust and the side that had been facing the sun was scorched. The stunted grass beneath had seen the last of its summer and was rotting with the leaves, giving off a mushroomy smell.

"Pick some," Stepan asked, still looking at the little tree.

I set to work willingly, broke off several branches with heavy clusters and tossed them into Stepan's lap. He lifted the branches to his mouth, pulled off the juice-spurting berries with his lips and murmured contentedly:

"Sweet as hell! Rowan and bird-cherry—they're the grapes of the Urals! " But the next moment he threw aside the branch with a frown of distaste. "Ugh, what muck! "

A cobweb on the half-dead branch had tangled into a small grey lump and it was full of writhing green maggots, living together in clammy comfort. They thrived in these webs, gorging themselves on the leaves and young shoots of the tree, and, when they grew a little bigger, breeding another swarm of loathsome green progeny which would not kill the tree altogether but would prevent it from growing and bearing fruit.

Stepan didn't touch the bird-cherry any more. He gazed up at the sky that was still blue but already longing for rain and snow, and gave himself up to certain unhurried thoughts. Eventually he turned towards me.

"Why are you so quiet? "

"I'm eating berries."

"Ah! They're good berries on that bush, they are. And they have memories for me."

And he began to tell me how at the end of a sunny August, when summer was on the wane, he and Nadya had been walking home from the hospital along this line.

It was before they were married. In fact, they had only just met, at a one-day rest home, where for their good deeds workers were sometimes sent to have a sound night's sleep, eat some tasty food and enjoy themselves. Nadya was a cleaner in the office and used to scrub out the pit-operations room with its grimy walls and grimy floor that was always smudged with coal dust and miners' boots. And before that she had lived in with a family for six years, looking after the children.

Three or four times they went to the pictures together at the club. Three or four times Stepan saw Nadya home. On Trinity Sunday they went out to the meadows to celebrate summer according to ancient Russian custom, with a samovar. In this settlement, as in many other settlements in the Urals, people enjoyed celebrating any holiday, old or new, and drank just as much at all of them. It was out in the meadows that Stepan kissed Nadya for the first time, and the next day both his hands were torn off at the wrists.

The disaster blinded Stepan to everyone and everything, the mine, the world at large, and Nadya. Everyone except his mother. He remembered her as soon as he came to after the explosion. The thought of her grief tortured him. At first he felt neither pain nor fear. The fear came later, in the hospital, when he wanted to pass water. He stuck it for two days, trying not to sleep for fear of disgracing himself. The other men in the ward offered their services. He refused. Burning with shame, he thought to himself, "Is it going to be like this all my life? "

At night Stepan got out of bed and crept to the window, but the ward was on the ground floor. He groaned and pressed his face into the gauze that had been stretched across the window to keep out the flies, and suddenly he heard a voice.

"Stepan, don't torment yourself. I'm here, beside you. Everything's all right at home. I'm not letting mother come to see you. Her heart's not good enough."

He lurched against the gauze, tore through it, found Nadya in the darkness with his burning stumps, drew her towards him and wept. Barely visible in the gloom, she clung to him, tearing at the gauze with her teeth, tearing at it so that she could put her lips to his face, so that he would feel there was a living person with him, at his side.

"Don't you think any bad thoughts," she kept whispering. "All will be well. Don't think about the bad...."

But this only made him weep all the more.

"It's my hands, they seem to be on fire! " he complained.

Nadya blew on his bandaged stumps, just as a mother blows on a child's "sore place", and stroked them.

"Ask for some sleeping powders. They have some funny name I can't remember. It'll heal quicker while you're asleep. Don't be too proud to ask. And don't think any bad thoughts." And all the time she kept blowing on his stumps.

Either Nadya's words or his own tears brought him relief and he fell asleep, his cheek resting on the windowsill.

In the morning he himself asked one of the men who looked a homely soul to help him.

Nadya came to his window every night. She could not get away from work during the day.

"You mustn't come so often," he would tell her. "It's eighteen versts there and back."

"Never mind that, Stepan. I'm used to going without sleep at night. I've nursed other people's children most of my life."

On the day of his release from hospital she came to fetch him. She appeared for the first time in the ward and began tying up his things in a bundle. He sat listlessly on the bed, keeping his stumps out of sight, and stared at her in silence. All the men in the ward looked at her too. Their attention embarrassed her and made her hurry. When she had collected everything, she smiled round the ward and made a shy little bow.

"Get better soon. Good-bye to you now." And she made another little bow. The patients chorused their good-byes and said a few words of encouragement to Stepan, to which he responded by looking even grimmer and hurrying out of the ward.

Half of the way they were silent, except once, when Nadya glanced sideways at him and asked shyly if he was thirsty.

He shook his head sullenly.

"No."

A jet that looked no bigger than a mosquito flew sound-lessly across the sad, quiet sky, dragging a thinning web behind it, then wove this web into a figure of eight over their heads and shot away like a spark into the sun.

"How it goes! " Nadya exclaimed. "You'd think those pilots would all burst their eardrums! "

Stepan shrugged. What did it matter about eardrums? Summer was coming to an end and there were the potatoes to be dug, and fire wood to be stored, and the hay to be brought in from the meadow. But how? What with?

At just the wrong moment he recalled fighter pilot Kostya. Stepan had often seen him in town. Kostya would sit in the middle of the pavement in the leather saddle of his trolley, legless but dapper, with a fashionable pair of sideburns, and not beg but demand alms, reciting his tale of trouble that he had learned by heart. "Three Messers for one Lavochkin, and then they grounded me like this, the bastards! Spare a ruble to clear a poor man's head, if you've got any conscience left...."

Yes, their folk still had plenty of conscience. They would give him their last kopek, and it was the easiest thing in the world to appeal to their pity, specially with a cripple's stumps, specially with no hands. But then what? Tumble out of a bar like Kostya the fighter pilot and bawl out a senti-mental song, then go to sleep on the pavement outside?

"Hell! As if I hadn't anything better to think about than him! " Stepan tried to turn his thoughts elsewhere. But nothing cheerful came to mind.

In an hour or two he would arrive at the settlement and all the few remaining inhabitants would turn out to meet him.

The women would start to snuffle into their aprons and his mother would stroke his shoulder fearfully and hide her tears so as not to "get him overwrought".

The mean old bee-keeper Feklin from the local farm would come round with a pot of honey. Secretively and with meaningful gestures he would slip it into mother's hands in the kitchen. With a long drawn-out womanish sigh he would say, "Dear-o-dear, fate's a fickle jade. Who knows what it'll bring us tomorrow! " Then he would make a tactful pause and wait for something.

Mother would fuss about laying the table and producing a bottle of vodka from the family chest. Feklin would shake his head for decency's sake, and then say, "Well, just one", and then settle down at table for the whole evening. He would drink his first glass with his palm cupped beneath it, then his second, then a third, no longer bothering about the cupping, and begin to talk on the subject of "How life should be lived". He would set himself up as an example, expecting everyone else to marvel at his astuteness, ingenuity and thrift.

And everyone would listen patiently to Feklin, although they knew he was not a good man, that he liked to drink at others' expense, that he was a gossip and a miser, and as sticky as the pot of honey that he brought to everyone—fire victim, sick man or bridegroom about to marry.

The thought of it all made Stepan quite sick. "Perhaps Nadya will turn him out sharp? " he glanced sideways at Nadya. Her brows nearly joined at the bridge of her nose. Her face was high cheekboned and stern, but with broad, smiling lips. There was something trusting and kind in those lips. Stepan turned away and swallowed a sigh; it was not for a man to go about sighing so that the whole forest could hear. And anyhow, he had better have it out with Nadya. What were they going to do now? What about the future? Surely it would be better to face his troubles alone. Why should she bear his burden for him?

The sodden peat squelched under their feet. They had reached the stream.

"What lovely black bird-cherry! " Nadya excl imed and

ran up to the tree, jumped and pulled a branch to the ground: "Hold it! "

Stepan's eyes butted her like a pair of horns. What could he hold it with? But the next moment he pinned the branch down with his knee and leaned close to Nadya, watching her quick hands plucking the berries, the cotton kerchief that had slipped to one side and the lobe of her ear recently punctured for ear-rings but already growing over because she hadn't been able to buy any. Cleaners earned enough to buy their bread and soap, and nursemaids were given worn-out dresses and down-at-heel shoes instead of wages.

She filled the hem of her skirt with berries, sat down on the grass and commanded him. "You can let go now. We're going to eat."

Stepan released the branch and it sprang away from them, stripped and tousled, swayed for a moment over their heads, then became anxiously still.

"Here you are! " Nadya said and held a bunch to Stepan's mouth.

The cool berries stung his lips. He drew back.

"I don't want any."

"Please yourself. I'll eat them. I love bird-cherry and I won't budge from here till I've had all I can swallow."

"That's up to you."

She ate the berries, making no further attempt to talk to him. It was obvious that she no longer wanted the berries, that the silence was embarrassing her and she was guardedly waiting for something.

Stepan stared fixedly at a dragonfly that had entangled itself in the mown sedges and was chirping desperately as it strove to free itself. Should he go and help it or crush it with his boot? He turned his gaze away from the exhausted insect. Before him, beyond the pylons of the power line rose the wall of the forest. The scrub along its edge had been slashed and the forest looked as though it had lost its trousers and the trees seemed to be hiding shamefacedly behind one another. Across the forbidden line the little stream was making its way between the peat hummocks towards this forest, afraid to utter a murmur. Flowers touched by the first frosts bowed their grey heads over it; they were weak and sad. There was nothing to gladden the eye; everything was at the crossroads between summer and autumn.

"Well, what do we do now, Nadya?" Stepan broke the oppressive silence. The effort of waiting for him to speak must have tired her and she gave a start. But she answered calmly,

"The same as everyone else."

His frown deepened.

"What does that mean?"

"The usual thing."

"That's great!"

Nadya shot a sidelong glance at him and her overlapping brows twitched angrily.

"Ah, what a man you are, Stepan! Why are you on your guard all the time? You look upon me as a stranger, don't you? I don't feel that way about you."

"I have no hands, Nadya."

"What of it?!" she bridled quickly. "What are these? Rakes?" And she showed him her hands, washed out, scarred with splinters from the floor-boards, the fingernails cut down to the quick. "Oh, I've had enough of you!" she said crossly, shook the remaining berries out of her lap and stood up. "Let's go! Why upset ourselves!"

He did not move. Looking at the bunches of bird-cherry that had fallen at his feet, he said huskily: "Forgive me."

"What have I to forgive you for? How silly you are!" And she ruffled his gentle, baby-soft hair. He caught her with his stumps and pushed his face into her belly, just as he had once buried his face in his mother's apron.

"But how shall we live?"

Nadya held him tight, kissed him on the head, then on the cheek, then on lips that responded readily and passionately to her kiss.

"Darling Stepan!"

"Nadya! I'll be so ashamed!"

"There's nothing to be ashamed of when you love someone," she whispered, clinging to him. "Nothing...."

"Yes, there is! There is!" he wept and ground his teeth.

It was one of those rare occasions when the woman broke the man's resistance and then, overwhelmed by what she had done, lay with her head turned away and silently bit the grass to stifle the accusing tears that had been in store for him and that she no longer had the right to shed.

Stepan stirred and said once again, as though from under ground:

"Forgive me."

She rose briskly, pulled down her skirt, told him not to look and went down to the stream. Some time later she returned. Tidy, severe, she stopped in front of him and let her hands fall to her sides.

"Well, we're married now." She paused for a second, touched the bird-cherry tree and gave it a friendly shake. "The bird-cherry married us. She was the only witness. So we can still part, if we feel like it. She won't tell anyone."

"How can you, Nadya! " Stepan blurted out, realising that this was the woman's humiliation that she had been unable to relieve with tears. "We'll go to mother and announce everything in the proper way."

She gave a dry little laugh. "What is there to announce? I moved to your place long ago. I came over with my bundle on the day of the accident. Why should the old woman grieve alone, I thought. It'll be better if there are two of us." She bit her lip and looked away. "See what a fast worker I am! Grabbed my man right away! "

"There's no reason for you to talk like that, Nadya," Stepan reproached her. "No reason at all! " Noticing that those kind, warm lips had begun to tremble, he stood up and pressed his cheek to hers. "If you want to know, I could climb a mountain and shout it out for the whole settlement, the whole world, to hear what a woman, what a great person you are. And I could drink the water you wash your feet in and do any other stupid thing...."

"Now he's off! " Nadya laughed, and wiped her eyes with her hand. "You haven't been drinking, but you're talking proper drunk. Come on, let's go home."

"Yes, we'd better. Why speak everything out? " Stepan

checked himself and shook his head. "You can't stop yourself sometimes."

"And that's how it was, friend," Stepan said thoughtfully
after he had told me the whole story and we had walked
about five kilometres in silence. "That's how two hands
turned into four. My son's growing up now. Toshka, we call
him. He'll be going up into the second form soon. Everything's running right, as it should be. But Nadya's the pillar
of the family, our roof rests on her shoulders. Without her I'd
have fallen apart like an overboiled potato. And finished up
under the table, I dare say. Get me? "

We were approaching Stepan's house. All at once he threw
me his gun and went rolling like a ball down the hillside.

"There's a woman for you! There's a woman! " he
shouted. "There's no holding her, she's always breaking
loose! "

From the ravine below Nadya was pulling a home-made
haycart herself. Stepan ran up to her, protesting hotly.
Nadya's words reached me as I descended the slope.

"But the hay's rotting! "

"They'll give me a horse at the pensions office. Why
should you make yourself a beast of burden? I'll go and
demand one."

"You think I'll let you go knocking at them office
doors? " Nadya retorted. "And don't make such a fuss. I'm
just bringing in the last lot. Let the helpless invalids take the
horse from the office. They need it more than we do."

"There's a character! You couldn't crush it with an
anchor! " Stepan complained to me and harnessed himself to
the cart, firmly pushing his wife aside. She stuck her fork in
the load and started pushing the cart from behind.

Still with the same mild sorrow the leafy forests were stripping themselves naked in the dales and over the streams; still
the mountains stood with the ruffled far-flung taiga hiding in
its breast a last warmth and the animals that had to moult
and grow new coats before the snow came; still the sky,
kindly as yet but already swelling with clouds, hung calmly
over the earth.

54

And these two people, who seemed so perfectly fused with all there was around them, went on pushing their haycart slowly and stubbornly up the mountainside. On the slope there stood a soundly jointed log cabin, and on the roof, nose to sky, was the wooden aeroplane with its tin propeller. There was no wind and the propeller was not making its usual whirring noise. But it seemed to me that at any moment the little plane might soar up out of the taiga, climb higher than the mountains and fly far, far away.

* * *

A TROUBLED DREAM

The gun had been pushed into a padded trouser leg torn from a suit of protective clothing, which had then been wrapped in a baby's vest, footcloths and other odds and ends, all soaked in oil. When Susloparov unswaddled it from its numerous layers of rags and it emerged with its two hammers sticking up perkily out of a yellow crust of old, congealed grease, Faina asked in a distant voice:

"It must be all rusty by now? "

Susloparov was about to say he must have a proper look at it, and already had a mutilated finger over the catch that would open the gun, when it struck him that Faina's tone had expressed neither disappointment nor regret over the gun's being rusty and the loss she would incur thereby. Not at all. There was even a trace of hope; it barely showed, but it was there.

"Now, look here, what good is it to you? " the reply formed on his lips but, instead of uttering it, he merely gave Faina a quick glance and lowered his eyes.

Faina stood with her back to the mouth of the big Russian stove, both hands resting on the white-washed ledge, ready at any moment to take the gun and put it back in the chest. Her frank, weary gaze expressed both confusion and resignation and the persistent hope that nothing would come of all this, nothing would change, and at the same time, though incapable of ill will, it harboured a certain estrangement, even hostility towards him, Susloparov, who might take the gun away with him forever.

Susloparov pressed down the catch, still without lifting his eyes. The gun opened with a grating sound. More out of habit than for any particular purpose Susloparov glanced down the barrels, then flicked along them with his fingernail, clapped his hand over the muzzle and examined the bluish rings that appeared on his calloused palm, as though they had been made by the local authorities' rubber stamp. After all this he breathed noisily on the gun's oily cheek and rubbed it clean with his sleeve. Then he breathed on it again and wiped it once more and the silvery cheek sent a bright blob of light across the wall of the hut.

Faina realised that this was merely the final weighing up,

that the main judgement had long since been made and the gun's fate decided, and gave a sigh of unconcealed regret.

"It never misfires. They don't make guns like that now."

And Susloparov, who knew the gun better than she did and was also for some reason convinced that guns had been better made before the war, took up her tone and added:

"No, they don't make them like this any more. That's why I'm taking it." He demanded a rag, thus blocking any further attempt at resistance on Faina's part.

Almost angrily Faina threw him a washed-out, blotchy strip of footcloth and sat down on a stool by the window with a skein of thread stretched on a pronged oven pole. She wound the strands of wool with her gaze fixed steadily on the window, sometimes missing the prongs altogether.

Susloparov wiped the gun dry, cleaning out every crack and crevice. He gave himself up entirely to this occupation, barely able to restrain a deep-seated hunting instinct that made him tremble with excitement. His hands darted over the gun, stroking it, and the blob of light darted about the room and once or twice caught Faina's eye, making her frown crossly and glance at him. But he was too carried away to notice. His heart was full of anticipation of the chase, but his head was troubled by memories, and with all the thoroughness of a peasant and the poignancy of his Russian nature he grieved as though he had offended someone or someone had offended him.

He and Faina's husband, Vasili, a childhood friend, had bought this gun in nineteen thirty-eight. They had bought it at the new shop that had just been built at the Lysmanikha Timber Mill. Vasili was working on the circular saw in the container shop and had been married for about two years to Faina, who also worked in the container shop, also on a saw, but a two-handled one, the kind you pull and then let your partner pull.

Vasili had dressed himself up real smart, in his new half-length overcoat and freshly repaired felt boots, which left finely perforated footprints in the snow, and set off with Susloparov for the shop. With the utmost zeal and thoroughness they had gone about making their choice from a dozen other equally greasy and forbiddingly strange double-barrelled shotguns.

In the end they put one aside.

A good many people had gathered at the counter by this time. Vasili had his hand thrust deep into his inside breast pocket, clutching his money, and was quite pale. A moment ago he had not known whether to take the money out or keep it there, but now he could neither tear his eyes from the gun nor change his mind. Eventually, seeking support, he stared helplessly at his friend and forced out a monosyllabic "Well? "

Susloparov hesitated. He spread his arms and turned with a questioning smile to the onlookers, the salesman, and then back again to Vasili. Susloparov knew, if anyone did, just how important this moment was.

Even as kids, the two of them together had made themselves wooden guns and blazed away, slaughtering animals, birds and people right and left. When they were at school, they had rigged up a kind of firestick with a barrel of brass tubing and a butt of dry birchwood bound with strips of tin. They had packed the barrel tightly with match-tips and sprinkled in a pinch of gunpowder from an old box as well, so that it would go off with a real bang. Then, since they both wanted to light the fuse, they drew lots.

Vasili drew the shorter of the two matches.

Screwing up his eyes, Susloparov scraped the matchbox on a match fixed in a hole in the barrel, and then there was such a bang that the whole contraption went flying together with some of Susloparov's fingers and half his ear.

Susloparov was left with three stumps instead of fingers on his right hand and a blue powder scar on his cheek.

But this had no effect on him whatever. He grew up and started tinkering with muzzle-loaders that must have dated back to the time of Pugachev, and various sawn-off guns and Berdanka rifles that always had something missing and would not fire. Up to now he had seen a real gun only in his dreams and was therefore even more at a loss than Vasili.

Still, in this affair he was not the suitor but only the match-maker, whose responsibility, as we know, is of quite a different order. So, after a moment's hesitation Susloparov banged his fist down on the counter with a force that set the scales rattling.

"We'll take it! "

They carried the gun proudly through the village, just as women carry their precious first-born. Vasili's broad face, with its shovel-like, pointed chin, became radiant with pleasure at the thought of what he had dared to do, and suddenly it would darken with fear as he realised that goods bought at a government shop could not be returned. But fear was quickly smothered by a surging love of this gun he now possessed that was still so shiny and steely blue, untried, not yet broken in.

"Wife! Open the gate! " Vasili bawled, loud enough for the whole barrack to hear, and the neat, shapely little Faina, who had long since stared a hole through the window (she, a woman, had not been taken with them to buy the gun on superstitious grounds), ran out into the corridor, where there were any number of doors but no gates.

"Goodness! " she gasped, clasping her hands to her breast.

She had known they would come back with a gun. She and her Vasili had saved up for it, kopek by kopek, ruble by ruble, and even so its purchase had still seemed a long way off, almost impossible. And now, here it was! Faina's voice and glance expressed genuine fright because she had grown up in an unadventurous family where there had never been any guns or shooting or anything of the kind, and now this terrible banging thing was to be installed in their little room, and right over the bed at that! Suppose it went off all of a sudden! Even an unloaded gun fired once a year, so people said. And Vasili was so fond of scaring her. Even now he was beaming with delight because he had given her a fright. But for him life had no meaning without a gun, without hunting. And she could see that herself, she wasn't blind; there was something lacking in his life, he was restless, and she imagined it must be some fault of hers as a woman.

Susloparov and Vasili carried the gun into the room, polished it with the tails and sleeves of their clean shirts, breathed on it and polished it again, and started clicking the hammers like children. At every click Faina shuddered, expecting it to fire. The men forgot all about her and kept peering up the barrels in search of three shadowy rings, but for a long time could discover only two or none at all, whereupon they would argue and swear and look again, each screwing up one eye. Faina began to feel jealous of the gun.

Susloparov, a big fellow with a large head, large hands and a small nose, was not yet married and had no gun, but he maintained his seniority. Noticing Faina's crestfallen mood, he boomed at Vasili, who by now, so Faina suspected, was quite prepared to go to bed with the gun in his arms:

"Well, that's that! Now all we have to do is test the sights."

Faina busied herself over a frying-pan of sizzling potatoes. Susloparov watched her softly rounded shoulders and vaguely imagined what kind of feeling might overcome a man if he were to put his arms round such a shapely little woman.

"Look after your gun! " he said significantly. "It's like a wife. It'll repay kindness and affection." And with this he moved up to the table.

The men had a drink, then went off down to the river with the gun and some cartridges. They tried it out on tree stumps and an old basin, and came back delighted with themselves and everything else in the world. Vasili's almost new cap was riddled, and the following day he took it to work and showed it off to all and sundry. The men wagged their heads approvingly and clicked their tongues. "Neat! " "On the mark! " "Great shooting! " they commented, adding some strong language besides.

Vasili ceased to take any notice of Faina, and this sudden estrangement hurt her almost to tears. Even before this he had not paid much attention to her at work, particularly when there were other people about. He never called her anything more affectionate than "Faika" and kept very aloof, avoiding her whenever he could. But Faina knew that he was really quite tame and gentle. At home he would call her by all kinds of affectionate names, like "Fainushka", "Little Pea" and "Chickadee", and sometimes he whispered words to her that he would never have said to anyone else on pain of death.

Faina realised that this was how it should be. He was a man. And this was his man's pride, deep-seated, ineradicable. But pride or no pride, it was not going to prevent her from putting the question squarely—which was it to be, wife or gun?

Having taken this decision, Faina raised her voice above the clanging and screaming of saws that filled the small workshop and in even higher and more commanding tones called Vasili to come and eat. She spread out a kerchief on her knees and began to take the shell off an egg. She did her own, he did his own. Before starting on his, he tapped it on her forehead to crack the shell, but she refused to smile at his playfulness.

They ate their food and drank milk from a bottle. Vasili went down to the river and washed the bottle in a hole in the ice and, when he came back, informed her that in a week's time he would be going away into the forest for three days, hunting. He said it in such a matter-of-fact way that all the granite crumbled off Faina and she realised it was useless to argue; a change had come over their life. She tried to imagine in advance how lonely and anxious she would be without her husband, but any real idea of what it would be like evaded her because they had never lived more than one night apart.

During Vasili's first trip Faina spent nearly a week without sleep or rest because he was away in the forest not for three days but for seven. She roamed restlessly about the barrack. She ran to the office and demanded that a search party be sent out and was astonished at the calm indifference that greeted her request. She cursed Susloparov, who had tempted Vasili to go after elk. Damn them all, Susloparov, the gun and the forest. As soon as they got back (if only they would!) she would show Susloparov the door and then start nagging her husband and nag him till she got her way. They would leave the mill and go off to live in town. He wouldn't find it so easy to gallop off to the forest from there! She was no fool either!

But by the time her husband returned, Faina was so ravished and weakened with suffering that all she could do was bury her face in Vasili's smoky padded jacket. His chin was prickly with sparse steel bristles and he had a wild look in his eye. The hands with which he squeezed her smelled of the wild. And he was tired out.

He began telling her something, then broke off and asked her to heat the boiler. He tried to eat but instead drank seven mugs of sweet tea and a glass of home-brew as well, which suddenly made him so tipsy that he went all weak and couldn't say or do anything that made sense.

The next day they brought in blood-stained sacks from the forest, and on his own shoulders Vasili carried in an elk's head with great branching antlers that looked like the petals of some huge petrified flower. He dumped it on a bench by the stove. There was a half-chewed twig in its mouth. The motionless eye was the colour of stream-washed pebbles, and its depths were speckled with tiny golden seeds of light from the quivering flame of the shot.

It made Faina start away from the stove, knocking over the dishes and stools in the little room, which now seemed even smaller. What could she do with the thing? How was she to deal with such a mountain of meat?

Vasili managed everything himself. He sold the meat to the butcher's, singed the head, cut it up for jelly and put the antlers away under the bed.

Faina was never able to get used to all the worry and waiting she had to put up with from then on. How much fuss and bother and hasty packing there was in the hunting season. How many wild, disjointed stories did she hear from Vasili, stories that broke off only when he fell into a dead sleep.

These tales of pitch-dark nights, of elk and wolf-dens and bears took her breath away and banished sleep, but life would have been impossible without them; she could no longer imagine it otherwise.

But on the whole they were rarely parted. Once Vasili went off to town for three months on a course, and three or four times he had to report to the military recruiting commission, and that was all. Not once did he send word of when he would be back.

He liked giving her surprises.

He liked everything between them to be gay and unusual.

With a woman's obstinacy, she pretended not to like these goings on. It just wasn't right. She would turn away at the sound of her husband's footsteps, pretending she had no idea he was opening the door and creeping up behind her. Of course, she had no idea except that her heart was melting sweetly and cold shivers were running down her spine.

One day, after creeping up behind her like this, he threw over her head something so light and fluffy that it seemed to be alive. It was an Orenburg shawl, something she had dreamed of for years.

And that was that. Now she couldn't be angry any more; all the sharp words she had saved up suddenly vanished. A weak woman was Faina. She felt the shawl and stroked it and kissed her husband for it on his beaming face and said something quite different from what she had intended: "What am I to do with you? My blood has turned black with misery. I shall have mad children because of you, you devil...."

But he just roared with laughter and refused to believe a word of it. His hands were too busy feeling for what they shouldn't. "Don't play about! " she said and smacked an exploring hand.

One day at work, as he ran past her in the shop, he cried: "Faika! Have you ever eaten grouse dumplings? " Suspecting some catch or other, she replied vaguely: "Why? What about them? " "Oh, nothing. Just an idea," he answered with a yawn.

But she knew well enough what was behind it all.

On Sunday Vasili dashed off to the forest before daybreak. He came back late in the evening all covered in spider's webs and gossamer and shouted: "Faika! It's a cert'! Tomorrow we'll be making grouse dumplings! "

The next day he showed her how to cut the meat off the bones of a hazel-grouse, and off which bones, and how to mix the meat with milk to just the right consistency for moulding tiny little dumplings, and how to make a deliciously smelling broth to boil them in.

As always, he showed her only once.

He himself learned everything in one fell swoop, and it

made him angry to see people going over a thing more than once.

Faina conceived a child and grew round as a pea. She started sewing and making things and scrubbing the tables and white-washing the stove, which was as white as snow already. Vasili set about building a house over the Lysmanikha near a stand of birches outside the settlement, where there was plenty of grass and wind and the river would be nearby, so that his son would gulp all this in and become a hunter right away. He even thought of a name for his son, an easy name that would roll round the mouth like a small pebble—Arkashka.

But it turned out to be a girl and they called her Marishka. By this time the house was half way to being built. They put in the stove, moved into the kitchen in spring and Vasili reckoned he would finish the living room in summer.

That spring Vasili had no time to run off to the forest. He longed to hunt. Sometimes of an evening, when it was too late to do any more carpentry, he would sling his gun over his shoulder, take his daughter in his arms and call Faina, and they would walk along the bank of the Lysmanikha together. Then he would leave his wife sitting on a dry hillock and slip away to the fringe of the birch grove. "I'm over here, Faina, not far away! " his voice would announce from the dusk.

Even so, she was a little frightened at first. But when she had been sitting there for a bit and got used to the surroundings, she would stop glancing round suspiciously and relax her hold on her little girl, whereupon all the sounds and rustles seemed to withdraw and she would be overcome by the peace, the tranquility of it all. Marishka would go to sleep at her breast, and in a little while begin to súck furiously.

Faina would feel herself being gently swathed in the weariness of the day and this work-weariness, this peace, that had come into her soul from the world, would seep with her milk into the little girl, endowing her with her mother's kindness and diligence and all that Faina possessed, all the juices, all her soul, all the love she felt for this humdrum yet always spring-renewed world which even with closed eyes, even in the darkness of the night she could see with perfect clarity.

And there was the Lysmanikha, lively and turbulent in spring, talkative and serene, like a godly old woman in summer, with its icy water that made tea strong and a bath soft. If you washed your hair in this water, it would go all curly and soft, and any scurf would disappear, and any skin blemish would vanish in an instant. But to look at, it was just like any other river. If you didn't know about it, you would pass it by without a second glance. But once you knew, you wouldn't dare as much as spit in it.

The slopes and bluffs round the settlement, particularly on the embankment of the small dam, were yellow with colts-foot. It was as if all the sparks that had flown from the chimneys in winter had been scattered over the earth by the spring breezes. Slim-legged wind flowers bowed to the ground at Faina's feet, closing the white ears of their petals as evening fell, and between them were little blue clusters of birth-wort with lacy leaves. Birthwort was always supple and cool, because even in daytime the dew never dried out of the blue-pink bells.

When Faina was a little girl she had sucked the dew from birthwort and lungwort, for people had told her it would make her beautiful. And they had not been far wrong. At least, Vasili told her she was the most beautiful girl in the world.

The scent of the grass was not very strong as yet, but there was a sharp, bitter tang from the birches. They were all draped in catkins and breaking into leaf at the crown. White wisps of bark fluttered and flapped from their trunks. They were changing their old skins for new. The new skin was reddish and beneath it the sap was rising and awakening the leaves in the branches. As soon as the leaves came out, the sap would stop. And then everything would be green all round, and it would be warm, and her little girl would crawl in the grass.... What a lovely time that would be!

But as yet the earth was still hard at work with all kinds of jobs to be done; everything was in a whirl and singing for joy. Yes, the earth managed everything with a song: clearing the old snow away, breaking the ice, covering the rubbish with grass, drying out the mud.

"How big the earth is, how bountiful. What would become of us without her? "

Thus Faina sat over the river, lulling her daughter and herself with quiet, unhurried thoughts. A light mist, low and cold, began to layer the earth. But it could not muffle the flood-heavy Lysmanikha and, leaving the creeping mist behind, the river poured on in all its springtime strength to the Kama, and there, as it ran into the larger river's big, soft side, it fell asleep like a child beside its mother. The mist melted away quickly, as though the earth had breathed it out in one puff and then frozen into stillness again, so as not to disturb Faina and her daughter, who had suddenly yawned in quite a grown-up fashion and opened her eyes; so as not to prevent them seeing, hearing, living both in themselves and at the same time in this chillingly tangible world.

In the distance, where the red sky was growing brown and peaceful beyond the birches, there was a sharp "brrr", like the cry of an alarmed wagtail, followed by a sound like the squeak of coarse leather. Then came another cry and another leathery squeak. There was perhaps a hint of music in it, a strange yet attractive melody. But just as Faina was beginning to get used to the leathery squeak, it was snipped off, as scissors snip thread, by an anxious shout.

Faina saw Vasili rise from a tree-stump, straightening up tensely with lifted gun. She became tense herself and the baby began to worry her breast because everything was taut inside her and even her milk had stopped flowing. She held her baby tight, not allowing it to move or even cry.

She waited.

Out of the sunset, now coated with dark-blue scale, out of the smouldering crowns of the birches, as though from distant silent centuries, rose the dark shadow of a bird, calling and crying for its mate, and the forest held its breath in expectation. It was as though a sentinel was making his round to see how things were in this still damp and untidy leafless forest. Seemingly clumsy, with its long beak, the bird let its calling notes fall to earth, as though it were counting the last seconds of its life. Faina wanted to shout to Vasili, she wanted to stop the bird in its flight, but she could not tear her gaze from it, just as the bird could not check its flight of expectant love.

Only death could stop it.

Faina waited for what she knew would come but, as always, it was unexpected when flame spurted from the gun and she heard the slightly delayed sound of the shot. The bird seemed to stumble and with one wing rigid dropped lightly and obediently to earth.

It was all over.

Once again the momentarily disturbed earth regained its calm, but now it was all sadness.

The three of them, father, mother and daughter, sat together on the bank above the Lysmanikha. A woodcock lay beside them on the ground, its round eyes narrowed a little, in all its gay plumage that might have been made from last year's autumn leaves with a few petals of coltsfoot thrown in and some luminous marsh-rotted branches for its back and wings, and the whole array gilded with sunshine.

Its song, its flight, its love had been cut off. But even now over the birches on the edge of the dark forest, in darkness yet emerging from the darkness with their black vigorous shadows, other birds were flying back and forth, crying and cooing, languishing with love and the thirst for eternal renewal of the life that every year, every minute was departing from the earth. Little Marishka freed her hand from the blanket, touched the bird's motionless eye with her finger and drew it away in fright. Even she could sense something!

The lights were going out in the settlement. The young, skimpy grass rose stark and rigid from the earth. Cold waves of vapour rolled up from the river, closing in on the forest and creeping in among the birches. It was as though the black knees of the birch trees had been submerged in a foaming white flood. But this only seemed so. The Lysmanikha was a mountain river and in spring or after heavy rain its waters roared loudly and rushed swiftly but could not overflow their banks; there wasn't the space. The snipe on the islets grew silent. Only on a great larch tree across the river a night bird was uttering a gloomy, steady "Bb-ee-een, bb-ee-een".

The woodcocks flew no more. Everything was plunged

into a wakeful spring slumber, and the little family of three—father, mother and daughter—returned to their half-built house through the cold grass. They walked slowly, in silence, although they felt chilled and longed for the warmth of their bed.

Their shoes darkened in the dew. The rebellious stalks of the hellebore, poking up like railwaymen's furled flags, broke loudly under their feet. Faina carried the limply swaying bird by its metallic beak, Vasili carried the child. There was scarcely a light or a sound in the settlement—only the lamps blazing over the sawing shed and a drowsy light in the office window, where the foreman must be sitting up over his returns.

The house, which still smelled of the resinous forest, of rotting shavings and drying oil, stood in estranged isolation from the settlement with its rows of backyards and lanes. Faina hastened to switch on the lights, and rejoiced that two other living souls were coming in after her, and then with a twinge of anxiety she thought that if she were alone she would never have dared as much enter this dark house, so far away from the settlement, let alone live in it.

But she was to enter that house alone many times and live there alone for many years.

War broke out.

Vasili hastily nailed slats over the two windows he had only just made, fitted the frames in the third and went off to the landing stage with a bundle over his shoulder.

On the quayside women were wailing, accordions playing; everyone was singing, weeping or kissing. It was all noise, muddle and heart-break. Faina grew confused and kept asking her husband about his footcloths and boots, and her glance kept wandering foolishly to his shoulder, where there was no gun.

Vasili went off to the army as cheerfully as if he had been going out hunting. He couldn't understand why everyone was hollering like this. What if there was a war? They'd just go and give those Germans what for and teach them not to poke their swinish noses into our Soviet garden, then come back home again.

Vasili played the fool, pressed his wife's nose with his hard finger that was red as a fox from tobacco, and admonished her jokingly: "Now look you here, little pea, don't you go gallivanting around without me!" And she beat his hands with her fists and cried out that he was a shameless, wicked man.

And only when the siren hooted and the boat began to pull out from the quay did something sharp strike Faina in the heart and make her reach out wildly towards the departing boat and her Vasili.

But already there was water between them.

The half-built house was cold in the winter and the little girl caught pneumonia; rations were short and Faina traded her soft woollen shawl for a loaf of bread. She was transferred from the sawmill to a raft on the ice in the Lysmanikha Gorge.

But this was not the worst. After three months the letters from Vasili stopped coming. That was the worst. Then an official notice arrived. Faina threw it in the fire.

Her Vasili could not be missing! It was impossible.

When she went off to work she stubbornly hid the key under the carved platband round the window and left some food on the kitchen table, under a cloth. At night, even in her sleep, she listened expectantly for firm, loud footsteps, the tread of a man coming to his own home.

The war ended.

Her daughter grew up and went off to the city. Faina let her go without much pain, for she had always loved her daughter apart from her husband. She was not one of those women who love their husbands till the first child comes.

The master of the house was forever.

The master should stay with his wife until his dying day. Faina had wanted them to part with life and with one another just as her ploughman father had done. When he was struck down and he realised that it was the end, he had stopped his wife who was about to burst into a fit of weeping: "It's all as it should be. We all have to die some time and one of us has got to go first. It's better that it should be me. You're a woman, you will lay me out, and weep for me, and see me on my road...."

"Lay me out and see me on my road...."

Why had she been deprived of this right? Why couldn't they live their life together?

She listened eagerly to the stories told by men who had come back from the front and, pitying not just herself but everyone, consoled herself with this woman's compassion and tears. When she heard how people had starved in Leningrad, she would think to herself, "Yes, that's how it was for my Vasya." When some of the men told her how they had stood all day up to their necks in frozen bogs, or others, how they had lain with their faces in the sand with bombs and shells raining down on them, she would heave a long sigh and think, "Yes, my Vasya must have gone through that too." What did it matter that the bogs were in the north and the waterless steppe in the south?

Her Vasya had been on the whole front. He had borne the whole war on his shoulders and suffered the whole war, and she was suffering with him and with everyone.

But sometimes she was overcome by such misery that she had to face her grief alone, and then the days were heavy as lead and the nights seemed to have no end.

The other women in the settlement would complain of their hard life, their rough and drunken husbands. What those women didn't understand was that the bruises and the wages spent on drink could be counted. But who could count the solitary nights, in which a still fierce woman's passion was burning itself out? Who would plant in her the seed of Arkashka? Of Arkashka's children, her grandsons and great-grandsons?

Often she had the same dream, over and over again. A field of sunflowers, endless, yellow, full of joy. But all at once her throat would contract and her heart would begin to thump and she would groan in her sleep and sob in dumb agony. And this was because she could see the heads of the sunflowers falling with their freckled faces downwards and only their shaven prickly napes showing.

Death had come to this bright living field like a streak of black lightning.

But then the field and its sunflowers would disappear and

she could see only the sharp-beaked bullet that had hit Vasili and was flying on into the depths of time, a bullet that would strike down a whole line of brown-haired, merry children whose faces were so like those of the big-eared sunflower.

Night after night she would dream of unborn children.

"Ekh-ma! " Susloparov sighed, having polished the gun and placed fifty rubles on the oilcloth-covered table.

It was good money, honestly earned, that he had put down on that clean table, but still there was no joy in the buying: in fact, he felt rather awkward.

"Ekh-ma! " he repeated and looked sad, propping his injured dumpling-shaped ear on his mutilated hand. But he shook himself out of it at once, pushed the gun into the corner behind the wash-basin and put on his cap. "Won't be a minute, Fainushka! " he called from the doorway.

Only Vasili and Susloparov, who for some reason had always been shy in her presence, called her Fainushka. Perhaps he was shy because he was such a big man and had not been at the front; those matches had done him a good turn after all. Or perhaps it was because he remembered Faina when she had been plump and blooming, when she had been at her best, with everything in its proper place. Even now there was nothing wrong with her. She still had the same flowery little apron tied in a bow on her shapely back, and her breasts were still buxomly round, and her face was not old. Sometimes it even flushed pink and she had only a few grey hairs, just a sprinkle.

But in her eyes you could see the inner sagging, the drooping of her soul and already she was beginning to look upon the world with all its fuss and joys and sorrows with a weary resignation and ingrained grief.

Susloparov was always trying to think of the most tactful way to persuade Faina that it was no use waiting any longer; he wanted to "fix her up" with a widower who had children, the skipper of the rafting launch Vakhmyanin. Susloparov had even thought of what to say to her, had even thought of a joke based on the advice in the Scriptures: "Love thy neighbour! "

For some reason he was sure that a joke would make it all much easier. But he couldn't start the conversation with a joke, and so one day when he had brought some firewood on the timber mill's horse, he looked over the house and blurted out: "Life passes by, you know. Do you think it will last forever?"

And Faina replied: "No, it won't."

Everything would have been settled in no time, but by some trick of the devil a long, heart-rending film was shown at the mill, about a soldier who came back to his country after many years of roaming abroad. Faina saw it and rejected her suitor out of hand.

There had been a purpose behind Susloparov's persuading her to sell him the gun. She must be in need of money, he had thought. The still only half-built house was badly in need of repair and for over a year now she had been working as a nanny in the village kindergarten, earning only enough to feed herself. Floating timber was beyond her now; her rheumaticky legs couldn't stand the cold.

"Maybe I was wrong about the gun? Maybe this was her last joy? And I've taken it from her. Ah, life's a hard lot!" Susloparov thought confusedly, cursing to himself as he hurried to the shop.

When he got back, he banged the bottle of vodka down on the table with deliberate boldness and declared in his most cheerful tone: "Well, we've got to wet the bargain, haven't we?"

Faina watched him, pursing her lips like an old woman, as he lumbered about the hut, and her eyes were warily alert. "Surely she doesn't think I'll start making passes at her if I get drunk?" he thought as he sat down at the table and caught her glance. And he made up his mind not to drink more than he could hold.

He dashed half a tumbler of vodka into his mouth, made a face and crunched some pickled cabbage. Faina pecked at her glass like a chicken and wiped her lips furtively with her hand.

"Still haven't learned the trick, Fainushka?"

"No, I haven't," she responded quietly and, lowering her eyes, said with a quiver in her voice: "Perhaps I ought to have learned to drink and swear. Perhaps that would have made it easier...."

A shot rolled down from the hill beyond the river. It was followed by another and another. That Sunday evening the hunting season had opened and the local sportsmen were out well before the townsfolk, patrolling the hunting grounds and hastening to bag the as yet unfrightened game.

Susloparov was about to talk of hunting but stopped himself in time. He thought of mentioning the launch skipper, a quiet-living, non-drinking man, a suitable mate for a widow from all points of view, but again he hesitated. Any subject of conversation, it seemed, was risky where Faina was concerned, but this only increased his feeling of guilt towards her and with the drink going to his head he began to feel a slobbering pity for the woman.

He finished the bottle as quickly as he could, rose silently, put on his jacket and cap, took the gun and, with the door half open, muttered in a dull, sober voice:

"Sorry, if I did the wrong thing...."

"But why?" Faina protested, glad that he had not worried her with his talk, not tried to paw her and not destroyed the respect she had always had for him. "Go and shoot to your heart's content. It never misfires...." There was nothing else she could think of to say about the gun. "But you know that. At least it's a good thing it was you who got it."

He was about to reply, but something stuck in his throat and he began to cough. He pulled his cap down over his mutilated ear, which felt the bite of even a light frost, swung round and went off up the hill to his house that was a couple of versts away from the settlement, at the mouth of the Lysmanikha. There was a multicoloured pole by the house with various river signals flapping from it. Susloparov was a light-buoy keeper and he also grew cedar and larch seedlings for the forestry.

As she cleared the table Faina breathed in the smell of vodka and male sweat that had long since quitted her house and regretted that her guest hadn't smoked.

She polished the tumbler and the wine-glass until they squeaked, brushed the crumbs off the table, then watered the feeble ficus that she had inherited from her mother, and the rose-bush that had spread half way round the hut but never bloomed. She swept the floor, dusted the elk's antlers nailed over the bed, those first antlers, which were still like the petals of a huge flower. She cleaned every stem, every crevice in the bone. There was not a speck of dust anywhere, not a scrap of tobacco ash; there were no cigarette butts among the flower, no stains on the striped matting that lay so flat on the floor. Not a single pellet or cartridge cap remained in the cracks between the floorboards. Once they had been full of them, packed there like yellow cockroaches, but now they had all gone.

All gone.

All those little things and gadgets that had belonged to her husband had disappeared as unobtrusively as they had once appeared. There were no mittens lying about, no tarry-smelling waders hanging by their straps from the rafters, no awl, no cobbler's needle wedged into the window-frame, and in the grooves of the frame there were no old lead sinkers, or fish-hooks or bent nails or any of the other odds and ends that a handy man needs.

The house was clean, tidy, everything was in its place, and there was no one to grumble at for male untidiness, which, it tuned out, was so essential to a house that was lived in.

In other houses, at least, there were letters from those who had died. But here even the letters had got lost. There had been only four of them altogether, but one day long ago Marishka had been left by herself at home and she had taken the letters out of the chest and thrown them into the fire. The charred paper had fallen on to the floor and burned a hole by the stove.

Faina had patched up the hole as well as she could, but the black patch still showed from under the metal strip.

And even now she was haunted by the memory of how she had slapped her little girl's thin bare bottom with all her strength, though the poor child was already half suffocated by the smoke.

She herself had wept even as she dealt the blows.

Without letters, without things, memory runs to holes.

Faina did her best to patch them up and now even the disappointments of her past life hardly seemed disappointing. But how much longer could she go on making the effort?

Often she took the photograph of her husband down from the wall. It was of a man with a flat face, like a shovel. The Vasili she remembered had been quite different. He had been someone that no photographer or anyone else in the world had ever seen except herself. But look at the eyes in this photograph. They were startled, frightened, as though the man's chair had been pulled from under him just as he was being photographed. In the eyes she had known there had been a joyful sparkle of welcome, generosity and mischief. Without those eyes, the picture was not worth looking at.

No eyes, no soul.

Faina straightened the runner on the chest and looked around with a fresh glance, and the house with the windows in the best room which had been put in many years ago but never caught the sun properly, this house with its sagging ceiling, its quiet, clean emptiness, all at once struck her as incongruous, like the old hulk of a boat that lay in the mouth of the Lysmanikha with no engine or hooter or steering gear. The wheel was there but there was nothing for it to turn because the boat had been converted into a sports club. Since autumn it had been deserted. The timber rafters made use of it to shelter from the wind. But for some reason a hush came over people when they went aboard, and even the children didn't like playing in a boat from which the heart had been removed.

Frightened by this unfortunate comparison between her own home and the useless hulk of a derelict ship that had no more voyages to make, and trying to escape the bleakness of the house, Faina climbed up onto the bed over the stove, that cosy, stuffy little nook, straightened the sack-cloth that had slipped of the mattress, turned the pillow over warm side up, pressed her face into it and began to cry. She cried for an hour or two, perhaps three, pressing herself deeper into the corner behind the chimney, but not so as to relish her loneliness and make sorrow sweeter, as girls do sometimes, when overcome by the first disaster of parting. There was no sweetness, no relief in her tears.

Shots rang out in the woods. Late in the evening a loud report boomed over the few birches that remained in the grove, most of which the women had cut down for firewood during the war, and rolled away over the Lysmanikha and the riverside hills. That put a stop to the rest; after that there was not a single shot, not a rustle.

Darkness poured in through the kitchen window. The Lysmanikha swelled with mist. Now it was a white streak running all the way to the Kama and drawing a line across Faina's window. But even at night, through the mist, just as before the war, although far less often, the woodcocks were winging their way across the sky, their sharp beaks and keen eyes trained on the earth with its rising scents of rotten leaves and newly sprouting grass; the snipe were twittering under the banks; the wind-flowers were closing their white earflaps for the night; the razor shoots of the hellebore were slicing through the skin of the earth; sap was fermenting in the trees, awakening the leaves; cold vapours were weaving their patterns at the foot of the hill and round the forest edge; the new moon was butting the sky with its sharp young horns; the little logging settlement was falling asleep to the chugging sound of the power engine; lights were going out, voices falling silent; the half-drunken riot of spring was subsiding, but only for a brief moment, while nature gathered her spent energies for an even more riotous festivity on the morrow.

It was night over the earth, the brief, restless night of spring. And a woman wept quietly all through the night in the empty house over the little River Lysmanikha. She wept quietly, as though fearing to hinder spring in its great and mysterious work of creation.

She was bidding her husband farewell. The last and final farewell, twenty years after his death. Farewell forever.

THE SIBERIAN

The march was over. It had, in fact, been a long gruelling journey. The men of the replacement company had made their way by steppeland tracks, country roads and forest paths, scrambling into passing lorries when they could, and yet it was still called, as in the old days, a march. During this "march" they had made their uniforms filthy and soaked them in sweat, and had eaten every scrap of the rations that had been issued for the road. On the last day they had existed on what was known as "Granny's coupons"—begging food in the villages and hamlets or trading their new footcloths and underwear for milk and potatoes.

At last they had reached the front-line area. And now they were lying in a gully on the spiky, dustcoated grass, listening. Some looked round nervously at the sound of every shot, some pretended not to care. The talk was almost entirely on one subject—would they get anything to eat today? The general opinion was that they ought to because this was the front-line area and the grub here couldn't be anything like the stuff they got in the reserve regiment and the attitude would be different too. The old hands, the men who had joined the company after hospital, would exchange understanding grins on hearing such talk and, just in case, take a closer look at the locality to see if there was a potato field nearby. They knew, if anyone did, that you could always trust the sergeant-major but there was no sense in not looking after yourself.

The front-line was very near. The ground was quaking, bursts of machine-gun fire cut the air like whiplashes, and every now and then there was a furious exchange of shots. Signallers ran past with their coils of wire, untended horses loped about aimlessly, lorries lumbered past, and soon a wounded man appeared.

He hobbled down into the gully, leaning on a stick. He had only one boot on. The other leg was wrapped in a footcloth, held in place over a bandage by telephone wire. The puttee that he no longer needed, was tucked in his pocket and the loose end was getting in his way. But he showed no sign of abandoning the spare puttee or his unused boot either, which he had fixed to his rifle barrel. Thrifty type, by the look of him.

"Hi, there! " this front-line man says perkily and points at his leg with the stick. "Done my bit of fighting for the time being, and what's to come—we shall see. Anyone got too much baccy? "

The new men reach obligingly for their pouches. But a soldier with a broad, slightly pock-marked face gets in first. The wounded man lowers himself without haste to the ground, winces and starts making a large cigarette. The soldier with the pock-marked face follows his movements with shy respect, obviously anxious to ask questions, but hesitating to do so.

"So this is what war's like? " he asks at last.

With a bit of a swagger the wounded man lights up from a captured German lighter, takes enough tobacco for another three cigarettes out of the pouch, tears off a strip of newspaper for the same purpose and, as he returns the remains of the tobacco and paper, says casually:

"Yep, this is it." And he points over his shoulder. "The front edge is only about six hundred yards from here." Then, after a brief pause, "Well, boys, I reckon I'll be on my way. Or, you never know, they may drop something on this very spot, and you haven't got a slit or a fox-hole among the lot of you. What could I do if I lost my other leg? I'd have to crawl to the medical company on my hands and knees."

And he hobbled on his way. The soldier who had supplied the tobacco watched him till he disappeared from view over the brow of the nearest hill. His face had grown sad.

A sharp word of command brought them all to their feet, straightening their belts and shuffling into line.

"At ease! Sit down, all of you! " a dark-faced lieutenant with weary eyes commanded, and himself sat down on a reel of cable which the signaller who was with him had promptly rolled into position.

Both the lieutenant and the signaller had popped up from nowhere. Looked as if they were pretty good at catching you unawares.

"Had anything to eat today? " the lieutenant asked, and answered his own inquiry, "You haven't. Well, never mind. I think they'll send us up something this evening." And with this for consolation he at once began asking questions. Who was from where? Who had done any fighting already? What had they been before the war? Who had a big family? Then he took down their names on a notepad and detailed them to their various sections.

The soldier with the small-pox scars at once caught the lieutenant's eye. His face with its scanty eyebrows had broken into a broad smile and his good-natured grey eyes were regarding the lieutenant as if he had known him years ago and this was their long-awaited reunion. The lieutenant couldn't help returning that smile. It was so trusting, and the soldier himself looked such a simple, homely kind of fellow. Obviously not born to wear uniform.

His service cap, though still quite new, had already lost its shape and drooped over his ears like a limp cabbage leaf. His belt buckle was all on one side, his tunic was stained with grease, and his puttees were wound anyhow up to his knees without a scrap of smartness.

"Well, you are a pretty sight! " the lieutenant said humorously. "You must have been a disappointment to your sergeant-major in the reserve regiment."

"I got it all ways, Comrade Lieutenant. Never off fatigues. Reckon I must have scrubbed about thirty miles of floor in that two months."

"Name? " the lieutenant cut him short, sensing that the soldier would be only too ready to talk if given the chance.

"My name's Savintsev, Matvei Savintsev. I'm from the Altai. Maybe you've heard of the place, the village of Shumikha, not far from Togul."

"No, I haven't heard of it, Comrade Savintsev. There are a great many villages in our country."

"Yes, but our village is something special! " Savintsev glanced round, as though seeking some comparison and, unable to find one, ended with a sigh, "Beats the lot, our village does! "

"Judging by what he tells us, Comrade Lieutenant, this Shumikha of his is nearly a town, only the houses are a bit smaller and the asphalt's a bit thinner," said a voice from the group.

This was followed by restrained laughter and an expectant pause.

"Well, where shall I put you? " the lieutenant bit his lip, trying to weigh up the bulky figure in front of him.

"I'm not finicky," Savintsev responded readily. "I'll go where I'm sent. If you want to find out how keen I am, try me out where there's plenty of work to be done."

The lieutenant considered a little longer and reached a firm decision.

"The command platoon, with the signallers? They always have plenty to do."

So, Savintsev joined the clan of "cobwebmen", as the signallers were called at the front. His open, easy-going nature, his readiness to help anyone at any time in any possible way, and a talkativeness that never became tedious, all helped him to fit in naturally with the front-line men. For some reason they never took him seriously and on the very first day gave him the woman's name of Motya, despite the fact that he was father of a family, and quite a large one at that. Did the name suit him? It must have done. There was a certain warmth in it and an inoffensive smile.

The numerous subtleties of a wartime telephone operator's work gave Matvei a lot of trouble at first. But since he had always found learning difficult he didn't let his failures worry him, and once he had mastered a thing, it was his for ever. He had done four years as a tractor's mate and taken two courses before he was allowed to drive a tractor, but eventually he became quite famous as a tractor-driver and even been written about in the newspapers. But when the surprised signallers questioned him about this, Savintsev merely brushed the matter aside.

"Me, famous? Get away! There aren't many of us men around in the collective farms nowadays. So we're all distinguished now."

On quiet evenings, when the war faded out of mind and the men's hearts turned to peaceful things, Matvei would talk about his native village, his home and family.

His tales were listened to with pleasure. They brought with them from afar the memory of home pastures, of a girl's song, of fresh milk, of the smoke from a bath-house, where it was good to steam yourself after a day behind the plough. Ordinary life with its daily round acquired a fresh beauty they had never appreciated before; it had all been taken for granted. But now....

Sometimes Matvei would produce a photograph from an old leather wallet that he must have inherited from his grandfather and examine it at great length. He was in it himself, with an unnaturally tense look on his face, and beside him was his wife with a baby in her arms, and another boy and girl in front. The boy's mouth had dropped open in surprise, and the little girl was scowling furiously and clutching a book.

"She goes to school now! " Matvei informed his comrades with pride. "She went up into the fourth form this winter. And Sashka will be going to school soon, too. They'll all need kitting out, new snowboots and books.... Pelageya will be up to her neck in worries right now! " And Matvei would fall into a thoughtful silence, and perhaps even give a sigh. "I wonder what they're doing now? "

"Having tea, I expect," one of the soldiers suggested playfully.

"Tea! " Matvei would exclaim, and indignantly attack this simpleton who had no idea of what country life was like. "Don't you know, you dimwit, that this is harvest time and there're only women to bring in the corn? A fat lot of time they've got for tea now. They're sweating blood, they are. Just you come to work at our place after the war and see how much tea you'll have at this season! "

Then they would remind him of the time difference. If it was evening here in the Ukraine it must already be night in the Altai, and quite likely the farm women would be enjoying a cup of tea after their day's work.

"Well, maybe they are. But I go to bed with my own folk and get up with them—we're never apart," Matvei replied quietly, and that put an end to the argument.

But the war was still raging and the enemy was rolling back out of the Ukraine towards the frontier.

For all his apparent clumsiness Savintsev tried hard at his

job. He would search the line for breaks and mend them, wind in and wind out new lines, lie flat with shells bursting all round him and, having picked the dirt out of his ears and nose, run on at a lively enough pace. Like any signaller, of course, he had various little dodges and ways of doing things that he had thought up himself. Fighting a war does not mean just shooting; it means hard work, sometimes harder than any man can bear. And victory in war goes to those who know how to work, who can sometimes accomplish what at any other time would have seemed beyond the bounds of possibility.

Matvei worked hard, found out new ways of doing things, and even got up to some quite cunning tricks. He learned to cut telephone wires with back-plate of his carbine, and strip them with his teeth, and do without an earth in emergencies. But front-line men are learning all the time, every hour, every minute, and such inventions surprised no one. Their usefulness was all that counted. A signaller, for example, usually mends the line alone and the telephone operators curse and bawl at him, but as soon as the line is operating again they forget all about the man who did the job. Who cares what ideas he had, what tricks he devised to restore communications under fire? Perhaps there has never been any work more tricky and unrewarding than that of the signaller in wartime.

But war is bound to show a man in his true colours sooner or later.

It so happened that Matvei Savintsev's unit was in action round the village of Mikhailovka. There must be hundreds of such villages in the world. Just an ordinary village with white cottages, storks' nests on the roofs, and flourishing vegetable patches and orchards all round, and streets with tall well-sweeps and mud up to your knees in wet weather. And this village was placed as most of such villages are placed—near to a stream, on a gentle slope, with a hill behind making a convenient position for defence.

The infantry stormed into Mikhailovka and went on to attack the hill behind it, but the hill was not so easy. The enemy was firmly entrenched. The infantry called up more fire power and blasted away at them, but that wasn't enough either. So, they waited for the artillery. One day passed, then another and another, and still the hill was not taken. The infantry had tackled mountains, high passes and broad rivers. They had overcome them and pushed on without delay, and now they were having all this trouble over one little hill like this. Mount Elbrus itself never had such attention as was granted to this unimposing bump on the landscape. Commanding officers, high and low, ringed it on their maps in red and blue pencil. The "Katyusha" rocket mortars, artillery and tanks were brought up to deal with it. The hill was mashed and pounded so that even now you can't get a plough into it because of the metal in the ground.

But nothing would shift the enemy. They stubbornly refused to retreat and, what was more, even managed to attack. At night an enemy patrol occupied two houses on the edge of the village. The engineers who had been living there were lucky to get out alive and their commander probably remembers those houses to this day. In the morning he and his "lions" would have to win them back. Not alone, of course. They would be given artillery support. The lieutenant who had met the replacement troops when they arrived took a reconnaissance scout and a party of signallers and went out to correct the fire and maintain contact with the men who would attack the hill the next morning.

In darkness, slashed from time to time by streams of tracer bullets, the signallers carried the wire out to the front.

"Wait, boys! " the scout's whisper reached them from the darkness ahead. "There's a bog here. We can't get through this. We'll have to go down along the streambed. There's a concrete pipe down there, makes a kind of bridge. We'll go that way."

In the morning a timid mist rose over the earth and stole away quickly into the gully, leaving tiny beads of dew on the grass. The dew was also timid. Its brief silver soon melted away. Yet, it did wash the dust off the grass and, when the sun rose from behind the hills that were still wreathed in the smoke of yesterday's fires, hundreds of tiny sparks were scattered over the fields and in the village orchards and in the branches of the occasional willows nestling against the bank of the duckweed-coated stream, and the birds began to twitter and a nightingale or two broke into song. How in the name of wonder had they survived? Why hadn't they died of fright, those eternal songsters with their tiny, fluttering hearts! Listen to them singing away, as if nothing had happened. While the weary harvest sun shone down just as it used to in the days of peace.

It was harvest time, the busy season.

But over on the right, far beyond Mikhailovka, a mortar bomb plonked into the ground, like a stone into a pool. It was followed by another, and for a minute after that there was quiet. Then the mortars on the other side snorted back, and soon they were all at it! Crump, thud, whine! The birds' voices faded into the din and the calm harvest sun was screened with smoke.

The day's fighting had begun.

The engineers made three charges, swearing and cursing to spur themselves on, and three times they beat a hasty but less voluble retreat into the sunflowers, shooting back as they ran, while their commander, who suffered from shortness of breath, fired threateningly in the air from his revolver and blasted his "lions" with the worst language he could think of. In the end the two houses the engineers had lost ceased to exist altogether, except on maps and artillery charts, and the engineers returned to a heap of bricks and mortar and a cellar lined with rotting logs, but they were right glad to be back all the same.

The lieutenant and his scout who had been correcting the fire went back to the infantry battalion.

Here as yet there had not been much progress. After the artillery softening up, the battalion had struggled across a reaped field, pushed half way up the hill and taken cover. So now the gunners got busy. The infantry wanted fire here and fire there. And they got it! Could that mortar battery be silenced? Yes, it could, and was! A tank embedded in the hillside was causing trouble—let him have it! Certainly! Crush that machine-gun nest! Shoot, gunners, shoot! Use those cannon of yours! That's what you're the gods of war for, isn't it?

But then the line broke down. The telephone operator Kolya Zverev, a young, nimble and, in the opinion of all the other signallers, pretty useless fellow, rattled the receiver and bawled hoarsely: "Mid-line. Mid-line! Motya! Motya! Savintsev! " and squirmed guiltily under the grim eye of the lieutenant.

A telephone operator on a dead line is the most unpopular person in the world. Not only is he an eyesore to his superiors. Everyone who enters his dugout looks daggers at him and, no matter how he huddles away into a corner, they all manage to jab him with a knee or a gun or anything handy, and then bawl at him to keep out of the way. The out-of-work telephone operator is fair game for everyone. Or rather, not quite everyone. There is always someone on whom he can vent his feelings—the signaller out on the line, for instance. In this particular case it was Savintsev. Yes, Kolya would give him a real blast this time. A real rocket, that's what Savintsev would get, no matter that Kolya was only half his age. This was no time for respecting the elderly. If anyone had touched Kolya Zverev with a wet finger at that moment it would have fizzed—he was that heated up. At last Savintsev's voice crackled over the line.

"*Dawn,* you can talk to *Moscow* now." The signaller's laboured breathing robbed Kolya of his fury. All of a sudden he didn't want to curse him any more, and merely said:

"Fine, Motya, switch off, then! "

Soon Savintsev's ungainly figure squeezed into the dugout, scattering around chunks of earth. He wiped off sweat with his sleeve.

"What a time we're having, eh! Fritz is giving us what for today. Quite a few of our chaps have been killed by that pipe bridge already. I managed to work my way round it."

"Sing us another tune," Kolya Zverev grumbled.

Matvei coughed guiltily, dithered a bit and added rather huskily: "I was bringing you something to eat, chaps. They sent it from the command post...."

"And you spilt it!" Kolya glanced at the empty can and spoke in the same impatient tone people used on him when the line went dead.

"No, I didn't spill it," Matvei began to explain. "You see, in that vegetable garden that the engineers have just won back I struck a potato pit and there was a woman in it, with her kids. More dead than alive and not a bite to eat for two days. So, there was nothing for it. We've had to put up with it before, but those kiddies...."

The scout, who up to now had preserved a grim silence, let his cracked lips break into a smile and clapped Savintsev on the back.

"Ah, Motya, you simple soul! You'll have plenty of time to go about without your pants in the next world."

"I shan't need any pants there anyway. It's nice and warm, they say, and the women are all fasting and don't take any notice of the old sinner," Matvei came back, encouraged by the scout's words, and hastily pulled out of his pocket some small white-topped cucumbers. "Here you are, boys. You can stop the rumbling with these for the time being. Cucumbers are good for you—food and water all in one. If I couldn't bring you dinner, at least I'll get you some water. I wanted to take some from the stream, but the water there is just concentrated slime and frogs. Ah, the water we have in our Altai streams—sets your teeth on edge."

The lieutenant entered the dugout. Sweat was streaming down his face, leaving dirty stains. He sent the scout out to take his place and sank down by the telephone with a sigh of relief.

"Phew, this heat! How's the line, Savintsev?"

"All in order so far. My mate's out on the mid-line."

The lieutenant settled his map-case on his knees, spread out a map and called up the command post, which was code-named *Moscow*.

"This is Twenty-four calling. What's the situation? Still the same. The infantry has got half way up the hill and now they're lying on their bellies, munching the rest of their rations and waiting for support fire. We can't move a step these days without support. We've got soft. Can you smash two machine-guns and a mortar battery for us? The Germans set them up during the night. And throw in a spot of covering fire as well. Then we'll get somewhere. Here's the map reference.... Hullo! Comrade Five! Five! Five! Damn and blast this line. It always breaks just when it's most needed! " the lieutenant angrily threw the silent receiver into Kolya Zverev's lap. The telephone operator's face at once grew sulky. "Savintsev, out on the line! At the double! "

Matvei flew out of the dugout like the wind. The joins in the wire scratched his palm but he ran without letting it out of his fist, darting from one shook to another, and dropping into the furrow by the field boundary when he was fired at. Down by the stream there were no shooks and Matvei had to crawl.

On the far side, another soldier was also running along the line. Matvei recognised his mate. Not far from the bridge the signaller seemed to stumble, threw up his hands and fell.

A sniper!

"Don't move! " Matvei shouted. "He'll finish you off! Don't move! "

The dust spurted once or twice round the fallen signaller and he lay still.

"The bloody murderer! " Matvei gritted his teeth. "He's done him in! And those lads down by the bridge too! "

When he was in a tight corner Matvei liked to reason with himself, aloud if the situation permitted. It soothed his nerves.

"So Fritz has shot through the wire where it crosses that pipe," he said to himself, "and now he's picking off our chaps one by one. That sniper's been set to watch for them. Crafty swine! You'll have to think this one out, Matvei, or you'll fail in your job and finish up in the next world into the bargain! "

He crawled cautiously away, switched on his set and heard the lieutenant's impatient voice:

"Hullo! This is Twenty-four.... Ah, it's you, Savintsev. What's wrong out there? "

"Plenty, Comrade Twenty-four. There's a sniper, the bastard, giving out free tickets to the next world. My mate's just collected one."

"I see! " the lieutenant's deep sigh came over the line. "But we've got to maintain contact, Savintsev. It's a matter of life and death! Understand? "

"Of course, I do. I wasn't born yesterday. All right then, I'll try crawling—"

"Wait, Savintsev—" the lieutenant paused and only his heavy breathing, muffled by distance, came over the line.

Matvei waited and gave a sad little laugh.

"What's the use of thinking, Comrade Commander? " he asked not the commander but himself. "There's a war to be fought. You can't think yourself out of that. We've got to keep the line working. You've seen plenty of deaths, you yourself have death at your elbow all the time, and yet you still feel guilty when you send a man out knowing he won't come back. Maybe you've caught a glimpse of that little wooden village of mine and a woman who lives there—Pelageya. Instead of a stained crumpled letter from the trenches, she'll get a short type-written notice and fall on her face, weeping and wailing like they do in the country. And three bareheaded little kids will gather round her. And they won't understand at first how it was that somewhere far away a young chap could send their father to his death.... No, commander, you needn't think about that. Don't weaken yourself and me. We've got to fight, there's work to be done." Matvei shifted his position and coughed.

The lieutenant also shifted and coughed.

"Right, then, get on with it! And be careful! " he concluded with a grudging warning.

Matvei switched off his set and took a good look round. About two hundred metres from the concrete pipe were some stunted willow bushes drooping over the rushes that lined the stream. "We're still alive so far," Matvei said to cheer himself up, and started to crawl.

Cautiously parting the rushes, he found himself in the muddy stream-bed. His arms sank elbow-deep in the clinging slime and it was hard to crawl, but he pushed on towards the pipe, taking a rest now and then and spitting out the evil-smelling water. The bank of the stream and the rushes kept him out of view of the sniper, but Matvei was afraid he would notice the wire bending the tops of the rushes.

Here at last was the pipe. Matvei slid into it feet first.

Slimy green water was trickling along its concrete bottom. Lying on his stomach, Matvei unscrewed the cleaning rod of his carbine and, using a crack in the concrete, bent it to the shape of a hook. Having admired his work, he tied the hook to a length of wire.

"Now then, who'll fox who! "

Poking his head out a little, Matvei tossed the hook on to the top of the pipe and pulled. It caught on something. He pulled harder and the hook came free, leaving several broken wires dangling over the edge of the pipe. "Fair enough! Let's do some more fishing. Maybe we'll catch something else."

A softnosed bullet grazed the pipe.

"Run away and play! " Matvei muttered, drawing the hooked wires into the pipe.

He found his wire at once. It was a captured German one— red. For some reason the commander of the signals section adored any trophy. He had gradually replaced all the Russian wire with German and was very pleased with himself about it.

"Here it is! " Matvei remarked with satisfaction and went on, thinking aloud, "This red stuff made a fine target for them. You can see it a mile away. That blooming sergeant! Any old rubbish suits him as long as it's foreign! Just let him wait till I get back. I'll throw out the lot." And reasoning thus, Matvei plugged the joined wire into the set.

"Dawn.... Dawn...."

"Savintsev, is that you? " came the lieutenant's relieved voice. "So you made it? All right, then. Thanks! "

"Don't mention it! " Matvei chuckled happily and, hearing that the lieutenant was sending *Moscow* the map reference, he put down the receiver and, without realising it, began to sing quietly to himself. While he sang, he sorted out and stripped the ends of the other wires.

> *My father was a plowman born,*
> *Side by side with him I toiled...*

He plugged in a grey wire and pressed the receiver to his ear with his shoulder. A woman's voice was reiterating wearily, without hope:

"Moon.... Moon.... Moon...."

"Hullo, lass! Who're you calling?"

"Who's that?"

"Signaller Savintsev on the line!"

"I don't know anyone of that name. How did you get on to our line? Switch off, don't interfere!"

"How can I interfere when your line isn't working anyway," Matvei reasoned good-naturedly. "Tell me who you want. Maybe I can help you in your trouble. And don't send any more signallers out to the pipe—there's a sniper on the look-out for them."

"I'm calling *Moon*, comrade signaller. Do try and find it for me, please."

"There's no line to the Moon yet. You'll have to wait till after the war for that," Matvei quipped. "Tell me the name of the operator you want."

"Golyba. His name's Golyba. Do try and find him."

Matvei plugged in a wire and started calling up *Moon*.

"Who's that asking for *Moon*," came a voice with a heavy Ukrainian accent.

"There's a girl round here seems to be missing you. I'll put you through." Matvei joined up the two broken ends and picked up the receiver.

They were already talking.

"Some signaller I'd never heard of—Savintsev—repaired the break."

"Hullo! Comrade Savintsev?"

Matvei pressed the receiver.

"Here am I. What's up now?"

"Very many thanks, Comrade!"

"What for?"

"For the connection. You've mended another man's line and given us great help...."

"I reckon there aren't any lines that don't belong to us on this side of the front."

Soon all the broken ends that Matvei had hooked were joined up. The lines were alive again and working. But Matvei, who knew he wouldn't be able to slip away unnoticed, soon grew tired of doing nothing. Besides, he was uncomfortable, lying in the wet. Soaked to the skin and filthy, he gazed at the edge of the village, just visible below the rim of the pipe. Some of the houses were burning. Great clouds of dust were mingling with smoke. There was a smell of burnt grain. The vegetable patches were dotted with shell holes. Trenches ringed the orchards. Bare stove pipes, all that remained of houses, raised their gaunt shapes everywhere. The sun beat down. Matvei found it hard to breathe. The smoke stung his nostrils and caught at his throat.

"Huh! That chap Golyba's got funny ideas! Doesn't he realise all this is ours? I feel as much for that little village over there as I do for my own Shumikha. Why do they do this to us? Why march into our country and ruin everything?"

The heavy guns spoke up. Invisible shells whined overhead and crashed into the hill beyond the village. Even before they landed Matvei knew whose they were. He knew the sound of Russian shells as well as he had known the sound of his own tractor before the war. From the hill came the wild chatter of machine-guns and the bark of mortars and grenades. Though he could not see them Matvei knew it was the infantry.

"Maybe I can get away while the rumpus is on?" he thought, and picked up the receiver. "*Dawn!* How are things with you?"

"Fine! We're advancing. What a show the gunners put up, eh? Tigers and carriers came out against us and they tore the guts out of 'em."

"So things are moving? Everyone's happy?"

"Sure, they are! Where're you speaking from?" Kolya Zverev asked suddenly.

"What a place, boy! I've got a mansion to myself here where I can't even breathe. And I'm so filthy my own mother wouldn't know me."

"Where are you then? Who're you kidding? "

"Where am I? In the pipe they use here for a bridge. That's where! And the sniper won't let me out."

"Twenty-four is here. He wants to speak to you."

"Savintsev, are you stuck in that pipe? "

"I am, Comrade Twenty-four! "

"Well, hang on a bit. No need to tempt fate. We're advancing."

"I'll hang on if you say so," Matvei agreed mournfully and put down the receiver.

But when the shells started coming over even thicker, he couldn't resist taking a cautious look around. Raising himself with his arms, he scanned the reaped field and its rows of shooks, and suddenly he muttered to himself joyfully:

"Ah, Fritz, you don't know a bloody thing about farming! How many sheeves do we put in a shook? Five! And you've got nearly ten. Just wait, I'll teach you how to count."

Matvei grabbed the receiver.

"*Dawn! Dawn!* Give me Twenty-four! "

"He's gone off to the infantry."

"Listen, boy! " Matvei spluttered hurriedly. "I've spotted that sniper. He's hiding in a shook. It's bigger than the others and it's just opposite the houses our sappers had to leave in a hurry. I'd like to pick him off myself, the blighter, but it's a bit awkward from this pipe."

"*Ein Moment*! I'll ring up battalion headquarters. They'll treat him to a few mortar shells."

"Hurry up, then."

Shivering with impatience, Matvei felt in his pocket and began to curse loudly:

"You, silly mutt! You've made all your baccy wet! "

The seconds dragged by with agonising slowness. Surely they wouldn't miss him? A batch of mortar shells landed with a crash.

"That's it! " Matvei said aloud, and, more boldly than before, craned his head out of the pipe. The shook had disappeared. Only a few scattered wisps of straw lay on the ground.

"Serves you right, you bastard! " Matvei shouted, but a glance downstream silenced him. Four enemy tanks were moving along the stream-bed, with German soldiers running beside them, not firing.

"*Dawn! Dawn!* " Matvei yelled frantically. But *Dawn* gave no answer.

"*Moscow! Moscow!* "

"This is *Moscow!* What's all the fuss about? "

"Shut that! Give me Number Five! There are tanks coming! "

"Where are the tanks, Comrade Savintsev? " the battery commander's voice came on the line.

"Comrade Major, I mean, Comrade Five! " Matvei shouted confusedly. "They've nearly reached the pipe! They'll cut off the infantry! "

"Don't panic, Savintsev! Get away from there at once! We're opening fire! "

Matvei grabbed his set and darted out of the pipe, towards the village, then he stopped and with a gesture of resignation turned back. Picking up the dead wire, he ran across the hill in search of the break that had silenced *Dawn.*

Matvei was spotted. Bullets whistled round his head. Grenades burst in front of him. He flung himself flat, and hugged the earth. The tanks stopped and opened up at the Soviet infantry on the hill with their big guns. The German tommy-gunners left their tank escort and charged. Our men on the hill swung round frantically to meet the attack, and at the same moment the shells from the Soviet howitzers churned into the marshy ground round the tanks. Belching smoke from their exhausts, the tanks backed away towards the stream. But another curtain of fire dropped behind them.

Matvei saw one tank grind to a halt in the stream, its skidding tracks furiously mashing the greasy peat. His mud-stained face broke into a satisfied smile and he ran on, letting the wire slide through his fist. All at once something cut into his belly like a saw. Bright circles span before his eyes, a carillon of tiny bells rang in his head, the ground became soft as peat and ceased to support him. He fell, arms outspread, and the prickly stubble dug into his cheek. The faint yet pervasive smell of dry earth and ripe grain, mingling with the even more pervasive, sickly smell of blood, poured into his nostrils and clotted in his chest. And he had no strength to cough up the lump or to free his mouth of the sticky spittle that held it fast.

"If only there was something to drink," was the first, dazed thought that came into Matvei's head. He opened his eyes a little and saw just above him a blurred flower that swung to and fro making his eyes sting, like a bright blob of sunlight. On the flower was a grasshopper, quivering as if in song. Aye, that was what a grasshopper was for—to sing all the time. A real worker the grasshopper! But now everything swirled before his eyes and there was such a ringing in his head that he could no longer hear the grasshopper or recognise an ordinary flower like wintercress. He would have liked to close his eyes but something inside him suddenly longed to know what flower it was and to touch it. It was then that he noticed the wire lying limp as a dead worm beside the flower.

"What about the connection? Too bad! " he tried to reach out for the wire and with difficulty managed to drag himself half a metre. And when he grasped the wire the feeling of being alone and helpless that always comes over a wounded man gradually left him. Inwardly he felt sure that while he could hold the wire it would give him strength, and his sweating fingers took a firm grip on the thin, hot vein of the telephone line. He crawled on and the wire and the ground under him seemed to grow very hot, and lumps of something hot and hard got into his stomach and rolled about his body, crashing into his heart. "If only I can keep my senses," he told himself, trying not to think about the wound.

Here was the break. Matvei spotted the other end of the line lying a short distance away, dragged himself to it and began to join the two ends. But his hands would not obey him. His fingers must have gone numb now, because he could feel neither pain nor the hot wire. "I can't do it! " Matvei thought miserably, and with a last effort squeezed his numb fingers into a fist. "I'll just get my strength back a bit, then...."

Kolya Zverev found Matvei when he ran out to the line. There was a trail of blood across the stubble. He turned Matvei over. In the furrow where he lay the blood had formed a pool which the earth could not absorb quickly enough. Kolya snatched at his belt, but he had left his flask behind. He felt in his pocket and pulled out the cucumber that Matvei had given him so generously only a short while ago, crushed it to pulp and forced it into the signaller's tightly closed mouth. Matvei's lips were caked with dirt, blood and chaff. He had been gnawing the stubble. The line was still working through his hand. Kolya tried to unclench the closed fist but the fingers had gone rigid and the whole big, toil-scarred hand was solid as a rock. Matvei opened his eyes. He stared at Kolya as though trying to ascertain something, then with an effort unclenched his fingers and moved his parched lips.

"There...." And a minute later he said in a childishly plaintive voice, twisting his lips, "I'm in a bad way, son."

The telephone operator could see that, but he did his best to soothe him and said the things that are usually said at such times.

"It's nothing much. People have got over far worse and you're tough, you're a Siberian. I'll just bandage you up and you'll be all right. They'll patch you up in hospital. You know our doctors—not to worry! "

Matvei frowned.

"That's not what I'm thinking about. It's those Fritzes I didn't spot in time. The infantry caught a packet, I reckon. And all because of that darned sniper."

"Stop carping about yourself, can't you! What a habit you country bumpkins have got! " Kolya snapped rudely, as he bandaged Matvei's stomach, trying not to let him see the wound. "You deserve a hundred commendations for your work today, and you say such things," he went on, hoping to divert Matvei with talk.

Matvei squinted up at him.

"You're only wasting bandage on that wound and it's no use trying to hide it from me," he said quietly but sternly.

"As soon as they hit me I realised it was all up." And sensing that he had very little time left, and mustering his last strength to speak in a firm, businesslike tone, he gave his instructions: "You'll write home all that need be written and do all my last will, won't you? "

Kolya was about to object but Matvei glanced at him sternly and in a failing voice, but with great persistence, continued:

"You will write I was killed in action, honourably, so that Pelageya and our folk out there won't have any doubts." Matvei paused and fell into a reverie. For a moment his lids fluttered. Then he made another great effort and, as though afraid he would not have time to finish, let it all come out at once. With the breath whistling deep in his chest, he said: "Write that ... I died quickly ... didn't have any pain...." And then very faintly, his head lolling helplessly, he whispered, "Make sure you put that in! ..."

Kolya Zverev sobbed and stamped his feet.

"You've no right to turn in your cards like this! You're a Siberian! Understand? And you're going to live! Understand?! "

Matvei opened his sad eyes and looked at Kolya with a father's patience.

"Ah, my son! When you've lived as long as I have, you'll understand better. We, country folk, are used to having things all in order, so as not to forget anything in our last hour.... But how can you.... I'm sorry if I offended you...."

Matvei's cracked lips closed firmly, the upper lip under the lower. Pain swooped down on him, crushing his strength and forcing him to groan.

Kolya heaved the massive body on to his shoulders and, marvelling at his own strength, carried him straight through the corn, sunflowers and grain. Tears mingled with sweat trickled down over his lips. He tried to check them but it was no use. He wanted to wipe them away but his hands were occupied. So he started shouting:

"We, country folk! ... And who do you think we are? Why perhaps I.... Yes, perhaps I respect you more than my own father.... And you ... you! ..." And feeling the increasing weight of Matvei's body as it sagged over his shoulders, he bawled: "Listen, Motya! Don't die! Hang on a bit longer...."

But Matvei could hear no more. An endless field of rye was waving before his eyes. It was dry and hot. Quite close he spotted an ear of grain that looked like the blond eyebrow of his youngest daughter. He reached out towards it with his lips, but the ear of rye changed into a bright Siberian flower glowing like a hot coal. A grasshopper leapt from the flower and rushed towards Matvei with a chatter that grew ever louder. First it chattered like a reaper, then like a tractor, then like an aeroplane. It bore down on Matvei with a crushing roar and thudded into his head. The world was split apart by a brilliant flash of lightning that left a huge dark chasm. And into that chasm, first as a flaming ball, then a spot of light and, finally, as a tiny flickering spark, flew Matvei Savintsev until he flickered out altogether.

And the smoky grain-scented earth received him with a gentle sigh.

A SIBERIAN POLONAISE

In a grassy clearing at the back of our village stood a long boarded shed built on piles. It was known as the "garnery". The people of our village used to store seed there. If someone's house, or even the whole village, was burnt down, the seed would still be safe and the village would live, for as long as there is seed and ploughed fields on which to sow it and grow grain, the peasant will still be his own master and not a wandering beggar.

A little way from the garnery stood the watch-hut. It was tucked away under a stony slope, in a sheltered, sunless spot. Larch and pine grew high up the ridge above the watch-hut, and behind the hut itself a little stream rose out of the rock, like a blue curl of smoke. It widened a little in the clearing at the foot of the slope and could be traced in summer by the thick sedges and dropwort along its banks, and in winter by the faint wisps of steam rising from under the snow, and by the crust of ice on the bushes that had crept down the slope with it.

The watch-hut had two windows, one by the door and the other in the wall facing towards the village. But the window that had once looked out on to the village was overgrown with bird-cherry, brambles, wild hops and other weeds nurtured by the stream. There was no roof to be seen. The wild hops had swathed the little hut so thoroughly that it looked like a shaggy one-eyed head. A chimney crowned with a bottomless pail stuck up through the hops. The door had no porch and, whenever it opened or shut, let fall a shower of raindrops, hop cones, bird-cherry berries, or snow and icicles, according to the season and the weather.

The watch-hut was occupied by Vasya the Pole. He was by no means a big man, lame in one leg, and he wore spectacles. He was the only man in the village who had a pair and they evoked a scared politeness towards him not only from us youngsters, but also from the grown-ups.

Vasya lived quietly and peaceably and did no one any harm, but he had few visitors. Only the boldest of the village children sometimes dared to peep through the watch-hut window, and even they had never been able to see anything. The garnery, on the other hand, was haunted by kids from early spring, right on into autumn. They played hide-and-seek there, crawled on their bellies under the log ramp in front of the doorway or hid behind the piles and even in the bins; in the clearing round it they played skittles and tipcat and the boarded walls of the garnery were pitted with the marks of our lead-weighted missiles. The sound of them echoing under the eaves roused a great commotion among the sparrows inside. It was here, by the garnery, that I had my first taste of work, when I took turns with the other kids at swinging the handle of the winnower, and it was here, too, that I heard real music for the first time in my life—violin music.

Seldom, very seldom, indeed, did Vasya the Pole play his violin. He was the kind of mysterious person who turns up once in the life of every boy and girl and makes them remember him ever after. He was just the kind of man to be living in a rickety little hut under a forest bank, with a light that scarcely glowed and an owl that laughed at night like a drunkard perched on the chimney, and a little brook streaming in the background, and no one in the world knowing what its owner did or thought.

I remember Vasya coming round to see Granny one day and asking her for something. She made Vasya sit down and have some tea, and herself went to bring in some dried herbs, which she brewed in an iron pot with many a long sigh and pitying glance at her visitor.

I was sitting on the ledge above the stove, peeping out from behind the chimney. Vasya drank his tea differently from us, not from the saucer but straight from the glass, holding down the spoon with a long clean finger. His spectacles glinted menacingly and his shaven head looked very small, no bigger than a turnip. His short black beard had a streak of grey in it, like the mark of a lightning flash, and, in general, he looked as if he had been sprinkled with salt and the big grains of salt had soaked all the juice out of his body. He ate shyly and only a little. He drank only one glass of tea and despite Granny's remonstrances refused to eat any more and, instead of crossing himself, rose and ceremoniously took his leave, carrying the brew of herbs in an earthenware jar in one hand, and his bird-cherry stick in the other.

"Lord, Lord! " Granny sighed, as she closed the door behind him. "What a misfortune.... The poor man's going blind."

And it was on the evening of the next day that I heard Vasya's violin.

It was early autumn. The doors of the garnery were wide open to let the draught in. The garnery was empty as yet. The grain bins were being repaired and the place smelled of shavings and the musty grain left over from last year. A little flock of youngsters who were too young to be taken out for the ploughing were playing "cops and robbers" in the garnery. The game was not going well and soon petered out altogether. Games never seem to go well in autumn, nothing like as well as in spring. One by one the boys slipped off home and I stretched myself out on the ramp and amused myself picking grains of wheat out of the chinks between the logs. I was waiting for the rumble of a cart coming down the bank, so that I could catch our folk on the way back from the ploughing and drive home with them; then, perhaps, they might let me take the horses down to the river for a drink.

As it grew dark over the Sentinel Bull, a crag on the other side of the Yenisei, a big star blinked itself awake amid the trees on its summit and began to shine. It was as prickly as a burr, was that star. But on this side, beyond the ridges that rose behind Vasya's hut, the sunset persisted as it rarely did in autumn. Soon, however, it, too, was attacked by darkness from both sides, from the forest and from the river, and its light was cut off till morning, like that of a bright window screened by shutters.

Darkness fell and everything became very quiet and lonely.

I could not see the watch-hut. It had disappeared into the shadow of the ridge, merged with the gathering night, and only the yellowing leaves of bird-cherry reflected a little light from the hollow dug by the stream. Bats began to whirl and squeak over my head and fly into the open doors of the garnery.

I crouched back against the wall and was afraid even to breathe aloud. Carts rumbled down the slope above Vasya's hut with a clatter of hooves as people started coming home from the fields, from work, but I didn't dare unstick my back from the wall of the garnery and couldn't shake off the fear that had come over me with the fall of darkness. Lights went on in the village windows and smoke from their chimneys drifted towards the river. Someone was looking for a stray cow in the thickets of the Little River, alternating gentle appeals with long outbursts of swearing.

A skinny moon, like a half-bitten slice of apple, placed itself in the sky along with the solitary star shining over the Sentinel Bull, and a long shadow from the garnery fell across the clearing. My own shadow was there, too, thin and long-nosed.

The crosses in the cemetery beyond the Little River—only a stone's throw away—showed up whitely; for some reason the old birches began to rustle their leaves, which looked black in the semi-darkness; something creaked in the cemetery, then squeaked, and a cold, clammy feeling crept under my shirt, up my back and all over my skin, to my heart. By this time I was crouching with my palms flat on the logs, ready to push off and make a wild dash for home and rattle the latch loud enough to wake all the dogs in the village.

But from the bottom of the slope, from the tangle of hops and bird-cherry, from the very depths of the earth, or so it seemed, came the sound of music and that sound simply nailed me to the wall.

Now I was even more frightened; on my left was the cemetery, ahead was the slope with the little hut at its foot, on the right, the creepy stretch of floodland beyond the village, where there were a lot of white bones lying about, and where a long time ago, so Granny said, a man had hung himself, and behind me was the pitch-dark garnery, and behind that was the village with its kitchen gardens all overgrown with thistles that from a distance looked like black wreaths of smoke.

Here I was, all alone, with terror lurking on every side, and on top of everything there was this music—this violin! A violin playing all by itself. But somehow the actual sound was not at all threatening. It was kind of plaintive, and there was nothing awe-inspiring about it. In fact, there was really nothing for me to be afraid of at all. What a fool I had been!

How could anyone be afraid of music? What a fool! Just because I had never heard it before....

The music grew softer and clearer and suddenly I realised that my heart was not beating as hard as it had been before. The gentle notes seemed to be bubbling out of the hill along with the little stream. Someone had flung himself down by the stream and plunged his lips into the water and kept drinking and drinking and could never drink enough because his mouth and everything inside him were so dry and parched. And for some reason I thought I could see the Yenisei flowing quietly in the night and a raft on it with a light aboard. And from the raft some strangers were calling, "What village is it?", and then drifting on down the river. Why? Where to? And then I saw a long creaking line of sledges coming along the frozen Yenisei. And this went past, too, and creaked away into the distance with the dogs running beside it and the horses plodding on drowsily. And after that I saw a crowd on the river bank and something wet and draped in slime, and there were our village folk all along the bank and Granny with her hair down and for some reason sobbing her heart out over me.

Now the music was all sadness. It spoke of how I had been ill with malaria all summer and how bitter the quinine had tasted and how frightened I had been when I couldn't hear anything and thought I was going to be deaf for the rest of my life, and how my mother had appeared to me in a feverish dream and put her cold hand with blue nails on my forehead, and how I had screamed out and been unable to hear myself screaming.

Granny had kept the lamp on all night and shown me all the corners and the space under the stove and under the bed to convince me that no one was there.

I also remembered a little girl whose arm was withering. She had been taken away to town in a sledge. And then that long string of sledges came into my mind again. It was still wending its way round a bend in the river and disappearing behind the ice ridges and into the frosty mist. The horses grew smaller and smaller until the mist closed over the last one. Everything seemed lonely and deserted; there was only the ice, the cold, and the dark motionless crags with their motionless forests.

But now I could not see the Yenisei any more as it had been in summer or winter, because the tiny living stream behind Vasya's hut was bubbling again. It had begun to swell and it was no longer just one stream but two, three, already an ominous flood gushing out of the cliff, rolling boulders before it, smashing down trees, tearing them up by the roots and carrying them along in a swirling torrent. In a moment it would sweep the hut away, rip the garnery off its piles and fling and avalanche down the mountainside; thunder would crash in the sky, lightning would flash and set light to the legendary flowers of the ferns. The flowers would set the forest alight and then the earth would catch fire and there would be no putting it out with the waters of the stream or even the Yenisei itself—nothing, nothing would stop this terrible storm!

"What's happening?! Where is everybody?! Why don't they do something?! Why don't they stop Vasya and tie him up?!"

But the violin quelled the storm itself. Again it was regretting something, again it was just one man grieving about some loss of his own, again someone was going away, perhaps on a sledge, perhaps on a raft, or perhaps just walking away on foot in the darkness. The world had not gone up in flames, nothing had fallen in ruins. It must have been someone's soul that had burnt itself out, like the blazing fern flower I had imagined, which blooms only in fairy-tales and legends, once in a hundred years, and is never seen by anyone.

Everything was back in its place. The moon and the star over the river. The village, now with darkened windows. The cemetery in its eternal silence and peace. The little hut under the bank, wrapped in the seared bird-cherry and the gentle song of the violin.

Yes, everything was in its place again. Only my heart, which had been fired with grief and exultation, having once begun to bound and leap, still kept pumping at my throat, wounded for ever by the sound of music.

What had this music really been telling me? Not about that train of sledges, about my dead mother, about the girl with the withered arm. It was something else, something very big. What had it lamented? Who had it been angry with? Why did I feel so distressed and full of heart-ache? Why did I want to cry as I had never cried before? Why was I sorry for myself, for all the people eternally asleep in the cemetery, and among them, under a low mound, my mother, and the two sisters I had never seen, because they had lived before I was born and only for a little while, and mother had gone away to them and left me behind in this world, where a worried, yearning heart was fluttering and beating against the glass like a beautiful Mourning Lady butterfly.

The music ended suddenly, just as if someone had placed a masterful hand on the violinist's shoulder and said, "That's enough! " The violin broke off in the middle of a note, giving out a last sigh of pain instead of a great shout. But another violin, quite independent and with a will of its own, soared higher and higher and with a last gasp of pain, with a groan held back between clenched teeth, broke off in the deep vault of the heavens, beside that solitary needle-sharp star....

I sat for a long time in the corner of the garnery, licking the tears that had rolled down on to my lips. I had no strength to get up and go. I wanted to stay here, in this corner, and die abandoned and forgotten by everyone, so that they would all be sorry afterwards.

Something had happened. The world had changed. I was filled with a foreboding of disasters and sufferings in the future. And the foreboding turned out to be true, for music does not deceive.

I don't know how long I sat there. There was no sound of the violin and no light in Vasya's hut. "Perhaps he's died?" I thought, remembering how suddenly the music had broken off.

I made my way cautiously up to the hut. My feet sank into the cold, clinging black soil moistened by the stream. Rough, sticky hop leaves brushed my face and the cones rustled drily overhead, giving off a smell of icy water and sweet birch sap. I lifted the tangled stems that hung over the window and peeped in. An iron stove was burning dimly. Its flickering light picked out a small table by the wall and a plank bed built into the corner. Vasya was lying on the bed with his left hand over his eyes. His spectacles lay upturned on the table, glinting now and then in the light of the fire, and on his chest lay the violin, and the long stick of the bow was clenched in his right hand, which hung down over the edge of the bed.

I opened the door quietly and stepped into the hut. Since he had been to tea with us and particularly since hearing the music that he had just splashed out into the world, I was not so frightened of going into his house.

I sat down on the doorstep and stared at the hand gripping the smooth stick.

"Play something else, uncle," I begged quietly.

"What shall I play you, boy?" From the tone of his voice I realised he was not a bit surprised that someone had entered the house. He seemed to take it for granted.

"Anything you like, uncle."

Vasya sat up on the bed, and turned the wooden pegs of the violin as he passed the bow over the strings.

"Throw some more wood on the fire."

I did as he had asked. The fire nearly went out and the hut grew quite dark. Vasya waited, without stirring. Then there came a crack from the stove, then another, and red roots and grass showed in its burnt-out sides and a flame coiled in the grate. Its reflection fell on Vasya. He tucked his fiddle under his chin and began to play.

It took me quite a time to recognise the tune. It was the same as the one I had heard while crouching by the garnery, and yet it was quite different. It sounded much more gentle and kind; the alarm and anguish were only hinted at. The violin no longer moaned. Its soul was not bleeding. The world was not going up in flames, the mountains were not falling apart.

The flame went on flickering in the stove and, perhaps, up there on the slope behind the hut the ferns had again caught alight. And if you found a fern flower, you could become invisible and steal all the rich men's wealth and give it to the poor, and rescue Vasilissa the Beautiful from that ogre Kashchei and bring back to life your own mother and the mothers of all the orphans in the world.

Some dry logs of pine that had died of having the sap tapped out of them blazed up in the stove, and the stove-pipe grew purple with the heat and a smell of hot wood and resin came from the ceiling. The hut was filled with a great warmth and a heavy red glow. The flames danced and the stove crackled merrily, shooting out big sparks.

The musician's shadow, broken at the waist, darted round the hut. The figure with the violin stretched across the wall, became transparent and erratic, like a reflection in water, then withdrew into a corner and vanished, and in its place the living musician, Vasya himself, appeared. His shirt was unbuttoned, his feet were bare, his darkcircled eyes were closed. He kept his cheek pressed to the violin as if he felt more comfortable and at ease like that and could hear something in his instrument that I should never hear.

I was glad when the fire died down a little, because I could no longer see Vasya's face and the pale collar bone poking forlornly from under his shirt and his right foot, so stumpy and short, as if it had been torn with pincers, and his eyes tight shut in their black sockets, fearing even the glimmer of light that now came from the stove.

In the semi-darkness I gazed at the quivering, darting or smoothly gliding bow, at the shadow swaying rhythmically in time with the violin. Again Vasya appeared to me like a magician from some remote fairy-tale, instead of just a lonely cripple that no one could be bothered with. I became so absorbed in watching and listening to this magician that I started when he suddenly spoke.

"This music was written by a man who had been deprived of the most precious thing in the world." Vasya was thinking aloud, as he played. "If a man has no mother or father, but still has his homeland, he is still not an orphan." Vasya seemed to muse for a while. I waited and listened. "Everything passes; love, regrets, the bitterness of bereavement, even the pain of the deepest wounds, but the longing for one's native land never passes and never fades."

The violin again touched the notes that had blazed in the music I had heard before, and that had still not quite cooled. Vasya's hand again convulsed with pain, but at once returned to obedience and the momentarily clenched fingers relaxed.

"This music, boy, was written by my countryman Oginski in a roadside inn," Vasya went on. "He wrote it on the border, when he said good-bye to his country. He wrote it as a last farewell. The composer died long ago but his pain, his longing, his love for his country—things that no one can take from a man—they live on."

Vasya fell silent and only the violin spoke. It sang its song and the last notes died away. Vasya knew it would say the rest. Its voice softened and fined down to a mere gossamer thread in the darkness. The thread quivered, sagged for a moment, and snapped almost imperceptibly.

I took my hand away from my throat and let out the breath I had been holding with my hand and chest, afraid of breaking the fine thread that had now broken of itself. The fire grew dim. The embers settled down under layers of ash. Vasya was invisible in the darkness. No sound came from his violin. All was quiet, dark, and sad.

"It's late," Vasya said from the corner, from the darkness. "Go home now. Granny will be worried."

I rose from the doorstep and grabbed the wooden latch, because I had nearly fallen. I had pins and needles in my legs and they hardly seemed to belong to me.

"Thank you, uncle," I whispered, heedless of my legs.

"For what, boy?"

"Because I'm not an orphan any more."

I staggered out of the hut on my flabby legs. With tears of love I thanked Vasya, his little hut and this world wrapped in darkness, and the sleeping village, and the forest sleeping beyond it. I wouldn't even have minded walking past the cemetery, I was no longer afraid. At this moment there was no evil in the world. It was kind and lonely, like me; there was no room for anything bad.

Confident of this kindness, which had flooded like the moonlight over the whole village, the whole earth, I went into the cemetery and stood for a while over my mother's grave.

"Mother, this is me. Tell me what you are like. I've forgotten your face and I don't see you in my dreams any more."

I knelt down and put my ear to the mound. Mother did not answer. All was quiet on earth and in the earth. The little rowan-tree that Granny and I had planted was shedding its sharp-feathered wings on mother's grave. Over the neighbouring graves long strings of yellow leaves hung down from the birches. Their crowns were bare and the naked twigs striped the half-moon that now hung right over the cemetery. Not a sound could be heard. The dew was thick on the grass. There was no wind. Then a chill air began to creep down from the hills. The birch leaves began to fall more thickly. The dew began to look like glass and its brittle cold crept into my feet. A leaf floated down inside my shirt. I began to shiver and wandered out of the cemetery into the dark streets of the village, past the sleeping houses and down to the Yenisei.

For some reason I had no desire to go home.

I don't know how long I sat on the steep cliff over the river. It was roaring over the big boulders on the floodland. Knocked off course by the boulders, the water tied itself in knots and swirled away from the bank, causing whirlpools in the mainstream. Ours was a restless river. Always troubled by strange forces, constantly at war with itself and the cliffs pressing down on it from both sides.

But this restlessness, this primeval defiance soothed me, just as one is soothed by the murmur of a weir or a tiny brook. Perhaps this was because it was autumn, and because there was a moon over the river and steely dew on the grass, and because the stinging nettles along the banks did not look at all like weeds but rather like some fantastically beautiful plants, and also, of course, because I still had Vasya's music about his undying love for his country inside me. The River Yenisei, sleepless even at night, the steep-browed Bull on the other side, the saw-edge of firs on its summit, the silent village behind me, the grasshopper hard at work despite of autumn among the stinging nettles, as though it were the only grasshopper in the whole world, the grass that seemed to be moulded out of metal—all this was my country, something that was always tugging painfully at my heart.

It was quite late when I returned home. Granny must have guessed from my face that something of importance had happened to me, and didn't scold. I am still grateful to her for that.

"Where have you been all this time? " she asked. "Supper's on the table. Eat it and go to bed."

"Gran, I heard Vasya the Pole playing his violin."

"A-ah! " Granny responded. "He plays strange stuff, my lad, stuff we don't understand. His music makes the women cry and the men get drunk and violent."

"Who is he? "

"Who should he be? " Granny yawned. "A man. Why don't you go to sleep? I've got to be up early for the cow." But she knew I was not so easily put off, and added: "Come into bed with me."

I snuggled down beside Granny and put my arms round her neck.

"Oh, how cold you are! And your feet are wet! You'll be taking ill again," she exclaimed and tucked the quilt round me, stroking my head. "Vasya is a man who lost his home and people. His father and mother came from a far-off country—Poland. The folk there don't worship as we do; they have different prayers. And their tsar is called a king. One day the Polish lands were seized by the Russian tsar. There must have been something those two couldn't agree about, the tsar and their king.... Are you asleep? "

"No."

"You ought to be. We have to be up with the dawn." And just to get rid of me Granny told me as briefly as she could that some people in this far-off country had rebelled against the Russian tsar and for that he had sent them out here, to us, in Siberia. Vasya's parents had been among these exiles and Vasya had been born on a cart, under the sheepskin of one of the guards. And his name was not really Vasya but Stasya—Stanislav in their tongue. It was our village folk who had given him a Russian name. "Are you asleep? " she asked again suddenly.

"No."

"Oh, bother you! Well, Vasya's parents died soon afterwards, first his mother, and then his father, a year or two later. You've seen that big black cross and the grave with the flowers on it, haven't you? Well, that's theirs. Vasya looks after it better than he looks after himself. He had aged a lot lately, and we never noticed it. But we're not so young ourselves any more, God forgive! ... Well, Vasya has lived here ever since, out there by the garnery. They didn't take him for the army. When he was still a little baby in that cart, his foot was frost-bitten.... And so that's how he lives.... He'll be dying soon. Like the rest of us...."

Granny's voice grew fainter and tailed off with a sigh. She was asleep. I didn't disturb her. I just lay there thinking and trying to understand what life was all about, but could not get to the bottom of it. Later I discovered that even grown-up people cannot always understand it either.

Some years after that memorable night the garnery fell into disuse because an elevator was built in the big village next to ours. Vasya was left with nothing to do. By this time he was quite blind and could not be a watchman anyway. For a while he went round the village, begging. Eventually, however, he lost the use of his legs, and then my Granny and other grannies started taking food to him in his hut.

One day Granny came home looking carestricken, pulled out her sewing machine and started making a sateen shirt, a pair of trousers without a fly, a pillow-case with tapes instead of buttons, and a sheet without any seam down the middle— all the usual things for a burial. People came in and talked with Granny in hushed voices. Once or twice I caught the name "Vasya" and the next moment I was dashing towards his hut.

The door was wide open. There was a crowd round it. People were going in and out, sighing; their faces were meek and sad.

Vasya was carried out in a small coffin that might have been made for a child. His face was covered with a cloth. There were no flowers. No one had brought a wreath. A few old women followed the coffin. There was no wailing. Everything was done in businesslike silence. A dark-faced old woman who had once been the verger at the church read prayers as she went along and cast bleak glances at the derelict garnery with its sagging doors and boards torn from its roof, and shook her head disapprovingly.

I went into Vasya's hut. The iron stove had been removed. There was a chilly hole in the roof and water was dripping in down the dangling roots of grass and stems of hops. Shavings were scattered over the floor. The bedding lay rolled up in the corner. The plank bed must have been used to put the coffin on because the table was too small and one of the legs was rotten. The watchman's rattle, a broom, spade and axe, lay under the bed. On the windowsill behind the table there was an earthenware bowl, a mug carved out of a birch fungus, a spoon, a comb and a little jar of water I did not notice at once, for some reason; in it there was a bird-cherry branch with buds that had just burst open. Vasya's spectacles gazed at me forlornly with their empty lenses.

"But where's the violin?" I thought as I looked at the spectacles. And the next moment I saw it. It was hanging over the bed. I pushed the spectacles into my pocket, took the violin down from the wall and ran out to catch up with the funeral procession. The men carrying the coffin and the old women following in a bunch behind had already crossed the log bridge over the Little River, tipsy with the spring floods, and were climbing the slope to the cemetery, now wreathed in a green mist of awakening grass. I tugged at Granny's sleeve and showed her the violin and bow. Granny frowned and turned away from me, then she lengthened her stride and whispered something to the dark-faced old woman. The old woman's thin lips moved and I heard the words: "Lot of expense ... not much from the village Soviet...."

I was ten and knew enough to guess that the old woman wanted to sell the violin to cover the cost of the funeral.

I tugged at Granny's sleeve and, when we had dropped behind a little, asked her grimly, "Whose violin is it?"

"Vasya's, squire, Vasya's," Granny replied mildly, watching the dark-faced old woman's back. All at once Granny bent down and whispered in my ear, "Put it into the coffin! Put it there yourself!" and hurried on.

Before anyone could set about closing the lid of Vasya's coffin I squeezed forward and, without saying a word, placed the violin and bow on his chest along with a few yellow coltsfoot flowers I had plucked at the spot where the bearers had changed shoulder.

No one dared say anything to me. Only the devout old dame gave me a piercing stare and at once raised her eyes to heaven and made the sign of the cross.

I watched the lid of the coffin being nailed down—had they done it firmly enough? I was the first to toss a handful of soil into Vasya's grave, as though I were a close relative and, afterwards, when the other folk had sorted out their spades and ropes and gone away down the cemetery paths to shed their pent-up tears on the graves of their own kin, I sat for a long time beside Vasya's grave, crumbling lumps of earth between my fingers, and waited. I knew it was no use waiting, yet I waited all the same.

But Vasya's violin had fallen silent forever.

During the last autumn of the war I was on duty by the guns in a small badly shelled Polish town. This was the first foreign town I had ever seen in my life. It was no different in any way from our own ruined towns. The smell was just the same: smoke, corpses, dust. Leaves, paper and soot were floating about among the misshapen houses and along the streets, strewn with mangled metal. A dome of fire hung menacingly over the town. It seemed to be caving in, collapsing on the houses, into the streets and side-roads, subsiding into weary embers. But a long muffled explosion echoed over the town and the dome was again lifted into the dark sky and everything was bathed in heavy, static light. Leaves from the trees were whisked into the air by the heat and shrivelled before they fell.

Sometimes a squall of artillery or mortar fire would descend on the burning ruins. Aircraft whined overhead. German flares lit up the ragged fighting line on the fringe of the town, then broke into sparks and dropped into the raging inferno where human homes were writhing in their last agony.

I found myself imagining that I was all alone in a deserted burnt-out city. It was a feeling I often had at night, particularly among ruins. But I knew that quite close by—I had only to slip through a hedge that had been spared by the fire—our gun crews were sleeping in an abandoned hut, and that thought gave me strength.

We had captured the town only that day, and by evening people with bundles, suitcases and barrows and often with children in their arms had begun to appear as if from nowhere. They had wept over the ruins, dragged a few things out of the fires and waved their fists westwards at their eternal enemy.

Night had come down and covered their grief and suffering, but it could not cover the fires.

The sound of an organ reached me from a building on the other side of the street. Half the building had been bombed away and the exposed inner walls were adorned with the wan faces of saints and madonnas staring out through the soot with blue sorrowful eyes.

Those saints and madonnas had been staring at me all the evening until it grew dark and I felt embarrassed for myself and for mankind in general under their reproachful glances. And even now the light of the fires would still sometimes pick out of the darkness a sad face with a damaged head or a brickbat scar on its cheek. It seemed to me that they, too, were listening, and comprehending in some way quite different from ours this music that reminded me of my distant, almost forgotten childhood.

The music stirred up old memories. I sat on the gun-carriage with closed eyes and my carbine pressed between my knees, and let my head sway as I listened to the solitary organ playing amid the din of war. At one time I had wanted to die of the strange sadness and exultation one solitary violin had stirred in me. I had been young and foolish. Since then I had seen so many deaths that there was no word more hateful to me than death. The music I had heard in childhood must have cracked and congealed inside me, particularly the part that had once made me weep. Now I was more attracted by the part of it that had frightened me in those days with its resilient, hidden power. Yes, just as on that far-off night, the music still held me, but it no longer forced me to tears, no longer sprouted into weak, white shoots of pity. It challenged me to do something, to act, so that there should be no more fires like this, so that people would never again have to shelter among burning ruins, and the sky would never again be shaken by bursting bombs.

The music sounded solemnly over the town, drowning the crash of shells, the drone of aircraft and the dry crackle of burning trees. Music dominated the grief-stricken ruins, music that a man who had never seen his homeland but had yearned for it all his life had kept in his heart like a sigh of his own, native earth.

THE HORSE
WITH THE PINK MANE

Granny came back from Uncle Levonty's and told me our neighbour's children were going up the bank for wild strawberries. I ought to go too.

"You'll pick a basketful. I'll take them to town with mine and sell them and buy you a gingerbread."

"One like a horse, Granny? "

"A horse it shall be, then."

A horse-shaped gingerbread! It was the dream of all the village children. He was so white, that horse. And his mane was pink and his tail was pink and his eyes were pink, and so were his hooves.

Granny never let me play with bits of bread. Eat at table or there'll be trouble! But a gingerbread was a different matter. You could slip a gingerbread away under your shirt and when you ran you could hear that horse kicking your bare tummy with his hooves. Sometimes you'd go cold with fright thinking you'd lost it. But no, here it was! And you would feel it through your shirt to make sure it was there, that fiery steed!

How much respect and attention you received with a horse like that! Uncle Levonty's kids would make up to you in all kinds of ways. They'd let you have first knock at the tipcat, or a shot with their catapult—all for the sake of a bite or a lick at your horse.

When you gave Levonty's Sanka or Tanka a bite you had to hold on to the place where they were allowed to put their teeth in, and hold on tight, or else they'd snap off such a lump that there would be nothing left of your horse but the tail.

Levonty, our neighbour, had a job cutting firewood which he did with Mishka Korshukov. Levonty collected the wood, sawed it up, split it and turned it in at the lime kilns that stood opposite the village on the other side of the Yenisei.

Once every ten days or, perhaps, every fifteen—I don't quite remember—Levonty would be paid, and then his house, which was full of children and nothing else, would be the scene of a real bean-feast.

Levonty's house and all the neighbours' houses as well would be gripped by a kind of fever. Early in the morning his wife, Vasenya, would come chasing round desperately to Granny's door with a fistful of rubles.

"Neighbour! " she would cry out in a half scared, half joyful voice. "I've brought you the money I'm owing! " And she would rush away, whisking up the dust with her skirt.

"Hi, wait a bit, you mad hussy! " Granny would call after her. "It's got to be counted."

Auntie Vasenya would turn back meekly and Granny would count the money while she shifted from one foot to the other, like a mettlesome horse straining at the bridle.

Granny counted the money slowly and thoroughly, smoothing out each ruble. As far as I remember, she never gave Levonty's wife more than seven, or ten rubles at the most, out of the "reserve" she kept for a rainy day, because the whole "reserve" consisted of ten rubles. But even with so small a sum to pay, the scatter-brained Vasenya contrived to miscount a ruble or even three.

"The way you treat money, you blind dummy! " Granny would rail at her neighbour. "You give me a ruble too much! And someone else another ruble! Where will that get you? "

But Vasenya would cause another whirlwind with her skirt and go running off.

"It's myself I've cheated, not you! "

Granny would go on railing against Levonty's wife and Levonty himself and slapping her thighs and spitting in disgust, while I sat by the window gazing longingly at the house next door.

It stood all by itself in the open and there was nothing to bar the view from its carelessly glazed windows—no fence, no gate, no porch, no beaded window frames, no shutters.

In spring Levonty's family would do a bit of digging round the house and rig up a fence of poles, twigs and old boards. But in winter this all disappeared into the belly of the Russian stove that squatted ponderously in the middle of the hut.

Little Tanya summed up the family's way of life in her lisping tongue.

"When Daddy goes for us, we jus' run and never s'op! "

Uncle Levonty himself would come out into the street on warm evenings in a pair of trousers supported by one solitary brass button with two eagles stamped on it and a calico shirt without any buttons at all. He would seat himself on the axe-scarred block that represented his porch, smoke and look around, and if my grandmother started scolding him from the window for being idle and enumerating all the jobs she considered he ought to be doing in and around the house, Uncle Levonty would merely scratch himself blissfully.

"I love freedom, Petrovna!" and he would make a sweeping gesture. "Fine, isn't it? Like at sea! Nothing to offend the eye!"

Uncle Levonty had been a sailor at one time and he loved the sea, and I loved him. The chief aim of my life was to get into Levonty's house the day after he had been paid. It wasn't so easy. Granny was up to all my tricks.

"Don't you go sponging on them!" she would thunder. "Those proletarians have enough hungry mouths to feed! And they haven't a penny to bless themselves with, as it is."

But if I did manage to slip out of the house and make my appearance next door, that was all I could wish for. I was the centre of attention and happy as a sandboy.

"Out you get!" tipsy Uncle Levonty would sternly command one of his little boys. And while the unlucky one was reluctantly leaving the table, he would explain his action to his children in a voice that had suddenly grown thick with emotion. "He's an orphan, you see, and you've got parents to look after you!" And with a pitying look at me, he would burst into tears. "Do you remember your mother at least?" And I would nod to show that I did, and then Uncle Levonty would sorrowfully rest his head on his hand and smearing the tears over his face with his fist, recall, "We chopped firewood together one year, she and I did!" And bursting into sobs, he would go on, "No matter when I came round ... at night, after midnight.... Oh, Levonty, you poor lost soul, she'd say, and ... give me a little drink to clear my head...."

At this point Auntie Vasenya, the children, and I with them, would set up a wail and the whole family would be overcome with such pity that every little scrap of food they possessed was placed on the table and everyone set about treating me and could hardly bring themselves to eat a morsel.

Late in the evening or around midnight Levonty would always ask one and the same question: "Wha's life all about?!" After which I would grab as many gingerbreads and sweets as I could and the other kids would grab anything they could lay hands on and take to our heels. Vasenya would be the last to flee, and Granny would "put her up" till the morning. Levonty would smash any glass there happened to be in the windows, curse and swear, rampage about the house and burst into a flood of tears.

The next morning he would patch up the windows with the fragments of broken glass, mend the benches and table, and then, full of gloom and repentance, set off for work. Three or four days later Auntie Vasenya would again make the round of the neighbours, but without any whisking of her skirt. This time it was to borrow money, flour and potatoes, or anything else that was going.

It was with Uncle Levonty's children that I set out to pick wild strawberries and earn a gingerbread by my own labours. The kids carried glasses with chipped edges, old birch-bark baskets that had been stripped of most of their bark for kindling, and one little chap had a ladle without a handle. Levonty's young daredevils threw their utensils at each other, tumbled about, once or twice started to fight, burst out crying and teased one another all the time. On the road they climbed into someone's allotment and, since nothing was ripe there, fell upon the spring onions, gorged themselves till they spat green, and threw away what they couldn't eat, leaving themselves only a few blades for whistles. They whistled through these chewed blades for the rest of the way and to the sound of this music we soon reached the forest and the rocky bank.

As soon as we got there the whistling stopped and everyone scattered over the bank to gather the wild strawberries, which were only just beginning to ripen. They were still white-sided, and there were not many, so they were a joy to find.

I picked zealously and soon covered the bottom of my neat birch-bark basket. The main thing when you were berrying, as Granny always said, was to cover the bottom of your basket. With a good two or three glassfuls in my basket I gave a sigh of relief and started picking all the faster, and higher up the bank there were more and more to pick.

At first, Levonty's kids behaved themselves, and only the sound of the lid tied to the copper kettle could be heard. The kettle was carried by the oldest boy and he rattled it to make it known that he, the eldest, was close by, so we had nothing to fear.

All at once the lid of the kettle broke into a nervous clatter and there were sounds of struggling.

"Guzzling 'em yourself, are you? What will you take home then?" the eldest boy was asking, and giving someone a kick after each question.

"O-o-w-ow-ow!" Tanka hollered. "Sanka's had lo's an' lo's, and no one minds him."

Sanka was dealt with too. He lost his temper, threw down his pot and rolled in the grass. The eldest boy went on picking, but the more he picked the sorer his feelings became. Here was he, the eldest, gathering berries, doing what he could for the family, while the others ate what they picked or just lounged on the grass. He went up to Sanka and gave him another kick. Sanka howled and flung himself at his brother. The kettle clanged to the ground and the berries tipped out. The two brothers rolled about scrapping wildly and crushed the lot.

After the fight the eldest boy lost his keenness. He knelt down to gather the scattered, crushed berries and crammed them in his mouth.

"So you can do it and I can't? You can but I can't, eh?" he repeated ominously, until he had eaten everything he had gathered.

Presently the two brothers made it up, stopped calling each other names and decided to go down to the Little River for a splash.

I, too, wanted to have a splash, but was afraid to leave the bank because I had not yet filled my basket.

"Afraid of Granny Petrovna! Booh!" Sanka teased, and called me a dirty name. He knew plenty of such names. I knew them, too, because I had learned them from him and the others, but I was afraid or, perhaps, too shy to use them, so I merely said:

"Granny will buy me a gingerbread like a horse! "

"Sure it won't be like a cow? " Sanka jeered. He spat at the ground and countered quickly, "Why don't you say you're too scared and too mean! "

"Me? "

"Yes, you! "

"Mean! "

"Yes, mean! "

"I'll eat all these strawberries, if you like!" The moment I spoke the words, I regretted them, realising that I had fallen into his trap.

All in scratches, with bumps on his head from fighting and various other causes, a rash of pimples on his arms and legs, and red, bloodshot eyes, Sanka was the most spiteful of all Levonty's kids.

"You haven't the guts! " he said.

"Oh, haven't I! " I boasted with a sidelong glance at the basket. It was more than half full. "So I haven't the guts? " I repeated, my voice failing, but rather than give in and be dubbed a coward, I lifted the basket resolutely and tipped out its contents on the grass. "There! Eat them with me! "

The whole gang pounced on them in a body and the strawberries vanished instantly. All I got was a few undersized fruit. How sorry I was to see them go. I felt quite sad. But I put on an air of bravado and threw caution to the winds. What did it matter now! As I scampered down to the river with the others I boasted, "And I'll pinch one of Granny's rolls, too! "

They egged me on joyfully and said they could do with more than one. Maybe I could snatch some cookies or a pie as well?

"All right, then! "

We splashed about in the icy water, roamed along the bank and caught a bullhead with our bare hands. Sanka hoisted out the repulsive creature, compared it with his private parts, and we tore it to pieces on the bank for its ugliness. Then we threw stones at the birds flying overhead and winged a sand martin. We tried to revive it with water from the river, but it couldn't swallow and only stained the river with its blood. Soon its head dropped on one side and it died. We buried the sand martin on the bank, among the pebbles, and quickly forgot all about it because we had taken up another, really thrilling game. We had started running into the mouth of a big cold cave where, as all the village knew for a fact, an evil spirit lived. Sanka ran farther into the cave than anyone. Even an evil spirit couldn't catch him!

"Pooh! That's nothing! " Sanka boasted on returning to safety. "I'd have gone even further, I would. Only I haven't got any shoes on and there's ever so many snakes! "

"Snakes? " Tanka retreated from the mouth of the cave and, just in case, pulled up her slipping panties.

"I saw a house sprite and his wife there," Sanka rattled on.

"Bunk! " the eldest boy contradicted. "House sprites live in attics and under the stove."

Sanka was put off his stroke for a moment but rallied quickly.

"Depends what kind. There's house sprites that live in houses and there's others that live in caves. He was all grey and covered in moss and shivering something awful. And his wife was thin as a rake and looked at me pitiful like and moaned. But she couldn't tempt me! If you got near her she'd grab you and gobble you up. I gave her one in the eye with a stone! "

Perhaps Sanka was lying about the sprites but his tale was terrifying to listen to and I fancied I could hear someone moaning in the cave. Tanka was the first to beat a retreat from this evil spot and the rest of us followed her in a wild rush down the hillside. Sanka whooped and yelled all the swearwords he could think of to prod us on.

And so in this interesting and jolly fashion we passed the whole day and I quite forgot about the strawberries. But the time came to go home. We sorted out the pots and baskets we had hidden under a tree.

"Granny Petrovna will give it to you! That she will! " Sanka chortled. "We've eaten all your strawberries! Ha-ha! We did it on purpose! Ha-ha! She can't do nothing to us! "

I knew myself that it was just "ha-ha! " for Levonty's kids, but it would be "oh-oh! " for me. My Granny, Katerina Petrovna, was not like Auntie Vasenya.

I trudged along after the Levonty's kids out of the forest. They ran on ahead of me in a gang, kicking the ladle without a handle. It clattered and bounced on the stones and lost what was left of its enamel.

"You know what? " Sanka came back to me after a word with his brothers. "Put some grass in your basket and some strawberries on top and no one will be any the wiser! 'Ah, my little child!' " he began in a perfect imitation of my grandmother. " 'The Lord in his mercy must have helped you, little orphan that you are!' " And, little devil that he was, Sanka gave me a wink and dashed away down the bank.

I stayed behind.

The kids' voices died away below, among the kitchen gardens, and I felt frightened. I could hear the village from here, it was true. But all around was the taiga and the cave was not far away, and in it there was an evil sprite and his wife, and lots of writhing snakes.

I sat down with a sigh and nearly started to cry, then set about pulling some grass. I pushed the grass into the basket, then picked some strawberries, heaped them over the grass, and soon the basket looked as though it were full to overflowing.

"Ah, my little child! " Granny declaimed when, trembling with fear, I handed her my basket. "The Lord in his mercy has helped you, little orphan that you are! I'll buy you a gingerbread, the biggest one there is. And I won't put your berries in with mine. I'll take them straight to town as they are, in this basket."

I breathed again.

I had thought Granny would discover my trickery at once and give me what I deserved, and I had been prepared to face the penalty.

But the danger had passed. I was safe. Granny put the basket down in the cellar, praised me again, gave me something to eat and it began to look as if there was nothing to fear for the time being and life was not so bad after all.

I finished my meal and went out in the street to play, and there I was so misguided as to let Sanka know what had happened.

"I'll tell your Granny! I'll tell her! "

"Don't, Sanka! "

"Bring me a roll, then I won't."

I crept into the pantry, took a roll out of the bread bin and brought it to Sanka, hiding it under my shirt. Then I brought another, and another, until Sanka had gorged himself.

Now I had not only cheated Granny, but stolen her rolls, too! What would happen to me now? I worried all night, tossing and turning on my bed in the loft. There was no sleep for me, inveterate criminal that I had become.

"What are you fidgeting about up there for? " Granny's voice croaked in the darkness. "You've been paddling in that river again, I'll be bound. Is it your legs hurting you again? "

"'S all right," I called back. "I was only dreaming."

"Go to sleep! Don't worry your head over anything. There's more to be afraid of in life than in any dream, young man."

What if I woke her up and confessed everything?

I listened. The sound of Granny's laboured breathing reached me from below. It'd be a pity to wake her. She must be tired, and she had to get up early. I should be the one to miss my sleep. I'd stay awake all night, catch Granny in the morning and tell her the whole story of the basket, the house sprite and his wife, the rolls—everything.

Soothed by this decision, I didn't even feel my eyes close. Sanka's leering unwashed face popped up in front of me, then the strawberries blotted out Sanka and everything else.

The smell of pinewood and the cold mysterious cave invaded the loft.

* * *

Grandad was out in the far field, about five kilometres from the village at the mouth of the River Mana. We had a strip of rye, a strip of oats and a strip of potatoes out there.

Folk were only just beginning to talk about collective farms in those days and the people of our village still farmed on their own. I liked being with Grandad in the far field. Life was so calm and steady there somehow. Perhaps this was because Grandad never made a fuss, and even worked without any hurry but in a very thorough, capable way.

If only the far fields had not been so far! I would have gone out there to lie low. But in those days five kilometres was an enormous, insuperable distance for me, and my cousin Alyoshka was not at home either. Auntie Avgusta had come over recently and taken him out to the logging camp where she was working.

I drifted about the empty house and could think of nothing better to do than go next door again.

"So Granny Petrovna's sailed away! " Sanka leered and spat through the gap between his front teeth. The gap was big enough to take another tooth and we were terribly jealous of it. It was so good for spitting!

Sanka had decided to go fishing and was sorting out his line. The younger children were crawling and toddling about on their bandy legs, and Sanka was handing out slaps right and left because they kept getting in his way and tangling the line.

"The hook's missing," he said crossly. "One of these brats must have swallowed it."

"Will he die? "

"'S nuffin'," Sanka reassured me. "You've got plenty of hooks. If you give me one I'll take you fishing."

"Done! "

I dashed home delightedly, grabbed our fishing rods and some bread, and we set off for the boulders beyond the meadow that ran down to the Yenisei below the village.

Levonty's eldest boy was not present this time. His father had taken him out on a firewood trip and Sanka was in sole command. Conscious of his great responsibility, he had stopped teasing and even pacified his "crowd" if any fights broke out.

By the boulders Sanka planted the rods in position, baited

the hooks with worms, spat on them for luck and made his casts.

"Sh! " he whispered, and we all froze.

Nothing rose for a long time. We grew tired of waiting and Sanka sent us off to look for sorrel, riverside garlic and wild radish.

Levonty's kids knew how to live off the land. They ate everything God offered and were not a bit finicky, and so they were all ruddy-faced, strong and quick, particularly at table.

While we were gathering greenstuff to fill our bellies, Sanka hooked two ruffs, a gudgeon and a white-eyed dace.

We built a fire on the bank. Sanka spitted the fish on sticks and started frying them.

The fish were eaten almost raw without salt. The kids had guzzled my bread long ago and now they took up various amusements. Some dragged sand martins from their holes, others skidded flat stones across the water, or tried to bathe, but the water was still cold and we hopped out quickly to warm ourselves by the fire. When we were warm we rolled in the as yet low grass.

It was a clear, summer day. The sun beat down fiercely. Mottled cuckoo tears bowed their heads round the cattle-field. Bluebells swayed to and fro on their long crisp stalks and only the bees could hear them ringing. Morning glory gramophones lay on the ground near an ant-heap and bumblebees were poking their heads into their light-blue horns. They stayed there so long with their fuzzy little bottoms sticking out that it looked as though they were listening to the music. The birch leaves shone, the aspens moped in the heat. The hawthorn had passed its prime and was shedding its last blossoms untidily in the water. The pines were wrapped in a blue mist. There was a slight haze over the Yenisei, and the red mouths of the lime kilns flaming on the other side of the river were barely visible. On the cliffs the forests stood motionless and the railway bridge in town that could be seen from our village in clear weather now quivered like fine lace and, if you looked at it long enough, the lace frayed and broke into holes.

It was from beyond that bridge that Granny would come rowing home. What would happen then? Why had I done all this? Why had I let the Levonty's kids lead me on?

How good life had been before! I had run about without a care in the world. But now? Perhaps the boat would capsize and Granny would be drowned? No, I'd rather it didn't. My mother had been drowned. What good had come of that? Now I was an orphan. A miserable creature. And there was no one to take pity on me. Levonty was only sorry for me when he was drunk. Granny was always scolding and she might let fly at me, too; she had that kind of temper. And Grandad was away. Out in the far fields was Grandad. He would have taken me under his wing. He even caught it from Granny himself sometimes. "Spoiler! You've spoiled your own children all your life! And now it's this one! "

Ah, Grandad, if only you'd come home for a bath! Or just for no special reason, and take me back with you.

"What are you moping for? " Sanka bent over me with concern on his face.

"Nothing! " But by the tone of my voice I let him know that it was he, Sanka, who had brought me to this pass.

" 'S nuffin'! " Sanka consoled me. "Don't go home! Bury yourself in a haystack and lie low. Petrovna noticed one of your mother's eyes was half open when they buried her. She's scared you'll get drowned, too. She'll start hollering, 'He's drowned, my little child, he's left me, my little orphan'—and that's when you turn up! "

"I won't do that! " I protested. "And I won't listen to you any more! "

"Go and fry then! I was only trying to help.... Hi! You've got a bite! Look! "

I slithered down the cliff, scaring the martins out of their holes, and tugged at the rod. It was a roach. Then I hooked a ruff. The fish had started to rise. There was hardly time to rebait our hooks and cast.

"Don't step over the rod! " Sanka howled superstitiously at the capering youngsters and went on hauling out fish one after another. The youngsters threaded them on to a willow branch and let them dangle in the water.

All of a sudden from behind the nearest boulder came the rap of iron-shod poles on the river bottom and a boat appeared round the headland. Three men drew their poles out of the water all together. The polished tips glinted in the light and plunged into the water again and the boat all but dipped her gunwales, then surged forward, sending waves to either side.

Another stroke with the poles, hands shifted for the downward thrust, and the boat lifted her bows and rode lightly forward. Nearer and nearer. A stroke by the helmsman and the boat nosed away from our rods. And it was then I caught sight of a fourth person seated under the awning. The shawl over her head was drawn under her arms and tied at the back. A crimson blouse showed under the shawl. That blouse was taken out of the family chest only for trips to town or on red-letter days.

It was Granny!

I shot away from those rods straight towards the cliff, jumped, grabbed a tuft of grass and pegged my big toe into a martin's hole. A martin flew up and pecked me on the head and I fell back on scattered chunks of clay. On my feet again, I raced away along the bank, leaving the boat behind.

"Where are you off to? Stop! Stop, I say! " Granny cried.

I pelted on as hard as I could go.

"You'll come home! You'll have to come! Swindler! " Granny's voice pursued me.

The men put a whiplash to my heels by shouting, "Stop him! " and before I knew it I was at the other end of the village.

It was then I realised evening had come and, like it or not, I should have to go home. But I didn't want to go home and so, just on the off-chance, I decided to go and see my cousin Keshka, Uncle Vanya's son, who lived here, at the upper end of the village.

This time I was lucky. A game of *lapta* was in progress in front of Uncle Vanya's house. I joined in and played till dark. Auntie Fenya, Keshka's mother, appeared and wanted to know what I was up to.

"Why don't you go home? Granny'll be missing you! "

"No, she won't," I replied as casually as I could. "She's gone to town. She may be away for the night."

Auntie Fenya asked if I was hungry and I joyfully put away all she gave me.

Keshka, a sickly, silent boy, drank only some boiled milk. "Always milk, milk, milk!" his mother told him. "Look at the way this boy eats. That's what makes him strong!"

I was beginning to hope Auntie Fenya would invite me to stay for the night. But she went on asking me about this, that and the other, then took me by the hand and led me home.

All the lights were out when we got there. Auntie Fenya knocked on the window. Granny shouted, "It's not locked! " We entered the dark, quiet house; there was no sound save for the beating of moths' wings and the buzz of flies against the window panes.

Auntie Fenya pushed me through the porch and into a little cubby-hole that was built on to it. There was a bed in the cubby-hole made up of floor mats with an old saddle for a pillow. It was kept like that in case anyone suffering from the heat during the day wanted to lie down in the cool. I bundled muself up in a mat and lay quiet.

Auntie Fenya and Granny were a long time discussing something inside. The cubby-hole smelled of bran, dust and the dry grass that had been stuffed into all the cracks and under the ceiling. For some reason this grass kept popping and crackling. I felt miserable in the cubby-hole. The darkness was dense and rough to the touch, and full of smells and hidden life.

A solitary mouse that had to go hungry because the cat was on the lookout for it was gnawing timidly under the floor. And the dry grasses and flowers lodged under the eaves kept crackling as they opened their pods and scattered seed in the darkness.

Stillness, cool and the sounds of night had taken over the village. After the heat of the day the dogs revived, crept out from under porches, doorsteps and out of kennels and gave tongue. An accordion began to toot by the bridge over the

Little River. That was where the young people of the village gathered to dance and sing.

Firewood was being chopped hastily at Uncle Levonty's. He must have brought in something that needed cooking and his kids had pinched a pole from someone. From us most likely. It would be too far for them to go anywhere else for firewood at this time of night.

Auntie Fenya left and closed the front door firmly behind her. The cat slipped furtively across the front steps. The mouse froze under the floorboards. It became very quiet and lonely. Not even a floorboard creaked. Granny wasn't moving about the house any more. She must be tired. I began to feel chilly, so I rolled myself up into a ball and breathed on my chest.

I was awakened by a sunbeam filtering through the bleary window of the cubby-hole. Dust was swarming in the beam like midges. From somewhere I caught a whiff of fields and ploughland. I looked round and my heart jumped for joy. Grandad's old half-length coat had been spread over me. Grandad had come home during the night! Hurrah!

In the kitchen Granny was relating loudly, in a flood of indignation:

"...A cultured lady she was, in a hat. 'I'll buy that lot of strawberries,' she says. Certainly, I says. By all means. It was a little orphan who picked them...."

At this point I wanted to fall through the earth along with Granny, and I couldn't make out what happened after that because I had buried my head under the coat and was choking myself with it so as to die as quickly as possible.

But the heat and the suffocation were too much and I uncovered myself.

"...Always spoiled your own kids! " Granny was booming. "Now it's this one! And he's already started cheating! What'll he come to later? He'll finish up in the chain gang, that he will! A convict for life! I'll have to set about Levonty's kids too! This is their handiwork, I'm sure! "

Grandad took himself off into the yard, out of harm's way. Granny came out into the porch and peeped into the cubby-hole. I closed my eyes tight.

"You're not asleep. I know! I spotted you! "

But I didn't give in. Granny's niece dropped in to ask what sort of trip Granny had had. Granny said thank the Lord and at once embarked on her tale.

"My young 'un! D'you know what he's been up to! ..."

We had many visitors that morning and to each of them Granny said, "My young 'un! D'you know...."

She went to and fro, gave the cow a drink, turned it over to the herdsman for the day, did her various jobs and, whenever she happened to pass the door of the cubby-hole, shouted:

"You're not asleep, I know! I spotted you! "

I knew she would eventually finish in the house and go out. She was bound to go out to retail the news she had gathered in town and find out what new events had occurred in the village during her absence. And to everyone she met she would proclaim, "My young 'un! D'you know what...."

Grandad slipped into the cubby-hole, pulled a pair of leather reins out from under me and winked as much as to say, "Don't worry. There's nothing to be scared of! "

I snuffled.

Grandad stroked my head and the tears that had been gathering so long gushed forth uncontrollably.

"Now, now, now! What's all this? " Grandad soothed me, collecting the tears off my face with his big rough hand. "Why do you lie here hungry? Go and ask forgiveness. Go along now." And he gave me a gentle push in the back.

Holding up my trousers with one hand, I put the other to my eyes and went inside.

"I'll never ... I'll never ... I'll never..." I began, and couldn't get any further.

"All right, all right! Wash your face and sit down to eat! " Granny said still unrelenting but without any more threats and thunderbolts.

I meekly washed my hands and face, wiped my hands with great care, still shaking now and then with a few unexpended sobs, and sat down to table. Grandad was busy in the kitchen, coiling the reins over his arm and doing some other job. Sensing his invisible but reliable support, I took a crust from the table and started eating it all by itself. Granny splashed some milk into a glass with a single sweep of her arm and plonked it down before me.

"Isn't he a good little boy now! Isn't he just! Wouldn't even ask for a glass of milk! ..."

Grandad winked round the door at me—stick it out! I knew that without being told. Heaven forbid that I should contradict Granny at that moment or do something she didn't approve of. She had to get it all off her chest, unburden herself completely.

For a long time Granny poured shame and accusations on my head. I wept again contritely. She scolded me again.

But at last her wrath was spent. Grandad went off somewhere. I sat smoothing the patch on my trousers and pulling threads out of it. And when I raised my head, I saw before me....

I closed my eyes and opened them again. Yet again. I closed them and opened them. Across the scrubbed kitchen table, as if across some great country with all its fields, meadows and roads, there came galloping on pink hooves a white horse with a pink mane.

"Take it! What are you staring for? But if Granny ever catches you cheating her again...."

How many years have passed since then! How much has happened! But I shall never forget Granny's gingerbread— that wonderful horse with a pink mane.

GRANNY'S DAY

Soon after the mowing was over, all our numerous relatives would turn up together at our house to pay us a visit or, to be more exact, to celebrate Granny's birthday. It happened only once in every two or three years; more often would have been too great an expense. No one ever arranged for Granny's sons, daughters, grandchildren and other offsprings to make their visit in any particular year, at any particular time. By some trick of intuition they themselves knew when to come.

Granny and Grandad also had the knack of guessing when the children were about to descend on them and would prepare well in advance to receive and provide for the multitude. Naturally the children would not come empty-handed, but it was Granny and Grandad who had to bear the main burden, and long beforehand, way back in winter, our house would embark upon a great fast, and all kinds of restrictions would be imposed on eating and spending.

When the cow had calved, the young bull or heifer would be kept under special observation—with a view to slaughter. A load of grain would go off along the sledge road to the mill at Bazaikha, to be turned into baking flour. While winter still reigned, eggs would be laid up, cream would be churned into butter, and all these supplies would be stored away in the cellar or the pantry or some secret hiding place known only to Granny.

To me alone would Granny sometimes grant a cracked egg, some skimmed milk, a crooked, yellow cucumber or some little morsel left over from the cooking.

Life in our house would become more and more hectic as the great day drew near. More and more often Granny would drop something or spill something and shout at no one in particular, "Oh, I'd sooner be dead! It would be a lot easier, that it would! "

Nevertheless, she managed to enter into the festive spirit sooner and more wholeheartedly than Grandad and Uncle Kolcha. The pressure would get both men down, and once they had "taken the bit between their teeth", as Granny put it, they were not so easy to handle.

More often than not it was Granny herself who drove her menfolk to rebellion by further disturbing the ruffled current of our life with sudden attacks and fits of suspicion or simply by laying too much stress on her own contribution to all the work and preparations.

Before this particular anniversary, which I have remembered ever since because I was then of an age to remember such things, Grandad blew his top at the worst possible moment. And once again it was Granny who drove him to this extreme because she was too worried and tired to feel when Grandad had reached the limit of his patience. Up to then she had been able to sense that limit in time to put a rein on herself. Sometimes of an evening Grandad's brother, Ksenofont, a lonely old fellow, would grow tired of sitting all by himself in his ancient, half-buried shack and would come round to sit with Grandad on the wooden coping beside our gate. The two brothers would sit together, smoking and exchanging their tobacco pouches. Sometimes they would spend the whole evening in this way, without a word spoken, and part well satisfied with each other. Sometimes they would smoke for a while in silence and then, just as silently, go off together. Once they were gone they were gone, and it was no good searching for them. Grandad would come in late, rather drunk and guiltily silent. Granny would toss him a pillow and blanket and he would go and make his bed in the loft over the barn.

Now, on the ill-fated evening in question, Ksenofont had come round as usual and Grandad had slipped out of the gate in an old pair of felt boots and coloured underpants, and he and his brother were sitting together, burning tobacco and thinking.

In the harassed, tired-out state she was in Granny could not help being irritated. There were those two men, wasting tobacco, while she was run off her feet and would never get all her jobs done. So out she came into the yard, shouting and scolding, gave Sharik the dog a kick, grabbed up a hen that had gone to roost among the stinging nettles and flung it into the hayloft and then lashed out at any empty pail that had got in her path. But even when the pail came rolling down to the gate and hit the timbers with a crash, Grandad didn't take a scrap of notice.

The trouble really started, so it came out later, when Grandad and Ksenofont went off to pull Ksenofont's boat higher up the river bank because the waters of the Yenisei were rising; the great heat that summer had set the glaciers in the mountains melting and Ksenofont's boat (he was a keen angler) was in danger of being swept away. Granny, however, took it into her head that they had gone off drinking, and this put her in a worse temper than ever, and she waited for Grandad's return so that she could pour out her wrath on his head. No one had ever seen Grandad rolling drunk. In fact, it was rather hard to tell just how much he had drunk and what condition he was in. To be on the safe side, it was better to wait until he had slept it off, as Granny usually did, exercising all due caution and restraint.

But not this time. First she flung a tantrum in the house, then she blew up in the yard, then she stamped out into the street and, finally, she stormed off to Auntie Avdotya's to break all her windows if she found Grandad there.

While she was at Auntie Avdotya's, investigating the situation, Grandad returned from the river, climbed up into his loft and calmly dropped off to sleep.

Granny, however, was still smouldering with spent-up fury and, in the morning, she let Grandad have it good and proper. He listened to her calmly, with perhaps just a trace of sorrow on his face, and his square, Pugachov-style beard twitched up and down once or twice, a sign which Granny, unfortunately, failed to notice, then without waiting for her to finish— obviously she was going to be at it for a long time—he went out into the yard, led the family horse out of the stable, took the cross-bar out of the gate and hurled it right into the stinging nettles, whereupon I, guessing what was going to happen, dashed into the house, shouting:

"Granny! Granny! Grandad's going away in the cart! "

Let him go, the devil! " Granny cried with as much temper in her voice as ever, but rushed out into the yard at once.

Grandad's revolt reached such a pitch that he didn't even close the gate behind him. He left it wide open and, what was more, instead of moving the board under the gate, he drove straight over it, grinding it to bits under the cart wheels.

"All right! You needn't shut it! " Granny screamed from the porch. "And neither shall I! Neither shall I! That'll be a proper disgrace! Just look at the state our gate's in, good folk! Look and wonder! It's wide open! Wide open to the world! You've left your own home wide open, that's what you've done! "

She went on shouting in this vein but it did't stop her from standing on tip-toe and craning her neck in the hope that Grandad had just been hasty and would change his mind and turn back. But the cart was beyond the cemetery by now. It rumbled on over the pebbles of the Little River, clattered away up the hill and disappeared into the pinewoods. Terrified at being lashed with the reins by such a peaceable man as Grandad, our dobbin charged along as far as any race-horse up the hill towards the meadows where our mowing patch and hut were. The little hut had not been taken over by the loggers because it was too far from the rafting pool. Uncle Kolcha had been standing in for Grandad during the mowing, so that Grandad could stay at home and help Granny. Now her helper was gone!

"Good! Goody! Very good! Fine! " Granny declared, hands on hips, when the rattle of the cart had died away among the trees. "All the children will come home soon. 'Where's Daddy? ' they'll ask. Even the little ones, our grandchildren, will want to know where Grandad is. And this is what I'll tell them. 'My dear children,' I shall say, 'the piss has gone to his stupid old head and our Grandad Elijah the Prophet has driven off to all the devils. So fast you could only hear the thunder of his cart. Well, now you know, my dears,' I'll say, 'what a life I've had with such a man! All the torment and suffering I've had to put up with, unhappy woman that I am! ' "

Granny had no time to waste on lamentations, so she said all this and sang it out for the benefit of anyone who might be passing, while busying herself with her household chores, but she left the gate open and told me not to close it either. With resentment and real pain underneath it, she kept on repeating that people should look and judge what kind of life and what sufferings she had been compelled to endure.

Almost till night-time the gate remained open, but we had to close it when it grew dark and there was no longer any hope of Grandad's returning. Granny and I both got well and properly stung before we retrieved the cross-bar from the stinging nettles. She poulticed my blistered hands and with what was left of her rage uttered a last, feeble threat:

"Very well, stay up there then, and go hungry! Dotty, that's what he is! What did I say to send him off like that? All right, suppose he hadn't been drinking for once. I get nervy myself sometimes, I, too, can say things I don't mean. What of it.... But he'll ruin that horse, that he will! He's such a cruel old devil, he is! "

Nearly all next day she kept on talking as if Grandad were still just round the corner. Then she gave in, packed some food in a knapsack and sent me off with it to the hayfield.

"It's Kolcha I'm sorry for," she said as though to justify her conduct. "The other one can die of hunger today or tomorrow for all I care. I shan't worry, I shan't shed a single tear. Not one! " She stamped her foot and shook her fist in the direction of the hayfield. But at the gate she started shifting from one foot to another and straightening the straps of my knapsack, and eventually she muttered confusedly, "Ask Grandad to come back. There's the calf to be killed and no end of other jobs to be done. Ask him to come back. He's obstinate but he'll listen to you. Ask him to come back, dear."

But that was easier said than done. I was in a difficult position. Even a small indiscretion on my part might result in Grandad's further estrangement from the family.

He greeted me surlily, so the first thing to be done was somehow to get rid of this surliness.

As though nothing at all had happened, I began by grabbing a pail and clattering down to the stream with it. Then I made a fire, washed the potatoes and started singing loudly:

> Oh, you nasty old potatoes,
> Aren't you ever going to cook?
> Our guests, all kissed, await us
> And you're cold as water in a brook!

And it worked! Grandad's nostrils quivered and he smirked into his beard.

"Where's the salt, Grandad?"

He eyed me with vexation, as much as to say, "Even out here they won't leave me in peace. They must come bothering me, won't leave me to my proud solitude."

"Where do you think, boy? In the hut."

Again I had him on the hook! He had actually uttered a sound. That was something! Quite a lot, in fact! If only Uncle Kolcha would come back from the hay-making now, we would soon bring Grandad round. After all, it was no fun for Kolcha to have to stay up here fasting with Grandad; he would much rather be back home in the village.

> Good old salt,
> Salty old salt! ...

I bawled louder than ever and tossed a handful of salt in with the potatoes, then made as if to throw in another, but Grandad's voice said:

"Salt costs money!"

Aha, Grandad, so you've still got an eye on your property, eh? You haven't turned your back on all your worldly possessions. If you can still think of things like that, it means you still care.

But as yet Grandad was not asking me any questions and pretended that everything could go up in flames for all he would worry. He didn't care a tinker's cuss about the forthcoming celebrations. He had shaken off his fetters.... But I had different ideas. I was going to get Grandad out of his sulks and back to the village.

The potatoes were soon cooked. I strained off the water and put the pot on the table. When I had cut the bread, I took Granny's potato patties and two bowls of soured milk out of the knapsack and put them on the table too. Grandad did not take a scrap of notice. He just sat there on an upturned log, puffing away. His gaze, focussed somewhere far away beyond the River Mana, was full of scorn for everything that concerned work or household matters.

"Shall I call Uncle Kolcha?"

"Can if you like. What do I care? "

I dashed off to the field and started calling and waving my arms from a distance.

"Uncle Kolcha! Uncle Kolcha! "

Kolcha was fencing in a haystack, binding the stakes with twigs and shaping the poles. His shirt was unbuttoned and hanging loose over his trousers. His wavy forelock was feathered with dry grass and shavings. I flopped down in the shade of the stack, while he went on with the fence, asking about Granny, the house and our affairs as he worked. On the way back from the field to the hut we decided on our further course of action.

On the pretext of having urgent matters to attend to Uncle Kolcha would leave the hayfield after dinner. Grandad, we reckoned, would not be able to put up with the loneliness for long and would also make tracks for the village.

"But don't go pestering him or rubbing him up the wrong way," Uncle Kolcha instructed me, "Mind you don't make a slip! "

He washed his face and hands in the stream, sat down to table and shouted at the open door of the hut:

"Hi, Dad, why don't you come? We're waiting."

Mumble, mumble from the yard.

What Grandad was mumbling into his beard we couldn't make out. At last he appeared and crossed himself sternly and sadly in front of the wooden icon. Uncle Kolcha and I busied ourselves peeling the hot potatoes, and tried not to look at Grandad. At first he ate unwillingly, as if it were torture, picking little misshapen, damaged potatoes from the pot, grunting and sighing as he peeled them, and salting them heavily. A picture of sorrow was our Grandad. Uncle Kolcha turned away to the window, as though to keep an eye on the horses, and it was all I could do to stop myself from tittering. That would have ruined everything.

Gradually Grandad got his appetite back and we finished off all the food I had brought from home; Granny had sent only just enough, so as to tease the men's appetite with her goodies and tempt them away from the hayfield. Subtle politics at every turn!

After dinner I climbed up into the loft, and Uncle Kolcha took himself off to the village.

Grandad pottered about the yard, muttering to himself and tapping with his axe. This was the critical moment. Grandad might overcome his resentment or he might make up his mind not to return to the village at all. A very self-willed old man was our Grandad.

But all at once there was a clank of harness. Grandad had stopped wandering aimlessly about the yard and gone to fetch the horse. He had given in.

Soon there was a clatter of hooves on boards. Grandad was backing our unwieldy dobbin into the shafts. Then he gathered up his belongings and groped about in the porch for the padlock and key.

"Are we here to spend the night? " he asked grumpily, addressing no one in particular.

I climbed down from the loft unwillingly stretching myself and yawning, as though I had just been disturbed in the middle of a good nap.

There was fresh hay in the cart. I flopped down into it and trotted the cart out of the yard. Grandad closed the gate. I waited for him. He was a long time closing that gate. I hoped he wouldn't change his mind. No. He was blowing his nose and lighting up properly for the road.

Throughout the journey I watched Grandad's unrelenting back. He said nothing to me and made no attempt to quicken our pace. He was going home as though under compulsion, without any desire. When we were half way there, he turned to me and asked grimly:

"Did she send you herself? "

I figured that since we had now passed Korolyov's Gully and would soon be on the slope down to the village, he was not likely to turn back, and answered affirmatively.

"Yes."

"Aha! ... Huh! "

From these sounds that Grandad forced out into his beard I concluded that he had enjoyed his revenge to the full and was now gloating. The "Aha! " meant, "That's what comes of driving a man beyond endurance! " and the "Huh! "

meant, "I may be a 'slowcoach' and an 'old grunter', but they can't get on without me because I've always been master in my own house and always will be, and no matter what tricks they play, the big day can't come off without me, and even at ordinary times it's still worth-while to have me around."

"Gee-up, Dobbin! Gee-up! " Grandad brightened up and flicked the reins and we rolled up to the house at a lively trot.

Granny was there to open the gate. She took Dobbin by the bridle and went tripping across the yard with him, looking gratefully at me and ingratiatingly at Grandad, and talking away all the time. As yet Grandad made no response either negative or positive.

"Perhaps you'll have a drink after your day's work? ' Granny suggested over supper, and rushed a small bottle o vodka in from the best room.

Grandad poured the vodka into a china goblet, knocked i back, grunted approvingly and set about his cabbage soup.

Peace had returned to our house.

* * *

The guests arrived by various means of conveyance. Uncle Kolcha Senior came down from town with his wife Natalya on the loggers' motor launch. They led an odd kind of life. They would work all the hours that are made, sell their stuff at the market, scrimp over every kopek, then spend all their savings on a grand outing and start saving again.

Uncle Vasya and Auntie Lyuba would come from Bazaikha on foot, across the mountains. They were very much alike, both very neat and kind, and Granny adored them. They both worked at the Laletinsk Experimental Nursery, Auntie Lyuba as a gardener and Uncle Vasya as a labourer. This time they brought some red apples that were still sharp and rather bitter. Since most of the children, including myself, had never seen an apple, we were overjoyed with the present and devoured those tart, mouth-binding apples in no time. Auntie Maria and her husband Zyryanov came down by boat from the Mana Rapids, bringing sterlet and salmon trout with them for pies. Zyryanov was a buoy-keeper. They had no children and so they lived closely and were rather well off. Granny was not very fond of Zyryanov and addressed him always by his surname. She was kind of Auntie Maria, but never interfered in their life. "Married life is nobody's business," she would say.

As usual, some new relatives turned up and, as usual, there was a guest in swaddling clothes—the son of one of Granny's nieces. Granny immediately unwrapped him and without making it too obvious had a look to see if his nappies were clean and he had no rash. Then she felt the bandy-legged little Siberian's chest and tummy, in response to which he stretched himself blissfully, frowned and emitted a loud noise that made everyone roar with laughter, while Granny cooed:

"And here's another newcomer! The more the merrier! A knot for his belly, legs round as jelly and smells of good black bread—he'll make a plowman! A plowman he shall be! " And the little fellow suddenly gave a smile, and his young mother, who had heard all about what a character Granny Katerina was and how hard she was to please, and had been standing in fear and trembling up to now, pressed her shawl over her mouth and nose. Granny, who, of course, knew all about everything, said sharply: "That's right! Now you'll start him off too! "

Meanwhile, in the yard the men would be strolling round recalling what the place had been like before and rejoicing that not much had changed. Vying with one another, they would recollect how Vasya had slid off the roof into the cattle pen and landed astride the cow, whereupon Granny, who had been milking the cow at the time, had nearly gone off her head; or else, how Vasya and Ivan had crept on to Timsha Betekhtin's allotment for cucumbers and he had fired gravel at them from his shot-gun; or how Vasya had been bitten by that fierce horse Karka, whereupon Vasya had lost his temper and had bitten Karka back, after which Vasya had been the only person Karka would allow to come near him, having no respect at all for anyone else; or how they used to bathe from morning to night in the Yenisei, and would even start among the shore ice; or how they robbed the birds' nests (what fools they had been!); or how they used to work in the hayfield and mother would come running over and tell all the boys and girls off for being slovenly, set an example herself by binding a couple of sheaves, and then rush off back to the village or to the next field, where she must also give orders and instructions because there was no one else to take on the responsibility.

"Remember? "

"Remember? " that was the word from all sides.

And my grey-haired uncles and aunts laughed and their faces looked younger. They were nearly all ginger-haired and freckled and had high cheekbones. The reddest of all were Uncle Kolcha Senior and Uncle Vanya, but there hadn't been enough paint left to go round for the rest, so they all claimed, and the colour had run rather thin. Uncle Kolcha Junior was just a light brown, and had been left with a mere sprinkling of freckles.

The gate was scarcely closed for a moment. The latch clanked back and forth like a festive bell as our folk kept rolling in. And the neighbours, too, friends of my uncles and aunts, who had not seen them for a long time, also dropped in to say hullo and have a word. They were invited to be our guests on the morrow, but not very insistently. After all, it was a family celebration and everyone in the village knew that strangers would not be welcome at such a feast.

Granny had said many a time that she had brought up her children strictly, perhaps too strictly, but at least she had something to show for it. Even now, she would put on an air of severity, just to make sure her sons and daughters—some of them were already grandparents themselves! —did not forget who she was and what she was. For their part the "children" gladly allowed her the pleasure of bossing it over them. The yoke was too temporary and unreal for them to feel the weight of it.

So now, with her headscarf all awry, Granny shot out into the yard and broke into all the reminiscing and idle chatter.

"Here you, men! Boys! What the devil are you sitting around for, wasting tobacco? "

"What is there for us to do, Mum? "

"What is there to do? Can't you go out for a night's fishing? I'd make a lovely fry for you."

"But where are the nets, Mum? "

"Nets? Mum's got everything! She lets nothing go to waste! " Granny declared, striking herself on the chest, and the men went into the barn and broke into loud exclamations, all meant for her to hear: "There's a mother for you! That's the way to look after things! We're in luck, we are!"

From the barn came the clink of the sinkers on the nets and the satisfied rumble of male voices mingled with the hopeless demands of the women:

"You might at least take off your clean shirts! " Then they would turn on Granny: "Once you get an idea into your head! They may get drowned! "

Granny was about to take up the argument when she was brought up short by the ringing, devil-may-care voice of Auntie Avgusta:

"Don't you need us to keep you company, or are you too many as it is? "

"Here she is at last! " Granny swooped down on her. "Why didn't you come tomorrow? Straight to the table, eh?"

None of the Potylitsyns had come off worse in life than Aunt Avgusta. Her husband had been killed, her son had been born dumb. She had no home of her own and was always moving from one strange house to another. Avgusta gave Granny a hand on holidays and week-days as well. Though she couldn't live without her, Granny was always scolding Avgusta. She would spend days on end, darting from window to window, because she thought something might have happened to Auntie on the logging rafts, but as soon as Auntie turned up Granny would have some reproach to utter.

"I've been at work, floating timber, Mum, I can't leave just when I want to. It's not mine to leave," Avgusta replied with a touch of bitterness, and everyone felt awkward and even Granny didn't know what to say to that. But Avgusta herself put everything right.

"So here we are, Lyuba dear! " she said and stretched out both arms to hug and kiss Vasya's wife, who was sweet to everyone and whom everyone loved. Then Auntie Avgusta hugged Auntie Talya and Uncle Kolcha, made some remark and laughed, and the whole family was united and cheerful once again. About ten minutes later Avgusta went rushing off to the shed with a milking pail, and a little later she was sifting flour and taken up entirely in her work.

Meanwhile we sat on the steps of the porch. Alyoshka, her son, who had come round the evening before, kept showing me in sign language how the water dragged the logs apart when you were rafting and what a sweet fruit custard they served in the canteen. I translated all this to my younger and older relatives. Everyone expressed their wonder at Alyoshka's powers.

"What a quick boy he is! And without being able to speak too! Think of that! He'd make circles round one or two who can! "

"He has even learned to play chess! " I shouted when I had at last understood some more of Alyoshka's signals. Granny was on the spot at once, very much alarmed.

"Wha-a-at? ! "

"Alyoshka plays chess! "

"Oh, what an awful thing! He'll lose all his own and Avgusta's money."

Uncle Vasya explained to Granny what chess was. It was not a card game, it was not pontoon.

"Ah," Granny was reassured. "But it'd be better if he didn't play at all. You never know! "

Katenka, Uncle Vasya and Auntie Lyuba's daughter, a little girl with a bow and wearing a sailor blouse with anchors on it, stood figuring the ground with her sandal.

"I know *shum* poetry."

"Do you really? " Granny asked in surprise and squatted in front of the little girl, making a delighted face. "Come on, then, dear, recite your poem to Granny." And she removed her kerchief from her ear, so that she shouldn't miss a word.

Katenka mounted the steps of the porch, as though it were a stage, Uncle Vasya called for silence, Auntie Lyuba strained forward and blushed with anxiety, not taking her eyes off her daughter and following every movement of her lips with her own.

> *Oh, you white-feathered magpie,*
> *Teach me to fly,*
> *Not very far and not very high,*
> *Jus' far enough*
> *To see Granny go by.*

This flattering little verse made an indescribable impression on all present, particularly on Granny. She disappeared into the house at once and came running back with a whole handful of sweets. With thoughtless generosity she tipped them into the pocket of Katenka's sailor blouse. Then she kissed her all over, and the uncles and aunts praised the little girl so highly and said such nice things about her that they nearly set me off, because I, too, wanted to climb those steps and recite loudly and with great expression a poem I had just learnt at school:

> *Two soldiers met in battle—*
> *One was foreign, one was ours....*

But that would make Granny shed a tear. "If only his poor dead mother could listen to him and see him now! " And she would look at the uncles and aunts in such a way as to make them pity both me and her as well. Uncle Kolcha Junior and my god-mother Apronya, who had been with my mother in the boat but had been saved, would become stony-faced and neither of them would say another word for the rest of their stay. The women who were less closely related to us would start asking Granny about it and she would go into a detailed account of what had happened and how it had happened, and how the river had been searched for my mother and what she had been like when they had found her—"we could hardly recognise her"—and what kind of funeral they had given her and what the burial robes had been. Half the guests would fall into a sorrowful mood and some would go off to the cemetery to weep.

But I wanted no tears now because there would be tears

soon enough anyway. There are no more tearful folk than
Siberians during a party. And this was why I made no
attempt to recite, but I did mutter the poem to my younger
cousins and they liked it a lot. They, too, hated to see the
girls doing better than the boys and winning more of
Granny's approval.

* * *

Towards evening the men, talking loudly, full of excitement over the forthcoming fishing expedition, which would
demand speed, agility and skill, set off for the river and
rowed away in two boats to the island to cast their nets from
its upstream end.

They took none of the boys with them and I was badly
disappointed. I loved the exciting and cunning game of
fishing with floating nets.

But I was not sad for long. There were plenty of other
guests; Granny did not call me indoors and we played until
dark at all kinds of games—skittles, "it", hide-and-seek, and
leapfrog. We played till we were tired out. Granny and
Avgusta, Apronya and Auntie Maria had by that time lighted
the stove, rolled out the buns on the table, pinched the pies
into the right shape, and made little bag-shaped loaves and
pastry nuts and all kinds of other nice things. We were fed by
Auntie Lyuba, who kept asking me in a whisper:

"Uncle Vasya wasn't drunk when he went off, was he?
They won't get drowned, will they? "

"Lyuba, dear! " Granny called from the scullery. "Make
up the beds for the band in the front room. They can all
sleep together on the floor, they won't get mixed up. And
you go to bed yourself, my dear, get some sleep. We're used
to this, but you're a tender one, from a good home...."

"Oh, but I couldn't, Mother, I want to be with you all. I'll
just put the children to bed and be with you right away."

"Now then, Lyuba, don't contradict! It's my rule here.
For better or for worse, I'm the one who rules! And no
arguing! What's come over the yeast these days? You used

to leave the dough to rise and it would come up lovely and soft, but with this yeast now the loaves all seem so feeble, blast and bother them! Or have I lost my touch? Perhaps my eye and hand aren't what they used to be? "

The aunts assured Granny that all was as it should be, that there was no cause to upset oneself, and told each other how they had been getting on and who they had seen lately, what illnesses they and their children had had, and what wages were being paid for floating timber.

Some time in the middle of the night a smell of baking pervaded the house. It was the smell of the first buns, fresh from the oven. The next moment Granny appeared in our room.

"Are you asleep, dears? " she whispered.

"Nunno."

"Oh, you naughty things! Well, here's the first bake for you! Careful! They're hot! You'll wake up the babies. And you try a bun too, Lyuba, my dear."

"Thank you, Mother. Oh, how hot it is! "

"Eat up, then! " Granny squatted down beside Auntie Lyuba for a minute. "How are you getting on with Vasily? Everything all right? "

"Right enough. We don't have any rows."

"The Lord be praised for that. Vasily's a good boy, a very good boy. He had more sense than any of the others...." Granny fell silent, and sniffed the air. "Oh, botheration! Once I start talking! Those girls won't keep an eye on anything! They'll just turn their heads the other way...." Granny shot out of the room and closed the double doors behind her.

We didn't hear the men come in, nor did Auntie Lyuba, because she was asleep. And in the morning she was very confused about it, specially when Uncle Vasya teased her that next time they went fishing he would row his boat all the way to town and there he would catch a "real sterlet"!

"That's enough talk from you! " Granny shouted from the store-room, and gave a loud, sighing yawn. "What did you catch? A couple of trout, and that's all I'll be bound?" She came out of the store-room, where she had slept for an hour or two at dawn, glanced at the two baskets full of dace and

said in a surprised voice: "Just look at this. So you did catch
something! "

"We cast in the name of your angel, Mum! "

"Well, she's not such a bad angel, is she? Nice and fishy! "
Granny assented, and ordered Uncle Vasya: "Stop hanging
about round your wife, now. Off you go into the hay-loft
with the others and have some sleep. You've been up all night
messing about, you'll be under the table with your first glass,
looking for the rest of the family. And this is my order for
you, Lyuba. You must feed all our band and keep an eye on
them to see they don't go falling in the river or getting lost.
Avgusta, Apronya, Maria! You've been dozing long enough!
Up you get, you great lumps! Sun says it's nearly dinner
time."

"Of all the devils!..." Aunt Maria's grumbling voice came
from the store-room. "She gets up at some unearthly hour
and won't let anyone else have a bit of sleep."

"Must do her bit of bossing! " Apronya put in.

"Real general, isn't she?! " Avgusta added.

One after the other the aunts came out into the yard,
stretching and yawning, clattered the stopper of the wash-
can, and before long were hard at it again, their drowsiness
vanishing and freshness returning to their tired faces as they
worked. By noon the tables in the front room were laid. The
aunts and Granny disappeared for a little while and reappeared in a state of unbelievable elegance and dignity. Actually it was only Granny and Aunt Maria who put on dignified
airs. Apronya and Avgusta were too humorously inclined and
sharp of tongue to keep it up for long.

At last, Grandad opened one of the double doors and
Granny the other, and in lilting voices that barely concealed
their emotion, invited the guests to table.

"Be so kind, dear guests! Be so kind as to try our modest
feast. Don't judge us too sternly. It's what God has sent."

And Grandad muttered into his beard:

"Come in, good folk, come in! "

All this ceremony went against the grain with him but,
having more than once endured Granny's reproaches for not
being able to welcome people properly and grudging them a

kind word, Grandad performed his duties to the full. His sons winked at him as they went by, made various approving remarks and even suggested he abandon his position and come to table himself. But Granny was on the watch and Grandad dared not slip away.

After some humorous scuffling and a brief but noisy spell of internecine strife, during which we tried not to knock anything over or spill something over ourselves or a neighbour, our large family took their places, the grown-ups at two tables, and the children, at a third. The tables had additional sections fitted to them and they stretched from wall to wall, just as in the rafters' canteen. At the end of the table under the icon there were two vacant places—for Granny and Grandad.

The tables were laid in accordance with Siberian custom: everything that was in the oven or the cellar or the pantry, everything that had been saved up, had to be put on the table. The more the better. So everything on the tables was wholesomely large, beautifully dressed up, roasted and baked to a turn, prepared with great care and skill.

The meat jelly—Granny's pride—with just a thin film of fat on the top, had started wobbling when the guests came into the room and it was still wobbling. It looked as clear and light as air, but you needed a knife to cut it. There was pickled cabbage in slabs and finely chopped. The salted cucumbers were all cut into thin slices. The boiled chicken reclined with its legs sticking out of the dish. Little plates of milk-cap mushrooms, smiled up at us cordially with their saffron lips. In Siberia they never wash this mushroom before salting. Instead they wipe each one separately with a cloth, so that it keeps its colour and crispness in the brine. Two large iron pans contained the dace, which had been baked in the oven. They were not a bit dry but they had been so perfectly browned that you could eat them head and all—and how delicious! They were dressed with pepper and laurel leaf, but no fat had been added—what kind of dace was it if it couldn't provide its own juice? Either it was a bad dace or the cook was no good. There was also a fish pie made of salmon trout, which the Zyryanovs had brought. We make our fish pies according to the size of the fish. They can be any size as long as they will go into the oven. This one was not very big, but it had a fine aroma. Salmon trout makes the best fish pie of all. Just as with the dace, nothing is added to the pie except pepper and laurel leaf. It provides its own juice, fat and fragrance.

Tarts and buns, meat cooked in all kinds of ways. Soused sterlet, eggs fried with milk, sweet pies, dishes of last year's cowberries, and of whortleberry jam made the year before last, biscuits, rusks, pastry nuts.... Mountains of everything, almost spilling off the table.

Now would be the time to start tucking in—but no such luck. At the very last moment Granny disappeared and we all had to sit waiting in suspense. Grandad shifted from one foot to another, muttered something into his beard and eventually took his seat at table, under the icon.

"Trust her to put on airs! "

Uncle Kolcha Senior and Uncle Vanya left the room, then reappeared, leading Granny gently by the arms. As they came in they winked at Avgusta and Apronya, warning them not to laugh and spoil the ceremony. Taking the longest route, past all the youngsters, Granny's eldest sons led her to the place of honour, moved back her chair and said:

"Yours is the place of honour, Mother! "

Granny knew how hard it was for these fifty-year-old children of hers to make speeches, and she had expected nothing more. How modestly and shyly she lowered her eyes and with a slight quiver of the lips said:

"Thank you, my children. Thank you for your respect and affection."

In passing she treated Grandad to a withering glance for infringing the ritual and not knowing his own worth. Grandad turned away crossly and his beard went up and down, up and down.

But this was not all by any means. Granny turned to the icon, making sure that she could still see all the tables out of the corner of her eye, and began to cross herself. Everyone moved back their chairs and benches, a fork dropped with a clatter, causing much hissing at one another, and all the grown-ups followed Granny's example and crossed themselves before the ikon. To Granny's obvious displeasure, the young ones, myself including, remained seated. She made no comment, however, since most of us were schoolchildren.

At last Granny was in her place, waiting. Now it was Grandad's turn. From under his chair he produced a three-litre bottle of vodka and without a word filled all the tumblers, while Auntie Lyuba went round filling the little wine-glasses that we eagerly held out with cowberry liqueur.

The three-litre bottle sufficed for only one round. Grandad lifted his thick glass tumbler and in a quiet, hesitant voice proposed:

"Come on, then, children, here's to our being together, here's to the health of the old lady! "

His was the first glass to touch Granny's wine-glass. Then the whole table was clinking glasses. We, youngsters, also clinked glasses and the moment had come to drink, but then a hitch occurred. Uncle Mitry, the black sheep of the family, had squeezed his way quietly into the room. Uncle Mitry was the trial of Granny's life. He was a hopeless drunkard. Without letting anyone know, Granny had made him put on one of Grandad's clean shirts and a pair of his trousers. Uncle Mitry was smaller than Grandad and the shirt was too big for him and the trousers hung baggily at the knees. He had also been given a hasty wash and brush-up. And now he stood tugging nervously at his shirt.

Grandad moved a stool up to the table with his foot and Granny straightened the ends of her silk lace kerchief at her throat and surveyed the table defiantly: "Yes, I invited him! Say what you like, but I invited him! "

Uncle Mitry's wife Tatyana was not present. She never visited us. Again because of Granny. Tatyana was a "proletarian", as Granny called her. She was an activist and organiser of the collective farm. She spent all her time at meetings and neglected her children and husband in a way that appalled Granny, who heaped abuse on her daughter-in-law wherever she went, even to the point of undermining her authority.

Uncle Mitry took his seat on the stool, a little to one side. Everyone hesitated, glasses in hand, clearing their throats. Avgusta was the first to recover and break the tension:

"Bottoms up then! Your arm's your own, so use it! Many happy returns, Mum! Dad—here's to you both! "

Tired of waiting, the men downed their vodka quickly and while the women, simpering and shy of each other, merely sipped their glasses coyly, they set about the dace and the meat jelly, and no one except Granny noticed that Uncle Mitry put his hands under the table and did not drink a drop.

The second three-litre bottle appeared, and now the sons took over from Grandad. He had done his job and it was time for them to fend for themselves. After the second round the tables began to ripple with laughter and talk and before long we youngsters were asked if we had had enough to eat and were dismissed with handfuls of nuts and sweets, the makeshift table at which we had sat being removed to make more room.

Granny's Day had begun!

We climbed up into the loft, from where we could see everything. Alyoshka gave an imitation of a staggering drunk and looked so funny that we all rocked with laughter.

Avgusta's powerful, mocking voice rang out from the best room. Imitating activist Tatyana, she tapped the empty vodka bottle with her fork and commanded:

"Now then, you men! Keep quiet there! Strike up, Mother! "

"Singing's not for me now, girls! I lost my voice long ago."

"We'll help you."

"Very well, then. Have it your way," Granny relented in a voice that sounded as if she had been giving in to everyone all her life.

> *Flows the river,*
> *Swift it flows....*

Granny sang standing up, not very loudly and a little hoarsely, and beat time for herself with her hand. For some reason something seemed to take hold of my spine and a thrill went right through my body. As Granny approached the chorus, her voice grew more tense and her face paled and needles of elation plunged into my flesh and I felt as if my blood had congealed and stopped flowing in my veins.

> *Aye, 'twas down that river,*
> *Down that river....*

The table responded with a roar of voices that were still strong and unspent, and it was not the song, so it seemed to me, but Granny herself had reached her sons and daughters at last, and they picked up and carried on lightly, joyously, sweeping aside all bad things from their path, taking pride in themselves and the mother who had brought them into the world, who had suffered for them and endowed them with their hard-working, songful hearts.

The song about the river rolled on majestically. Granny sang her part with growing confidence, making it easier for the others to take up. Even in song she tried to provide well for her children, to arrange everything to suit them, and to make it so that the song should awaken only good feelings towards one another and leave for always an indelible memory of the home, the nest they had now left, that which there was none better and never would be.

Now the tears were running down Granny's face, and down Avgusta's and Aunt Maria's, too. Uncle Mitry, who still had not touched either food or drink, covered his face with his sleeve and began to shake, and the front of Grandad's shirt bounced like a horse collar round his neck.

Even though she was crying, Granny did not spoil the song. She kept it up right to the end and, when the final words of the song flew out through the open windows, making the panes rattle, and echoed over the Yenisei, over its dark cliffs, everyone started kissing one another and declaring their eternal love, and the kissing and the declarations were almost drowned in the tearful snuffling of Potylitsyn noses, which could stop even a strong wind if it got caught on them.

"Mum! Mummy dar-ling! "

"And where's Daddy? Where's Daddy! Da-dd-yy! "

"Brother! You're our br-o-ther! " Uncle Kolcha Junior declared, hugging Uncle Mitry.

Uncle Mitry nodded assent and glanced around him in fright. He was perfectly sober, lost and lonely here. I felt sorry for Uncle Mitry. I was crying, too, hiding in my corner, but not loudly, just to myself, and wiping the tears off my nose, which was also a Potylitsyn nose, with my fist.

Just when and how Levonty and his logging mate Mishka Korshukov turned up at our house and found their way to table, I cannot explain. Mishka Korshukov with his accordion, the wood and the bellows of which were all patched with rags, and Uncle Levonty with that eternal smile of his from ear to ear.

"Peace to this honest company! "

"Levonty! Mishka! Come on, play something! "

"Let them wet their whistle first! " Granny interposed and poured them each a full tumbler, since wine-glasses and similar vessels were not their measure at all.

Uncle Levonty and Mishka Korshukov stood together and clinked glasses with Granny and Grandad.

"Many happy returns, Katerina Petrovna! Your anniversary! To the gathering! "

"Eat, my dears! Eat and enjoy yourselves! "

Granny put her lips to the glass and set it down again.

Mishka and Levonty drank valiantly, as a team, as though they were splitting logs together, and their Adam's apples moved regularly, emitting loud, well-trained gurgles.

Then Mishka picked up his accordion and let his agile fingers run over the keys. The children crowded at the door of the room, breathlessly awaiting the music.

And then it came! Mishka pulled out the accordion to its full width, then twisted it into an unbelievable shape. And from this patched-up cornucopia a melody, rather wheezy and creaking, because Mishka had several times ripped his instrument in half, a melody that was familiar and yet difficult even for a fine ear to place, came pouring forth. It was Mishka himself who gave us a lead:

> *Once a field was Masha reaping,*
> *Golden sheaves she bound for heaping,*

Oh, how young and fair was she....
And everyone joyfully took up the song:
Oh, how young and fair....

How was it they had not known the song at once! Having made a start, Mishka let himself go, bouncing up and down on the bench as if it were a galloping horse. Someone offered him a glass and whenever he could retire into the background and the singers could get on without him, he would keep up the tune in the bass with one hand and with the other down a glass of vodka.

"Have a bite to eat with it, Mishka!" Granny suggested, but Mishka shook his head, implying he was too busy. Avgusta presented him with a slice of cucumber on a fork. He took it with his lips and winked at her and she winked back, as though in secret agreement. Mishka went over to another tune and while the men were still obliviously roaring:

Oh, how young and fair!

the women were already dancing a *barynya* round the table and tumbling out of the best room into the more spacious middle one. Wheezing, creaking and hissing, the accordion's ragged bellows pumped out a wild Russian dance.

The party reached its height. Roused by the dancing, the guests shouted, squalled and stamped their feet. Now they were all at it, each man for himself and all together. At the table there remained only Grandad, the old ladies, retiring Auntie Lyuba and sober Uncle Mitry, sitting there like a tree-stump, afraid to bring his hands out from under the table because they were dirty and scarred and might grab a glass and cause a shameful scene.

Auntie Vasenya appeared and eyed her husband severely, as much as to say, "So you're here already!" By this time Uncle Levonty was really worked up.

"And here's my wife, Vasilissa Semyonovna!" he bawled. "A fine woman! Now what's up, what are you staring at? You disapprove of me, do you? Why should you? What for? I'm one of the family here! And what a one! Am I not, Auntie Katerina?" And this was followed by a smacking kiss and such a hug that Granny implored:

"Oh, botheration! He's crushed me, the devil! What a grip you have, to be sure! "

"That's because I love the Potylitsyns better than any of my own family! Maybe I set them above the whole village! "

Auntie Vasenya was dragged to the table and given a seat beside Uncle Levonty at the now ruined feast. For decency's sake she sat primly and gave her husband a powerful nudge with her elbow, whereupon he jumped up clownishly and uttered a loud yelp. Everyone laughed, and so did she.

Meanwhile the women were dancing and whooping to Mishka's accordion, which he was ripping without mercy.

They danced themselves into a state of utter exhaustion. The men and women staggered back to the table, fanning themselves with handkerchiefs and all talking at once, each on his own favourite theme.

"Here, Dad, have a city fag for a change."

"No, Vasya, it'd be wasted on me. The city cigarettes make me cough. But perhaps I'll try one, all the same."

"'Sixteen' I says to him! 'Ten! ' he says to me. 'Sixteen! ' I says. 'Ten! ' he comes back." Uncle Kolcha Senior chopped the air with his fist.

"What did you settle for?"

"Twelve."

"Aye, that's all you can make now. What a life, eh! "

"...And that elk crashed right into a bear's den! " Uncle Vanya, who had long since given up hunting because he now had a job as a groom at the collective farm stables, was telling one of his gains. "And out comes the master himself! Bang! I go with the left barrel! Still he comes on! Bang! I go with the right! On he comes at me! "

"On he comes! "

"Aye, that he does! His jaws all dripping with blood, but on he comes. So I reaches for my cartridge pouch, and there's not a single cartridge in it! They'd all fallen out while I was chasing the elk...."

"Pure fiction! " Zyryanov, the learned man of the family, remarked sarcastically. "You're making it all up! "

"Oh, is it! What do you know about hunting anyway? You with your rupture! You'd better keep quiet...."

6-794

Granny squeezed herself between Zyryanov and Uncle Vanya. They would come to blows before you knew what! And meanwhile someone was telling Uncle Mitry:

"There's two kinds of people as don't drink, Mitry. Them as don't get offered, and them as has no money. But you've got to know when to stop! Got to know your limit! "

And Mishka Korshukov was crooning into Avgusta's ear, "As soon as the priest goes out to look for that treasure the Russian soldier pops into bed with the priest's wife! "

"Keep your hands to yourself! Mother sees everything! "

"Now this is salmon trout we're eating, isn't it? " Uncle Levonty was asking the women next to him, as he tucked into the fish pie. "But when I was at sea with the navy, I had some fried octopus! "

"What? "

"Octopus. One of the marvels of the sea! Something like a snake. Very tasty reptile, I must say. Couldn't stop eating it! ".

"Brrr! How horrible! " the women shuddered. "How Vasenya manages to kiss you after that! "

"All you women can talk about is kissing! " Levonty retorted.

"What are the girls coming to these days! Yours have snowed you under with their babies, Avdotya! You let them have too much of their own way, you do! "

"But we were no angels in our young days either, Maria. They made us marry young. And that was our salvation. Otherwise.... Oh, bother them all, girls and men! Let's have a song instead, women? "

And Aunt Avdotya's thin, high-pitched voice sliced through the talk like a knife cutting a pie:

> Love me, my darling, while I am free,
> And I'll be yours as long as I can.
> Fate will soon part us, in prison they'll keep me,
> And you'll belong to another man.

Aunt Avdotya put her own, special meaning into this song. The family understood this and sympathised with her and were again plunged into a state of high emotion. They swung into the chorus with such fervour that the window panes rattled and the smoke in the room swirled about and it seemed that the ceiling would be lifted off and come crashing down on all of us.

They sang fit to burst their throats. Even Grandad moved his lips, although no one ever heard him singing. Widowed, childless Ksenofont joined in with his rumbling bass. Avgusta thrust her sharp voice into the song. Aunt Apronya's voice struck the highest and most tearful note. Aunt Maria took up the solo in a well-fed but sorrowful tone. Zyryanov hummed it with a faint smile of superiority. Kolcha Junior's wife, Nyura, led the song well, bringing the chorus in at the right moment and rallying those who looked like dropping out. With his ear pressed to the accordion to catch the tune Mishka Korshukov sang with a real tremolo, like someone on the stage.

Everyone sang, old and young, except Auntie Lyuba. City-bred, she did not know our songs. She sat with her head on Uncle Vasya's chest, no longer at all embarrassed, and a pallor crept into her girlish face and in her eyes there was pity, love and happy pride at having joined such a family, with such people, who could sing like this and honour one another like this.

Aunt Avdotya, who had choked with tears during the song, was taken out for a drink of water. But the song lived on without her. She soon returned, her face still wet and, gathering up her hair, joined in the chorus. Everything was fine and very moving, but all of a sudden Uncle Levonty stood up at the table and asked everyone at once:

"What's life all about?" And thumped the table with his fist.

"Botheration! Levonty's started!" Granny cried in alarm and began clearing away the bowls and other more valuable pieces of china.

"Levonty! Levonty!" came the shouts from all sides, as though to a deaf man. "Stop that! What are you up to? You're in company!"

Aunt Vasenya clung to her husband. His face hardened, the skin grew tight over his cheekbones and jaw and his teeth gnashed like caterpillar tracks.

"Yes! I'm asking you! What's life all about?" he repeated.

"We'll tie you up with a pair of reins and put you under a bench, and then you'll know what it's all about," old Ksenofont declared calmly.

"Tie me up!? With reins?"

Uncle Levonty brushed off his wife like a fly and ripped the cloth off the table. Plates, cups and forks clattered to the floor. The women and children rushed out of the house. But Uncle Levonty was not allowed to get out of hand. The Potylitsyn men were not a timid lot, and no weaklings either. They piled into Uncle Levonty, pressed him against the wall and, after a brief but futile resistance, he lay helpless under a bench in the middle room.

"Yes, that's the right place for you! " Aunt Vasenya stood over him pointing an accusing finger. "Other people behave like people, but you.... Let them see what a life I have with you, you old hooligan."

The table was quickly cleared, the cloth straightened, a fresh bottle of vodka brought up from the cellar and the party continued its course. Uncle Levonty was forgotten at once.

While everyone else had been busy pacifying Uncle Levonty, Granny had quietly placed a glass in front of Uncle Mitry, who was still sitting miserably alone.

"Here, have a drink. Don't torture yourself! "

Uncle Mitry furtively tipped the vodka down his throat and pushed his hands under the table again.

"And have something to eat."

But he ate nothing and, as soon as Granny's head was turned, he grabbed someone else's unfinished glass, and then another, and another. Soon he swayed and toppled off the stool. Granny caught him as he fell and led him away, meek and unresisting, to the store-room, where she locked him in. After that she inspected the hay-loft. There were several sprawling bodies there; some of the men were sleeping it off already.

Gradually the party began to flag. Late at night Granny and Grandad packed off the toughest of the men to their various corners or to their own houses. Then Granny put on her apron, cleared the tables, swept the floors, made sure once again that everyone was comfortably asleep, crossed herself once again and said: "Thank the Lord! "

She sat on a bench by the table for a while, said her prayers, took off her party clothes with a sigh of relief and went to bed.

The family slept heavily, snoring, groaning and muttering. Now and then someone would break into song and at once smother it with sleepy lips.

I was the only one who could not sleep. I was guarding my beloved Uncle Levonty. He seemed to know that I was on watch and, when morning was near, I hear his husky voice calling:

"Vitya! Vitya! "

I was at the bench in an instant. Uncle Levonty was lying with his head on a pillow that Granny had provided, uttering weak moans.

"Untie me, laddie."

In his struggles he had drawn the knots very tight and it took me a long time to free him, working with my teeth and nails and even a fork. He grunted and quietly offered me his advice.

At last he got up, swayed for a moment, and asked:

"Did I do any damage? "

"You didn't have time. They tied you up."

"Well, that was all to the good, then. Everything's ship-shape. Have you got a drop of anything to clear my head? It's just about falling apart."

I gave Uncle Levonty a glass of vodka, which Granny had casually left on the windowsill. He drank it with a great effort and disgust, wiped his mouth on his sleeve, sat down for a while, then put his finger to his lips:

"Sh! I'll be going! Don't tell Granny Katerina."

"All right."

He staggered away, as though walking on a heaving deck, tried to control his legs but banged his forehead against the doorpost and hissed at himself "sh-sh! " In the yard the dog Sharik went for him and he had to speak:

"Sharik! Sharik! Keep quiet, brother! "

In the morning Granny found the reins under the bench but there was no sign of Uncle Levonty.

"Who let that villain go?" she exclaimed, and looked at me.

I shrugged as though I didn't know.

"Well, he got away in time, did our neighbour! I'd have given him beans! That I would! "

In the afternoon the seeing-off began. Uncle Vasya, Auntie Lyuba and Katenka packed up for their journey to Bazaikha. Tears, kisses, and one for the road. Avgusta went off to work at the run. Zyryanov and Aunt Maria left in their boat. Uncle Kolcha Senior set off to visit Aunt Talya's relatives, the Shakhmatovs, and the rest of the family also broke up, some going to the cemetery, others to their friends.

Offshoots of our celebration persisted for several days in various parts of the village.

In our own house Auntie Avdotya, quiet and hollow-cheeked, scrubbed the floors, Grandad tidied up the yard and the hay-loft, Granny put her holiday clothes away in the chest and returned to her household chores.

The great day was over. We were back in the old routine.

* * *

AUTUMN SORROWS
AND JOYS

At the end of autumn, when the forests are bare and the mountains on both sides of the Yenisei seem even higher and huger, and when the river itself, which only in September was still pebble-clear, lifts its sleepy waters from their bed, and the hoar-frost breaks out on the empty kitchen gardens, there comes to our village a brief but bustling time, the time of the cabbage cutting.

The laying in of cabbage for the long winter, for the big Siberian families, is a thorough-going business, demanding annual preparation, and so I shall begin my story of the cabbage-cutting in a thorough-going, far-sighted way.

The potatoes in the kitchen garden have been dug and dried and stored away, those for eating, in the basement, those for seed, in the cellar. Carrots, swedes, and beet-roots have also been cut, and even the radishes, whose blunt snouts used to peep out of the edges of every vegetable bed, have been pulled, and their plump, mottled bodies lie at rest in the gloom of the cellar on top of all the other vegetables. Tangled strings of peas and bluish bean plants with charred black pods are spread about round the porch for wiping your feet on.

Sometimes when you're rubbing your boots on those plaited stems and letting your eyes grope in that yellow mangled heap, you suddenly spot a crinkly white pod with a few hard peas inside. So you wipe that pod on your trousers, split it open and sorrowfully pour the hard little kernels into your mouth, and while you chew them you remember how only a little while ago you feasted in the kitchen garden among the peas propped up with sticks, and how the bees and bumble-bees were there, too, investigating the violet and white flowers clustered along the stems. And how Sharik, that omnivorous dog, rummaged in the pea thickets and snapped off the sugary pods and with much smacking of the lips gobbled them up.

You couldn't tempt Sharik into the muddy, forsaken kitchen garden today, not for worlds. There are only cabbages in the garden now, their green garb flopping all over the rows. The rain and the dew have seeped through their outer leaves and they have drunk their fill and swollen to such a size that nothing worries them any more. Glistening with raindrops, wallowing in satiety and indolence, unafraid of the light frosts, they await the hour for the sake of which they were nurtured and watered to this state from bluish two-leaved seedlings.

In the middle of the kitchen garden stands the cow, either dozing or wondering ponderously why people are so fickle in their treatment of her. But a short time ago she had only to show her face in the kitchen garden and they would drive her out like an enemy from another country, lashing her with anything they could lay hands on. But now they have thrown the gate open and she is free to roam where she likes.

At first she went in with a rush, her tail flying, stripped two heads of cabbage, gobbled up the green grass under the bird-cherry tree, munched the birch twigs she found behind the fence round the bath-house, then came to a halt and didn't know what to do. Now, either from boredom or misery she suddenly lets out a great moo, and from all the other kitchen gardens, from behind the banks covered with flax or stinging nettles she is answered by other puzzled cows, similarly separated from the group.

In the daytime the chickens also flap down from the barn into the kitchen garden, peck about lazily and rummage in the tufts of grass left over from the distant days of weeding, but for the most part sit about with ruffled feathers, and gaze crossly at the young cocks that are strutting about, standing on tiptoe and trying their voices. They produce such a wretched sound, nothing like the glorious war-cry beloved of hennish hearts.

It was in this season on the verge of winter that I was awoken one morning by a terrific roaring, rumbling and hissing of I didn't know what, for at first I could scarcely see anything; the house was full of steam and people were darting about round the stove lugging red-hot stones, like devils in purgatory.

At first I was terrified. Only half awake, I hid behind the chimney. But then I remembered that it was late autumn outside and the time had come to steam out the barrels and tubs. Soon the cabbage-cutting would begin! Fine!

I skipped down off the stove into the kitchen.

"Gran!   Gran!..." I pursued my bothered, perspiring grandmother about the house. "Gran! "

"Keep off! Can't you see I've no time for you today! And why, for goodness sake, are you paddling about this wet floor with bare feet? Want to be choking and spluttering again? Up on that stove now, quick! "

"I only wanted to ask when we'll be bringing in the cabbage. All right then, if you can't tell me a little thing like that...."

I climbed back on to the ledge above the stove. It was hot and steamy up there, under the ceiling. My face felt as if it were wrapped in a damp cloth and I could hardly breathe. Granny pushed a hunk of bread and a mug of milk on to the stove for me as she hurried by.

"Eat that and make yourself scarce! " she commanded. "We'll be carting cabbage tomorrow, God willing."

I finished off the bread in two bites, drank the milk in three gulps, pulled on my boots, clapped my hat on my head, tossed on my coat and set about getting out of the house. I had to grope my way through the kitchen. Everywhere there were tubs, bowls and barrels, covered with mats, from which there came a muffled rumbling and hissing. This was caused by the red-hot stones that had been tossed into the water—imprisoned elements raging to escape. The air was thick with the smell of currant leaves, heather, mint and bath-house heat.

"Who's that flinging the door wide open? " Granny shouted from the stove. The flames in the stove-mouth surged and leapt, throwing reflections on Granny's face, and she looked like a bedraggled devil.

Once outside I almost choked with fresh air. I stood on the porch, shaking my shirt to let the cool reach my sweating back. In the shed was Grandad in an old pair of top boots, standing at the grindstone, turning the wheel with one hand and holding the axe to it with the other. I could see it was awkward for him to be turning and sharpening at the same time. Wasn't it just the job for a boy—to turn the grindstone!

I hurried over to the shed and Grandad relinquished the crooked iron handle to me without a word. At first I put a real spin on it, and the reddish, rusty water went flying from under the stone. Soon, however, my energy began to fail and I had to change hands more and more often, noting in dismay that there was rather a lot to be sharpened this morning: about five iron cabbage choppers, and several knives as well, and, now that he had started, Grandad would be sure to put a fresh edge on all his axes too. I began to regret having volunteered so readily and to hope secretly for something to go wrong with the grindstone, or for some other means of escape from this gruelling task.

When I had very little strength left and was really steamed up and it was not so much I turning the wheel as the wheel turning me, the gate-catch rattled and Sanka appeared in the yard. That Sanka, just like God or the devil he was! Sure to appear whenever I needed a helping hand or a push towards disaster.

I gave him as cheerful a smile as I could muster and waited, expecting him to ask at once for a turn at the wheel. But what a menace that boy was! First he said hullo to Grandad, chatted to him about this and that like an equal, and only when Grandad had nodded in my direction and grunted, "give the workman a breather", did Sanka casually take the handle from me and without a scrap of effort, almost as if he were playing with it, give it such a spin that the stone began to hiss and send the water flying and Grandad had to caution him and jerk the axe away.

"Easy there! Can't you see I'm sharpening the point."

I sat down on an upturned log. This was all rather disappointing for me to see and hear.

"We're going to chop cabbage soon," I announced.

"I know. Katerina Petrovna is going to steam our barrels as well. We've been asked in to help."

Of course, there was no surprising Sanka. He was perfectly informed about all our household affairs and ready to work anywhere or with anyone as long as he didn't have to go to school. He was getting "unsatisfactories" for conduct now and the teacher was writing notes to his parents about him. When she read one of these notes, Auntie Vasenya would either blink helplessly or chase Sanka with an iron hook.

Uncle Levonty, if he was sober, would show his son his own hands with their iron-like callouses and try to impress on him by the example of his own life how hard it was for an uneducated man to earn his daily bread. When drunk, Uncle Levonty would always question Sanka on the multiplication tables.

"Sanka!" he would say, raising his finger and putting a serious, schoolmasterly expression on his face. "What are five times five?" Whereupon with unconcealed satisfaction he would answer himself: "Five fives make thirty-five!"

And it was no use trying to prove to Uncle Levonty that he was wrong and that the answer was not thirty-five at all. Any correction would offend him and he would start insisting that he was a right-living, hard-working man, that he had once been a sailor, and had voyaged to many lands, and it was only lately that he had sprung a bit of a leak; there had been a time when the skipper used to shake hands with him and one of the high-ups had presented him with a repeating watch for meritorious service. True, he had been discharged after that and had to spend the proceeds from his watch on drowning his grief. But he still had his pride.

Meanwhile Sanka would quietly slip out of the house. Uncle Levonty would turn on Auntie Vasenya and complain. And she would complain back. And while they were shouting at each other they would forget what had made them so indignant in the first place and Sanka's education would end there.

If there was anyone in the village whom Sanka really respected and feared it was my grandad. Sanka couldn't live a day without him. He would exert himself at any job just for a nod or a glance from Grandad. I think he would have moved a mountain if Grandad had wanted him to.

When we started bringing in the cabbage, Sanka humped such huge sacks that Grandad could not help reproaching Granny.

"Anyone'd think you were loading a horse. He be only a child, you know!"

The word "child" did not sound exactly convincing as applied to Sanka, and Granny, of course, answered Grandad to the effect that he had never shown any pity on his own children and had always been fonder of other people's, and that this recruit for the chain-gang, Sanka, received far more affection from him than his own grandson—meaning me—but all the same she did put fewer cabbages in the next sack. Sanka demanded more and Granny shot a sidelong glance at Grandad.

"You'll strain yourself! You're only a child, you know...."

"'S nuffin'! " Sanka retorted, shifting his feet impatiently and crunching a white cabbage stalk between his teeth. "Put some more in! "

Granny added one or two more cabbages and gave him a push.

"Off you go! That's enough! "

With a wild whoop Sanka charged away from the cabbage patch into the yard. Up the steps he went like a race-horse and, slithering to a halt in the porch, shot the cabbages out on to the floor with a great rumble.

I pelted after him with a cabbage under each arm, enjoying myself no end. Sharik chased us, barking and snapping at our trousers, and the chickens went squawking on all sides.

It was after midday when we cut the last cabbages and threw them into the bath-house. Granny bustled off to make a meal, and we sat down on the grassy bank round the bath-house to rest and heard the calling of the wild geese. Everyone looked up at once and silently traced with their eyes the fine thread woven slantwise across the sky above the Yenisei.

The geese were flying high and for some reason I felt as if I were seeing them not in reality but in a dream and, just as in a dream, their cries grew fainter and softer as they flew further away and the thread grew finer until it melted altogether into the red, windy weather that came with the sunset.

Either it was the calling of the wild geese or the fact that the kitchen garden had been cleared of its last vegetables, or the lights going on early in the windows of the neighbouring cottages, or perhaps just the mournful lowing of the cow, but I began to feel sad, and I think Sanka and Grandad did too. Grandad smoked the rest of his big hand-made cigarette, crushed it with his boot and heaved a rather guilty sigh, as though he were saying farewell not to a mere vegetable patch that had done its job for the year but to a sick friend; the kitchen garden looked so chilly and bedraggled with its scraps of cabbage leaf, its scattered bunches of potato tops, its few surviving tufts of thistle and hawkweed, its trampled divides and its forlorn, lonely bird-cherry tree standing black against the sky.

"It'll soon be winter," Grandad said softly, when we had left the deserted kitchen garden.

He closed the gate and fastened it firmly with a rope. He must have forgotten that we should have to open it again to collect the rest of the cabbages from the bath-house, and to let in the cow, so that she could again stand motionless in the middle of the patch for hours on end and give out her village-shaking moos of regret for the green meadows and the well-organised herd.

Next morning I ran off to school, suffered impatiently till lessons were over, and dashed home. I knew what was going on in our house at this moment and how essential it was for me to be there.

While still in the street I heard the thudding of many choppers and the ring of the pestle in its iron mortar and the song of the women who had come in to help.

> *Wicked folk with envy curs't*
> *Want to steal my love from me....*

The leading voice was so high-pitched that it tickled your eardrums. And suddenly, like an avalanche down a mountainside:

> *Money and jealousy, do your worst—*
> *No more shall this man my lover be.*

Anyone called in to help was sure to be offered a drink. That was why the women were singing so loud and well together; they had had a drop to make the work and the song go better.

In two bounds I was up the steps and had thrown the kitchen door open. Holy saints, what was going on here! The house was full of people! Such a racket and a rattle you'd never imagine! Granny and the older women were squeezing the cabbage by hand on the long kitchen table, and the cabbage was squeaking like frozen snow under your boots. The women's arms were plastered with bits of cabbage-leaf up to the elbows and all red with beetroot juice. A great heap of taut white slices was piled on the table along with thin round slices of carrot and little chopped sticks of beetroot. There were cabbages all over the place, under the table, under the benches, by the stove. The floor was so thickly strewn with leaves and stumps that you couldn't see a single floorboard. By the door stood a tall cabbage barrel, already full and covered with a lid held down by huge stones, from under which the murky beetroot juice had begun to ooze. There were aniseed and fennel floating in it; Granny used to add just a little of each, for the aroma.

I could feel it drawing my mouth already.

I wanted to take a pinch of cabbage from the barrel but Sanka spotted me and beckoned me over. He was not with the other youngsters who, as I well knew, were romping in the middle and front rooms. He was with the women. He looked a bit dazed. Either the women had treated him to a glass or it was the general merriment that had set him off. Anyway he was pounding away with the pestle with such vigour that the mortar rang like a bell all over the house and little pebbles of salt went flying out of it.

> *Vicky-Victor, cheeky cheat,*
> *One of Granny's pies did eat.*
> *Granny scolds him loud and long,*
> *Vic says he done nothing wrong!*

Sanka roared, beating time with his pestle.

I had been in such a hurry to get home and so much looking forward to the feast of joy I knew there would be in our house, and here was Sanka dousing my spirits with his song about a pie that I had indeed eaten on the quiet once. But when had that been! I had repented long ago and made up for my misdeed, but I still got no peace from that wretched song, summer or winter.

I was about to turn away and go out but Granny wiped her hands on her apron and wagged a warning finger at Sanka, and Auntie Vasenya swept the flat of her hand over Sanka's bristly top-knot, and all was well again.

Granny took me into the middle room, pushed the empty plates and glasses to the corner of the table and gave me my meal, then she took a bottle of vodka from under the bench, poured a glassful as she walked back into the kitchen and in a gentle sing-song voice cried:

"Now then, women, dear girls, all of you, here's to the cabbage not going sour and keeping crisp and wholesome."

One chopper stopped banging, then another, and another, and my Auntie Apronya, letting herself go, drained the glass and gave a valiant little grunt.

"Here's to that hubby of mine, Pashka Gryazinsky, always getting his stuck in his throat like a bone, while mine always goes down light and lively! "

The women all roared, and then each of them, having drunk a glass, said something about her husband that at any other time she wouldn't have dared think of, let alone speak aloud.

There was no admission to the house for the men that day; they were barred.

Uncle Levonty, it is true, managed to sneak in on the pretext of not being able to find something he needed badly in his own house, but the women raised such a hullabaloo and bore down on him so menacingly, brandishing their knives and choppers, that he quickly tumbled out of the house with cries of "They're all mad, the wildcats! " But Granny, who was in an exceptionally kindly mood that day, took him out a glass of vodka, and from the yard he boomed in his cracked bass:

"Hey girls! Here's to your cabbage tasting as good! " I swallowed down my dinner and joined in the work. I banged away with a wooden pestle, pressed down the chopped cabbage in the barrel, stripped the green leaves off the heads, took turns with Sanka at crushing salt in the mortar, slithered about on the wet leaves and joined in singing with the women, and in the end struck up myself with a ditty I had learned at school:

> *Dunya let her tresses down.*
> *Caught all the sailors in the town.*
> *Dunya, Dunya, Dunya, do—*
> *Dunya, be my sweetheart too!*

Granny clapped her hands and let them fall to her sides in despair. "Oh, botheration! Listen to what my young workman's been a-learning now! What a scholar he is, eh! "

The praise went to my head and I bawled even louder than before:

> *Let 'em stick us in the nick!*
> *We'll break their windows with a brick!*
> *Dunya, Dunya, Dunya, do—*
> *Dunya, be my sweetheart too!*

Meanwhile the work went along easily, as if it were no effort at all. The women sitting in a row chopped the cabbage in long tubs and if one of them missed the beat and hit the wooden side of the tub, another would cry out in affected horror:

"Botheration! Tired out that I am! Don't you give me any more, Aunt Katerina! "

"I've had enough too! Or I'll be sprawling on the cabbage leaves! "

"Me too! "

"Aye, it don't take much to knock us over, worn out and trampled on as we are...."

"Don't let's be thinking about trouble, my dears," Granny interrupted. "Our troubles will go to the grave with us. Let's have a song instead. Come on, Avgusta, strike up! "

And again Auntie Avgusta's ringing voice would pierce the fumes of pickle and vodka that filled the hut and all the women in a kind of tearful joy and desperation would come in with her and sing one of their long drawn-out songs.

Granny sang with them and at the same time dipped two halves of cabbage pressed together into the brine, then packed them away into a barrel with great care and forethought, covering them with a layer of well-squeezed chopped cabbage that was already oozing with juice. This task she always did herself and never entrusted it to anyone else.

Many women would come to us later and try our cabbage and express their admiration for Granny's skill.

"Well, I'll be damned! What's the magic spell you know, Petrovna? It's like sugar! "

And Granny, moved by such praise, would respond to this with a touch of modest pride:

"It's not the words but the hands that count in any job. Don't spare your hands. They're what make the taste and look of everything. They hurt at night, these hands of mine, because I've never spared them."

The work would ease off by evening, and one by one the youngsters crept out of the middle room. They all had tummy pains from eating too many sweet cabbage stumps and were moaning to go home.

The women wrapped them up crossly, gave them a few light cuffs and wished them out of their sight for ever because there was never any peace while they were about. Regretfully they left our house, thanking Granny for her hospitality and inviting her to visit them. And Granny thanked them for their help and promised to be on the spot whenever and wherever she might be needed.

In the twilight we swept the leaves and scraps of cabbage out of the house. My aunts scrubbed the floors hurriedly and threw down the mats again, and no sooner was the work finished than Grandad and Uncle Kolcha Junior would come in from the far fields. They had put everything away for the winter, swept the straw into the shed and packed away the ploughs, harrows, forks and rakes in it.

Granny laid the table, poured Grandad and Uncle Kolcha a glass of vodka that appeared to have been left in the bottle by chance.

Supper was eaten wearily, without much being said.

The men asked if we had managed the cabbage all right. Granny replied that, thank the Lord, we had. The cabbage was nice and juicy this year, it ought to keep well, but she didn't like the look of the salt; it was such grey, unsalty looking stuff. She hoped it wouldn't spoil everything. And they reassured her and reminded her how bad it had been in nineteen nineteen and twenty, but all the same they had had some good cabbage from it and it had been a great help in feeding the family then.

After supper Grandad and Uncle Kolcha sat and smoked and Granny talked to them about the cellar and the shelves that needed mending there. Yawning till the tears came into her eyes, she warned Kolcha not to be out late in the evening, and not to go gallivanting with that flighty Nyura of his till cockcrow, because there was no end of work to be done in the yard and he would miss his night's sleep again.

Uncle Kolcha Junior listened obediently but both he and Granny knew that this was just talk and not to be taken much notice of and soon he left the house, humming a tune to himself before he was out of the porch.

"Hi, Mishka? How much longer you going to be?" he shouted outside the gate.

The homeless Mishka Korshukov, "befriended" by Auntie Avdotya and temporarily accommodated in her house, answered briefly, "I'll be out in a tick."

Presently Mishka's accordion began to croak from the street and Mishka and Kolcha Junior would strike up a salty ditty under the village windows while Auntie Avdotya's girls, whom Auntie Avdotya held onto very tight but sometimes not quite tight enough, peeped after them between the drawn curtains. Sometimes they would slip out of the house and then Auntie Avdotya would race after them along the village streets, seek them out in some dark corner and drag them home by the hair.

Granny puffed into the lamp glass and whispered in the darkness as she listened to the lads' voices growing fainter in the distance.

"They'll be getting into a fight again! Why can't they sit at home quietly? But no, they must be out gallivanting of an evening! Let's hope they don't get a knife in the back. The kind of people there are around nowadays.... God protect us!"

She would shift about restlessly, sigh, mutter to herself and pray, and it suddenly struck me that Kolcha was not the only one she had been worried about in this way. My other uncles and aunts who had now settled down and were living their own lives had also had their nights out and Granny had tossed in her bed just as uneasily and worried as much about them. What strength, what a great heart she must have to be able to worry about us all, and me as well, and be worrying still!

"Ah, my hands, my poor hands?" Granny murmured to herself. "What can I do with you? What can I rub you with?"

"Gran! Here, Gran! Let's rub them with ammonia?" I don't like ammonia. It makes my eyes sting and gets up my nose, but for Granny's sake I would bear anything.

"Haven't you settled down yet?" Granny replied. "You go to sleep. You're too green to teach me, my lad! Thinks he's a doctor!"

The shutters muffled the hut and cut off every glimmer from the outside world. From the kitchen came the smell of the fermenting cabbage and I could hear it beginning to bubble and subside gruntingly under the weighted lids.

The clock on the wall ticked. Granny fell silent and stopped tossing and turning on her bed. She must have found a place for her aching hands and made them comfortable.

With the first glimmer of dawn through the shutters she would be on her feet again, busying herself about the house, and then set off to help someone else with their cabbage, and in another hut the same commotion would reign, with banging choppers and bursts of song, and the youngsters who had eaten too much cabbage and cabbage stumps would run behind the sheds.

For a whole week, and sometimes two, the banging and clattering would be heard throughout our village. The women would slip in and out of the village shop, hiding little bottles of vodka under their shawls, and the men, banished from the houses, would hang about round the threshing floor or the coach shed, smoke their tobacco, taking pinches from each other's pouches, talk weightily about the threshing, about squirrel shooting, and about the sledge road that the snow would soon provide and the frost harden.

And so it was that winter came to the village to the sound of banging cabbage choppers and the long, drawn-out songs of the women.

While the women and children were moving from house to house, while the cabbage was being cut, the bank waters of the Yenisei froze, sprinklings of snow and frozen rain appeared in the furrows of the kitchen garden, sludge came down the river, and a white rim formed round the base of that great crag the Sentinel Bull, leaving a dark strip of unfrozen water below. Even the belated flocks of wild geese would pass over our rocky shores that now offered no shelter or resting place for them on their long journey south.

One night there was a fall of snow. The cow was given her first forkful of hay and plunged into it, burying her head to the horns in the fragrant bundle.

Sharik went bounding about in the snow, rolling in it and barking as if he had gone off his head.

In the daytime the men trundled the cabbage barrels and tubs out of the kitchen and rolled them down the smooth boards into the cellar. The kitchen at once became much roomier. Granny wiped the floor and brought in a slab of pinkish juicy cabbage in an enamel bowl. She sliced it up with a knife and put forks and bread on the table.

But we tried the cabbage without bread.

Kolcha Junior munched it for a minute or two. I munched. Grandad munched. Granny stood waiting in suspense for our verdict.

"That's the stuff to help down a glass!" Kolcha concluded at last, and with a grunt of satisfaction took another forkful of cabbage.

"Grand!" I said, and lifted my thumb.

And Grandad simply said: "Not bad. Worth eating."

Granny crossed herself in relief and whispered: "Thank the Lord, thank the Lord! Now we'll get through the winter. We've plenty of good potatoes, enough for ourselves and for market as well. We'll buy Kolcha some new snowboots, and a coat for our man. Vitya ought to have something to wear too. He tears everything you give him to shreds, the little devil."

All day Granny pottered about the house, as lively as a girl, chatting to herself, telling me off and stamping her foot at Sharik.

But neither Sharik nor I had any fears of Granny at a time like this. If she got angry with anyone today, she would only be pretending; it would be just for show.

The long, stubborn vigil of winter was about to close in on our lives with its frosts and snow. From now on we should live mostly indoors and in the yards. And the thrifty folk who had tried hard enough and laid in their stock of vegetables, berries and cabbage would weather the winter, cracking their cedar nuts and telling fairy-tales in the evenings and, when the Epiphany came round, set about celebrating the feast days in the fiercest of frosts.

And in every hut, in the middle of the table, like a fruit centrepiece, there stood a beautiful plate, bowl or earthenware jar of pickled cabbage, scourge and succour of Siberia, now rising in a hump of pink slabs, now sprouting with wet, juicy leaves, now chopped fine.

What force there was in that cabbage—that I shall never know. But our folk ate it all through the winter with potatoes, in soup, steamed, fried and raw, whole barrels and tubs of it, and were healthy and cheerful and kept their teeth into old age, and could each do the work of two men and, with a plate of cabbage to go with it, drink enough for three.

ON A FAR
NORTHERN PEAK

He had been standing motionless on this crag for hours. The crag was huge, bare and black, rising out of the dreamy mist like the ruins of a medieval castle. Scattered for a mile or more around this relict were boulders as big as houses, and from these had split off lesser rocks that resembled a great grey flock of sheep grazing till first snow on the grass-tangled, boggy clearings at the foot of the cliffs.

There are many such crags, boulders, screes and cliffs carved by the wind, in the Great Ridge, and they are nearly all named after the shape that nature has given them—Bear, Tent, Trident, Cartridge, even Armoured Train.

For some reason he had chosen the Cartridge. He stood looking down from its blunt, skyward-pointing tip and, but for his massive, branchy antlers, he himself might have been taken for a whimsical creation of the wind and rain, so well did he merge with this peaceful, rugged world that slumbered in a thousand miles of perfect stillness.

He would appear on the crag just before sundown, when the blue haze lifted from the peaks and all was distinctly visible from afar, and the setting sun would drop cosily into the fork of his antlers and rest there for a while, as though held by two kindly outstretched arms; then it would roll down on to his back and sunrays would shoot forth from every branch of his antlers and he would suddenly blaze with a blue, mysteriously alluring light, like some brilliant new planet rising above the Great Ridge. And every beast and bird for miles round would pause and turn its head timidly to where for many evenings now this wild stag had burned with a pure, smokeless flame and still had not burned out.

The leader of a herd of two thousand reindeer which was moving slowly eastward across the Great Ridge, cropping its way back to the collective farm, dropped behind a little and, planting his sinewy legs firmly apart like a peasant, looked up at the crag where the wild stag stood shedding its alarming light.

The leader's nostrils pulsated feverishly until moisture oozed from them with the strain and he could hear the blood roaring in his ears. He swung his head to shake off this oppressive, all-enveloping sound.

The leader was deep-chested, thick-set and stern. It was his strength that had given him mastery of the herd, and his leadership was acknowledged not only by the other stags but also by the herdsmen, who talked with him trustingly and gave him salt to lick as a reward for faithful service. Many a time had he saved the herd from the agile and fearless northern wolves that would fight to the death for their food. The leader knew where to find pasture moss among the screes on the desolate, windswept ridge; he could sense the threat of an impending landslide and spot the rusty fur of moss that concealed the pitfalls in bogs; he could hear the stealthy, cat-like tread of the white-necked mountain bear, and there was much else the leader knew and could do that was of use to both man and reindeer. But there was one thing he could not do, and that was to fight for the perpetuation of his race, to win love in combat.

Man had relieved him of this age-long necessity. Man had made him docile and obedient and had helped to quench in him the flame that had consumed the heart of many a stag, the fire that made them swift as the whirlwind and selflessly proud in love.

But the wildling that stood poised on the crag wanted to fight. In his bold, rigid stance, in those rearing antlers, in that pawing foot, there was a challenge. Any moment now, it seemed, he would fill the sky with a mighty roar, awaken the mountain-tops from their white slumber and plunge down in the wake of their foaming torrents, roused to blind fury by the fatal sweetness of his lust.

The leader was troubled. He guided the herd farther and farther away from the Cartridge Crag. The figure of the wild deer was now no bigger than a mosquito, and yet in the long northern sunset that almost encompassed the whole ridge he could still be seen, and so could the nestling of the sun in his antlers, and the way he himself turned for an instant into a bright tongue of flame and rose above the earth like a wonderful new planet, and then faded slowly in the ash-grey dusk.

But at last the herd drew so far away that the crag itself seemed to quiver and rise, melting phantom-like into the air, and then the leader's muscles relaxed of their own accord and he lay down in a broad mossy glade and allowed his thick white lashes to droop wearily. In place of the leader two sturdy reindeer stationed themselves alongside the herd, lifted their heads and with quivering nostrils sifted the streaming air, disentangling every current, every thread, as though deciphering an infinitely complex manuscript to which they alone knew the key. The young plump-breasted, tender-eared hinds roamed about round the resting leader, curving their necks playfully.

The leader watched them with a look of drowsy satiety, munching the succulent moss.

In the morning the herders drove up with their sledges and barking dogs, stopped for a while, gave the leader a lick of salt—his reward for good service—and went on to make their camp on the other side of the next pass, in a sheltered spot beside a stream that rushed down the mountainside with a grating of pebbles. In two or three days the leader would bring the herd to this camp and the herders would let him go on ahead, then overtake him again and make another camp further on. In this way the herd would gradually cross the ridge and, having grown fat on the mountain mosses, they would descend by winter to the plain, to the peaceful and carefree life of the home range.

But this desperate wildling would remain alone in his rebellious solitude, and in winter, no doubt, a wolf pack would pick up his scent and pursue him till the frost plugged his nostrils with ice and he stumbled panting and doomed to a standstill in the deep snow. Without undue haste the wolves would then close in like a tightening noose, throttle him, tear him to pieces and each grab his own share. They would even lick the blood off the bare rocks, would those starving wolves.

Where was he from, this fearless guest? Why had he come?

It was many years since wild deer had roamed these parts. Man had driven them further and further north, into the windswept deserts of the Arctic. Perhaps he had broken away from a domestic herd and gone wild? Perhaps this was the end of a wild chase after hinds during the rutting? Or perhaps he could find no mate and was searching the ridge with a ferocious desire to love and fight for love?

But now, he had a mate. In fact, he had two. How he had found them among the screes, among the piles of bare rock in the ravines, in the sparse stunted woods, he alone knew. He was young; this was his first nuptial autumn and he, sired by a great stag and mothered by a fleet, willow-like hind, was ardent in love and forever seeking new mates. But even more than for love he thirsted for battle, for ferocious combat, to use up his overflowing strength and quell the fire that blazed ever fiercer in his heart. But there were no more wild, slim-legged hinds to love and no long-maned stags to challenge on that vast ridge. He bellowed, he called, and the two hinds he had miraculously discovered pricked up their ears and obeyed his angry, peremptory voice and followed him farther and farther south, towards the wooded slopes that frightened them with lurking perils. The yearning for motherhood was stronger than fear, and they never lagged far behind their lord. But he had caught the languorous, attractive scents in the streaming autumn wind and was heading straight for the huge herd of reindeer.

And now he had found it.

For one, two, three evenings he had taken his stand on this crag, waiting for other stags as proud and frenzied as he to come and fight with him. And his bellow sent a quiver of excitement through the dumb, patient, devoted hinds hiding among the rocks below.

But no one responded to the wild stag's challenge.

He could himself have come down to the herd and stamped the ground and sent the stones flying and the grass and moss whirling like a swarm of mosquitos and filled the air with premonitions of battle, but the smells of smoke and dogs and another, even more persistent smell, of settled and contented peace, frightened him.

This was the smell of man. He never ceased to fear man, even during the rutting.

And yet, love proved stronger than fear. When the herd moved on across the hump-backed ridge towards the source of the rushing northern stream, he followed. Fired with the excitement of the chase, of the unknown and the sense of approaching battle, he quickened his pace. The two light-footed hinds glided after him like silent shadows, scattering spark-like leaves from the dwarf birch-trees and pendulous blue raindrops from the bilberries.

He caught up with the herd on a slope where the moss ended and the forest began and unmown grass lay in tangled swards on the sloping clearings.

He advanced to the middle of a glade, stood for a while amid the wiry stalks of burnet grass, the fluffy sprigs of fire weed, and the wild rosemary whose scent was now especially pungent with winter in the offing. He snorted belligerently and stamped the ground with a powerful hoof. The grass trembled and sprinkled its ripe seed, a flock of partridges flew up from the rocks, the purple pods of the burnet spurted rain and sent red ripples across the glade. Then he began to bellow threateningly, imperiously, and with each of his front hoofs, flinging up clods of earth in turn he lowered his massive head with its redmisted, unseeing eyes closer and closer to the ground.

He had brought with him his two hinds and he had to prove to them, and to this obedient, law-abiding herd, to this sky, this earth, to the whole world, that he had the right to love.

He would win that right or die!

The leader stepped out of the herd and took his stand protectively before his charges. In his posture there was both hesitation and annoyance. The other stags in the herd formed up respectfully behind him, like soldiers in several ranks, and behind them stood the hinds, twitching their long ears and craning their necks in womanish curiosity.

The wild stag bellowed again and kicked earth even farther. He seemed to strike what had once been fiery lava, and draw sparks from it. The leader did not stir. Thick-set, broad-chested, with big, clumsy hooves, he stood curiously regarding the frenzied young stag and was at a loss what to do.

But then once again, just as when he had first seen his

challenger, the leader heard the blood roaring in his ears and felt a great heaviness in his body, and he shook his head to rid himself of this oppressive noise and weight. The wild stag took this as a challenge and with muscles youthfully tense and rippling sprang forward to meet the leader, his antlered head held high.

The herd stood still in timid, confused suspense, while the two wild hinds, realising what was afoot, moved aside and began to nibble moss in a clearing, as though they had nothing to do with the mortal combat that was about to take place.

The newcomer approached the leader with a dignity and animal grace that was, of course, noted by the female members of the herd. He bellowed even louder, again and again, so that all the hinds, those he had brought with him, and those from which he was barred by a forest of antlers, should hear the bite in his voice and should see how strong, handsome and fearless he was, and feel what sultry strength lurked in his young, fresh, unspent body.

He was not thinking now of victory.

He was not thinking at all. He was on fire, and this fire that raged within him was of such elemental force that no power on earth could have stopped him and called him to reason. Yet some noble instinct did restrain him until his adversary was ready for battle. But when the leader of the herd lowered his head and, having awakened his slumbering impulses and a frenzy long since overgrown with fat, at last shook his antlers and snorted, the wild stag struck him antler to antler.

It was a dry, naked blow, like the clash of two flints, and it made the whole herd rear and stamp. Jaws stopped chewing, eyes stared in dim astonishment at the battling males.

The wildling charged again and, no longer seeing the leader with his blood-misted eyes, yet by some instinct guessing his position, struck another even more terrible blow and, as their antlers met, he felt his enemy's neck give for a moment and his head go back. Without disengaging, the wild stag stood his ground and his legs sank deep into the marshy rock-strewn earth. A sharp stone slit the skin of one of them and ripped it off like a stocking, exposing straining sinews and muscles like slabs of red-hot steel.

The strain forced a bloody froth from the wildling's nostrils.

But the leader was beginning to tire. His head was going back farther and farther. Both stags had reared up on their hindlegs, driving each other down crutch-deep into the marshy soil, snorting hot breath into each other's snarling faces and scattering bloody foam from mouth and nostrils. The leader was strong and well knit, but he was beginning to stagger drunkenly and it would not be long now before he crashed down on his back, smashing his antlers on a boulder, while the stag from the far northern peak gave tongue in victory and trumpeted to the mountains, the earth, the sky, his lawful right to the wild, untamed love which he had won in fair fight.

But by some imperceptible twist of the head the leader freed his antlers and dropped on his knees before the wild stag into the churned and trampled mire. He seemed exhausted, vanquished, beaten into submission and only his eyes, which were not blinded by blood and ferocity, were intently watching the young, unreasoning stag that had attacked him.

For a fraction of a second, a mere fraction, the wildling stood poised on his hindlegs, then with a triumphant snort hurled himself upon his vanquished enemy.

He did not even feel the branch of the leader's deliberately and accurately placed antler as it entered his body like a soldier's bayonet with a slight crunch and its cool point touched that pulsating thing which was no longer a heart but a molten ball of fire, burning through his chest, about to explode in an exultant cry of victory.

The smell of overheated blood rose to the nostrils of the wild stag and the inner fire died down at once and the red film cleared from his eyes. As though in a transparent, shimmering stream he saw the stags crowding in the distance, the frightened long-eared hinds beyond them and the two wild ones still calmly grazing on one side, awaiting their fate. He saw a white-capped peak that suddenly rippled and swung upside down along with all the narrow runnels of its streams and the blunt crowns of its larches advancing in thin lines up the desolate slope.

He died before he could utter the cry of victory. His mouth remained open in a silent roar of exultation and his eyes retained for ever a look of astonishment and the thirst for love. The leader tossed aside the carcass of what but a moment ago had been a wild and beautiful creature and shook his head in distaste. The smell of blood annoyed and depressed him. He went over to a rock and carefully wiped his antlers clean of the red blood. Then without a backward glance he ran after his charges and ill-temperedly drove the straying hinds into the herd, prodding them viciously with his antlers and chest.

Night overtook the herd at the foot of the Trident, a huge crag with three sharp peaks. In one of the clefts between these peaks there lay several heaps of antlers, fraternally intertwined like the roots of a tree. Some had crumbled to dust, others were black and splintered, others had been bleached white by wind, snow and the torrents of spring. Grass and flowers had sprung up among the antlers and the dry pods were now cracking open to sprinkle seed in the cracks between rocks.

Although the leader and his herd did not have to shed their antlers—they were sawn off for them by man, who thus relieved them of a sad and essential ritual and the gruelling trek it entailed—nevertheless a faint gleam of memory made them halt at the foot of the crag and a strange sacred feeling of attachment to this place revived in the leader and all the stags of the herd.

All that night the herd lingered under the crag, not daring to graze or utter a sound. Until the first sunray the stags stood like a guard of honour at the entrance to the antler-strewn cleft and their nostrils pulsated and quivered as they drew in the scent of mouldering bones.

Their leader was troubled and preoccupied. Mingled with this sorrowful smell of decay he fancied he could catch the persistent, pungent scent of the stag he had killed at sundown.

The leader bowed his head nearer and nearer to the ground

in mourning. He saw a young stag carrying his first set of antlers to the ancient burial ground. He had come down from a far northern peak inaccessible to man, from the bare frost-seared crags that have only a few stunted bushes at their foot.

He had braved rivers and torrents, rockslides and treacherous bogs, avalanches and wolf packs, trouble and storm. When he had brought his antlers to this place and with painful jerks wrenched them from his skull, and when they had fallen, linking their branches with the antlers of his ancestors, two great blue tears had flowed from his eyes. He had heard the faint ringing sound as they trickled down those horny branches to the very earth, to the harsh, unyielding earth with which he was forever kin.

That night he had lain in the shadow of the Trident, relieved and tranquil, filled with a sweet sorrow. And the wisdom of a grown stag, who was now to know the joy of perennial renewal, had become his for all the days of his life.

Just before dawn the leader noticed the herd stirring uneasily. He turned his head in displeasure and saw two hinds approaching. Those two.

The leader did not drive them away, and at dawn he led the herd down from the Trident.

The stags and hinds went their way slowly, leaving bare nibbled patches on the mossy mountain tundra and blackened stamping grounds that would not grow over for many a year. Now and then the stags would turn their heads and their nostrils would quiver as they glanced back at the Trident.

The leader did not quicken his pace or attempt to hurry his charges.

A few sunsets later, when the herders pitched their tent in a forest on the eastern slope of the Great Ridge and the herd reached the fringe of the forest tundra and was moving along over patchy moss interspersed with grass, the wild hinds began to drift away from the herd.

In the daytime they would graze in the forest clearings, lie among the grey scrub, rebuffing the thick-legged bucks of the herd, who were neither discriminating nor persistent in love. At night, however, they would snuggle into the warm depths

of the herd they had joined, and sigh as only cows and reindeer can sigh—with a long, noisy sadness.

Day by day the two hinds lagged further and further
behind the herd, and one night they did not rejoin it.

On a bright, frost-whitened morning the leader led the
herd down into dense and boundless forests, leaving the
mountain peaks, the crags and passes gleaming in the radiance
of a cold, idly sparkling sun. Before quitting the mountain
tundra, whose narrow ledges and vast spaces would await him
till the following summer, the leader cast a farewell glance
over the Great Ridge, the scrub-tangled slopes, the seed-
shedding berry patches, the unmown grass and the black
ruins of the crags, whose thick century-chilled chests were
already weathering the first frosty winds, which would later
gather strength and fury and start tearing them to pieces and
fling down now a rattling torrent of stones, now an avalanche
of huge boulders crushing everything in its path.

On one sharp prong of the Trident that glittered like steel
on high, he espied two slim-legged, long-eared figures. They
stood there very close together, abandoned and sorrowful,
until the whole herd and the very last stag had disappeared
into the forest, which now lay hushed in expectation of snow
and winter.

And now the leader himself, that wise and considerate
father of the herd, disappeared. He, too, had withdrawn into
the forest. The wild hinds strained their eyes and nostrils
until darkness fell, but there was nothing more to be seen.
Even the scent of the stags had been dispelled by the keen,
rising wind. In pitch darkness the hinds crept down and lived
at the foot of the Trident until the antlers in the glen were
covered with snow, until the frost had suppressed the scent
of that rebellious newcomer who had brought his first antlers
to this sacred burial ground.

Then the two hinds set out for the western slope of the
Great Ridge, plunging deeper and deeper into the sparsely
wooded glens. By the spring they would reach a place which
men call the Island. There is such a place amid these great
mountains where the wild beasts seek refuge from danger.
This is where the wild deer, goats and she-elk give birth to

their young, and sick or wounded beasts of prey take shelter. It is a place where not a single beast, either in hunger or in rage, will touch another.

A small mountain—some five miles long and one across— but densely wooded and entwined with thorn bushes and brambles, it is walled on all sides with treacherous, impassable screes that make it quite inaccessible to man, who nowhere in the whole wide world can find himself such a safe and sheltered refuge.

In the cunningly twisted gorges of this mountain, among the huge boulders below and the smaller rocks above, where it would seem that only a snake could pass, there are animal trails.

When their time comes, the two hinds will climb one of these trails with silent stealth and on the soft, thick moss spread with bilberries and cranberries, under the stocky cedars and spruce with their beards of lichen, they will bring forth their young to replace the loss that nature suffered in autumn.

And in a year or two, on some far northern peak of the Great Ridge, a wild stag will once again give tongue with all the power of his passion-chocked heart and demand fair fight for what men have from the beginning of time called love.

CAPERCAILLIE

The taiga thinned out as we neared the high pastures of the Urals, where the cattle we were driving were to spend the summer.

Nearly all the trees now were conifers, warped by the winds and the intense cold of the north. Only here and there amid the spare-branched spruce, fir and larch did a birch or an aspen show its timidly fluttering leaves or the ferns uncoil their snail-like fronds.

The jostling herd of calves and bullocks plodded on wearily up an old cutting bestrewn with fallen trees, and so did we, scrambling over the spiky windfalls with difficulty.

A low mound covered with pale-leaved bilberries that had just finished blooming showed up on the path. The small green pimples of the future berries had put out barely visible grey petal-like anthers and these had quietly dropped off, and now the berries would begin to swell and turn purple, then blue, and finally black, with a greyish down on them. The bilberry is sweet and strong-flavoured when it ripens but it blooms more modestly, perhaps, than any other berry.

A clamour broke out at the bilberry mound. The calves went galloping about with their tails flying and the little boys who were driving the cattle with us began to shout.

I hurried up to the mound and saw a capercaillie running in circles with outspread wings.

"There's a nest! A nest!" the boys shouted.

I stared around, scouring the mound with my eyes, but could see no sign of any nest.

"There! There it is!" the boys pointed to the green stump by which I was standing.

I glanced down and my heart jumped with fright—I had nearly trodden on the nest. It was built not on the mound, but right in the middle of the path, under a springily protruding root. Overgrown with moss on all sides and on top as well and draped with grey tresses, the little house had a small opening on to the bilberry mound. Inside there was a nest, also proofed with moss. And in the nest was a clutch of four mottled light-brown eggs only a little smaller than hen's eggs. I touched one with my finger; it was warm, almost hot.

"Let's take them!" the boy standing next to me breathed excitedly.

"What for?"

"Just for fun!"

"But what about the capercaillie? Look at her!"

The capercaillie was threshing about a little distance away. Her wings were still outspread and she was sweeping the ground with them. She had been sitting on the nest with outspread wings, covering her eggs, keeping them warm. Her wings had grown rigid from lack of movement and she could not fly. At length, however, she managed to fly up on to the branch of a fir-tree and perched over our heads. It was then that we saw that her belly was bare right up to her neck and the bare pimply skin of her breast was pulsating. The bird's heart was beating with fright, anger and a desperate courage.

"She pecked out her down herself and is warming her eggs with her bare belly so as to give every drop of warmth to the little ones that will hatch out," said the schoolmaster as he came up.

"She's like our Mummy. She gives us everything. Every little drop..." one of the little boys said sadly, in a grown-up fashion and, probably in embarrassment at having said something so gentle for the first time in his life, he shouted gruffly: "Come on, let's round up the herd!"

And they all ran away merrily from the capercaillie nest. The capercaillie sat on the branch, craning her neck after them, but her eyes were elsewhere. They were fixed on the nest and, as soon as we had moved away, she flew down smoothly from the tree, crept into the nest, spread her wings and grew still.

Her eyes became filmed with drowsiness, but she was still on her guard, every muscle tense, and her heart beat with powerful strokes, filling with warmth and life the four large eggs from which in a week or two or, perhaps, in a few days the big-headed chicks would appear.

And when they grew up, when on one clear, light-filled April morning they dropped their first song into the great and kindly mystery that surrounded them, perhaps there would be in that song words in the bird tongue that we cannot understand, words about mothers who give their children everything, and sometimes even their own lives.

SHEPHERD AND SHEPHERDESS
A Modern Pastoral*

* Reprinted from a *Soviet Literature* magazine publication, 1972

And she trudged across a wilderness, a field unploughed, uncared for, unknown to the scythe. Her sandals were full of grass seed, thorns clung to her old-fashioned coat with its trimming of grey fur on the sleeves.

Faltering, slipping, as if on ice, she walked up to the railway line, and started off along the sleepers. Her step was nervous and irregular.

As far as the eye could see there was silent steppe all around covered with late autumn grass turning to rusty stubble and stained with patches of salt marsh. The Urals were a dark and distant hulk against the sky. There were no people. No birds sang. No livestock cropped the grass. Only solitary trains passed by.

Nothing disturbed this hushed wilderness.

Her eyes were full of tears, everything before her was swimming, rocking, as if at sea, and where sky began and sea ended she could not tell. The rails swayed like trailing seaweed, the sleepers rolled on like waves. Breathing became harder, as if she were climbing an endless, rickety staircase. At the kilometre sign she wiped her eyes with her hand. The striped post with the big figure on it swayed, rippled, and then settled down in front of her. She left the line and walked down towards a mound which had perhaps been made by firemen for a beacon or in ancient times by nomads; she found the grave with an obelisk upon it. Once upon a time there had been a star on top of the obelisk but evidently it had rotted away.

The grave was overgrown with wormwood and wiry weeds. A thistle grew beside the obelisk but did not venture higher than its top. It clung timidly by its barbs to the weathered column, its ribbed stalk emaciated, prickly.

She knelt before the grave.

"All these years I've searched for you! "

The wind stirred the wormwood on the grave, tweaking the down from the thistle heads. Ringwort seeds and dry frozen grass filled the brown cracks wrinkling the earth's face. A dull ashen bloom covered the steppe, above it loured the ancient mountain range, tired and weary, slumped deep into the plain, and the wall eyes of the salt flats gleamed cold and silent.

But that was farther on, towards the horizon. Here only the feeble grass rustled mournfully and the withered thistle rasped.

She undid her headscarf and pressed her face to the grave. "Oh, why must you lie here alone, in the heart of Russia?"

She said no more.

Just stood there—thinking.

Remembering.

Part One
THE BATTLE

The roar of guns shattered the night silence, cleaving snow-clouds and darkness, exploding into flashes of light. Underfoot the troubled earth swayed, shuddered, stirred, together with the snow, and the men clinging to it.

The night was full of alarm and confusion.

Our troops were wiping out the almost defunct grouping of German troops whose command, like that in the battle of Stalingrad, had refused to accept the ultimatum for unconditional surrender.

Boris Kostyaev's platoon, together with other platoons, companies, battalions and regiments were waiting for the enemy to strike to attempt a break-through. Lorries, tanks and cavalry had been rushing back and forth along the front all day. In the evening the Katyushas were rolled out onto an elevation, disrupting telephone communications in the process. The infantry, seizing their rifles, cursed the Katyusha's gunners. The hooded guns were thickly covered with snow, and the rocket-launchers' lorries looked like beasts, poised to spring. From time to time a rocket flared up above the front line and then the barrels of small guns and the long trunks of the anti-tank weapons could be seen protruding from the snow. In their helmets and caps the soldiers' heads stood out against the snow like scattered, unpeeled potatoes.

At midnight the quartermaster's platoon arrived bringing soup and the vodka ration. There was a stir and a bustle in the trenches. The quartermaster's platoon, scared by the treacherous silence of the snowstorm—it seemed the enemy must be out there crawling up to attack—rushed everyone so they could collect up the thermoses as quickly as possible and beat it, bravely promising to bring food again in the morning, and with any luck vodka as well. The troops were in no hurry to let the quartermaster's platoon go and they increased their panic with tall stories about how many enemy troops were in the vicinity and how they might spring a lightning attack.

No one brought food or drink to the rocket crews for their rear detachment had forgotten how to walk on their own two feet. The infantry men proved to be of sterner stuff in this weather. Good-hearted, they gave the gunners soup. "But see you don't fire at us!" they laid down the condition.

To right, to left, from near and far, came the thunder of battle. But on this sector there was an uneasy hush. The almost infinite patience of the troops had worn thin. Young soldiers were seized with a desire to rush into the pitch darkness, to fight and put paid to the unseen enemy, to expend their pent-up fury. Older men who had run the gamut of suffering during the war staunchly bore the cold, the lashing wind and snow and the uncertainty, and hoped that they would come through this time, too. But just before dawn, a kilometre, or perhaps two to the right of Kostyaev's platoon heavy firing broke loose. Behind, out of the snow, the 150 mm howitzers thudded and hissing shells flew over the infantry-men so that they hunched up in their snow-covered, frozen greatcoats.

The firing grew heavier, mounting in intensity, swelling into a great thundering wave. Mortars howled, rocket-launchers screeched metallically, and ominous flashes lit up the trenches. Ahead the batteries of the regimental guns barked frantically.

Boris drew his pistol from the holster and hurried along the trench, floundering in the snow. Although they had been clearing the trench with spades all night, throwing up a high breastwork of snow, all the same, the way was blocked in places almost to the breastwork and then it was not always clear where the breastwork started.

"Plaa-aa-toon! At the ready!" Boris shouted, or rather tried to shout. His lips were frozen and the command was unintelligible. Sergeant-Major Mokhnakov, deputy platoon commander, caught Boris by the skirts of his greatcoat and pulled him down. At that moment a stream of bullets came whistling out of the snow, they heard the frozen chatter of the machine gun manned by Karyshev and Malyshev; submachine guns rattled, rifles cracked out smartly.

Out of the whirlwind of snow, there appeared a dark mass of people. With coughs, hoarse cries and howls, the mass hurled itself at the trench, fell in, sank into the snow, floundered.

Hand-to-hand fighting had begun.

The starving Germans, demoralised by encirclement and frost, came forward frantically, blindly. They were quickly despatched with bayonets and spades. But behind that wave another came rolling and then a third. Everything was confusion in the darkness: roaring, firing, cursing, the cries of the wounded, the shuddering of the earth, the frozen, creaking recoil of guns, which fired upon the enemy and upon their own troops, too, unable to distinguish what was what—that was beyond anyone now. Boris and Mokhnakov stuck together. Mokhnakov was a left-hander; in his strong left hand he held a spade and in his right a captured pistol.

He did not fire haphazardly, did not get excited. In snow or darkness he could see the right place to be. He would drop into a drift, dig himself in, then jump out and make a short thrust, hacking out with the spade, or shoot and fling something out of the way.

"Keep cool! Otherwise you're a goner!" he shouted to Boris.

Marvelling at his composure, at his cool and accurate calculation, Boris himself began to see the battle more clearly and he realised that his platoon was still alive and fighting, but that each soldier was fighting alone and that he had to let the men know he was with them.

"La-a-ads! Let them have it! " he cried in a strangled voice.

Guided by the sound of his voice Germans poured in to get him. But the way to the platoon commander was constantly barred by Mokhnakov. He defended Kostyaev, defended himself and the platoon. Then either his pistol was knocked out of his hand, or he ran out of ammunition. He snatched a submachine gun from a wounded German, used up all the ammunition in that, and then had to resort to his spade. He trod down the snow to provide himself with a firm stand by the trench, and then flung first one and then another emaciated German over his shoulder, but the third gave a dog-like whine and clung fast to him and the two of them rolled together into the trench, which was swarming with wounded, who were attacking one another and howling from pain and blind rage.

Rockets, many rockets, soared into the sky. In their brief light, scraps of battle scenes came into prominence and in the hellish confusion snarling faces pressed close, then fell away and disappeared into the fiery Gehenna and into the darkness yawning beyond. In the glaring light the powdery snow looked as black as gunpowder and smelled like gunpowder. It stung the face and took away the breath.

A giant of a man, an immense shadow with a blazing torch trailing behind him was moving, no, flying, on wings of fire into the trench and crushing everyone in his path with an iron crowbar. Men fell with skulls cracked open, and screams of pain rent the air.

"Kill him! Kill him! " Boris fired with his pistol but missed, and, backing along the trench, pressed himself to the wall, shifting from one foot to the other, as if in a dream, unable to understand why he could not run away and what was stopping him.

It was a fearful sight, that burning man with the crowbar. His shadow darted here and there, one moment swelling to vast proportions, and then disappearing, and he himself, like some visitor from the nether world, kept flaming up with fresh force, and then fading again. Baring his teeth he wailed like a wild thing. He even seemed to be covered in thick hair, holding not a crowbar but an uprooted tree. His hands long, with claws.... He emanated lethal cold, darkness, primeval horror. The burning torch at his back was like a reflection of those fiery storms from which this monster sprang, rising from all fours and coming down to our age with the unchanged visage of the caveman.

Mokhnakov leapt from the trench, ploughing through the thick snow and came face to face with the giant, now completely enveloped in flame.

"Ser-er-geant! Mokh-na-a-kov! " Boris was trying to push a clip of cartridges into the pistol and to jump from the trench, but someone caught hold of his coat from behind.

"He-e-e-elp! He-e-elp! " came a desperate wail from Shkalik, Boris' orderly, the youngest in the platoon. He would not let the commander get away from him, he tried to drag him into the snow. Boris threw him off and waited, with pistol raised, for the next rocket to flare up. His hand was firm, without a trace of a quiver. Everything in him had suddenly turned to stone, was frozen solid—now he would get him, he knew he would get him for sure.

One rocket, then another. A whole bunch of them splashed into flame and Boris caught sight of Mokhnakov, trampling on some burning thing. A ball of fire rolled from under Mokhnakov's feet and burning fragments flew in all directions.

The fire went out.

Mokhnakov fell heavily into the trench.

"Alive! You're alive! " Boris seized hold of the sergeant-major, feeling him all over as if to make sure he really was alive.

"It's all over! All over! The Fritz went crazy! Off his nut! " Mokhnakov shouted breathlessly, thrusting his spade into the snow to clean it. "His camouflage sheet caught fire.... Horrible it was! "

Black soot whirled overhead, grenades exploded loudly, shots came thick and fast, the big guns thundered. It seemed as though the whole war was now concentrated here, in this spot, raging in the trampled pit of the trench, giving off suffocating smoke, roars and whines, shell fragments, and the bestial snarls of men.

Suddenly, for an instant, everything died down. Only the howling of the snowstorm sounded in their ears.

"Tanks!" the many- voiced yell went up from the trench.

Stifling, noisome fumes came at them from the darkness. The tanks—eyeless monsters—rose out of the night. They heard a raucous grinding of caterpillar tracks in the frost, which immediately skidded to a halt in the deep snow. Beneath the tanks and on the tanks the snow bubbled and melted.

They had no way back and anything that crossed their path they smashed and ground to dust. The guns, now only two of them, turned and fired after them. With a stealthy sound that made the heart sink the rocket launchers rained down a salvo upon the tanks and a hellish fire lit up the battlefield, rocking the trench like a cradle, melting everything in it—snow, earth, metal, the living and the dead. The noise of battle swelled.

A howitzer shell exploded by the side of a heavy tank, which shuddered with a grinding of metal, and began swivelling to left and right. It swung its gun, the muzzle brake fell into the snow, the barrel dipped, and ploughing up the snow ahead of it, the tank dived blindly for the trench. This monster, now out of control, scattered both Germans and Russians. The eyeless hulk appeared over the trench, its treads clanking; turning with a screech, it tossed clods of dirty snow at Mokhnakov and Boris, enveloping them in its hot exhaust. The machine toppled into the trench sidewise, skidded, then tore onward.

The motor whined, strained to the limit, the tracks churned and chopped the frozen earth.

"What *is* he doing? What *is* he doing?" Boris, almost breaking his fingers, was crawling along, pressing into a frozen crevice. Mokhnakov shook him and pulled him out of the snow.

"The grenades! Where are the grenades?"

Boris stopped struggling in the snow and recalled that he had two anti-tank grenades hanging at his belt beneath his greatcoat. The evening before he had issued out two apiece, and had taken two himself. Now he had forgotten about them. Mokhnakov had either lost his or had already used them. Pulling at his mitten with his teeth, Boris thrust his hand beneath his coat—there was only one grenade there now. He whipped it out and began to pull out the pin. Mokhnakov groped at Boris' sleeve, trying to get the grenade from him, but Boris pushed him away and crawled along after the tank, which was ploughing through the trench, slowly, metre by metre, chewing up earth and snow, seeking a support for the second track.

"Stop! Stop, you bastard! You wait! I'll get you.... Right now!" Boris flung himself after the tank, but his legs, as if torn from their sockets, would not support him and he kept falling, stumbling over crushed bodies. He lost his mittens, and got a mouthful of earth, but he kept hold of the grenade as if it were fragile glass, glass, afraid of setting it off, almost in tears because he could not reach the tank, because he had so little control over his legs.

The tank fell into a deep shell-hole, was seized with convulsions and just then, freeing himself from the snow, Boris rose and lobbed the grenade like a boy playing ball. There was a great roar, the lieutenant was enveloped in snow and flame, clumps of earth flew at his face, filling his mouth, and he was sent rolling along the trench like a pup.

The tank shuddered, recoiled and was silent. The track fell off with a metallic clatter and unwound like a soldier's puttee. A hail of bullets flicked against the armouring, where the snow was hissing as it melted, and someone else flung a grenade at the tank.

The anti-tank riflemen came to life and hit frenziedly at the tank, striking flashes of blue flame from its surface, annoyed that the tank did not catch light. A German appeared, bareheaded, close-cropped, in a ripped tunic, with a sheet tied round his neck. He shot from a submachine gun held at his stomach, shouting and jumping about. When the ammunition ran out, the German threw the gun away. Then he began to pummel with his bare fist on the sealed armour of the tank, his skin sticking to the frozen metal and tearing. Just then he was cut down by a bullet. He sank beneath the caterpillar track, quivered in the snow and was quiet. The sheet he had been wearing in place of a camouflage cape fluttered in the wind and covered his frenzied face.

The battle receded to one side, into the night. The howitzers redirected their fire; rocket-launchers, shuddering with a hoarse sound, now sprayed flame on other trenches and fields, and those Katyushas which had been standing since the previous night by the trench were burning, stranded in the snow.

Ahead, the regimental gun—now there was only one—continued to bark. What remained of the infantrymen in the trench fired spasmodically with their rifles and the battalion mortar went into action. Soon two more mortars started up, and a submachine gun cracked out late but joyfully. The anti-tank riflemen ran out of ammunition, and the machine-gun was silent too. Here and there from the trenches the dark figures of enemy soldiers leapt forth and rushed into the night to join their own side, with cries and shouts.

A few shots rang out after them, but there was no pursuit.

Straw stacks were blazing in the distance. Multicoloured rockets flared up like fireworks. But here all was quiet. Would it be for long? The snow was blanketing the dead. Cartridges and grenades exploded on the almost burnt out Katyushas. Flaming cartridge cases split from charred machines smoking and hissed in the snow. The crippled tank, a frozen hulk, reared black above the trench and the wounded were dragging themselves towards it, to find shelter from the wind and the bullets. An unknown girl with a first-aid pouch hanging from her neck was bandaging their wounds. She had lost her hat and mittens, and was blowing on her finger-tips to warm them.

Mokhnakov had managed to light a cigarette. He drew on it and kept his gaze on the tank, dark and motionless.

"Let's have a puff!" Boris held out his hand.

Mokhnakov did not give him the cigarette but pulled out the platoon commander's mittens from beneath his coat and then his tobacco pouch and paper. When Boris had rolled himself a clumsy cigarette, lit up and had a fit of coughing, Mokhnakov exclaimed cheerfully: "Made a fine job of that tank!"

Boris looked uncertainly at the vanquished tank: such a giant, and such a tiny grenade! Such a tiny human being! He was still partly deaf from the explosion. And his mouth still had earth in it, gritty on his teeth, and his throat was burning. He was coughing and spitting. His head was throbbing and rainbow circles swam before his eyes.

"The wounded..." Boris said, picking in his ear. "We have to collect up the wounded! They'll freeze."

"O.K." Mokhnakov took his cigarette from him, threw it into the snow and drew the commander closer to himself. "We must move," Boris heard him saying remotely, and started pulling his ear again, picking out the earth with his finger.

"There's something in it.... Something there...."

"Never mind, it's a good thing you're alive! Who on earth throws a grenade that way!"

Mokhnakov's back and shoulder tabs were spattered with dirty snow, the collar of his sheepskin coat was half torn off and flapped loose. Everything swayed before Boris' eyes, Mokhnakov's flapping collar seemed to hit at Boris' head—not painfully, but deafeningly. On the way Boris scooped up some snow and devoured it, but it was also polluted with soot and gunpowder and his stomach gained no coolness from it, on the contrary, it even burned. Above the open hatch of the damaged tank the snow was dancing in a whirlpool. The tank was cooling, and the metal was ringing and cracking, painful to his ear. Mokhnakov caught sight of the hatless nurse, took off his own cap and crammed it onto her head. The girl did not as much as glance at Mokhnakov, she just paused for a second and blew on her hands.

Karyshev and Malyshev, both from Boris Kostyaev's platoon, were dragging the wounded towards the tank, into shelter.

"So you're alive and kicking!" Boris rejoiced.

"And you too!" Karyshev echoed joyfully, and sniffed at the air so energetically that the tape hanging loose from his fur cap flew into one nostril.

"But our machine gun's out of action," Malyshev said rather guiltily.

Mokhnakov climbed up onto the tank, and pushed the still limp body of a German officer into the hatch. Then, just in case, he fired a round into the tank from the submachine gun he had picked up somewhere. He peered inside by the light of his torch and, jumping down into the snow, reported: "A tankful of officers! Fixed it up nicely, they did. The soldiers were out in front, for cannon-fodder, but the officers were under the armouring...." He bent towards the nurse: "What about dressings? "

"Communications! " the half-deafened platoon commander shouted loudly and hoarsely, and wiped his nose on his frozen mitten.

Mokhnakov knew himself what to do. He summoned those who remained of the platoon and despatched one soldier to the company commander. If he did not find him he was to hurry to the battalion commander.

From the damaged tank they got petrol, they splashed it on the snow and lit it, throwing on broken butts of rifles and submachine guns and all kinds of stuff they had captured. The nurse warmed her hands, and tidied herself up. Mokhnakov brought her a pair of officers' fur mittens and gave her a cigarette. After finishing his cigarette and exchanging a few words with the girl, he climbed into the tank, rummaged about with the aid of his torch, and yelled, as if from the tomb: "Got it! "

Flourishing an aluminium flask, Mokhnakov got down, all eyes upon him.

"One mouthful each for the wounded! " Mokhnakov said sternly. "And ... a little for the doctor," he winked at the nurse, but she made no response whatever to his generosity, and the whole of the schnapps was shared out among the wounded, who lay on groundsheets behind the tank. The driver of the Katyusha, who was badly burnt, screamed with pain. His cry pierced the heart but the soldiers pretended to notice nothing.

A sergeant who had been wounded in the leg asked them to take away the frozen German lying beneath him and they rolled the dead fascist out of the trench. His mouth, open in anguish, was filled with snow. They pushed aside and dragged out of the trench other corpses, and put up a canopy over the wounded, made of groundsheets fixed at the corners to rifle barrels; in the course of the work they warmed up a little. The groundsheets flapped resoundingly in the wind, the teeth of the wounded chattered. At times quiet, drained of strength, at times crying out desperately to the vanished sky, the driver lay in agony. "There, there, brother," the soldiers said soothingly, not knowing what they could do to help.

One after the other three soldiers were sent off to battalion HQ but not one of them came back. The nurse called Boris to one side. Hiding her nose in the collar of her quilted jacket, which was stiff with cold, she banged one boot against the other and gazed pointedly at the lieutenant's ragged mittens. Slowly he took them off and, bending over one of the wounded men, he drew them on to the willingly outstretched hands.

"The wounded men will freeze," said the girl, her swollen eyelids drooping over her eyes. Her face and lips were swollen, too, her crimson cheeks looked as if they were spattered with flour, her skin was cracked from wind and dirt.

The burnt driver was whimpering weakly now as if someone had thrust a dummy in his mouth.

Boris thrust his hands into his sleeves and looked down with a guilty air.

"Where is your nurse? " the girl asked, without opening her eyes.

"Killed. Yesterday."

The driver was silent. The girl reluctantly raised her eyelids. Beneath them, dimming her sight, stood tears. She waited, tensed, to hear the man cry out again, and the tears in her eyes flowed back to whence they had come.

"I must go." The girl hunched her shoulders and stood there for a couple more seconds, listening. "I must go," she added, bracing herself and began to clamber up onto the breastwork of the trench.

"You need an escort. I'll give you a soldier."

"No need to," he heard from the distance. "People are short. Suppose...."

A minute later Boris climbed out of the trench. Wiping the frozen moisture from his eyes with his sleeve, he tried to make out where the girl was but nothing could be seen in the darkness.

The snow fell in slanting sheets. The flakes were wet and Boris decided that the snowstorm would soon be over: it was falling thickly, blunting the force of the wind. He returned to the tank, and stood there a moment resting his back against the track.

"Karyshev, collect everything you can for the fire!" the lieutenant ordered grimly, and added quietly: "Remove the clothes from the dead to keep them"—he indicated the wounded—"warm, and find me some mittens somewhere. Sergeant-major! How about sentries?"

"It's all seen to."

"Someone should go to the gunners. Perhaps they've got communications."

Mokhnakov got up unwillingly, pulled his belt tighter around him, and himself went off to the gunners who had fought so staunchly during the night. Before long he was back.

"There's one gun left with four men. They're also wounded. They've no shells left." Mokhnakov banged the snow from his collar and only now noticed with surprise that it was torn. "Shall I bring the gunners here?" he asked, pinning his collar together.

Boris nodded. The indefatigable Malyshev and Karyshev moved off behind the sergeant-major.

They got the wounded gunners into the trench. The men's spirits rose at the sight of the fire and people, but their commander would not leave the firing position and asked for shells to be brought from damaged guns.

So, without communications, just relying on their eyes and ears, they kept going until morning. Straggling groups of lost Germans appeared like ghosts out of the gloom from time to time but, on seeing the Russians and the crippled tanks and charred lorries, they made themselves scarce, disappearing forever into the drowsily swaying snowy haze.

In the morning, at about eight o'clock, the howitzers ceased to thunder in their rear. Guns to left and right of them fell silent too. The little gun ahead of them gave up, also, after one last resounding roar. The gun commander had either used up his ammunition or had been killed at his post.

Lower down, Boris estimated, two mortars were still in action, although there had been many of them the night before; the rat-tat-tat of large-calibre machine-guns was heard; somewhere, huge guns began to boom, striking at an unknown target faraway. A respectful hush descended upon the infantry, and firing points along the forward area timidly stopped firing one by one; after a delayed salvo which echoed all around, the giant guns (the pundits declared that a man could easily crawl into the barrel!), which use more fuel on the journey than powder and shells in battle, grew disdainfully quiet, but from the distance earth tremors reached them for a long time still, and the soldiers' mess-tins clinked at their belts from the quaking.

Air and snow ceased to shake. The trembling in the ground and in their limbs died away. The snow settled and clung silently. It fell eagerly, heavily, as if it had been accumulating, suspended there above the earth, waiting until the fiery holocaust came to an end.

All was quiet. So quiet that the soldiers began to stick their heads up out of the snow and look uncertainly around them.

"Is it over?" someone asked.

"It's over!" Boris wanted to shout, but the faraway drumming of machine guns and the barely audible reverberations of explosions reached his ears.

"That's over for you!" the platoon commander growled. "Fall in. Check weapons!"

"Ya-a-aev! Ya-a-aev!"

The voice came nearer.

"Ya-a-aev!"

"Seems like someone's calling you?" the quick, sensitive ears of the former fireman Pafnutiev, now an infantryman, pricked up. Without waiting for permission he hollered; "Hey there-ere-ere!" the effort warming him a little.

As soon as he stopped shouting and jumping, a soldier with a carbine appeared out of the snow and fell beside the tank, which was up to the top of its caterpillar tracks in snow. He fell upon the frozen driver, passed his hand over him, moved away and wiping the thawed snow off his face grunted: "I've been looking for you all over! Why didn't you answer? "

"Why don't you report, man? " Boris muttered, pulling his hands from his pockets.

"I thought you knew me! The battalion commander's runner," the messenger said, shaking his mittens out.

"Should've started with that."

"The Germans have had a walloping, and you're sitting here knowing nothing," the soldier rattled on, hoping to smooth over his blunder.

"Stop blabbering! " Sergeant-Major Mokhnakov boomed. "Report what you've come for and share out the booty if you're well off."

"So, Comrade Lieutenant, you're summoned to the battalion commander. You see, you've been made company commander. The company commander's dead."

"And we're to stay here? " Mokhnakov compressed his blue lips.

"And you're to stay here." Not favouring the sergeant-major with a glance, he held out his tobacco pouch: "Here you are, our poison weed! Nothing like it for warming a man up...."

"To hell with you and your poison weed! It's enough to make you sick. You didn't meet a girl anywhere on the way? "

"No. What, did she run away? "

"Never you mind whether she ran away or not! Probably got frozen...." Mokhnakov cast a reproachful glance at Boris. "Shouldn't have let her go by herself...."

Drawing on tight, oil-stained mittens, which probably came from the dead driver, and drawing in his belt, Boris said quietly: "I'll send for the wounded as soon as I get to the battalion." Ashamed at being obviously pleased at the idea of leaving this place, Boris added loudly, raising the groundsheets covering the wounded: "Hold on, brothers! They'll be coming for you soon."

"For God's sake do your best, Comrade Lieutenant. It's cold, we can't stand it."

Boris and Shkalik wandered across the snow, with no paths or roads to guide them and relying entirely on the runner's instinct. It turned out to be totally unreliable. They got lost, and, by the time they arrived at the battalion position there was no one there apart from an angry telephonist with a scratched nose. He sat huddled up in a groundsheet, like a Bedouin in the desert, shouting loud, unprintable curses at the war, at Hitler and especially at his fellow-operator, who had fallen asleep at the intermediate point. The telephonist had almost exhausted the batteries, trying to wake up his opposite number with the buzzer.

"Just imagine! Some more lunatics have turned up! " the telephonist declared venomously, without taking his finger off the buzzer, which sounded like an angry wasp. "Lieutenant Kostyaev, is it? " On receiving an affirmative answer, he pressed the jigger: "I'm off! Report to the battalion commander.... The code? To hell with you and your code! I'm frozen to death...." Still grumbling, the telephonist switched off the apparatus and kept repeating: "I won't half give it to him, I will! " Removing the mess-tin, on which he had been sitting, from beneath his behind, he grunted and stumped off over the snow awkwardly, his legs stiff from inaction. "Follow me! " he gestured. He rolled up the cable, the reel creaking sharply, and advanced ferociously towards the intermediate point. If the other operator had not frozen to death, he'd get what was coming to him.

* * *

The battalion commander had taken up quarters across the river, on the edge of a hamlet, in a bath-house. The bath-house was an old-fashioned type, without a chimney, quite a rarity in the Ukraine. Born into a Semirechye Cossack family, Battalion Commander Filkin—it was a rather comic surname, quite inappropriate to his energetic character—had been Boris' classmate at the regimental training school. He greeted his platoon commander warmly.

"We've got the Russian spirit here! " he announced gaily,

"a real Russian bath! Let's have a good steam, Boris! " He was highly excited at the military success, and had perhaps had a drop or two. "What a war, Boris! A hell of a war! The Germans have surrendered—masses of them. Absolutely masses. And what about us? " He snapped his fingers. "The second company has practically no losses—about fifteen casualties—and they may simply be off womanising somewhere!"

"But we were hit badly. Half the platoon gone. Have to get the wounded away."

"Really? And I thought it'd passed you by. The main fighting was elsewhere.... But you've come through." He slapped Boris on the back, then took a drink from an earthenware flask. It took his breath away. He wagged his head in delight. "Ah, what a drink for you! Real rotgut! Shan't give you any, even if you're freezing. We'll have to get the wounded. God knows where the transport is! I'll give them what for! For the time being, Boris, you'll act as company commander.... Oh, yes, I know you love your platoon. I know you're a modest type. But you've got to do it. Take a look here! " Battalion Commander Filkin opened a mapcase and began to tap the map with his finger. The skin was coming off its frozen tip, and the end of the finger was red and round like a radish. "The position is this: we're occupying the hamlet, but beyond, in the ravines and in the field between the hamlet and the village there's a big enemy concentration. We have to get them. The Germans have no guns or machines, and practically no ammunition, they're half dead, but what the hell.... They're desperate. So let Mokhnakov remove the platoon and you choose a place to station the troops. I'll gather all that's left of the battalion there. Get going! Look after the soldiers, Boris! It's still a long way to Berlin...."

"Get the wounded away! Send a doctor. And give them some spirits," Boris pointed to the flask.

"All right, all right," the battalion commander waved his hand. "I'll take the wounded, I'll take them." He began talking to someone on the telephone. Boris relentlessly picked up the flask with the home-brew. Hugging it awkwardly to his chest, he walked out of the bath-house.

He looked for Shkalik, handed him the flask and told him to return as fast as he could to the platoon.

"Leave someone with the wounded and light a fire," he instructed the runner. "And don't get lost."

Shkalik put the flask into a bag, slung his rifle over his back, waved goodbye with his mitten and reluctantly made his way across the vegetable plots.

Dawn came, and perhaps it was lighter now, too, because the snowstorm had died down. The hamlet was up to the chimneys in snow. By the houses stood German tanks with open hatches, and armoured troop-carriers. Some of them were still smoking. A green car lay flattened like a frog in the middle of the road, a dirty stain spreading from it over the snow. Everywhere there were shell holes, and clods of earth flung up by explosions. Earth had even landed on the roofs. The wattle fences were all smashed: some of the cottages and sheds had been overturned by tanks or hit by missiles. A shaggy black flock of crows would circle above the ravines in silent concentration, then disappear.

A squad of soldiers in shabby uniforms were working in time to their own chanting, pushing the damaged lorries off the road, clearing the way for their own vehicles. A fire was burning by the cottages, and round it some elderly soldiers from an auxiliary quartermaster's platoon were warming themselves. Some war prisoners were sitting by the fire, too, timidly stretching out their hands to the flames. On the road leading to the hamlet stood tanks and other vehicles, extending in a dark, broken ribbon, and beside them their crews were trying to keep warm, jigging about with a bit of horse-play.

It did not take long for the platoon to reach the hamlet. The soldiers made for the fires and cottages. Answering Boris' unspoken question, Mokhnakov reported briskly: "That girl, that nurse, rustled up some captured transport and took all the wounded away. The artillery are a far cry from infantry—they're a cooperative lot."

"Okay. That's good. Have you eaten? "

"Eaten what? Snow? "

"Okay. The rear detachments'll catch up with us soon."

Warmed up by the quick march, the soldiers were already foraging for themselves. They were boiling potatoes in helmets and crunching captured buscuits, and some had even managed to get a drink. They roamed about, looking into the bath-house, sniffing around. But Battalion Commander Filkin came, drove them all away and gave Boris hell over nothing. It immediately became clear why he was furious.

"Have you been behind the bath-house? " he asked.

"No."

"Go and have a look then."

Behind the bath-house, which had not been heated for a long time but still smelled of smoke, behind that bath-house, the very sight of which made one's body start itching, there, by the potato pit, which was covered with a straw mat, lay the bodies of an old man and an old woman. They had been hurrying from the house to the pit, which by all appearances had served them as shelter more than once and where they were used to sitting it out for long periods, for the old woman had taken a bast bagful of food and a ball of thick homespun wool. They had been caught in the artillery softening-up barrage and killed there, behind the bath-house.

They lay pressed to each other, the old woman's face hidden in the old man's armpit. Their bodies had been riddled with splinters, their clothing was torn, grey wadding protruded from the patched wadded jackets.

The ball of wool had rolled out of the bag, pulling with it the ribbing of the socks the old woman had begun, together with needles of rusty wire. The old woman was wearing socks knitted in the same wool and those she had begun had no doubt been intended for the old man. On her feet were galoshes, tied on with a string, while the old man wore makeshift footwear cut roughly from German high-boots. Boris thought to himself that the old man had cut them down because the instep of the German boots was low and he could not get them on his swollen feet. But later he realised that the old man had kept cutting scraps from the uppers to mend the soles and had gradually got down to the instep.

"I can't.... I can't bear to see the bodies of old people and children," said Filkin, who had approached quietly. "After all, you expect it to happen to soldiers, but when it's children and old folk...."

The two men looked grimly at the old couple, who had no doubt had their ups and downs—rows and other unpleasant moments—but had embraced each other devotedly in the hour of death.

From the neighbours the officers found out that the old people had come here from the Volga regions during the famine. They had grazed the collective farm flock. The shepherd and the shepherdess.

"In the bag there are cakes made from frozen potatoes," the runner announced, after removing the bag from the old woman's dead hands. He began to wind the wool onto the ball. He wound it all on, then stopped, at a loss what to do with the bag.

The battalion commander gave a long sigh, looked around for a spade and began to dig a grave. Boris also picked up a spade. Some soldiers turned up from nowhere, men who by no means loved digging the soil—war had made them browned off with this job; and they took the spades from Filkin and Boris.

The grave was soon ready. They tried to part the hands of the shepherd and the shepherdess, but it was impossible, and they decided to leave them as they were. They laid them with their heads to the east, covered their sombre, lifeless faces— the old woman's with her shawl fringed with tassels, and the old man's with his worn out leather cap. The runner threw the bag with the food into the grave and started to shovel in earth.

The unknown old couple were buried, the mound was patted smooth with the spades and one of the soldiers remarked that in spring the grave would settle—the earth here was frozen and mixed with snow—and then perhaps neighbours in the hamlet would re-bury them. Lantsov, an elderly, lanky soldier, read a quiet, well-sounding prayer over the grave, and no one reproached him for it—after all they were old folk.

Part Two
THE MEETING

Although the fighting had finished, the soldiers had still not got over it and continued to live through the nightmare over and over again. For them the snowstorm and the battle were still raging.

They were drinking home-brewed spirit.

They drank it hurriedly, silently, not waiting until the potatoes were done.

They used their fingers to fish sour cabbage from the crock, they crunched, grunted with satisfaction, and avoided one another's eyes.

The mistress of the house, whose name was Lusya, looked at the soldiers with a scared expression, as she piled dry acacia twigs and little bundles of straw into the stove, hurrying to get the potatoes boiled. Lantsov, who had been spreading straw on the floor, stood up, wiped his hands on his trousers and sat down sideways at the table.

"Pour me out some, too."

Boris sat by the stove, warming himself, and being careful not to stare at the mistress of the house who was bustling about at his side. Sergeant-Major Mokhnakov picked up a German canister from the floor, poured out a good mugful, held it out to Lantsov and attempted a crooked smile.

"Knock it back, lad! "

Lantsov busily straightened his tunic as if he were getting ready to dive through a hole in the ice. Shuddering convulsively and spluttering, he swallowed down the liquor, then sat for some time unable to speak. Finally he got his breath back and said wretchedly, wiping away a tear with his finger: "Oh, Lord! "

Before long, he overcame his shyness, he livened up and tried to chat with the soldiers and the sergeant-major. But they remained stubbornly silent and went on downing the home-brew. It was becoming more and more stifling in the cottage owing to tobacco fumes, the persistent smell of musty sugar-beet spirit and the oppressive expectation of something bad.

If only they'd pass out quickly, Boris thought uneasily. It gets on your nerves....

"You ought to have a drink, too," Lantsov said to him, "it's true, you should ... it seems to me it helps...."

"I'll wait for the food," Boris said, turning towards the stove and stretched out his hands to warm them. The chimney drew badly and belched out a great deal of smoke—it was obvious there had not been a man about the house for a long time.

Since the night everything had been swaying and ringing hazily in Boris' head. Once in the past he had worn his boots out to the stage where soles and uppers had parted company. He had fastened them together with wire, and then he had caught cold and was driven to taking the boots from another young lieutenant like himself, whose body lay in a gully with those of his platoon. He had pulled the boots off and put them on himself—and for three days his feet had been like ice in those boots. He changed them as soon as he possibly could. Now he had a feeling as if all of him had been squeezed into a dead man's boot.

"You're frozen through? " asked Lusya.

He rubbed his hands on his temples to stop the dizziness, then looked at her with a clearer head.

"Right you are," he wanted to say, but he said nothing, concentrating his bemused attention on the stove. Shadows flitted over the woman's face, which was lit up by the fire. In her small features there was something that seemed slightly unfinished, as if it were illuminated from below by the smoky light of an icon lamp or one of the old country rushlights, so that only separate features were etched in clearly. She felt his keen, stealthy gaze upon her and bit her full lower lip. She had a straight nose, with fine nostrils, and on it was a smudge of soot. Her eyes were long and beautifully shaped and fringed with eyelashes which curled upwards like those of a doll. When she raised her eyes, from beneath these eyelashes there appeared dark and also slightly elongated irises. In them danced the reflection of the fire, they were constantly changing, growing dark, then light, and seeming to have a life of their own. But the expression of deep, lasting sorrow never disappeared from these mysterious eyes which seemed to have come from some other, bigger face. And Boris also noticed how restless her hands were. The whole time she seemed to be trying, unsuccessfully, to find a place for them.

The straw was consumed by the flame. The acacia branches lay there, a heap of red hot nails, giving out waves of dry heat. The woman's mouth opened slightly, and her hands came to rest calmly at her throat. It seemed that if you frightened her, she would shudder and drop her hands.

"Perhaps they're done? " Boris touched her tentatively on the elbow.

"Eh? " She started and stepped abruptly to one side. "Yes, yes, they're ready. Probably they are. Now we'll try them." Her pronunciation was not Ukrainian. In fact there was nothing that seemed Ukrainian about her, except her headscarf tied tightly, Ukrainian style, and the braid-trimmed apron. But the Germans had taught all the women hereabouts to conceal themselves under tightly tied headscarves, to hide away and to fear.

Lusya took the poker and moved the pail-sized iron pot to the edge of the hob. She tried a potato with her finger, shook her hand and popped her finger into her mouth.

Picking up the pot with a soldier's foot-cloth for protection, Boris emptied the water into the trough in the corner beneath the washstand. Thick clouds of steam rose from the trough. Lusya removed her finger from her mouth, tucked her hand beneath her apron and watched Boris, embarrassed.

"Now you can pour me out a drink, too," Boris said, putting the pot on the table.

"Not really? " Mokhnakov wondered in a loud voice. "By the end of the war, you'll see, you and Lantsov will be seasoned hands! " and again the corner of his mouth twitched.

Boris did not even look at him.

"Move up there! " he shoved against Shkalik's side.

Shkalik jumped as if he had been stung and almost fell off the bench.

"You've given the lad a drop too much! " barked Boris, to no one in particular.

"Won't you sit down please," he said to Lusya, who was standing by herself with her back pressed to the cooling stove and still hiding her hand beneath her apron.

"Oh, never mind me! You eat! " for some reason she was unnerved and began to fuss with her headscarf and her blouse.

"Nay, lass, you mustn't refuse," Pafnutiev sang out. "Sit ye down and don't turn your nose up at soldier's grub. We won't do you any harm. We...."

"Oh, come off it! " Boris banged his hand on the bench from which Pafnutiev had obediently risen. Then turning to Lusya: "I beg you...."

"Very well! Very well! " Lusya seemed to be ashamed that they were begging her to sit with them, that the lieutenant was even cross with the soldier for some reason. "I ... won't be a moment...."

She disappeared behind the door into the front room and soon returned, now without the kerchief and apron. She had a plait, coiled on the nape of her neck. The touch of pink on her cheeks stood out distinctly on her pale face. She would be intruding here, among the dirty, crumpled, angry soldiers, she thought, and she felt uncomfortable.

"You shouldn't have stayed here," she said stiffly and explained to Boris: "I kept asking them to go in there," she waved towards the door into the front room.

"We haven't washed for a long time," Karyshev said, and his fellow-villager and kinsman, Malyshev, added: "We'd leave some livestock behind us...."

Mokhnakov poured out a drink all round, with one for Lusya. They began to clink glasses. Mugs and tins clanged, a glass rang—out of delicacy they had given it to Lusya. She waited with raised glass to see whether the commander would say anything. He remained silent, and Lusya, looking down, spoke herself: "To your return..." and she turned towards the stove. "We've been waiting for you so long. So long..." she spoke with a slightly guilty air. Desperately, in one gulp, Lusya drank down the raw spirit and put her hand over her mouth.

"That's the way to do it! Now we can see you're real glad to see us! " Karyshev said in his deep bass and held out some American spam spiked on the blade of a pocket-knife along with a hastily peeled potato. Shkalik wanted to beat Karyshev to it, but he dropped the potato. Bits of hot potato fell into his fly, he started popping up and down like a cat on hot bricks, but immediately shrank back, embarrassed. The platoon commander turned away in annoyance. Shkalik shook the hot bits of potato down his trouser leg and felt better.

This man, Shkalik, was a teetotaller. Boris and Lantsov were non-drinkers, too, and because of it had sometimes felt themselves second-class people, not such staunch fighters as the rest of the troops, who although they usually took a drop just to warm themselves up somehow managed to put on a convincing air of being desperadoes and rakes. In general, our muzhiks, our Russian muzhiks, are fond of making themselves out to be real dare-devils, and more often than not give a highly coloured picture of their dealings with women and drink. Only Mokhnakov drank heavily, but he held his liquor well; anywhere, even in the most deserted places he could find something to tank up with and Pafnutiev, the former village fireman, was always hovering servilely about him in the hope of a free drink. Malyshev and Karyshev drank rarely but when they did, they made a good job of it. On receiving their ration, they would pour it into their flasks and when they had got a litre, or even more, they would wait for a blessed moment of calm and then, settling down in a glade or in some cottage, have a leisurely drink, clinking glasses and giving themselves up to reminiscences, "having a consultation", as they explained it. And afterwards they would sing— Karyshev in a bass with Malyshev adding in the descant:

O'er the ta-ree-ees aro-o-ose the su-u-un.
A big b-er-lack cro-o-ow caw-haw-hawed the-e-ere
The hou-ou-ours have go-ho-hone, the minutes flo ho-hown
When I walked ou-ou-out with a mai-hai-haiden fair.

"Where d'you hail from, daughter? " Karyshev, who loved all mankind, and was flushed with liquor, asked Lusya. "From your face and your talk you're probably Russian? "

and he tried to strike up a conversation with her but Boris said hurriedly: "Can't you let a person eat! "

"Well, I can eat and talk at the same time." Lusya was pleased that the soldiers had relaxed, and become friendlier. Only Mokhnakov was imperceptibly weighing her up with his sidelong glances. This fixed, all-knowing glance disconcerted her. "I'm not a local."

"Ah. I can see there's something about your face.... You're not Siberian, by any chance? " Karyshev went on questioning her, his expression softening.

"I don't know."

"Would you believe it? You're an orphan? "

"Uhuh."

"A-ah. That's a different matter. Then of course.... Life does treat people in all sorts of ways...."

Boris loved these two fellow-villagers from the Altai who were born and had lived and worked in what—according to them—was the most beautiful village in the world, Klyuchi. Boris had not understood these soldiers, had not taken to them right away. To begin with, when he had first joined the platoon, they had seemed to him to be rather dim-witted, and he had even been annoyed to hear their jibes and laughs at each other. Karyshev had ginger hair, Malyshev was bald. This distinction they made the subject of many jokes. As soon as Karyshev took his cap off, Malyshev would begin to needle him: "What did you do that for? Some German'll get the idea a Russian soldier's lit a fire to cook potatoes, then gun drill'll begin! " Karyshev grabbed a handful of grass and threw it at Malyshev's bald head: "You light up the whole region, the way you shine! Fritz'll think there's a mortar here and he'll get you! "

The soldiers would roll on the floor to hear these exchanges of repartee, and Boris thought: How stupid you have to get to be pleased with these flat jokes, so awkward for middle-aged men. But gradually he became used to the war and to his men and began to understand them in a different way, and now he no longer found anything awkward in the soldiers' jokes.

The pair from the Altai fought as they worked, without

fuss, without malice. They fought because it had to be done, and they did the job properly. They rarely went in for "intellectual" talk, but if they did, you found yourself listening to them.

Karyshev now sat expansively at the table, he was eating carefully and with respect for every mouthful and kept looking at Lantsov with a kind of wise cunning. The Altai man's tunic was unbuttoned, his belt was unfastened, he was confident, and obviously feeling at home. He was peeling the potatoes with his fleshy finger-tips, and gave the peeled potatoes unostentatiously to Lusya and Shkalik. The latter was now absolutely drunk, he sat swaying on the bench, eating nothing. He raised some sauerkraut to his mouth but it did not get there, and festooned the front of his tunic. Karyshev gave his tunic a shake and ribbons of sauerkraut fell to the floor. Shkalik dully followed his movements and suddenly blurted out: "And I'm from Cherdynsky district! ..."

"You'd better lie down, you from Cherdynsky district," Karyshev growled in a fatherly way, and pointed to the straw.

"You don't believe me? " Shkalik opened his eyes wide, wretchedly, like a child. He still was a mere boy. He had added two years to his age so that he could get into a trade school and receive free food. But they had taken him into the army—and so it had turned out that Shkalik was at the front, in the infantry. "There is such a place in the Urals," Shkalik continued to insist, ready to flare up or to burst into tears. "Do you know what kind of houses they have there?"

"Big ones," Pafnutiev sniggered.

"All different, not big," Shkalik corrected him, "and the window-bands and the gateway are all ... c-c-c-carved and decorated ... and a merchant used to live there, he sold grouse ... and ... made mi ... millions...."

"He's not your uncle, by any chance? " Pafnutiev continued to question him, and Lusya felt that he was being nasty. Shkalik didn't notice it, and was running on blissfully.

"No-o, my uncle looks after the horses."

"And your aunt, too, I suppose? "

"My aunt? My aunt looks after the horses, too. You think it's funny, eh?" Shkalik ran his eyes, filled with pain, round the table, frequently blinking his straight white eyelashes, like those of a sucking pig. "The writer Reshetnikov lived in our parts!" he shouted resoundingly, and banged his fist on the table: "Have you read *Under the Limes*? It's about us...."

"We've read it, we've read it..." Lantsov tried to soothe him. "About Pila and Sysoika, about Ulka, the girl they buried alive.... We've all read it. Let's go to sleep now. Time for bye-byes," he took hold of Shkalik, and pulled him onto the straw in a corner. Pafnutiev called out: "What good is a milksop like you?"

"See that!" said Shkalik. "And they don't believe me! Our place is famous for its horses, too! ... The Stroganovs lived there. Counts they were."

"And where might such a small person get such a big memory?" Pafnutiev gestured with his hands.

"Shut up!" Boris called out. "Leave him be."

"I'm being serious...."

Everything within Boris seemed to sag. In his clouded mind objects and soldiers' faces were all mixed together. Everything around seemed to fade, was covered by a shimmering veil. A heavy drowsiness pressed on his eyelids, weakened his muscles, and it was even difficult to move his hands. I'm worn out! Boris thought sluggishly. I mustn't drink again.... He began to eat cabbage with potato, he drank some cold water, and felt more sure of himself.

Mokhnakov was smoking unhurriedly, blowing smoke up to the ceiling and all the time smiling a sardonic smile.

"Excuse me," Boris said to their hostess, as if he had just woken up, and offered her the tin of American spam. All the time he kept catching the elusive glance of those unbelievably beautiful eyes upon him. It was as though she were looking out from a screen a long way off. A shadow would pass over her face and then it would clear again. "I keep him with me as an orderly, although I'm not entitled to one," Boris explained, referring to Shkalik, for want of something to say and not just sit, staring at the hostess. "He's a nuisance really, can't sew or cook ... and he loses everything.... He was wasting away in a reserve regiment, suffering from night-blindness."

"But he's one of those tender-hearted, kindly boys," Mokhnakov unexpectedly said, looking at the ceiling and addressing no one in particular. His look and his face were heavy, there was a rasp in his voice. For some reason he was getting at Boris. The soldiers pricked up their ears—that had never happened before. The sergeant-major had protected and taken care of the lieutenant like a father. So something must have happened between them. Well, they'd sort it out later. But after the night battle, here, in this cottage with such a young and pleasant hostess, they all felt they wanted to be good and kind. Lantsov, Karyshev, Malyshev and even Pafnutiev looked reproachfully at their commanders.

Boris did not react to the attack of the sergeant-major and did not touch the mug of home-brew again, although the soldiers pressed him to drink, knowing that a glass of liquor was always a good way of bringing people together. Even Lantsov let himself go and pestered Boris drunkenly to have a drop.

Lantsov was born in Moscow. In childhood he had sung in the church choir, but later on he had joined the atheistically minded proletariat, and had got a job at a big publishing house where, sparing neither time nor his head, he had read indiscriminately a vast amount of literature of all kinds, which had inclined him towards wordy reflection.

"Ah, Lusya, Lusya! " clutching his head theatrically, the lanky Lantsov swayed, then came to a stop, his eyes closed. "What have we seen! One such night will last a lifetime...."

Just like on the stage! Boris thought, frowning. Anyone would think he was the only one who lived through it.

Overcoming his irritation, Boris laid his hand on Lantsov's shoulder and said: "Come on now, for goodness sake! Let's talk about something else. Maybe we'll sing? "

Willingly responding, Pafnutiev struck up loudly:

> *The be-e-ell rang loud fo-o-o-or a ro-o-ll call,*
> *Lantsov's missing, he'd r-u-u-n away....*

But Lantsov put a scraggy hand over his mouth. "You can go on about Lantsov later. I want to say something. I've kept silent for a long time. I've kept thinking, thinking and saying nothing." Boris smiled faintly at the soldiers—let him have his fun. "I was thinking today. Yesterday I was thinking. At night, lying in the snow, I was thinking, too: surely such bloodshed must teach people something. This war must be the last one! The ve-ery last! Otherwise people aren't fit to be called people! Not fit to walk this earth! Not fit to enjoy its blessing, to eat its bread, potatoes, meat, and fish, not fit to live...."

"Stop, soldier! " Mokhnakov banged on the table and caught a spoon as it flew into the air. "What you say is right, but the guard's walking past the window...." Mokhnakov looked meaningfully at Pafnutiev, and thrust the spoon into his boot. "Off you go, cool down and don't forget to do your business while you're out there, you'll be clearer up here," he said tapping himself on the forehead.

Lusya started, looked from Lantsov to Mokhnakov and it was obvious that she felt sorry for the soldier who had for some reason been picked at by the sergeant-major and the lieutenant.

"Pardon me! " Lantsov bowed in her direction, conscious of a sensitive soul. "Pardon me! " He bowed ceremoniously to those at the table and, clutching at the wall, walked out of the cottage.

"What a performer! He ought to be in comedy, and here he is, in the infantry! " Pafnutiev sneered.

A man with a large head, a narrow chest and long thin legs, the former fireman looked like a walking toadstool. Pafnutiev was a combative, cunning and agile soldier. All the same, the platoon would have been better off without him.

Shkalik was sitting on the straw, rocking himself, frowning and stretching out his hand for the tin: "Don't take other people's drinks! " Mokhnakov came down on him and thrust someone else's mug at him. Shkalik sniffed at it but did not drink. He vomited.

"Get out! Disgusting! " Boris, reddening, turned away from Lusya and stared at Mokhnakov. Mokhnakov looked away at the window, yawned with a bored air and began to scratch the ice from the window.

"Never mind, I've seen everything in my time! " Lusya tried to cover the awkward pause. "I'll clean it up. Don't be cross with the boy." She wanted to go for a cloth, but Karyshev stopped her and held out the tin of spam. She began to eat. "Oh! " she said, hastily taking some. "Wouldn't you like some home-cured pork fat? I've got some! "

"Give us pork fat! " Mokhnakov swiftly turned to her and gave her a brazen look from narrowed eyes. "And give us something else," he flung, with a leer at Lusya's back.

He wa-a-aashed in de-e-e-w shook from the gra-a-ass
Turned to-oo-oo the Ea-ea-east and pray-ay-ayed to God....

His head resting on his hand, Pafnutiev drawled out the song about Lantsov who had run away, in a high, thin voice. His eyes would not focus.

Mokhnakov hung over the table, rummaged in his pocket, and fished something out. He produced a metal button, threw it up, caught it and with exaggerated firmness walked out of the cottage, more awkwardly than usual. He walked in an odd, dispirited way, the soldiers noticed, he kept flinging up the button or a coin, and the way he caught it was not playful but a vicious snatch from mid-air. Then he started to play about with a darkish blue German grenade instead of the button. It was like an Easter egg—quite a jolly toy. But the men protested. If the sergeant-major wanted to blow off a bit of himself, let him go and juggle somewhere in the distance. The others, after all, wanted to get to their homes whole.

Lantsov came back into the cottage and signalled to Boris.

The lieutenant jumped up, and rushed out, kicking open the door.

In the darkness of the entrance he ran into Shkalik, who was fumbling for the door handle. Boris thrust him into the cottage and stood listening. He heard a noise and Lusya's agitated voice in a dark corner: "Oh don't! Please don't! You shouldn't, really you shouldn't! Comrade Sergeant-Major! "

"Mokhnakov! "

There was a hush. Mokhnakov emerged from the gloom, coming towards him, breathing heavily and foully.

"Come outside! " Mokhnakov hesitated, then reluctantly walked ahead of Boris, remembering to duck beneath the low lintel. They stood facing each other. Mokhnakov was breathing stertorously, drinking down the ice-cold air. Boris waited until the door banged to and Lusya went into the cottage.

"What can I do for you? " Mokhnakov drew nearer. His breathing was now even, the air no longer rasped in his nostrils.

"Look here, Mokhnakov: If you ... I'll kill you! Shoot you. Got it? "

Mokhnakov took a step backwards, ran his eye over the lieutenant from head to foot, and indolently, reproachfully said: "You've got concussion from when the grenade went off, that's why you're going up the wall."

"You know what's done it."

Mokhnakov pulled his sheepskin coat round him and flashed his torch at Boris. Boris did not flinch or look away. His chapped lips were twitching convulsively. Beneath his eyes were dark rings, from dirt and sleeplessness. His eyes were bloodshot, his neck was held stiffly—the collar of his greatcoat rubbed, probably an old wound had become inflamed. There he stood, staring like a righteous schoolboy.

"Don't I just! Thanks very much! " Mokhnakov understood that this gawking Boris, the next-door kid, who was putty in his hands and allowed him to run the platoon, would kill him! No one would dare to lay a hand on the sergeant-major, yet this boy....

"That's all I need, a sharpshooter like you! " Mokhnakov laughed nervously and threw up the torch. The bright stain of light shot up, fell into his hand and went out. Mokhnakov banged the torch against his knee and when it lit up, once again directed it right into Boris' face, as if he wanted to singe the lieutenant's scarcely noticeable beard. "You just wait, me lad," Mokhnakov's eyes warned from the darkness. "I'll spend the night in another cottage," he said and went off, the patch of light marking the way. "Go to blazes, all of you! " he shouted, already a long way off.

Boris leant against the door jamb, something was gnawing at him from within, his lips were convulsed in a rigid line, his legs were like jelly, his body felt limp. There was a pressure in his ears, something was swelling, breaking within them. He looked at the two slender, sharp-pointed poplars standing opposite the house. Bare, dark, like motionless birch brooms—and beyond them the young cherry or sloe bushes billowed like smoke after an explosion.

Fragments of stars shone down restlessly, with a frozen light. The lights of vehicles darted back and forth along the streets, there were cheerful blast from accordions and explosions of laughter, a creaking of carts was heard, and somewhere a frightened dog barked hoarsely.

"Oh Mokhnakov, Mokhnakov! " Boris sank down onto the threshold, his hands hanging between his knees, his head sunk on his chest.

The barking grew faint in his ears.

* * *

"You'll be cold, Comrade Lieutenant," he heard Lusya's voice. In the darkness she touched Boris and gently ran her hand over the back of his head. "Why don't you come inside." Boris shivered and opened his eyes. The field, ulcerated with shell holes, the old man and the old woman lying by the potato pit; the giant in flames; the groans of tanks and people; the whine of shell fragments; fiery explosions, shouts, all these crumbled before his eyes, vanished, and his heart, which seemed to be in his very throat, contracted, stood still for a bit, then returned to its place.

"My name is Boris," he said, coming to himself again, heaving a sigh of relief, "Why should you call me Comrade Lieutenant? "

He moved away from the door, not comprehending why everything was in turmoil within him; his mind was unclear and full of fragmentary visions, strung together on a thread down which they slipped one by one, to disappear beyond some sharp but imperceptible edge.

It was still difficult for him to take in the night, filled with crackling frost and the noisy rejoicing of people who had come through a battle, and this woman with the theatrically unreal eyes, huddled up against the door jamb.

"How quiet it is! Everything's stopped. You just can't believe it. Shall I bring your greatcoat? "

"No, what for? " Boris did not reply immediately. He was trying not to meet her gaze. "Let's go inside, otherwise they'll be gossiping about us...."

"Well, most of them have collapsed. After all, you've been sitting here for a long time. I was beginning to get worried.... Lantsov keeps talking to himself all the time. He's an interesting man...." She wanted to ask him something, but could not bring herself to, and stood there shifting from one foot to the other. "What about the sergeant-major? Is he coming back? "

"No! " Overcoming his embarrassment, Boris replied briefly, and Lusya's spirits rose. She hurried into the cottage.

She did not open the door immediately, and Boris' outstretched hands touched her back—beneath the thin print housecoat he felt her smooth, unexpectedly strong shoulders and below the fastening of her brassiere.

Lusya started, and hurried into the cottage. Boris followed her. Averting his eyes, he warmed his hands at the stove and began to take off his boots.

It was warm and stuffy inside. The fire was crackling merrily—the soldiers had found some good pine logs. A boiler on the stove was singing like a samovar. Boris looked for a place to dry his footcloths, but the soldiers' clothes hung everywhere, filling the air with a pungent, stale, sweaty odour. Lusya took the footcloths from him and arranged them on some logs by the fire.

Lantsov was sitting at the table swaying, his head nodding.

"Why don't you go to bed? " Boris pressed against the stove, and felt the warmth going deep within him, relaxing his whole body. "Everyone's asleep already, and it's time you were, too."

"It's barbarous! " Lantsov philosophised, not listening to Boris. "Deaf Beethoven created for radiant spirits. But the

Führer's made his empty-headed murderers march to Beethoven's music! Poverty-stricken Rembrandt painted immortal pictures with his blood! Goering stole them. When things get difficult he'll throw them in the fire.... What's the reason for it all? The more brilliant a work of art is, the more all sorts of things are drawn to it. Like they are to a woman! The more beautiful a woman is, the more the ravishers want to paw her...."

"Perhaps that's enough, eh? " Boris cut him short. "Our hostess needs to have a rest. We've disturbed her enough as it is."

"Don't think of it, it's quite all right! You can't begin to imagine how wonderful it is to see and hear your own people! And after all Lantsov's talking like a human being. Here, we've become unaccustomed to hearing really human words."

Lantsov raised his head and with an effort focussed his attention on Lusya.

"Forgive an old man," he said, running a skinny hand over his stubby face. "Overdone the drink, made a pig of myself! And Boris, you forgive me, too. I beg you! " He slumped, his head coming to rest on the table, and he gave a drunken sob. Boris grabbed him under the armpits, and laid him on the straw. Lusya rushed to get a cushion from the front room, and thrust it under Lantsov's head. Feeling something soft beneath his cheek he snivelled. "A pillow! Nice children! " With a farewell whistle through his nose, he sailed far away from these shores, breathing evenly, softly smacking his lips.

"That's my last grenadier down! " Boris forced himself to smile.

Lusya was clearing the table. Picking up the canister containing the home-brew, she looked inquiringly at the lieutenant.

"No, no! " he said hastily, waving it away. "The smell's enough to kill the cockroaches."

Lusya set the canister down on the window-sill, gathered up the crumbs from the table, and shook the rag into the trough. Boris tried to find himself a place among these soldiers lying any old how, overpowered by sleep. Shkalik, the small fry, had been pushed to the top of the mass by those big fish from the Altai and he lay across some of the others, gasping, his mouth wide open, like a fish out of water. Lantsov was drooling, cuddling the cushion. Malyshev was snoring and the straw quivered near his mouth as if in a hurricane. The ribbons of five medals rose and fell on Karyshev's mighty chest. The medals themselves were in his pocket. He claimed the lugs were weak, and might come unfastened.

Boris tossed his damp overcoat down by the soldiers' legs, yanked out from beneath them a little crushed straw and began to arrange a padded jacket for his head. Lusya stood watching him, then apparently coming to a decision, she picked up the lieutenant's greatcoat and padded jacket, and threw them onto the stove. Climbing up onto the ledge, she spread them out so they would dry faster, and when she had finished she jumped lightly down.

"Why did you do it, I could have managed it myself...."

"Come here! " Lusya called him. Trying to tread quietly, Boris fearfully and obediently followed her.

The light was on in the front room. Boris blinked, it seemed so bright to him. The room was furnished simply and neatly. There was a wide bench with a back, and on it a runner embroidered with Ukrainian designs. The floor was earthen, but it was smooth, without cracks, surfaced with clay. In the middle of the room, in a wooden box, was a plant with spreading foliage and two bright buds. On the window-sills there were also flowers, in boxes and old pots. There was a homely feel about the air. There was neatness all around, and after the crowded kitchen with its stuffy atmosphere it seemed unlived in, somehow had a hothouse smell.

Boris stepped onto the cold floor, ashamed of his dirty feet, and with exaggerated interest gazed at the light bulb, which was not Russian in form, but flattened towards the bottom.

Lusya, seeming equally lost in this spacious, well aired room, said that their village had been lucky. There beyond the river the hamlet had been hit but here nothing was touched, although the German HO had been here for a whole month. Apparently the Soviet fliers had not known this. The

Germans had stationed a mobile generator here. An important general had been billeted in the cottage, and it was because of him that there was electricity. But he had practically never managed to spend the night in the cottage, sleeping at headquarters. The Germans had retreated in haste across the river, forgetting about the generator, and so there it was, still going full blast.

Explaining all this haltingly, she pulled apart some linen curtains decorated with appliqué work. Beyond a narrow plywood door, there was another little room. It had an uneven wooden floor spread with a brightly coloured rug; there were the bookshelves, with books and the broken comb, a thimble, scissors, a thick needle, stuck in an embroidered napkin. By the wall opposite the window was a clean, neat bed with one pillow. The other pillow, as Boris guessed, was the one she had taken for Lantsov.

"You can sleep here," Lusya said, pointing to the bed.

"No! " he said, startled. "I'm so..." he added, running his fingers over his tunic and feeling beneath it his long-unwashed body, encrusted with dirt.

"But then you'll have nowhere to sleep."

"Perhaps I'll sleep there," Boris hesitated, indicating the door. "Well, on the bench. And then..." he turned away, reddening. "It's winter. And you know it's worse then. In the summer there are less of them, for some reason...."

He infected Lusya with his embarrassment, and she did not know how to arrange things. She looked at her hands. Boris had noticed how often she looked at her hands, as if she were trying to understand what she had them for and where to put them. The awkward moment dragged on. Lusya bit her lips and walked resolutely into the front room. She returned with the print housecoat and held it out to him: "Now take everything off! " she ordered. "I'll get the trough ready for you and you can have a bath. Don't be afraid of me! I've seen everything." She spoke boldly, with a confident air, even winking at him, as if to say: Don't be shy, soldier-boy! But then she herself was overcome with embarrassment and slipped out of the room.

He unfolded the housecoat and saw that its buttons were

of all sorts and sizes. One was even from a soldier's uniform, and there was a half-belt at the back. The housecoat looked funny on Boris, he started muttering something gaily, then pulled himself up, threw off the garment, and pushed open the door to fling this feminine object through.

"I shan't let you out! " Lusya pressed against the plywood door. "If you want your things to dry by morning, get them off at once! "

Boris was taken aback: "Here's a pretty kettle of fish! " He scratched the back of his head. Well, what am I, after all? I'm an Armyman, aren't I? Acting with decision, he took everything off, put on the housecoat, buttoning it up and, after making a bundle of his things went in to where Lusya was, and swaggered in front of her, so that the housecoat came apart at the bottom to reveal his knobbly knees.

Lusya smothered her mirth. Sneaking a glance at the lieutenant, she took his documents and some papers from his tunic pockets, removed his Order of the Red Star and his guards badge and unpinned his Military Service medal. She carefully unpicked the red insignia which meant that he had been seriousy wounded.

Boris felt the leaves of the plant, sniffed at the red buds and was surprised that they had no smell. Then it dawned on him that they were made from shavings! The crimson flower made him think of a raw wound, and once again there was that painful feeling deep within him.

"What's that for? " Lusya pointed to his wound stripe.

"For a wound," Boris answered, and for some reason hastened to add: "A light one."

"Where?"

"Here," he poked a finger at his neck. "Bullet just glanced off. It was nothing."

Lusya scrutinised the spot he was pointing to—just above the collar bone was a mauvish, bean-shaped scar. There was earth in the lieutenant's ears and his inflamed eyes were rimmed with black dirt. The prickly collar of his damp greatcoat had chafed his neck and he looked just as if he were wearing a tie. She had a physical sense of his smarting neck, of his bodily weariness—from the sweat, the dirt and a uniform that was permanently damp and saturated with the smell of gunpowder.

"We'll leave it all on the table," she said and moved off. "Just bear with it a little longer, and you can have a bath.... Why not take a book?" Lusya added, opening the door.

"A book? What book? Oh, a book!"

Boris stooped before the bookshelves in the little room. The housecoat stretched dangerously taut on his back. He got up quickly, flung the garment open, looked at himself stealthily and was not pleased with what he saw: he was rawboned, with goose pimples, either from cold or embarrassment, and sparse colourless hair on his legs and chest.

Most of the books were about trade. "There, you wouldn't dream that she had anything to do with trade...."

Among the textbooks and manuals on trade he found a well-worn book in a home-made cover.

"Olden Times," Boris read aloud. He read and somehow could not believe that he was standing here in a little white room with one bed, wearing a girl's housecoat with a belt. From both housecoat and bed came a titillating smell. Or perhaps there was no smell at all, perhaps he was imagining things. He hardly felt the weight of the housecoat on his body after the many layers of winter clothing which seemed to have grown into his skin, and every now and again he wriggled his shoulders.

Everything was still ringing in his head, pressing in his ears, giving him an unpleasant feeling of nausea. If I could just sleep for two or three hundred minutes, or better still four hundred! He looked at the tempting cleanliness of the bed, yawned and ran his eyes over a page of the book: "I once chanced to visit the large village of Zaborye. It stands on the Volga. It's a wonderful free, rolling countryside here...." Boris stared amazed to find this classic here, and then with enjoyment repeated the beginning of this old story, cruel in a typically Russian way and sentimental in a typically Russian way, too.

The music of the words, even the rustle of the paper pleased him so much that for a third time he repeated the opening phrase, just to hear himself, and to make sure that everything really was as it was: that he was alive, that he felt cold, that his skin was covered with goose pimples, and he held in his hands a book which he could read, and listen to himself doing it. As if he were afraid someone would interrupt him, Boris hastily read the words, not understanding them but simply listening.

"Who have you got here? "

The lieutenant looked at Lusya as if from a long way off.

"Look, I've found Melnikov-Pechersky," he answered her at last. "It's such a good book."

"I like it, too," Lusya said, wiping her hands on a linen cloth. "Go and have a wash." With her kerchief on, she again looked older, more severe, and once again her eyes mysteriously receded into the distance.

Behind the big stove, as in most Ukrainian cottages, there was a sleeping ledge. On it Lusya had placed the wooden trough, and had left by it a tin of home-made liquid soap, a sponge, a bucket of hot water and a jug.

"Baptise thyself, slave of God! " Boris said, having waited for Lusya to shut the door to the entry and, almost overturning the trough, settled down in it with some difficulty.

He washed himself with his legs bent beneath him, and he felt the dirt slipping from him, like a thick, rough skin. From beneath that rough, salty skin, there appeared a young body, tensed with fatigue, and it gradually grew so light that he could even feel his bones. His heart began to come alive, and a delightful languor stole over his body. The trough began to rock like a boat on the waves, and bore the drowsy lieutenant far away.

He tried not to splash the floor, not to slop water onto the wall and the stove. All the same, he did slop water on the wall and on the stove, and he splashed the floor.

The space behind the stove became quite stifling, with its clayey, earthy smell, which tickled the nose. Boris remembered how he had enjoyed himself when they had reconstructed the stove at home. He saw it all, down to the last detail. Everything at home was upside down, in thorough confusion—and a few days' absolute liberty set in: he could run around as much as he liked, spend the night at the neighbours, and enjoy cold snacks whenever he fancied. Returning from lessons, his mother would wrinkle her nose fastidiously, and pick her way across the damp clay and crushed brick. Her whole appearance expressed impatience and discouragement, and she would vanish into the best room as fast as she could, giving his father a killing look on the way.

His father, also weary from school, tied a sack round himself with a somewhat guilty air and got down to work. The stove-builder approved of him, saying that here was a member of the intelligentsia who did not mind soiling his hands with manual labour. Father would look now and again at the door of the best room and suggest, appeasingly: "Perhaps you'd like to eat in the canteen, my dear?"

The only answer would be a haughty silence.

Boris would carry bricks, and puddle clay, getting in the way of the men; dirty and wet, he would shout excitedly: "Mum! See! The stove's coming on nicely!"

And it really was: from the mass of bricks, from the clay a structure was coming into being—with a gaping maw and two eyes—extra little hearths, and a pattern along the chimney breast.

At last they heated the stove and the workers waited anxiously to see how it would turn out. To begin with, it hissed and belched smoke through its great maw, and then the fire took hold. Still dark and unfamiliar in appearance, it livened up, began to splutter and crackle and to shoot off sparks, gradually drying out piebald like a horse, and becoming something essential and accustomed.

At the kitchen table father and the stove-builder were drinking their way through half a litre of vodka—"Here's to the stove burning up fast and merrily!"

"Now then, housewife! Take over your stove!" the stove-builder demanded.

The housewife did not respond. The stove-builder put the crumpled notes my father gave him into his pocket with an injured air, shook my father by the hand and both sympathising with him and encouraging him at the same time, nodded towards the tightly closed door as if to say: I wouldn't live a day with a biddy like that!

That had all been in some distant life which suddenly came back to him. Boris wiped the floor behind the stove and did not hurry away, wanting to prolong the surge of memory— that fragment from the past in which everything was now seen to have had particular purpose and significance.

After wringing out the cloth under the washstand, he rinsed his hands and went into the room.

Lusya was sitting on the bench, unpicking the under-collar, which seemed to have been welded to the tunic with stains of grey mould.

"The servant of the Lord hath risen! " Boris announced with bravado, faintly hoping that there was no livestock of any kind on the under-collar.

Putting down the tunic, Lusya looked at him closely and affectionately, in a maternal way, now quite openly. The lieutenant's fair hair, naturally wavy, was now a mass of tiny curls. His eyes also looked as if they had been well washed. The chafed scar on his thin neck stood out redder. The whole of this youth, without a single blemish on his face, with an innocent look, dressed in a print housecoat, was so embarrassed that no one would have imagined him a commander in the trenches.

"Oh, Comrade Lieutenant! More than one girl'll lose her head over you! "

"What nonsense! " parried the lieutenant, and immediately asked: "Why? "

"Just because," Lusya declared, getting up. "The girls know your kind of boy and love them, and then they get married to louts. Well, I'm off to bed! Pleasant dreams! " In passing, she stroked his cheek, and in her caress and her words there was a kind of maternal sense of superiority. He still could not make her out. Not even when she laughed—her eyes retained that unmoving sadness, continued to live their separate life in her face, the stern, intent, and all-understanding life of a wise elder.

But surely she's younger than me, or at most the same age? Boris thought, slipping into bed, and was unable to carry his reflections any further. His eyelids were overcome with heaviness, he was engulfed in heavy slumber.

* * *

The orderly of Battalion Commander Filkin, a presumptuous lad who fitted himself out well in the commander's store—with sheepskin coat, good felt boots and a white fur cap—took a wicked delight in waking Boris and the other commander long before dawn.

"Oh dear! And I haven't managed to wash your things. I was scared to go down to the river at night to get water. I thought I'd go in the morning," Lusya said guiltily. Leaning against the stove, she waited while Boris dressed in the other room. "You come again," she added, with the same guilty air, when he appeared in the kitchen, "and I'll wash them then...."

"Thanks. If we can make it," Boris replied sleepily and coughed, thinking to himself that it was the sergeant-major she was frightened of. Looking with envy at the soundly sleeping soldiers, he nodded to Lusya and left the house.

"You've been napping, been napping, you young upstarts! " This was how the battalion commander greeted his officers. When he was feeling out of sorts he always used this insulting form of address. Some of them were annoyed, and would get into arguments with him about it. But that morning no one felt like talking back. They were huddled up resentfully in the hard frost, hiding their faces in the upturned collars of their greatcoats.

"Oh, you young upstarts! " Battalion Commander Filkin sighed, and led them from this cosy little Ukrainian place to the ruined hamlet to meet the dawn, which lit up the far edge of the sky with a steely gleam and showed dully against the snow-carpeted fields.

The battalion commander was no longer smoking good cigarettes but home-made ones of crude shag. He had probably been up all night, and the fearsome tobacco had helped him stay awake. Generally speaking, he wasn't a bad sort at all. He'd flare up like birch bark and crackle a bit, he liked to send the soot flying. But he cooled down quickly. It was hardly his fault if the Germans wouldn't surrender. They'd dug themselves in along the ravines and in the fields, and were holding on. But holding on to what? And why? If they surrendered they would not be shivering with cold.... And the battalion commander would be able to sleep, and he'd let his young upstarts sleep, too, and Lusya would be able to wash his things. How strange she was, somehow....

"Dozing, Boris?"

Boris started. Would you believe it—he had learnt to sleep on his feet.... What was it Chekhov had said? If you thrashed a hare long enough you could even teach it to strike matches....

It was quite light now. It seemed colder, too. Everything inside him seemed to be on the verge of disintegrating, he was shivering so violently.

"You see that field beyond the ravines and the big village?" Filkin asked, and thrust the binoculars at Boris with the words: "It's time you got your own.... That's the last fascist stronghold, Comrade Commander," he continued, pointing to the village across the field. Holding up the cold-rimmed binoculars some distance from his face, Boris waited for what was coming next. "When the rocket signal goes up we attack from two sides."

"Us again?" the platoon commanders expostulated weakly.

"And us!" Battalion Commander Filkin flared up again. "What do you think? That they sent us here to pick mushrooms? In an hour I want you all ready in position. And no whimpering!" He looked sharply at Boris. "We've got to bash the nazis so their teeth fall out.... So they never want to fight again...."

After adding a few expressive words to heighten the effect, Filkin snatched the binoculars from Boris and hurried off somewhere, wallowing in snow to the knees.

The platoon commanders went back to the now awakened little village and drove the soldiers out of the warm into the bare field, energetically, as the battalion commander had instructed them.

The soldiers grumbled at first, but they took up their positions in the snow and were silent, even attempting to doze, mentally cursing the Germans. What were the damned nazis waiting for? What were they sniffing around for? Were they praying to their lousy gods for salvation? But what god could help now, when they were surrounded, and by such a powerful force that even a mouse couldn't escape....

A red flare shot up across a ravine, then a whole series of green ones. Tanks and lorries revved up all over the hamlet. The column on the road stirred and began to dissolve. First tanks and self-propelled guns started off slowly in various directions, crushing the remains of wattle fences, driving through sparse orchards on the sides of the ravines, then, as if finally managing to shake off their fetters, they charged forward, trailing black smoke, dipping into shell holes, plunging through snowdrifts.

The artillery struck. The Katyushas began to spew out their rockets. Pulling out his much-used pistol, Battalion Commander Filkin dashed towards the ravines. The soldiers rose from the snow and followed him. Before the tanks and guns reached the ravines they stopped and opened fire. From the direction of the hamlet came whining mortar shells, and the battalion commander halted the infantry and ordered them to lie down. The situation was still not clear. Many firing points had not moved to their new positions and communication wires were buried under the snow. In such a situation mortar men and gunners could easily hit their own side, and then beat their breasts and treat infantrymen to vodka in the hope that no official complaint would be made.

True enough, the infantry almost copped it. The same 150 mm howitzers that during the night battle had boomed in the infantry's rear now began to pummel the ravines and a couple of times cut it a bit too fine. The soldiers crawled towards the vegetable plots and the broken wattle fences, and got to work with their spades to dig themselves in. With a frozen screech of caterpillar tracks, the tanks drove along the ravines towards the field in pincer movement. There was scattered firing from rifles and machine guns.

The wind dropped, and with it the snowstorm. In one side of the sky hung the dim moon, which also seemed to have been pitted with shell splinters, and on the other, the cold, gloomy sun was struggling through the mist.

Why is it that during the worst hours for men Nature must always have...—Boris had no time to finish his thought—the battalion commander thrust the binoculars into his hand without a word. But the lieutenant could now see everything, even without the binoculars.

From the big village beyond the ravines and the field, a great crowd of people appeared on a flat eminence itself slashed by ravines and dotted here and there with trees—so big a crowd that you could not see the snow. Wave after wave of men came up from out of the ravines, running towards the crowd, which continued to pour from the village like a tidal wave. The white space between them grew narrower and narrower. The earth seemed to be swarming with locusts. Crushing the locusts, tanks drove at them from two sides. Suddenly, raising clouds of snow, there appeared an irresistible whirlwind, with a flash of toylike sabres.

"Cavalry! " gasped Boris, and his heart gave a leap and beat madly, as it had in his childhood when he watched a cavalry attack in a film. He had never seen a real cavalry attack. After all, what cavalry there was in this war did their actual fighting as infantry. So now the Germans are really in for it, he thought.

Everything was milling, whirling, circling on the field. A fine dust of snow hung in the air. Clouds of smoke rose from the tanks. The neighing of horses, the roaring of tanks, the screaming of men could he heard in the hamlet. At first the infantrymen were shouting, swearing, trying to get to the ravines, but after a time they quietened down.

It was quiet, too, in the field across the ravines. The tanks had burst into the village. Two of them lay burning like bonfires in the field, sending up a great column of smoke to the sky, to the sun, which was growing brighter and brighter. The cavalry was rounding up the fleeing enemy. Shooting continued, now frantic and disorderly as at a retreating quarry.

"That's that! " said Battalion Commander Filkin, in a whisper for some reason. As soon as he had said it, he himself was surprised at his own whisper, and he barked: "That's all, comrades. The German grouping's kaputt! "

Pafnutiev obligingly emptied his submachine gun into the air, jumped about and in a croaking falsetto shouted: "Hurrah! " The soldiers did not support him.

"What's the matter with you? Shagged yourselves out? It's a victory! The nazis are done for! "

The soldiers looked grimly at the field beyond the ravines, now mauled, stained and black. Those near the hamlet were for the most part rank-and-file infantrymen, and each one was now saying to himself: God forbid I should ever get into anything like that!

Battalion Commander Filkin began pressing German cigarettes on everyone, he cracked jokes to cheer them up, and promised to send them a field kitchen with plenty of porridge and vodka rations for the nominal strength of the battalion. He would have promised much more, but he was called to the telephone.

He came back from the bath-house in a different mood. Nibbling at a baked potato, he turned to let Boris take another from his pocket, then nodded and grinned: "This is instead of the forage I promised. Leave your sergeant-major in command, and come with me to receive orders. It looks as if there's no peace for us, and won't be for quite a time." He wiped his hand on his sheepskin coat and produced his tobacco pouch. "Take Lantsov or Shkalik with you. That bloody orderly of mine's vanished again. He'll go too far one of these days! I'll second him to you, and he can cart around an anti-tank gun and do a bit of digging."

Boris took both Lantsov and Shkalik. He wanted to bypass the field and was on the point of setting off for the edge of the hamlet when they saw Battalion Commander Filkin, who had decided on the direct route, sink waist-deep in snow. When he reached the other side he said: "You can't bypass war at the front," swearing half-heartedly as he shook the snow out of his pockets.

In the field—in the foxholes, shell holes and especially around the mutilated trees—lay heaps of Germans, killed by shots, sabre thrusts or tanks, and some of them still alive, their breath rising in little clouds of steam. They clung to the passing men's feet, crawled after them over the battered, bloodstained field.

Pushing off pity and horror, Boris kept shutting his eyes: "Why did you come here? ... Why? This is our land! This is our country, where's yours? "

Like a man with a back wound, Lantsov had to support himself on his rifle. "Could it ever happen again? Won't they learn from it? If not, they deserve what they've got...."

"Shut up, you stinking philosopher," Filkin muttered through clenched teeth.

Boris fed handfuls of snow to Shkalik, who had turned green.

"Call yourself a soldier! " Filkin sneered, looking at Shkalik. "Give him a baby's dummy of milk! "

On the outskirts of the village, people were crowding outside the kolkhoz threshing barn, a thatched building pitted with shell splinters, its walls damaged by shell-fire. By the wide-open gates of the barn, slender-legged cavalry horses, harnessed to peasant sleighs, were pawing the ground impatiently. As they drew nearer, the infantrymen realised that this was no ordinary crowd. There were several generals, many other officers, and—they saw suddenly—the Commander of the Front.

Boris' stomach went cold and a shiver ran down his sweaty spine. He had never seen the Front Commander before, and here he was, at close quarters. Boris hurriedly adjusted his belt and tried to untie the tape of his fur cap. His fingers would not obey him, he wrenched at the tape and tore it off, together with a piece of the fur. Before he had time to adjust his cap, a major in a yellow sheepskin coat with a shoulder belt across his chest, asked them who they were.

Battalion Commander Filkin reported.

"Follow me," the major ordered.

The Front Commander and his entourage stood aside to make way for the dishevelled, grim-faced men from the trenches. The Front Commander glanced quickly at them, and looked away. He himself, though he was immaculate in his long greatcoat, tall astrakhan hat and neatly pressed scarf, looked, in contrast to the officers around him, in no better state than the soldiers fresh from the battle-line. Deep folds ran down from his nostrils to the sides of his anguished, stern-set mouth, his face was the colour of wax, and in his old man's eyes—though he was not an old man, not an old man at all—there was infinite weariness. Lively conversation and laughter was heard among his entourage, but the Front Commander was evidently thinking his own joyless thoughts.

All sorts of legends made the rounds of the front about the past and present of the Front Commander, and the soldiers readily believed them, especially one of them. It alleged that one day the Commander had come across a platoon of drunken submachine gunners, and instead of despatching them to a punishment corps, he said, appealing to their reason: "If you stand on tiptoe you can see Berlin from here, and I promise you that when we take it you can drink your fill! While we generals stand sentry guard round you! Because you'll have deserved it. Only bear up now, bear up...."

The infantrymen followed the major into the barn and stood accustoming their eyes to the darkness. On some sheaves of faded maize mixed with broken straw and powdered clay, lay a dead German general, in uniform, with bright medal ribbons and silver-embroidered collar and shoulder tabs. In one corner of the barn, on an upturned winnower covered with a rug stood telephones, a thermos flask and a small transmitter with earphones. A deep armchair with sagging springs was pushed close to the winnower and on it was a crumpled check rug resembling the shawls worn by Russian village women.

By the side of the dead general knelt a puny German in a putty-coloured greatcoat, old-fashioned jackboots, gleaming like anthracite, and a forage cap of the type worn by the Good Soldier Schweik, only with fur ear-flaps added. He was crying as he brushed the dust with the palm of his hand off the general's face and uniform.

There was an interpreter here, too. She was wearing a beautifully fitting sheepskin coat and a fur hat, from beneath which showed her softly waving hair. She was saying something in German to the elderly soldier, but judging by everything, the words failed to reach his mind.

From one blue finger on the general's open hand hung a pistol. Hardly a pistol but a lady's trinket that looked as if it could shoot nothing bigger than a fly. The holster at the general's belt was also toylike, with a coat-of-arms embossed upon it. However, it was with this weapon that the general had shot himself. A small spot like a squashed cranberry was spreading on his chest·beneath the row of ribbons and insignia. The general, who wore glasses, was a thin man. His face was ashen, as if touched by hoarfrost. In his half-open mouth one could glimpse false teeth. The spectacles had remained on his nose even after he collapsed in death. A thread of blood also powdered with dust trickled through his grey, bristly moustache. The long strands of hair which had been combed over his bald pate were hanging down, exposing his practically bare bony skull. Above the stand-up collar of his tunic his neck was covered with a web of fine wrinkles and with blood-vessels darkened by death. The steel hook on his collar had burrowed deep into his neck like a tick.

"The commander of the grouping," the major said. "He didn't want to desert his soldiers while the Reichskommissar and the higher officers made a dash for it. The swine! They broke the ring of encirclement just for a few minutes, and got away in tanks, ramming and crushing their own soldiers, the scoundrels! It's unthinkable! "

"They tried it on us, too. It didn't work! " Filkin boasted, but the moment was inappropriate and he shut up, embarrassed.

The major looked at him with interest and was on the point of asking something when a tank rumbled behind the barn and a lorry hooted.

The major ordered them to remove the general's body. Boris was watching the spruce, clean-shaven officer from beneath his eyebrows. "A fine gentleman. Afraid of straining himself, so he gets us to do the dirty work...."

Battalion Commander Filkin took the pistol from the general's hand and held it out to the major. There was a shifty look in the major's eyes; evidently he wanted the pistol so that he could swagger in front of the girls on HQ staff with his trophy. But he could not do it in front of that thin, bony soldier with the melancholy air who stood there like a graven image, that green-faced boy who was standing trembling in his hunched up overcoat, and the lieutenant with the tape torn off his cap who looked at him with frankly hostile eyes—a hungry, angry, young lieutenant.

"What would I want a thing like this for? " The major waved his hand negligently. "Give it to him—in memory of his benefactor." The major turned up his nose fastidiously as he helped the old man to get up.

Battalion Commander Filkin drew out the cartridge clip with a click and threw it into a corner, behind the winnower, scaring away a flock of sparrows, and lobbed the pistol so that it landed at the feet of the elderly German. The man did not pick it up but shrank back, and the girl-translator persuaded him with a sugary-sentimental remark. The old man gave a peck of a bow, snatched it with dry, clinging fingers like the claws of a bird, and pressed it to his breast as if it were an icon. "*Danke schön,*" he said, then immediately checked himself and caught up with the infantrymen, who were clumsily carrying out the stiffened body of the general, and removed Schweik's cap from his head. His hair was wispy, and the whole of him seemed moth eaten, like some old-fashioned plush knick-knack. Hovering around the infantrymen, this stranger from the dusty centuries of the past, was saying something, trying to help them carry out his master. Down his flabby cheeks tears were running, and his whole being radiated infinite, unfeigned grief.

The sharp-witted, fearless front-line sparrows flew back onto the winnower and dived into it as soon as the people had gone.

By the side of the threshing barn an open Studebaker was waiting, attached like a trailer to a tank. The soldiers wanted to shove the body aboard but the old German, hopping about like a fussy hen and clinging to the sides, clambered into the back. The major gave him a bunk-up and the soldier once again muttered his gratitude, made some fawning remark. Taking the general's head carefully in his hands, he dragged the dead body into the back of the lorry, kicked some empty shell cases out of the way, and putting his hat on the floor, lowered the general's head upon it. The interpreter threw up a smart high-peaked cap, and the soldier fielded it deftly like a goalkeeper, going down on one knee.

"*Danke schön, Fräulein!* " Not forgetting to bow respectfully to her, he placed the cap on the general's head, and immediately the pitiful old corpse was transformed into someone important, of high rank.

The Front Commander already stood by the sleigh, at the head of which knelt an elderly submachine gunner, with the reins wound tightly round his hand.

"Razumovsky! " the Front Commander called, and the major, who had been supervising the despatch of the German general's corpse, rushed to the sleigh.

"Yes, Comrade General! " the major said smartly. The old German raised his head, folded his bird's claws in prayer, rolled his eyes heavenwards, a respectful entreaty for silence.

The Commander sniffed impatiently and ordered imperatively and with annoyance: "Bury the general fallen on the field of battle with all military honours! Coffin, salute and so on. Although we can't manage the so on." The Commander turned and sniffed again. "We don't keep priests at the front. They'll have a burial service for him in Germany. There'll be plenty of burial services! "

Boris liked the fact that the Front Commander, who emanated calm, unshakable strength, set such an example of conduct. But in the Commander's last few words the pent-up hate showed through and Boris realised that any pretence at nobility after what had happened the night before and this morning in the field behind that very village was out of place. Evidently the Commander had long ago been taught by war never to pretend, and now he was just carrying out somebody's orders. None of it was to his liking, and many other cares and urgent matters awaited him, and he was sorry to have been torn away from them. He had no doubt seen enough dead and captured generals, and he was sick to death of them.

Why did that foreign general come here, to the Russian snows? the lieutenant wondered morosely. To this threshing barn, to these sheaves of maize? Why hadn't he accepted the ultimatum for surrender? Some strategist! I suppose his heart had so turned to stone that he'd forgotten how to value human life, and so tens of thousands of soldiers died. Why didn't he shoot himself earlier? Out of duty? Fear? Indifference? What made him tick? If that high-up German couldn't live in a fitting way, then for the sake of the soldiers, his compatriots, for the sake of their children, at least, he could have died earlier and in a different way. After all, the experienced old soldier knew the grouping was doomed, that it was a dubious business hoping for a miracle and divine intervention, that defeated invaders do not even get graves, and that all that is anathema to the people would be swept off the face of the earth. What aims did he serve? What did he die for? And who was he, to decide for other people whether they should live or die?

The interpreter willingly, as if she herself were moved by his words, translated the Front Commander's order about the burial of the nazi general with full honours, and the elderly soldier, standing up in the body of the lorry, began bowing servilely to the Commander, clasping his bird claws to his stomach and repeating one and the same phrase, which seemed to have been hammered for good into his toadying head:

"*Danke! Danke schön, Herr General....*"

The Commander barked out something, spun round sharply, pulled his astrakhan hat down over his ears and, tucking the skirts of his greatcoat peasant fashion behind his knees, settled himself in the sledge. There was something rather bristly and at the same time infinitely sorrowful about his narrow, altogether unmilitary back, and even in the way he wiped his nose on his mitten, some kind of human defencelessness. Without turning round again, he drove off over the field. The sledge was rocked and tossed about on the hillocks, its runners uncovering corpses and the remains of corpses.

The horses bore the Commander's grey figure off along some tank tracks and galloped briskly towards the village, where tractors and tanks were already roaring, setting the road to rights. And when the horses and the sorrowful figure of the Commander had disappeared behind the snowdrifts there was a long and depressed silence.

"What's to be done with the batman—did you ask?" the interpreter broke the silence, her beautiful, slightly made-up eyes open wide.

"Oh, let him stay with his master," Major Razumovsky said, annoyed, and fastened the side of the lorry. "I'm not going to lay out that beauty! " He turned towards the infantrymen. "You're free now. Thank you."

"Not at all," Battalion Commander Filkin answered for them all, and tramped off with his men to look for the regimental commander.

Before long the tank with the lorry in tow caught up with them. The driver, who had evidently had to break his journey somewhere to do this job was jerking the wheel this way and that. A damp cigarette dangling from the corner of his mouth, he was saying something angrily to the major, shaking his head towards the back of the lorry, where the brass cases of artillery shells were rattling and rolling about, and the old German was shielding his deceased master from them. The major made some reply to the driver, then raised a hand encased in a leather glove in farewell to the infantrymen walking over the snow. The interpreter, who was standing in the back of the lorry, did not even look at them, and Filkin spat resoundingly in the lorry's wake:

"Stuck up hussy! " Stepping into the ruts made by a tank, he grimaced squeamishly. "The stink from that general or his batman! Did they fill their pants, or what?"

No one took up the conversation. The fatigue that always sets in after a battle was making everyone terribly sleepy. They had an almost irresistible urge to lie down right there in the snow, to curl up there, to bury their ears in the collars of their greatcoats and switch off from this life, from the frost, from themselves.

* * *

The hamlet was now crowded, packed with German prisoners. Among them Mokhnakov was pushing his way about, animated, his cap tilted onto the back of his head.

"Sergeant-Major! " Boris shouted loudly.

Mokhnakov unwillingly made his way out of the throng of prisoners.

"What are you yelling for? " he hissed. "They're all freezing, like dogs! "

"Enough! "

"Enough, then it's enough." Mokhnakov dragged along behind him and, thinking that Boris was still having trouble with his hearing, started swearing: "Bloody weakling! How did we get him for our commander! "

Boris had one wish: to leave this ruined hamlet, to leave this mutilated field piled with corpses as far as possible behind him and to take with him the remnants of the platoon.

But he was to see still more today.

A soldier climbed out of the ravine in a camouflage cape, his face smeared with clay. It seemed to be made from cast iron—black, bony, with inflamed eyes. He walked quickly down the street, and, without slowing down, turned into the vegetable patch where POWs were sitting round a burnt-out shed, eating something and warming themselves.

"Resting like civilised beings, are you? " the soldier bellowed and began to pull the belt of his submachine gun over his head. He knocked his cap into the snow, the weapon became entangled in the hood of his cape, but he jerked it off, the buckle scratching his ear.

The Germans fell back from the bonfire and watched the soldier as if hypnotised.

"Warming yourselves, you knackers! I'll warm you up! Right now! " The soldier raised the safety catch with trembling fingers. Boris rushed towards him but was too late. Bullets splashed in the snow and one German fell shot by the fire, and lay jerking, and a second crashed into the fire. The prisoners squawked like frightened crows, dashed this way and that, some of them going down on all fours in their panic. The soldier in the cape jumped up and down as if the earth itself was thrusting him up, he was snarling, shouting something wild and primeval, blindly firing rounds from his submachine gun.

"Down! " Boris fell upon one of the prisoners and pushed him into the snow.

The ammunition ran out. The soldier pressed again and again at the trigger, still shouting and jumping. The Germans ran behind the house, got into the shed, fell and floundered in the snow. Boris wrenched the submachine gun from the soldier's hands. The man began to feel for something at his belt. Someone knocked him down, and the soldier, sobbing, tore at the camouflage cape on his chest.

"They burnt Marishka! Burnt my fellow-villagers in the church! And my mother! I'll kill 'em by the thousand ... by the thousand! Where's a grenade! I'll chop them up, gnaw them to pieces! "

Mokhnakov pressed the soldier down by his knee, rubbed his face and ears, and shoved snow into his contorted mouth. The soldier spat, kicking Mokhnakov. "Easy, chum, easy! "

The soldier stopped struggling, sat down and with big inflamed eyes kept looking around him as if he had just had a fit. Then he unclenched his fists, licked his bitten lips, seized his head in his hands and, plunging into the snow, started crying soundlessly. Mokhnakov took the man's cap from someone's hands, put it on its owner's head, clapped the soldier on the back and heaved a long sigh.

In a nearby half-ruined cottage, an army doctor in a blood-stained overall with rolled-up sleeves was bandaging the wounded, not asking or looking to see whether they were Soviet or German.

All the wounded lay together—Soviet, German, groaning, shouting, crying; some were already smoking, waiting to be sent to the rear. A senior sergeant with a bandage slanting across his face and bruises beneath his eyes was licking the edges of a home-made cigarette, lit it and put it into the mouth of an elderly German who lay motionless gazing up at the damaged ceiling.

"How're you going to work now, man? " the senior sergeant muttered indistinctly from beneath his dressing, nodding towards the German's hands, which were wrapped in bandages and footcloths. "You've got everything frostbitten! Who's going to feed you and your family? The Führer! Sure, the Führer'll feed you! "

Cold air rolled in great waves into the cottage, wounded men ran or crawled in. They were shaking, wiping away tears and soot from their frostbitten faces.

The soldier in the camouflage cape was led away, stumbling, his head hung low; he was still crying silently. He was followed by a grim-faced soldier from a rear detachment, rifle atilt; he wore a short, scorched greatcoat and grey puttees.

The medical orderly who was helping the doctor could not cope with everything—undressing the wounded, cutting their clothing, having dressings and instruments ready for the doctor. Lantsov was drawn into the work, and a lightly wounded German, probably from the medical corps, also helpfully and deftly began to tend the wounded.

The pockmarked, one-eyed doctor silently stretched out his hand for an instrument, impatiently flexing and unflexing his fingers if he did not get what he needed immediately, and chided the wounded indiscriminately: "Don't holler! Don't fidget! Sit properly! I'm telling you, sit properly! "

The wounded, as if at the barber's, freezing into immobility, obediently bore the pain, silently biting their lips.

From time to time the doctor stopped work, wiped his hands on a calico footcloth hanging on a poker by the stove, and rolled himself a cigarette from light tobacco.

The stove, which had not been repaired or whitewashed for a long time, was heating up. Burning in it were pieces of fencing and empty ammunition boxes. It was smoky and crowded in the cottage.

The doctor, who was one of those eternal country doctors who served in remote forest hamlets or old provincial Russian towns, receiving small pay, a great many reprimands and even more thanks from the general populace, towered over the people lying at his feet. He smoked, screwed his eyes up from the smoke, looked indifferently out of the window and it seemed that nothing here concerned him at all.

Lantsov was shaking, his teeth chattering; as he came out of the cottage he wiped his hands on the snow and said:

"How ghastly war is! He's standing neck-deep in blood, and doesn't bat an eyelid."

"You don't understand a thing! Stop nattering! " Boris said, almost adding: after all, it's more difficult for the doctor than for you, Lantsov. You shout about your pain from the house-tops, don't give anyone any peace over it. But Boris kept himself in check and said something quite different.

"Where's Mokhnakov? "

"Gone off somewhere," Shkalik replied, lowering his eyes.

"More trouble! " Boris wiped his wet hands on the bottom of his coat and pulled his mittens out of his pocket.

"Go along to where we stayed last night, or someone else'll take it. I'll be there soon...."

In the ravines, which from above looked like fallen, branchy fir trees, everything was ploughed up, chopped to pieces by bombs and shells. Dead horses and people lay half-buried in a mixture of clay and snow. There were weapons, wheels, tins, mugs, photographs, books, pieces of newspaper, leaflets, gas-masks, spectacles, helmets, rags, blankets, pots and kettles, even a Tula samovar lying on its side, icons picturing Russian saints and pillows in darned country-style pillow-cases—all torn, crushed, battered, as if after an earthquake—and the bottom of the ravines looked like fresh clearings, where the trees had been chopped down and taken away, leaving bits of broken timber, and stumps.

Familiar tracks made by felt boots led to a dead German officer. Boris covered the man's face with snow and ran down along the ravine like a drunk, no longer able to stay among these twisted corpses.

In the depths of the ravine lay a dead horse covered with clumps of earth. A dog tore at its entrails, its tail between its legs. Beside it a lame crow was hopping about. The dog rushed at the crow yelping, but the bird flew a little way off and waited.

The eyes of this dog of unknown breed, an animal almost without hair, with a fancy, expensive collar hanging loose round its neck, were dim, savage. It was shivering from cold or greed. Its long, frozen ears, flopping like cabbage leaves, and the expensive collar brought to mind some rare breed of dog from a European nobleman's castle.

"Off with you! Shoo! Off with you!" Boris stamped and unfastened his holster.

The dog jumped away, pressing its tail even deeper between its sunken flanks, and no longer yelped like a pup but growled menacingly, baring its teeth. It was snarling and licking the blood from its scanty whiskers, and its flabby, bare skin, which had once concealed a noble, well-groomed body, trembled. The crow, sitting on the edge of the ravine, was cleaning its beak in the snow.

Boris cautiously walked round the dog and, constantly looking back at it, hastened away into the depths of the ravine. The crow turned and followed him with its eyes and then fluttered down. With a sense of relief Boris took his hand off his pistol.

He came upon Mokhnakov round the next bend in the ravine. He wanted to shout to him, but his convulsed lips only stirred soundlessly. Mokhnakov, bent over something dark in a snowdrift, turned sharply. His face began to pale, and he watched the lieutenant's hand to see whether it would reach for the holster. But Boris did not move, he did not even blink. His bloodless, taut lips continued to move, his throat was racked with spasms.

"What's up?" Mokhnakov walked up to Boris and slapped him on the chest.

"Don't touch me!"

"I won't touch you." Mokhnakov retreated, disguising his embarrassment and fear with a calm, ordinary tone of voice. "Where the hell have you sprung from? You get about, don't you...."

Boris suddenly doubled up and, dragging his legs and almost touching the snow with his hands, he lurched to the side of the ravine, leaning against the frozen, fresh-smelling earth. His throat contracted spasmodically, and sticky saliva welled up in it. He stood almost unconscious, his eyes unseeing, then gradually came to, wiping his lips on his sleeve. He looked up at the sky for some reason, saw light, and walked towards it. But everything was heaving, he saw double, another step and he fell into a shell hole, banging against a frozen clod of earth and the pain brought him to his senses.

Two frozen SS men were sitting in the shell hole, looking straight at him with their frozen cod's eyes.

Mokhnakov dragged Boris out, splashed some liquid into his mouth from the flask and Boris felt the fiery fluid to fill the frozen emptiness within him. Something grated on his breast and rang out in his ears—Mokhnakov was cleaning his greatcoat with a knife.

"No-o.... No-o...."

"Oh, stop it! " Mokhnakov morosely flicked the looted knife shut. "After all, war's not like going to the pictures! You've seen it here? The naked steal from the naked, and you worry about the niceties of it." Sniffing like a dog, Mokhnakov finished, now in a quite ordinary tone: "The Slavs smoke meat! Cook food to eat! Heat the bathhouse.... The living concern themselves with the living.... And you can't get this into your head." He snorted loudly and got out his tobacco pouch. He turned out to have two: one red, made of parachute silk, the other of canvas, with tassels, embroidered in crooked letters. Nice girls, far, far away, sent such pouches to the front with touching inscriptions, like: "Let's have a smoke! ", "In eternal memory and eternal love! ", and "May my love preserve you...."

"...You're getting on for twenty." Boris realised Mokhnakov was talking and strained his ears to listen. "You don't understand the least little thing about women. The Germans have got their whore houses, and they get leave! But we...."

What's he talking about? Boris forced himself to listen. Ah, he's on about women again....

"You can't get it from a decent woman. As for the pros, it's all the same to them—Germans, Russians, as long as you pay. And you don't understand that! "

"You should go to the prostitutes then. Why pester a decent woman? You've become no better than a beast! "

"What makes you think she's decent? They're all...." Mokhnakov bit his tongue—the platoon commander couldn't tolerate anyone saying anything bad about a woman. He'd go pale with indignation, and choke with fury. "My head's not quite clear. I had a drop too much..." Mokhnakov muttered. "All those people, dead, wiped out ... so I think, what does one woman matter.... And would you really have shot me? " Mokhnakov looked askance at Boris, probing.

"Yes!"

Mokhnakov cleared his throat harshly, drew on his home-made cigarette and a veil of smoke obscured his face, as he said with grudging approval,

"You're an honourable lad! I've got respect for you." Mokhnakov pinched his cigarette out with his fingers and wiped his hand on his boot. "I respect you for a quality I haven't got myself.... Otherwise...."

"Listen to me," Boris said heavily. "Don't dare to take liberties in front of me any more! Why do you behave that way? Punching, pawing, cursing! "

"You don't understand. You're too young and sure of yourself," he said dispassionately into the empty ravine, and then, shielding his face with his mittens, he continued in a bitter voice: "And I've seen all sorts of things, spent myself. I've no pity for anyone. I'd willingly be the hangman for the nazi criminals. I'd...."

"What's the matter? Are you all right? " Boris recoiled in horror. "Perhaps ... we should ask the doctor to take a look at you...."

"Little id-i-ot!" wiping his face, Mokhnakov smiled weakly. "Don't poke your nose into what you don't understand."

"Let's get out of here, Mokhnakov! Let's go, eh? "

Mokhnakov shook the snow off himself and stood still for a moment. Suddenly he seemed to sag and with a terrible despair said: "Where's the bullet with my name on it? Why do they take so long making it? "

Then he walked on along a blind branch of the ravine, filled to the brim with blinding-white, powdery snow, making a new path through it. In his whole rough-hewn figure, in his back, firm as a sackful of flour, even in the bear-like set of his shoulders there was something powerful and grim. Strength and ruthlessness emanated from the man, properties of the taiga where he was born and bred, where he had hunted wild beasts.

Boris gazed at Mokhnakov's back, heard him puffing away like a steam engine, and tried not to interrupt his thoughts, even muffling his cough with his mitten. People like the sergeant-major opened their hearts to you only in moments of extremity. It meant that such a moment had come.

Mokhnakov began his war record with the days of the retreat from the border, he had had several spells in hospital, had known cold and hunger, encirclement and breakthroughs, but had never been taken prisoner. He had been lucky, he said and, probably, it was because he stuck to the hallowed rule of the Russian troops—better death than captivity.

He had become part of the war, had grown used to it, and was able to overlook all sorts of small things which are often superfluous in war and harmful to life at the front. Until today he had never told anyone of himself, and he never had said a word of how he would live after the war, of what he would do.

Suddenly Boris bumped against Mokhnakov's hard-frozen greatcoat and, shuddering, opened his eyes.

People were moving along the roads, beneath a clear, cold sun with a frosty halo. All around was quiet, all sounds were muffled in snow so that the ears rang.

Along the road from the hamlet to the little village stretched columns of prisoners. In the ditches dead horses lay, sprinkled with snow. Outside the hamlet, in fields and along the road, were large numbers of crippled tanks, skeletons of lorries. On all sides field kitchens were steaming and fumigation was in progress: on wooden slats in tightly closed petrol drums soldiers' underwear, tunics and trousers were baking. The soldiers, in boots, caps and greatcoats were dancing round the fires. They would do that for half an hour. Then they'd put the things on, and their greatcoats, felt boots and caps would go into the drums....

Somewhere motors were humming peacefully, lorries skidded here and there. Charred straw ricks were black stains on the fields. The vans and tents of the medical companies stood by a thick wood on the side of a low hill, and a film was being shown on a sheet fixed to the trunks of pine trees.

Boris and Mokhnakov stopped for a little, watching a mischievous lad, Antosha Rybkin, singing songs and making fools of the ineffectual enemy who were running round in circles.

The audience sincerely rejoiced at the successes of the screen hero. They themselves were in quite a different kind of war.

Footsteps creaked and creaked in the snow. Columns of prisoners were strung out endlessly along the road which at intervals was marked by posts from which the wire had been cut, the posts themselves were listing sideways or had been sawn off altogether for firewood.

Mokhnakov and Boris were forced by Studebakers to the side of the road. The lorries were packed full of prisoners wrapped in scarves, balaclavas and rags. They were all huddled up, with their hands tucked in their sleeves, all similarly colourless and silent....

"How do you like it! " Mokhnakov grumbled. "The nazis in lorries and us on foot—whether at home, in captivity, even in the other world...."

Dusk was gradually falling. Blue shadows lay over the ravines, giving the white earth a sinewy look. The shadows of the posts lay long across the fields, long and thickened by the trees. Even the ditches were filled with blue. Sappers were going along with probes, and they, too, were blue, and ghostlike. The fields were criss-crossed by tank and lorry tracks, as if fastened with belts. As far as the eye could see the snow was glittering. A radio could be heard from the wood. A quiet twilight spread over lacerated, uncomplaining Old Mother Earth.

Lusya was not at home. The soldiers were settled for the night on the floor, with Pafnutiev on duty. His face was suspiciously red, his cunning little eyes shone excited and bright. He felt like talking and even singing, but Boris ordered him to bed while he himself settled down by the stove, utterly exhausted, everything dank and chill within him. He kept licking his lips, dry and rough like a fir cone. He could neither move nor think, all he wanted to do was to get warm and forget about everything in the world. Somehow he felt pitiful, lonely, and was glad there was nobody to see him like that—Mokhnakov was sleeping elsewhere again, and Lusya must have gone somewhere on some business or other. Who was she? What kind of business could she have to see to—a lone woman who was a stranger in these parts?

He felt himself dozing off, yet growing numb with cold. Then a feeling of oppressive, uneasy calm gripped him, and a thought as yet unformulated—the thought of death—began stirring like a maggot in his head, and instead of scaring him it awoke his curiosity by its very simplicity—just to fall asleep like that in some unknown little hamlet, in a stranger's house and be cut off from everything. Swiftly, imperceptibly and forever.

It would be so good....

What's the matter with me? What idiocy's come over me again! ... thought Boris, coming to; and, clutching at the wall he made his way to the little room, the furthest one. Without opening his eyes, he undressed, flinging his paraphernalia any old how into the darkness, and fell onto the low bed.

* * *

So far no staggering experiences were able to rob his young body of the urge to rest, and restore its strength.

He had a long dream: the earth was flooded with water—smooth, without waves, without even a tiny ripple. Pure, pure water and above it the pure, pure sky. Sky and water were bathed in a sunlight. On the water a railway engine was travelling pulling a string of cars, a whole train, and on the surface of the water the engine left a wake, then vanished in the distance. The sea had no shores, no end, you could not see where sky and sea merged. There was no end to that world, and there was nothing, but nothing in it—everything had been submerged, covered with a thick layer of water.

The engine, it seemed, was about to plunge into the depths any moment with a hiss like a burning log, and the little box-like cars, clicking away, would follow, along with the soldiers and their makeshift stoves, berths and all their belongings. The water would close over them, and the surface would resume its calm. After that the whole sunlit world would become peaceful, and there would only be water, sky, sun—and nothing else! A phantom world—without earth, without woods, without grass. He felt like soaring, flying to some shore, to some kind of life.

But his body seemed to have taken root. All around emanated hopelessness and futility. Tired birds, exhausted with their endless flight, fell one after another onto the cars, beating their wings loudly against the metal roofs. Whirled by the stream of air, the birds were thrown into the doors and they flitted about madly inside. Sergeant-Major Mokhnakov chased them, wringing their necks and throwing the bodies under the berths. Boris tried to stop him. "Got to have some grub, haven't we! " The sergeant-major struggled to free himself. "Here's something off the ration flying into our hands! ...." There were terrified cries from the birds, they fought their way outside, and flapped their wings soundlessly against the water....

His dream went on and on like that, there was a terrible feeling of expectation—at any moment something would happen. Boris put his foot forward over the abyss to jump out of the madly speeding train, and suddenly froze, feeling a fixed gaze upon him.

He stirred, gripped the sides of the bed, and woke up. Lusya was standing beside him.

"Your light was on," she explained hurriedly. "I've washed your tunic and trousers. I ought to wash your underclothes.... I thought you were awake...."

He was still in the grip of his sleep, and he understood nothing. When he went to bed, the light had been off—someone must have switched it on later.

"I thought you—" Lusya started again, and stopped in confusion. She stood for a long time bent over him, gazing at his face. At last she could! Quickly, hurriedly, mixing Russian and Ukrainian words, not allowing herself a single pause, she continued: How good it was that the same lot of the soldiers had come to her house for another night, she had got used to them. A pity she couldn't persuade them to sleep in the front room—they'd settled in the kitchen…. How frosty it was outside. So good that the battles were over … better still if the war were over, too…. His soldiers had managed to get dry firewood, but tonight they weren't talkative, they'd gone to bed right away and only that ex-fireman had stayed up for a drink….

"What a strange dream I had!"

He had not heard what she was saying; he was still under the spell of his dream, was talking to himself or thought she was somebody else.

"Terrible, was it? Nobody has any other kind nowadays…." Lusya hung her head, adding: "I thought you'd never come again."

"Why?"

"I thought you might be killed…. There was such shooting across the river…."

"D'you call that shooting?" he answered, rubbing his eyes with the back of his hand, and the next moment he suddenly saw her quite close. The swell of her breasts began above the low neckline of her housecoat. The vital spring swept downwards, became a stream, and from somewhere beyond the rounded breasts beckoned the mysterious radiance of a female body. He felt its intoxicating warmth. Close to him was her face with its elongated eyes, now confused and avoiding his glance. Boris even seemed to feel her improbably thick, upturned eyelashes brushing his cheek. His heart beat madly, taking a giddy plunge down and down. Trying to still the furious drumming in his breast, the desperate racing of his heart, he swallowed hard.

"What a … quiet … night…." A moment later he was able to say, more evenly: "I dreamt of the train that brought us to the front across the Barabinsk Steppe…. The steppe and the railway—everything was flooded. It was spring. It was frightening…." He felt instinctively that he had to talk and talk, that he mustn't look that way—he knew it was shameful, bad. She must have forgotten herself for a moment, must have relaxed, and there he was sneaking a look, and shaking all over! "What a night…. That silly dream…. What a quiet … night…." His throat went dry, his voice broke, everything within him seemed to break—his breathing, his body, his mind.

"War—" Lusya said breathily, also with an effort. Something had happened inside her too. With a feeble gesture she tried to indicate that war had gone away, had receded.

His eyes could hardly see her, everything was dim, elusive, was being carried off on those rhythmically tapping wheels. The woman swayed over him, a faceless shadow in a burning, all-consuming heat which enclosed him almost bodily, turning to ashes the very air in the room, his mind and his body.... He could not breathe. Everything corporeal within him was consumed, and only that all-powerful feeling remained, and now, entirely at its mercy, he muttered helplessly: "I feel ... so good ... here," and, thinking she might misunderstand him and overwhelmed by the shamefulness of the hint in his words, he indicated with his hand that he felt good to be here, in that house, in that bed.

"I'm glad." The words reached him from a great distance. His own words seemed far away, too, he could hardly hear them.

"I'm glad, too," he said. No longer in command of himself, resisting and by that resistance sapping his strength still more, he stretched out his hand to her—to thank her for her kindness, for the refuge she had given him, and to make sure that this misty shadow swaying in the uncertain nightmarish light was that very same woman with those swelling breasts, that mysterious fascination that sent his blood surging, made his heartbeat sound like a tocsin. A woman! That was what a woman was! Oh, what had she done to him? She had plucked him like a leaf from a tree; she had whirled him up into a mad eddying, and borne him off above the earth. He had no weight, no earth beneath him.... There was nothing any more, there had never been anything. Only she, the woman to whom he belonged entirely, to his last drop of blood, his last breath, and no one could ever change that, ever! It was the most powerful thing in the world!

Somehow, far, far away, somewhere in the boundless expanse he found her hand, and felt under his sensitive fingers every invisible pore of her body, every tiny hair as if his fingers were without skin and he had touched her hand with his exposed nerves. Suddenly he could not breathe, his heart beat in a frenzy. And Boris sunk into delirious darkness, into a hot, fiery tempest consuming everything.

He remembered nothing after that.

He was dazzled by a searing flash of light, and fell face down onto the pillow, nearly losing consciousness.

Grasp of reality came back slowly and gradually. Suddenly he was aware of the blinding bright electric light, of the woman lying beside him, shielding her face with her hand. He so longed to fall through the earth, to die with shame or run away to his soldiers in the kitchen that he groaned.

So that's what it's like! What's it all for? Whatever for? thought Boris. He bit his lip, at the same time feeling his heart beginning to calm down and his breathing returning to normal. He did not seem to have experienced any special pleasure; all he remembered was that a woman in one's arms for some reason felt very small and defenceless, and that made him feel even guiltier. If only he could forget everything, if only he could undo what he had done—then he would never again dare to hurt a woman with all this silly business. One could live perfectly well without it, he did not need it at all....

That was what the lieutenant thought, and he was amazed to feel that the oppressive load that had constantly weighed upon him was no longer there, his body seemed to be lightening and rejoicing after this sensual fulfilment.

A beast, that's what I am, just an animal! the lieutenant cursed himself, but even this cursing had a separate existence, had nothing to do with him. There was shame and turmoil in his mind, but through his body flowed a blessed, drowsy calm.

"And so, I, too, helped the army."

After these words, which the woman uttered quite clearly into the quiet of the room, Boris submissively waited for her to slap his face, to start sobbing, threshing about the bed, tearing her hair. But she lay without stirring, and a tear rolled down her cheek.

He was overwhelmed by a sense of weakness and guilt he

had never known before. He did not know how he could lighten the suffering he had inflicted on her so roughly, taking advantage of her meekness. And she had taken such good care of him; had fed him, had given him that chance to have a bath, had washed his dirty foot wrappings.... With his eyes fixed at the wall, Boris made a confession which for some reason all men seem to find shameful: "It's the first time...." And after a pause, he added, scarcely audibly: "Please forgive me, if you can."

Lusya did not answer. She seemed to expect him to say more, or else was waiting to become used to his breathing, to the warmth and smell of his body. To her he was no longer a stranger. Crushed as he was now under a double load of shame and guilt, which was especially pleasant to her, he appealed to her womanly devotion and forgiveness. Lusya brushed the tear away with a finger, turned to face him and said, sadly and simply: "I know, Boris," adding with just the hint of a smile: "Never mind me—women can never do without tears and emotions, it's like bread to them.:.." She touched him lightly, soothing and encouraging him.

"Switch the light off, will you." In her tone there was an unspoken promise.

Still not believing that he would not be punished for what he had done, he got up obediently, getting entangled in the blanket he had dragged with him. He walked barefoot to the chair, stood on it, and unscrewed the bulb. He remained standing thus in the dark, not knowing what to do next. Lusya did not call him, did not stir. Boris adjusted the blanket around his body, cleared his throat and sat down awkwardly on the very edge of the bed.

A night plane roared overhead, and a faint green light etched a line on the window. The plane flew low—the pilot had no fear.

After the small plane came heavy aircraft with their full load of bombs. Or perhaps they were ferrying back the wounded. The sound of their engines was laboured, like the breathing of a horse going uphill.

A faint bluish ray of light, diluted by distance, touched the window, and immediately a gnarled apple tree was conjured up on the pane, as if drawn with a pen, and one could now see the bookshelves, something white lying crumpled on the chair, and the dark, elongated eyes that looked directly at Boris as much as to say: "What's the matter? "

No, he could not join his soldiers in the kitchen. But how he wished to run away and hide. Yet his feeling of guilt kept him in this room, it demanded atonement, demanded he say something.

"Why don't you lie down," said Lusya and he thought she sounded offended and depressed. "Your feet will get cold from the floor."

His feet really were getting very cold, and, once again obediently, trying not to touch the woman, he crawled across the bed to the wall, and was on about to say something, to squeeze some remark out of himself, when he heard her say: "Turn round to me."

So she did not hate him, her voice held no pain, no repentance. A remote, hitherto well-hidden tenderness seemed to awaken in her voice.

How is it possible? ... Boris wondered, bewildered. Trying not to touch her, he slowly turned to face her, quickly hiding his hands under the pillow, and himself taking shelter behind the pillow as if behind earthworks, considering that it behoved him to lie as quietly as possible, hardly breathing, so that she might not notice his presence.

"Oh how green you are," Boris heard her say, and a wave of heat swept over him—she was moving closer. Lusya gently blew into Boris' ear, played with it, touching it gently with her fingers and pressing her face against his neck, and asked: "May I? " She touched the scar on his neck, "May I kiss you here? " and immediately she pressed her lips to the uneven scar as if frightened he might refuse. "D'you think I'm silly? "

"Oh no, not at all! " he answered awkwardly and immediately realised how foolish it was. He was sure that the scar could only be unpleasant to the lips, and in general that it was an idiotic thing to do. But he had to give in—after all, he was utterly in the wrong. "Well, if you like," he began, on the point of passing out with shame. "You can do it again...."

She lightly brushed her lips against his collar bone, then sought and found the scar with her lips, and again touched this old wound—kissing it lightly, tremulously.

Once more there was no breath left in him. His blood pounded in his temples, pressed on his ears, intensifying the turbulence still lingering within him. Again came that hot haze; the rustling of her words disarmed him utterly, plunging him into an echoing emptiness.

"My darling.... You shed your blood and I wasn't there.... Oh my darling.... My poor boy...." She kept kissing his old wound, which had suddenly began aching. Remarkably, her words seemed neither silly nor comic, though with some part of his mind he realised they were both.

Overcoming his awkwardness, and swept by an answering tenderness, Boris gingerly touched her hair—she must have undone her long plait meanwhile—then buried his face in it and asked, wonderingly: "What is this? What's the matter with me?"

"I don't know." Lusya ran her lips over Boris' face, then she found his mouth, and repeated, hardly audibly, as if falling, sinking somewhere: "I don't know...."

Her hot, feverish breathing evoked sympathetic echoes within him, and unexpectedly even to himself, he put his lips to her ear and uttered a word which came of itself from his wandering mind. "My dearest...."

He did not say this word, it came out in a groan, and he felt it run through her like an electric current, immediately softening her, making her very close to him, ready to be one with him, as he was with her. Utterly happy, he breathed out: "Oh, my darling."

And then again everything was quiet and there was a feeling of awkwardness. But this time they did not separate, and their bodies, so heavy, as if full of molten metal, were now resting, cooling.

They dozed off for a little, but even in sleep they were aware of one another, and soon woke up.

"All my life, ever since I was seven or may be even earlier, I've been in love with a thin slip of a boy like you, and all my life I've been waiting for him," she said, caressing him, and her words seemed as smooth and as rounded as if she were reading from a book. "And at long last he's come to me!"

Lusya assured him that she had never really known a man before him, that she had always felt nothing but disgust. She herself believed her own words. He, too, believed her. She swore she would never forget him, and he made the same vow to her. He assured her and himself that of all the girls' names he had ever heard he had found only one memorable, a name that was flower-like, had a sound that might have been Chinese or Japanese. It was Lusya. He told her that as a boy—no, not as a boy, as a mere child of seven—that's right, he remembered now—he was seven when he had heard her name and he had dreamt, he remembered it very well, he had dreamt many, many times about Lusya and had called her his own dear girl.

"O repeat it again, please repeat it! "

He showered kisses on her face salty with tears.

"My own dear girl! My sweetest! My own! "

"I could die now! " exclaimed Lusya, deeply moved.

Something snapped inside him. His memory conjured up the old man and the old woman, the grey-haired general lying on the sheaves of maize, the burnt Katyusha driver, the dead horses, the dog run wild, the soldiers crushed by the tanks—corpses, corpses and more corpses....

"What's that? Are you tired? Or..." Lusya propped herself up on her elbow and gazed at him, struck by a new thought: "Or are you ... frightened of death? ! "

"It's like looking at the sun—you can't look directly at death ... so I've heard. But that's not it," said Boris quietly, turning away, as if talking to himself: "What's far more frightening is to get used to death, to get accustomed to it—that's what's so frightening.... It's frightening when the very word death becomes a commonplace, just like the words 'to eat', 'to sleep', 'to love'...." He wanted to add something, but restrained himself.

"You're tired. Relax. Try to relax." Lusya attempted to catch the look in his eyes and could not, for he avoided her gaze. She lay her cheek on his chest. "Listen to your heart, how it's beating!" And she pressed her hand over it: "Easy now, calm down, calm down...."

"Don't let's talk about death any more."

Lusya withdrew her hand immediately, rubbed her temple with the palm of her hand, and said: "Forgive me ... I'd forgotten about the war."

Once again the little plane rattled overhead, its light cutting across the window-pane, and the motor faded into the distance. Now they could hear the sounds in the street.

The street was not sleeping.

On the other side of the wall the army's life was going on, the soldiers were moving about. They heard a song:

> A stern, determined voice rings out:
> To countrymen, to family,
> While we still live, we swear to show
> No mercy to the enemy!

A lorry droned. The beam of its headlamps swung into the window, and the apple tree seemed to move: one moment it came close to the window, almost touching the glass with its boughs, then it receded, disappearing into the snow-filled darkness. The frosty, sparkling snowflakes flashed onto the window-pane and faded, and by contrast the warmth and comfort of the cottage felt especially desirable. A tank or a tractor started up with a deafening roar. It clattered, then stopped, and the motor went on running idly.

"One, two, three! Heave! " men were shouting in a variety of voices outside the window, then the voices began to fade, too.

They're going to the front. They're catching up with the front line, Boris told himself.

Someone in the kitchen began clearing his throat loudly, spitting and blowing his nose. It's Karyshev, guessed the lieutenant, a hardened smoker. Even at night he gets up for a smoke, lights up his stinking shag. A door creaked and banged, too—Karyshev came back from the street; then a dipper clattered against the bucket—he must have drunk some cold water. He coughed some more and was quiet.

Somewhere among the ravines on the other side of the

river an explosion was heard; the echo sounded like some-body banging a metal basin, the reverberations rippled far into the frosty night, the window tinkled, snow fell from the apple tree, and Shkalik exclaimed in his sleep out there in the kitchen, then muttered something and was heard no more.

"Perhaps another man has lost his life," said Boris after a pause, during which he strained his ears for another explosion.

Lusya pressed her hand against his lips and they stayed like that, lying side by side, listening to the night, waiting for something to happen. With his lips Boris gratefully touched the palm of her hand, which smelt of soap, ordinary washing soap. It was such a familiar, homely smell, one going back to his childhood, and it touched some chord within him. Annoyed with himself for their momentary estrangement, he again buried his face, childlike, in her hair, remembering with surprise his squeamishness at seeing somebody else's hair left on a comb once. It was laughable, too, to recall his squea-mishness about old buttons cut off from outworn garments.

"I thought you were cross with me," Lusya said, sensitive to his change of mood, and put her arm round his neck, now without hesitation. "Don't let's be angry with one another. We've no time for that...."

For a short time they lost all shame. Lusya's open lips were hot, her breasts rose and fell, her long hair was tangled around her neck. Passion spent, she pressed her face to his shoulder and muttered, half asleep: "You ought to have a sleep, why don't you try to doze off...."

"Don't sleep. Stay with me a little longer, don't sleep!..." That was what he heard in her words, and to please her—it was nice to please her—he slipped his arm under her head and said: "You know, when I was little my mother took me to Moscow. All I remember is an old house in Arbat and an aged aunt, who assured me that the stone floor of reddish and white flagstones had survived since before the Great Fire when Napoleon was there...." He stopped, thinking she was asleep, but she nodded to show she was listening. "I also remember a theatre with columns, and music. You know, that music was the colour of lilac ... the tune was simple, easy to listen to, and it was some shade of lilac.... I could hear that music just a moment ago and now I remember how they danced to it—a man and a woman, a shepherd and a shepherdess, a green meadow, white sheep, and the shepherd and the shepherdess. They loved each other, they weren't ashamed of their love, nor were they frightened for it. They were defenceless in their supreme trust. I used to think that those who are defenceless can't be touched by evil...."

She listened to him, hardly daring to breathe; she knew he would never, not to anyone, tell what he was telling her now—he could not tell it again because such a night would never be repeated.

"And do you know," Boris smiled, and Lusya was overjoyed that he still remembered her presence, "do you know, that ever since then I've lived in expectation of something. In olden times people would claim that an evil eye cast a spell on me, that it was the work of the devil." He stopped and sighed, as if disapproving of himself. "So you see...."

"We were born for one another, as they used to write in the old novels," Lusya said after a pause. "If you like I'll tell you about myself. Later. Because I feel so good now, I can hear your music. By the way, I used to study at a music school—oh yes." With one finger she touched Boris' mouth, which opened in surprise. "I can hardly believe it myself now. And anyhow, what does it matter?" She settled sleepily against him with a soft sigh. "I'm listening to your music...."

An old road overgrown with grass stretched on and on leading somewhere, and along it walked he and she. The road was endless and the wanderers were unreal. And the lilac music was hardly audible....

Boris came to with a jerk, and sat up, clutching his head between his hands: "I think I've slept again...."

"You trembled, you trembled so much.... Were you dreaming about the war again?"

Overjoyed that he was able to conquer himself and shake off his sleep, that beside him was a live person, immensely dear to him, Boris pressed her body, which had grown cold, close to his.

"My head's reeling...."

"Let me bring you something to eat and drink. You had nothing last evening."

"How did you know? You weren't at home...."

"I know everything. You must have something to eat and then have a rest."

"There'll be plenty of time to rest later, when I'm no longer with you. But eating's not a bad idea. We won't wake them up? "

"Don't you worry, I'll be very careful! " Lusya smiled mischievously and shook her finger at him: "You mustn't look at me, turn away." But as he went on looking at her, she took his head between her hands and turned it to face the wall: "Don't look at me. D'you hear? "

They were playing like a couple of kids, forgetting about the noise.

"Bad boy! You mustn't do that! I could do with a bite, too." She slapped him lightly, grabbed her housecoat, slipped out of the room and started dressing.

"Hey, waiter! "

"Stop it, Boris, or I'll give you what for! " she said, thrusting her face between the curtains, and in the quick gaze of her black eyes, which had entirely lost their remote look, there was so much that Boris jumped up and dashed towards her. But she drew the curtain and when he pushed his face against hers through the hard cloth she cried out: "I love you."

Boyish feelings overcame him. He struck the pillow with his fist, then threw it up and fell chest down upon it, as if onto a bird whose body was still warm. He caught sight of the impression left by her body in the bed.... He gently touched the sheet.

Beneath his hand was emptiness.

Lusya appeared in the doorway with the crockery, bread and potatoes, and was on the point of saying that thank God, the fireman had not drunk all the moonshine. But catching the expression on his face, she froze. He seemed not to recognise her; no, he did recognise her, he saw her, but as if from a distance.

"What is it? "

His eyes were filled with tears and his features stood out, sharpened in agony.

"I'm here! " she touched him. He came to himself with a start and grasped her hand, crushing it in his.

Lusya hugged him and immediately released him, then set about arranging their simple meal. Silently they drank home-brewed spirit from the same mug, kissing after every mouthful. Silently they ate the potatoes and pork fat, he peeling the potatoes for her and she for him.

The meal was over, there was nothing else for them to do and it seemed there was nothing for them to talk about. In silence they stared ahead into the emptiness of the retreating night. Boris guiltily stroked her hand. Lusya squeezed his fingers gratefully, and the next moment he grabbed her roughly in his arms, pushed her on to the bed, shouting: "Life or death? ! "

"Oh, what a boy you are! " she closed her moist eyes.

"You mean a fool? "

"You're a case!... And I'm a case and all around us there are cases...."

"I'm just drunk, I'm not a case."

"You can't have any more," Lusya dodged his hands.

"Yes, I can! " He proclaimed, shivering with assumed passion.

"You listen to me. I'm getting on for twenty-one! "

"Is that so? Let me tell you that I myself am getting on for twenty! "

"There you are, I'm a hundred years older than you are! " Very gently, as if he were a baby, she made him comfortable on the pillow. "And look at the time, it's after two in the morning...."

Once again one of the soldiers stirred in the kitchen, got up, and, stumbling over a wash-tub, cursed hoarsely. Lusya and Boris waited, tensely. A vague, hardly perceptible light came from the window, picking out Lusya's naked shoulders, setting aglow the hoarfrost on the window-pane, glistening in Lusya's hair, lighting up her eyes. There were shadows under her eyes and under her firm chin. Already seized with a premonition of the morning and parting, they sat pressed closely against each other, wishing for nothing more: they wanted neither to speak nor to think, they wanted to remain as they were, sitting together, half asleep, half awake, and feeling one another—two frank, living bodies experiencing untold bliss which melted the heart.

Part Three
THE PARTING

The window was lit up and the room began to fill with a red glow. A neighbour's dog along the street set up a monotonous howl and then a bell started ringing with a cracked frosty sound. The shadow of the little apple tree outside the window trembled, stirred, and moved close. Everything within the room came alive, shadows began to flit and move, and the dark cross of the window frame flickered on the floor and the walls.

Lusya clung to Boris, her nail sinking painfully into his flesh. He pressed her to him. "Now, now my little one! There's nothing to be scared about...." There was nothing to be scared about. Had there been any danger the lieutenant would have known at once—he had a remarkable nose for that, developed by the war.

On the other side of the line of tall, slim poplars which grew beyond the vegetable plot like a wall, a house was burning brightly, briskly, its thatched roof slipping to one side like a hat, sending forth showers of sparks and even bits of burning straw all over the vegetable patch.

They must have made a good job of drying their footwrappings, our brother Slavs! Boris said to himself gaily for some reason—perhaps because the house was burning so quickly and brightly. He knew that while they heated the stove with straw in such houses it was all right, but that if they used anything more substantial, like proper firewood or wooden furniture, especially with a splash or two of petrol added by the soldiers—then you could say goodbye both to the house and to the footwrappings drying inside it.

"They're frying the *polizei*," Lusya's words came low and she wrapped the blanket closer round her shoulders. "The bastard! He deserved it.... He helped the fascists pick people for slave labour. They sorted our people at those transportation points like rag-and-bone men: some they sent to Germany, others to Krivorozhye to work in the ore mines and some to other places...." Lusya's voice shook. Patches of light flickered all over her face and bosom. Her face, pale, then ashen, disappeared entirely in the shadow and only her eyes fringed by her thick lashes glowed with anger and fury.

"When the fascists occupied our village one of them came to live in our house. Quite a grand gentleman he was. He had come to Russia with his dog!... And the dog had a gilded collar, but it looked just like a frog, a great big frog, slippery and pop-eyed ... that gentlemanly fascist used to bring home girls from the transportation points, he chose the curvaceous ones ... and what he did with them! O God, what he did with them. He demonstrated something he called Paris love. One of the girls poked him in the eye with a fork for that Paris love.... Unfortunately he only lost one eye—his dog got hold of her and mauled her to death...." Lusya buried her face in her hands, pressing it so hard with her hands that it looked drained of blood. "It'd been trained to kill people, that dog.... It sank its fangs in the girl's throat as if she were just a bird, then licked its chops and settled down by the window.... There, in that very place! There! " With one hand Lusya pointed at the place while she pressed her other hand against her eyes, and Boris, feeling a chill in his back and head, realised that Lusya was seeing something fearful at that very moment. He asked her almost chokingly. "What? ... You saw it with your own eyes? "

Lusya nodded her head once, twice and, unable to stop, continued to nod, convulsed with sobbing....

He pressed her against his body and kept her in his arms until she recovered a little. We must crush them, wipe them off the face of the earth, beat them until their teeth begin to rattle in their heads! he thought. The battalion commander's right! He thought of Filkin, recalled the morning battle, the ravines, he recalled the dog with an expensive collar tearing the flesh of a dead horse. "That must be the dog! It must be shot...."

"Our partisans caught up with him." From her strange revengeful smile Boris decided that it had not been without Lusya's help. "They hanged him in the forest on a pine tree. His dog howled and howled, gnawing at the feet of its master. It chewed off his legs to the knees. It couldn't jump any higher and then it left for the front—there's plenty for it to feed on there. As for the nazi, that legless bastard's still hanging in the dark pine forest, his bones rattling, and until our entire generation, every one of us dies—we'll go on hearing that sound...."

The dog in the street had howled itself hoarse, there were no voices and the bell had stopped ringing.

"All these bastards should be—" Lusya forced through her clenched teeth. "They should all be done away with, every single one of them...."

Boris could not recognise her as the woman so passionate and exultant in her love, who had come to him in that now so very distant evening hour.

"Won't you tell me about your father and mother, Boris? What sort of people are they?" Lusya asked him a little later.

Boris sensed that she wanted to forget, to crowd out those ghastly visions.

"They're both school-teachers," he answered, not at once, but quite willingly. "My father is now a deputy headmaster and mother teaches Russian and literature. Our school was once a lyceum. My mother went there as a girl." He stopped, and Lusya's feminine intuition, especially keen that night, told her that he was drifting away from her again. "A long time ago one of the Decembrists, Fonvizin, was exiled to our little town. They say that Pushkin took the wife of General Fonvizin as the model for his Tatiana. My mother is some kind of cousin of the Fonvizins—twenty or thirty times removed, but very proud of it all the same. Like an idiot I never could remember mother's family tree," he smiled to himself, looking up at something only he could see as he lay on the bed with his hands beneath his head. "The streets and lanes in our little town of wooden houses are green with grass every spring. There's an embankment with weeds growing between the facing timber, and birds nesting in the cracks. When spring comes sage begins to bloom in the sunny patches, and in summer campion and thyme, and there are old, old birches there. And so many churches. The Siberian gold-diggers were a sly lot: after years of plundering a man would build a church on his own 'earnings'! And that would take care of all his sins. How simple-minded people are.... And now those churches are garages, bakeries, and workshops of all kinds. Bushes grow on the roofs and jackdaws and swifts nestle in the belfries. You should see the swifts come out in flocks before a thunderstorm—the whole sky looks covered with little crosses! And they're twittering away!... Are you asleep?..."

"Oh no, no! " Lusya shifted a little. "Tell me ... does your mother wear her hair in plaits? "

"Plaits? What have plaits to do with it? " Boris was surprised. "She has a fringe, she had plaits when she was young. I'm actually a late child, a cross between a son and a grandson, you might say...." He plumped up the pillow and lay chest down on it.

He was in the grip of those happy cloudless memories of long ago. They beat in his heart, coursed in his veins, they lived in him, bringing joy and solace, they were him—and how could one put oneself into words?

There he was, inhaling the morning aroma of his native town.

Those mornings—redolent of dew and mist, cold mist, fragrant with grass. It clung longest to the dilapidated wooden facing of the embankment, filling the cracks between the logs; it hung over the cupolas of the churches like winter fur hats. From the river rose an odour of rotting bark, and the mist carried a smell of dead, hacked trees. The river in spate attacked the dam, washing away the ground from under the wooden embankment, carrying rotten chunks of timber with it.

When the river returned to its banks, the boys always found mysterious treasure trove by the dam: pieces of bottle glass and crockery, coins covered with green mould, bones,

and copper crosses. In pools by the dam, shoals of small fry
were stranded. The crows hopped along the dam, poking
their heads under the logs and gulping down the fish with a
greedy gurgle.

The boys threw stones at the crows, and rescued the small
fry from pools contaminated with all kinds of decayed
things. The little fish struggled weakly in their warm hands,
slithering between their fingers. Released into water, the
small fry would lie on the surface at first, seemingly whispering, their mouths opening convulsively, and then swaying
drunkenly they would go deeper into the water for a while.
But they came up like dry willow leaves. Gathering strength,
the fry, now with conscious fear, nosed their way downwards
and clung to the bottom, swarming together and searching
for food.

In autumn the people rolled barrels to the dam, stacking
them against the wall, on their sides. This was a time when the
mists and the whole of the little town reeked of fish and
decay. The stacks of barrels grew higher and higher, more and
more steamers and barges put in here, and the town was full
of northern fishermen—crowds of weather-beaten men,
grown wild, and nostalgic for the company of other human
beings. Accordions played on the bank, from behind the
stacks of barrels full of *omul* and grayling came the squeals of
women, and the urchins secretly watched the adult goings-on.
The nights were unquiet, disorderly: the whole town seemed
to be drinking, to be on the spree as in olden times when the
gold-diggers arrived with their loot.

"Our lads and girls simply love to meet the steamers—all
the passenger boats. They stand waiting, swishing at themselves with twigs all the time—the midges and mosquitoes tear
us to pieces," Boris continued with a smile, and Lusya
guessed that he was now seeing scenes known only to himself, and was going on watching them in isolation from her.
She moved away from him, but he did not even notice. He
kept gazing in front of him, smiling blissfully.

"The lads treat the girls to handfuls of bilberries and
blueberries, or cedar nuts. Everyone's mouth is black from
the berries, and the streets are scattered with nutshells....

What's the matter with me? Talking about mosquitoes and berries! " exclaimed Boris. "Let me read mother's letters."

Lusya noted to herself, rather sadly, that he did not offer to do it right away. He wasn't used to sharing things with her: it would take time for everything between them to be as one—thoughts, feelings, life itself.

"Only you'll have to fetch them. I'm afraid, the letters are in my bag."

She got up and screwed in the bulb. Blinking at the bright light, she told herself that this was how it would be all her life—he would command and she would never tire of doing his bidding.

"That little soldier of yours feels bad. He just can't get over that carousing yesterday. It's agony for him. Why do they make a boy like that drink so much?" Lusya reproached Boris, on returning with the bag. "Oh, Boris! " she wagged her finger at him. "You're a spoilt boy, I can see! "

"Am I really? It's my mother's fault.... You know," he smiled, "once my father took me to the boxing section of the timber works club, and right away I got my nose blooded. That was that—mother wouldn't let me go there any more, but my father took me everywhere with him: fishing, or into the forests to shoot game or gather nuts. But he never allowed me a single drink. This Cherdyn lad wanted to have a real go at it...."

Lusya smoothed out the furrows over the bridge of Boris' nose and ran her fingers along his eyebrows, which began as a fine line, swept up towards the temples, then curved sharply down.

"Are you like your mother? "

Not knowing what pleasure it is for a woman to "discover" a man—sometimes this takes a whole lifetime, and is considered to be true love—he hurriedly intervened: "My person is not worth your attention...."

"What a well brought-up boy! " Lusya dug him in the ribs. "Read the letters, then, but wait till I lie down. Go on, you can read now! " He noticed the dark circles under her eyes and felt an unaccustomed manly pity. "Tired? " he asked.

"Go on and read the letters! "

It was quite a bundle of letters. Boris chose one, smoothed it out—and, as if in a flash of light, he could see his mother with a white shawl round her sloping shoulders, and a yellow wooden penholder in her ink-stained fingers; he even seemed to hear the scratching of the pen as it ran along the lines of fine handwriting: "My dearest, you know what sort of a man your father is. He's a despot, says I shouldn't write so often to you because you have to answer, or so he says, and lose time you need for sleep. But I cannot help writing to you every day.

"Here I am, just finished marking the exercise books and now I'm writing to you. Your father is in the kitchen mending a dragnet and thinking about you. I can read him like one of these exercise books, and see every comma he misses, and all the other little things. Your father is suffering because he thinks he's been too reserved, too unemotional with you, hasn't shown you enough love, has left things unsaid. He's mending that net, hoping you'll return by spring. He's changed so much that he sometimes calls me 'my little girl'. He used to call me that when we were young, in our courting days. Funny. Even then we were both over thirty.

"I think I've told you how difficult it is at school nowadays. But it's really amazing that the schools are still going strong even in these very terrible days of war. And we're continuing to teach children, to prepare them for the future— and that means we're not losing our faith in that future....

"...My dear Boris! It's evening once again, the day is gone and there's been no letter from you. How are you there? Our stove is alight, and the kettle lid's rattling away. Father isn't at home—he's giving maths lessons at the evening school. Boris dear, why were you so off-hand about your award? You didn't tell us even what kind of order you got. You know your father and his ideas of honour and duty. He'd so like to know what you got it for. I'd like to know, too. We're both very proud of you.

"By the way, your father told me how he taught you to guide a boat with a pole. As he was telling me I seemed to see you just in your bathing trunks: skinny, naked, your ribs showing. The boat was big and it was hard for you with the rapids near, while your father sat on the bank angling for those miserable gudgeons, watching your boat swing round and be swept towards the rapids. Eventually you almost reached the big rock, near where you were supposed to fish. But once again the current swung the boat and swept it away. You went up the river five times and five times you were swept back. Your nose was covered with beads of perspiration (your nose always used to perspire). At the sixth attempt you did it and shouted triumphantly: 'I've brought the boat, daddy! ' while he answered: 'Well, that's fine! Now tie it to a rock, and hurry up. We need plenty of tiddlers as bait for the evening.'

"Yes, it's no easy matter to be the child of a pair of school-teachers—they never stop giving him lessons, and as a rule when the children grow up they prove to be singularly foolish folk (you're an exception, of course, don't be sore!).

"I don't know what to do with your father. You should have seen how badly he took it when shoulder tabs were introduced in the army! He said we'd torn the shoulder tabs off the officers, and now our children had got to wear them! On the other hand, I was quite pleased to hear of it. I rejoice at everything that is sensible and doesn't affront the dignity of a Russian. Perhaps it's the blood of my ancestors that speaks in me?

"I must finish here. Once I begin thinking about my ancestors it means it's time to stop. It's just like your father: if he starts dancing after a drink or two it means he ought to go to bed—he's no good at dancing. That's between us, too, though it's no secret to you.

"My dearest! It's late, it's night in our parts, a frosty one. Perhaps where you are it's warmer. I've forgotten all my geography. It's because I feel you're at my side.

"It's amazing that as soon as I get towards the end of a letter I become tearful. Please forgive me. I'm a weak woman and I love you more than life itself. You're always here—I'm touching my heart ... forgive me. I should say something more, something heartening, but I can't. I'll just pray for you—please bear with me. All mothers are mad ... they're ready to give their lives for their children. Oh, if only that were possible!...

"Your father caught me out in a moment of weakness. I was saying my prayers before going to bed, whispering them, thinking your father was asleep when he said, 'No need to do it on the quiet if it helps him and you....' I burst into tears, and he said, 'My dearest little girl!' You know your father. He thinks he has two children—you and me.

"I bless you, my dear boy. And wish you a good night, if this is at all possible at the front. Ever, your mother, Iraida Fonvizina-Kostyaeva."

The letter ended, but Boris continued to hold it in front of him, gazing fixedly at his mother's hurried signature, seeing her clearly in his mind's eye: her prominent nose and ears, her white shawl falling off her sloping shoulders, the old-fashioned bun at the nape of her neck, the thin fringe on her forehead, which always made her pupils grin. He saw his mother put away the letter, wrap her shawl tighter round her shoulders and draw aside the curtains at the window, attempting to gauge in her mind's eye the distance separating her from her son.

Outside the window was a sprinkling of lights in the little old town, and beyond the lights she could make out the dark expanse of the river, covered with hummocky ice, and further still—the hardly perceptible silhouette of the mountains with gloomy, silent taiga on the slopes, and mysterious, frightening deep gorges. The town, the house and his mother were one world, an enclosed circle on one side of the river. Somewhere, on the other side of the river, the other side of an invisible chasm was he, her son; she, his mother, was separated from him by thousands of versts, by endless lines of trenches between the two conflicting worlds.

Boris came to with a start and folded the letter. "I have an old-fashioned mother, I am afraid," he said in a purposely loud voice. "And her style of writing is old-fashioned."

Lusya remained silent.

Boris turned round and saw that her face was wet with tears but for some reason he dared not comfort her. She grabbed the canister of home-brew from the shelf, put it to her mouth, splashed the drink over her breast, took a gulp, and said jerkily: "I must tell you about myself.... So there are no secrets between us...." Boris made an attempt to stop her.

"Everything has been so good.... I'm a hysterical fool, that's what I am! " She hurried on and her lips trembled; she kept running her hand over her face as if washing it. Boris wrapped the blanket around her. "How sweet and kind you are! You take after your mother. I think I know her well now. What are wars for? Deaths? Whatever for? A mother's grief alone.... Oh God, how can I express it? "

"I understand you. Before I got to the front, even up to last night, I couldn't understand...."

Night was coming to an end outside. The earth unhurriedly began to turn towards the sun and the day, that side of it where our troops and the enemy's were sleeping amidst the snow.

The *polizei*'s house had burnt through, collapsed. A heap of embers were now peacefully eating away what remained of the rafters. Here and there individual flames darted along them like so many agile stoats, and disappeared down a slowly thawing hole in the ground.

Lusya lay flat on the bed, her eyes fixed upon the ceiling. Boris let her stay like that. The reflection of the fire stirred like a little red bug in the window-pane; their room once again was filled with darkness, but the darkness did not bring them closer together, created no sense of communion. It lay oppressively over them, cold and miserable, like a premonition of something bad to come.

"I'd like a smoke," Lusya pointed to the shelf. Showing no surprise, and asking no questions, Boris felt about inside a wooden box until he found a packet of tobacco and started rolling a clumsy cigarette. Lusya put her hand under the mattress and brought out a lighter. Smiling wryly at something in her own mind, she undid the mis-shapen object Boris had given her, rolled it anew and lit up, momentarily illuminating Boris' face. The smile still hovered around her lips. "The cigarette lighter once belonged to that officer," Lusya tapped it with her finger-nail and blew out the flame. "The officer was hanged out there in the forest, but his lighter stayed behind ... an ivory lighter full of petrol...." A gurgling sound came from Lusya's throat.

"Why are you telling me that, what for? "

"Oh, Boris! " Lusya threw the cigarette on the floor and collapsed against him. "Where have you been all this time? Would we have met if it wasn't for the war? Did it have to be the war? Oh, my darling! My pure, my sweet darling! How terrible life is! How frightened I am to go on living!..." The next moment she took hold of herself and patted her tear-stained face dry with the corner of the sheet. "That's all right. That's all. Please forgive me. I'll be calm now." He felt like pushing her away from him, but he responded to her caresses as if out of duty.

"You're no good at pretending, you know," Lusya moved away from him and, sinking her fingers into his hair, she started playing with it. "And you haven't combed your hair.... How soft your hair is!... A man should know how to pretend."

"What about you.... You know everything? " He froze, shocked by his own audacity.

"I? " Again she began inspecting her own hands, and that annoyed him. "I've already said I'm a hundred years older than you. Women have to be believed sometimes...." And she laughed in a false, strained way. "My goodness, how clever I am!... Don't you feel we're on the point of quarrelling? Everything's following the established pattern."

"There'll be no quarrelling. Look, it's almost morning." The pale square of the window stood out now and a diffused light was filling the room.

"Do not wake her up at dawn..." Lusya quoted the poem in a whisper, and fell silent. Then she raised her head decisively, brushed her hair away from her face, and laid her hands on Boris' shoulders: "Thank you, my dearest, my bright sun! Like a sun you appeared in my sky, and warmed me up! ... It's been worth living just for this night alone. And now give me a drink and don't say a word, not a word...."

Boris got up and splashed some spirit into a mug. Lusya shuddered as she gulped it, then waited for him to drink, and lightly, momentarily clung to him. "Do bear with me just a little longer. Just a little...."

Boris touched her mouth with his lips, and Lusya's eyelids fluttered, and this somehow melted his heart. He wanted to do something good for her, something unexpected, and he remembered in a flash what it should be. Awkwardly, as if lifting up a sheaf of wheat, Boris picked her up and carried her about the room in his arms.

Lusya felt that she was too heavy and awkward for him to carry, but as this was what men did in romantic novels, then let him carry her about in his arms, since he was so well-read! She listened avidly as he talked unrealistic, nonsensical, but nevertheless pleasant-sounding words: the war would end, he would come for her, he would pick her up in his arms and carry her all the way to the railway station for everyone to see—a distance of three kilometres, a whole three thousand steps....

Oh, my poor dear! Lusya thought, her heart drawn to him in pity, but aloud she said, after brushing her lips against the hard wiry scar of his neck wound: "No, it'll be different. I shall rush to the station to meet you. I'll pick an enormous bunch of roses. White roses, snow white ones. I'll put on a new dress—white, snow white. There'll be music. There'll be masses and masses of flowers. There'll be crowds of people. Every one of them happy...." Lusya stopped her recital, and sighed, barely audibly: "There won't be any of that."

He didn't want to hear her say this. He talked on, muttering like a woodcock during the mating season, talking all kinds of nonsense about eternal love, about happiness and being faithful.

They came to when they heard the soldiers moving about the kitchen, stamping their feet, exchanging remarks; someone could be heard shaking out his greatcoat.

Lusya dressed, slid onto the floor and lay at Boris' feet: "Please take me with you, Comrade Commander," she pleaded with him, laying her cheek on his knees, looking up at him. "I'll wash soldiers' clothes and cook for them. I can learn to nurse the wounded. I'm quick to learn. Please take me with you! Other women can fight, why can't I...."

"Yes, they fight; we haven't been able to manage without women at the front so far," he said quickly, in a staccato manner, turning away from her towards the window. "We sing praises to them. And we don't even feel ashamed, as we should...."

"What a clever man you are, Lieutenant! " Lusya gave him a resounding kiss on the cheek, and left the room, tying the belt of her housecoat. Boris lay down on the bed, and the very next moment sank into a profound bottomless sleep of a kind he had never known before.

About two hours later, Lusya tiptoed into the room. She hung Boris' now ironed tunic, with the order and the medal already fixed on it, on the back of a chair; beside it she laid the trousers and the foot-wrappings, also newly washed but still a little damp; then she sat down beside him on the bed and touched his nose. He woke up but kept his eyes shut, luxuriating.

"There you are! " Lusya started to say, indicating his clothes, as she tucked loose strands of hair under her kerchief. "I've just learnt that it's very pleasant to see to the comforts of a man you love! " And she ruefully shook her head. "Well, a woman remains a woman, and no equality can help her."

Her cheeks pink from the recent ironing, Lusya looked very housewifely and sweet at that moment. Boris wiped the perspiration off her forehead with his hand, embraced her lazily, gave her a soft but passionate kiss and pulled her to him.

"No, no, you mustn't! Everyone's up! " She pressed her hands against his chest, but Boris held her firmly.

"But what if your soldiers hear about it?...."

"The soldiers always come to hear about everything before the commander-in-chief—whether it's a German offensive or our own, and as for our relations...."

Boris was dressing, and Lusya was plaiting her hair, when a discreet warning cough came from behind the curtains.

"Comrade Lieutenant, can we have some drink? " Pafnutiev's brisk voice was heard. "That is if anything's left, of course...."

"There is, there is."

"So there could be no ignition without fuel, eh? "

"Don't talk too much! " Boris answered with assumed severity.

Well, there'd be plenty of talk now, that was certain!

His soldiers would, of course, approve—their CO was a smart lad even though he did look like one of those intellectuals! Everything that had taken place between Boris and Lusya would be regarded by the soldiers as a brief, war-time adventure on the part of their lieutenant, and there was nothing he could do to change their opinion. He would be forced to condone, to agree with such an opinion. There'd be a whole barrage of questions about how it had been, and so on. Yes, it would be very difficult, almost impossible to avoid the perspicacity of his soldiers!

Boris handed the jar and the mug to Pafnutiev through the curtains; "Shkalik isn't to have a single drop! You and the rest may have no more that a hundred grams each! "

"As you wish! " Pafnutiev winked at his officer.

"What are you winking for? You won't be able to see straight if you don't watch yourself! " growled Boris.

Lusya was putting on a yellow dress, with black ribbons running down the front of it, Gypsy style; the sleeves were also trimmed with black. Her plait lay over one shoulder. She wore an almost new pair of high-heeled shoes. Now she was like a naughty little girl who secretly puts on her mother's finery. Behind Lusya's back the window-pane was scintillating with fairy-tale frost patterns—fabulous trees, ferns, flowers, and palms.

"How beautiful you are, Madame! "

Lusya tugged at the ribbon and wound it round her finger: "When I was still a girl I made this dress myself...."

"Is that so? A beautiful dress! A real beauty! "

"Go on and laugh!... But never mind, I haven't another one. So there." Lusya pressed her face against the crumpled, almost chewed up, shoulder tab of the lieutenant, and something stirred in her: the persistent smell of burning, of earth and sweat had not washed out. "I'd like to do something,

something...." Trying to fight the anxiety welling up within her, she made a vague gesture with her hand. "To play some old tune, to have a good cry.... But there's no piano in here and I've probably forgotten how to play anyhow." Her eyelashes trembled once or twice and she looked away. "Ah well, the waterworks have been switched on. It's remarkable how easy it is for you men to sweep us women off our feet...." Boris touched her plait, her neck, her dress as if she were being borne away from him—this sad, submissive woman with those eyes—so near and at the same time so far—borne away into the new day, into ordinary life, while he wanted to keep her back, to hold on to what had happened between them, and only to them....

She kept catching his hand in hers, trying to press him to her, as much as to say: here I am, beside you, with you....

* * *

They had breakfast in the kitchen, and though Lusya tried to avoid the eyes of the others, she acted more of the hostess now than she had before. The soldiers cracked jokes, good-humouredly, letting drop broad hints, maintaining that their lieutenant looked quite tired after the heavy battle he had had to sustain, dealing single-handed with the enemy onslaught, while they, the lazybones, had slept and slept, and hadn't done the first thing they'd been taught to do at army school—to go to the rescue of their commanding officer. Fancy them forgetting their duty—and hadn't they sung once upon a time a song that went: "We all march on together, the CO with his men! " What sort of men were they, sleeping through the whole night! A poor show, that's what it was! Political and educational work in the platoon must have been neglected, something would have to be done about it so that their young commander would not have to labour for the lot of them!

Shkalik alone understood nothing. Weak and trembling, his lips blue, he sat at the table meekly, like a green novice in a monastery, weighed down by worldly sins. They offered him the hair of the dog that bit him. He waved them away, covering his face with his hands, as if from Satan himself. So instead they gave him the juice of the sauerkraut, saying: "If you can't hold your liquor, don't drink! "

Lusya cleared the table and rummaged in the drawer. Among the buttons, threads and rusty thimbles she found a lipstick. Taking it with her to the front room she wetted its dried-up tip and painted her bruised and aching lips; then she swept out of the house carrying a can.

The soldiers got busy, some preparing to wash their clothes, or to shave, others cleaning their uniforms and boots smoking their vile tobacco, exchanging remarks lazily and poking fun at Shkalik. Boris listened to their leisurely chatter and was pleased that there was no summons for him to go to the battalion commander, no orders, and if his luck held they would stay here a little longer.

The talk centred around the same old subject to which the Russian soldier returns invariably as soon as he recovers from fear, as soon as he has rested a little. Pafnutiev was honing his razor, sucking at his tailor-made cigarette, screwing up his eyes from the smoke, and telling a story to his fellow soldiers: "So we had our dinner, and the children weren't at home. You must know that my father and mother had been dead for quite a while. Well, Zoya, my wife, was clearing the table, while I was smoking, watching her run about the house, showing quite a bit of leg, as a matter of fact. The windows were open, the curtains moving slightly; the smell of manure drifted in from the yard. It was all so quiet. Not a soul anywhere—not a single one! When Zoya'd finished I said: 'How about it, old woman, how about a little fun?' You should have seen her reaction—she ran about double quick, shouting: 'That's all you've got in your lousy head, you're all the same—tomcats! The vegetable plot needs weeding, the house is all upside down, the children are off doing goodness knows what...' 'Suit yourself,' I told her, 'vegetables are important, of course, go on and do the weeding. As for me—I think I'll go and look for some willing girl!' I was a strong man then, and I played the accordion. Well, my Zoya ran away when she heard that. She was gone a

minute, then two, then five minutes.... I went on smoking,
my imagination running on.... Then before you could say,
'Snip-snap, a flip and a flap' my Zoya flew in, all ready,
threw herself across the bed and shouted: 'Go ahead, and
may it choke you, you bastard! '"

The burst of laughter that greeted his words shook the
house. Pafnutiev himself laughed and laughed, his eyes
glistening with lascivious recollections, his razor almost cutting through his belt. Shkalik, who was eating sauerkraut,
almost choked. Malyshev pounded him on the back so that
Shkalik fell off the bench and the sauerkraut slipped down
his throat unnoticed. Karyshev snorted so hard that it sent
the onion peelings flying up into the air, spiralling. Even the
shyly silent Lantsov crinkled his pale lips into a smile.

Lusya returned and made a sign to Boris to come out of
the room. When he did, she pushed the can into his hands
and made him drink milk warm from the cow; then she
wiped the traces of milk from his hardly discernible moustache, and announced with a cunning smile: "I've found out a
military secret! "

Boris' mouth opened in surprise.

"Your detachment's to stay here for a day or two more! "

Boris made a strange choking sound, swept Lusya off her
feet and whirled her around the room, brushing a little mirror
off the window-sill. "Oh dear! " exclaimed Lusya. "It's a bad
omen! "

"What bad omen can it be? " laughed Boris. "D'you tell
me you believe in silly things like that? Superstitious, are
you? You said yourself two more days—isn't it enough? "

Lusya picked up the splinters in silence, and Boris helped
her. Somewhere a door banged to. Lusya pushed the broken
mirror into a pot with a plant, and hurried out into the
kitchen.

"To arms, soldiers! " thundered Mokhnakov in his hoarse
voice, trying to sound cheerful; then banging one felt boot
against the other, he reported to Boris: "Comrade Lieutenant, the order is for everyone to be in the square. The lorries
are waiting."

"Lorries? What lorries? We've got two more days...."

"Who's been talking out of turn? " Mokhnakov's inflamed eyes bored into the soldiers. They shrugged. Pafnutiev tapped his forehead and winked at Mokhnakov, who was on the point of letting fly with something blasting on the subject, but caught sight of Boris' white face. "The convoy! " Mokhnakov explained. "The same convoy that took the POW away is now at the regiment's disposal. We couldn't possibly catch up with the front line on foot even if we were to walk the whole winter."

Lusya stood pressing her back against the door. Her white shawl hung loose, exposing the black ribbons running down the front of her dress, and the low neck. Boris stood in the middle of the kitchen, riveted to the spot. "What's the matter with you? " Mokhnakov's look seemed to ask him.

Soldiers growled at one another, and cursed the war as they gathered their belongings; they kept bumping into Boris. Shkalik was rummaging in the straw, searching for his belt. Mokhnakov shifted the straw with his felt boot, lifted the snake-like belt with his boot and kicked it up so that it landed on Shkalik's head. "You need a wet-nurse! "

A soldier has very few things to gather, so that however slow the men were they soon had everything ready, then all at once they started saying goodbye to Lusya, shaking hands with her. They were quite used to doing it: maybe they had seen a thousand or two billets as they moved along with the front line.

"Get a jerk on, look sharp, brother Slavs! " Mokhnakov urged them, as he kept tossing up a coin, displeased with something. "A lorry's not a horse, it won't wait for you! "

The soldiers lit up and one after the other left the house, dragging the straw all over the kitchen with their boots. The house grew empty and cold. Lusya pushed the door shut with her back and seemed to fall into the room, as if into a cellar.

"Do I have to apologise, or what? "

Cramming a stack of letters and a towel into his mapcase, Boris looked up unseeingly at Mokhnakov. The latter returned the look with a sidelong glance, muttered something, slapped on his cap over one ear, and tossed up a coin to the very ceiling, but failed to catch it. Then he left, banging the door. Boris watched the soldiers snatched from the warm house out into the cold and, before entering the front room, he stood waiting for a moment, as if on the very edge of a chasm. Then with a single movement he put his mapcase over his shoulder, adjusted the collar of his greatcoat and pushed the door.

Lusya was sitting on the bench at the window, her chin cupped in her hands. She was looking out. A button slipped from its button-hole on the cuff of her dress, and the open cuff looked like two wings. Boris buttoned it up, joining the wings, and touched her hand. He had to say something, and the best thing would have been something jocular. But no jokes came to his mind.

"They're waiting for you," said Lusya turning round. Once again her eyes seemed to have that distant look in them, and her voice was calm and ordinary.

"Yes."

"Go then. I won't see you off. I can't." She turned away again, cupping her dimpled chin in her hands. There was something touching and yet comic in her poise, in her firmly pressed lips and her fluttering eyelashes. She was like a schoolgirl who suddenly becomes capricious at a school-leaving party.

A minute passed.

"But what can I do?" Boris shifted from one foot to the other and adjusted his mapcase. "It's time for me to leave." Once again he shifted from foot to foot, and again adjusted the case. Lusya said nothing. Her chin trembled, her eyelashes fluttered, the cuff came unbuttoned again, and the tail of her plait slipped into the wet groove of the window-frame. Boris squeezed the moisture from the end of her plait, and unwillingly let it fall. "You can't blame me," he said scarcely audibly, keeping his hand on her back above the low neck of her dress. He could feel the tender, silky warmth under her plait like the warmth of a bird's nest. "My dearest!" With a great effort Boris restrained himself from pressing his lips against the warm skin, as tender as a child's.

"Of course," said Lusya, looking at her hands, sensing that he had managed to overcome his feelings. Her fingers immediately came to life and fluttered about, adjusting the ribbons on her dress; then she pressed her hands to her throat: "Or course, nobody's to blame...."

"Goodbye then...." Clumsily, like a new conscript at his first drill, Boris turned round, shut the door after him softly and carefully, as if it were the door of a sick-room, and stood waiting a little, glancing round the kitchen to see if anyone had left anything behind.

Nobody had.

They've forgotten to clear away the straw. They mucked up the room and went away. Like they always do.... Well, never mind, what does it matter now.... One should say his goodbyes quickly and go.... Boris kicked the straw into one corner, and ran out to catch up with his platoon.

Outside soldiers were heading for the square from all directions, the snow crunching under their boots like crisp cabbage. Whitish smoke—the people here used straw for heating—hung in a cloud above the village, which was situated between two wooded hills, in the wide valley of a small river which broke into two arms here and joined another river, a bigger one. On the other side, along the bank, were the houses and the orchards of a hamlet, with a chapel in the middle.

Boris looked at it in amazement, for he did not remember noticing the chapel before. The houses across the river were badly damaged; the cupola had been knocked off the chapel. The wooden bridge had been burnt, the railings had collapsed, the ice on the river had broken up, and the black water was steaming. The stoves in the houses were being heated, and the smoke was trailing along the river. In the village on this side the house that had been burning in the night was smoking black beyond the vegetable patches.

Why on earth had the Germans not defended this side of the river, instead of retreating into open country, hiding in the ravines, apparently hoping to break through our lines from there? Every war has a character of its own, its own laws. Sometimes a platoon or even a bigger detachment may be practically wiped out, yet one or two men may come through it without a scratch. Sometimes a whole village may be smashed to pieces with bombs and shells, yet one house may remain intact right in the middle of it. All around such a house would be ruins, with only the stoves standing exposed, yet that one house would even have every window intact.

Now that the battalion commander had transport, he felt quite the great military leader and immediately showed it to the others. He looked Boris over, seemingly from a distance, as if searching for the changes in Boris and in himself. With his hand encased in a tight-fitting leather glove—a lady's glove, by the look of it—the battalion commander was imperiously indicating which lot should travel in which lorry and what interval should be maintained between them.

The soldiers boarded the lorries in high spirits, cracking jokes. There is no crowd better-natured than soldiers who have had a good night's sleep and a hot meal and who in addition have just learned that there is no need for them to foot-slog it to the front line.

The Ukrainian girls in similar yellow sheepskin coats trimmed with fur and wearing brightly coloured shawls on their heads materialised from nowhere. These white-toothed, strong, healthy girls seemed to come from some picture by Malyavin or Kustodiev, or more likely from some prewar poster.

There was not a soldier who could pass the girls just like that. Some tried to say a pleasing word to them, others gave them a pat, and there were some who tried to put their hands inside their coats. The girls giggled and protested shrilly, repelling the attacks of the infantry: "Get away with you! ", "What d'you think you're doing? ", "Now, now! Goodness me! ", "You'd better get going! "

But it was obvious that they did not want to see soldiers go and were thriving on their attentions.

So far Boris experienced no pain from the parting. All he felt was the pressure of the collar of his tunic, still damp and frozen hard: the collar of his topcoat again rubbed his neck, and the chafed part was inflamed; either the cold or the hard collar made it difficult to breathe, his thoughts seemed to congeal in his mind, to come almost to a standstill, but his heart, his very life which had been given such an impetus the previous night, sped on as if independent of him. They would speed on for a long time yet, but before they came to a standstill he would be overtaken by grief and pain. But Boris did not know this yet. He busied himself around the lorries, his excitement growing every minute, he even joked with the Ukrainian girls and patted them on the back. He had changed greatly in a short time. He had never even dared give girls the glad eye before, let alone touch them.

Battalion Commander Filkin was astonished: "You're getting to be a real man, Boris! "

Boris was on the point of cracking a joke back when he saw Lusya. She was running, rushing towards him, the woollen shawl thrown over her head, wearing the same black shoes. She threw her arms round Boris in view of everyone, and started kissing him, then getting into the lorry she kissed every one of the soldiers who had stayed at her house—saying that she'd come to regard them as her own kin and kith, exhorting them to look after their lieutenant and to be sure not to give Shkalik any drink....

The soldiers who had spent the night in other houses looked on with envy and loudly demanded their share of attention. Lantsov pulled one shoe off Lusya's foot and shook the snow out. Supporting herself on Malyshev's shoulder, she stood on one foot, laughing through her tears, talking on and on....

"May God preserve you, daughter! " said Lantsov, as he put the shoe on Lusya's foot, while Karyshev, adjusting the shawl over her head, stroked her hair lightly.

The lorries started off quickly, like restless horses. Boris embraced Lusya hard, so that her nose pressed painfully against the buckle of his mapcase, and for some time afterwards that pain was all she felt.

"Lieutenant, Lieutenant! " the driver chivvied Boris. "The others are off—and I don't know the way."

Soldiers passing in other lorries shouted laughing remarks.

"In olden times I would have prayed," said Lusya, tugging at the lapels of his coat. "I'd have howled, keened...."

"Don't you dare! That's all I need! " growled Boris and began disentangling himself from her, looking back at the lorries with apprehension. "You'll catch cold. You'd better go." He jumped into the cabin of the lorry, banged the metal door, and at once opened it again to apologise for everything but the engine came to life with a growl of satisfaction and the lorry shot off at top speed, so that Boris' body was pressed against the back of the seat, while Lusya's receding figure was immediately obscured in a cloud of exhaust. And that's how she stayed in his memory—lost, with a look of bewilderment.

The soldiers in the lorries were singing, whistling and exclaiming cheerfully. Behind them in the trampled snow cigarette ends were still smouldering, clouds of bluish exhaust smoke hung above the road, but the convoy was already outside the village, climbing the hill, the head of the column crawling into the forest.

"The address! " Lusya shouted as she darted after the lorries. "Oh God, you don't know the address! " Stunned, almost beside herself, Lusya made a futile attempt to run after the lorries.

On the outskirts of the pine forest—quiet, indifferent and almost gloomy—the very same forest where the skeleton of that German still hung from a pine tree, the first blunt-nosed lorry brushed its roof against low-hanging pine branches and the snow cascaded, obscuring everything from Lusya like a curtain descending upon a stage.

She stopped, exhausted, breathless.

What good would the address be? What could it change? Time seemed to have stood still for a single night, and now it was speeding on, inexorably counting off the minutes and hours of human life. The night had gone, disappeared beyond the rim of the new day. It was impossible now to put matters right, to bring anything back.

Everything had been and everything was gone.

Another convoy was moving past her. The soldiers gestured at the snow, at the houses, at Lusya's feet. Unable even to raise her hand and wave to them, Lusya swayed, as if bowing to them, repeating the same words all the time: "Win the war quickly.... Come back alive...."

She got home half-frozen. Her shoes sounded like stones against the floor. There was snow in her hair, the end of her damp plait was frosted over, and it swung like a plumb line against her back. Without bothering to undress, whimpering like a lost puppy, Lusya climbed into bed, unconsciously hoping that it might still retain some of his warmth.

Her house had been commandeered by a rear detachment, and an elderly but smart sergeant came in without knocking, and began apologising: "Everything was open and we thought the house was deserted...."

"You can stay if you like."

Lusya shook the shoes off her feet, and tugged feebly at the blanket, seeking something to cling to, moaning, howling through stiff lips and chattering teeth. Her dark, tearless eyes had an absent look, and suddenly acquired a strange gleam as if they had been touched with frost, had lost something vital, been emptied of life.

Part Four
QUIETUS

Gathering the ragged skirts of its white cloak, winter hurriedly receded northwards from the front. The naked body of the war-torn earth was healing in the sun, helped by the snow water and the fresh green grass. The willows came into leaf, the sunny slopes were spattered with violets, coltsfoot gleamed here and there and snowdrops shot through to the surface like bullets. Flocks of birds flew above the dug-outs, growing silent over the front and breaking ranks. The farm animals were taken out into the pastures for the first time. Cows, sheep and goats cropped the low-growing grass. Their herdsmen and shepherds were not there—schoolchildren and old people had taken over.

Warm, moist winds blew. The soldiers in the dug-outs were overwhelmed by nostalgia, which came flooding into the trenches along with the melting snow.

This was the time when the infantry regiment, which had suffered heavy losses during the winter battles, was withdrawn from the front for reforming. As soon as it was put in to reserve, the deputy political instructor of the regiment got a visit from a young lieutenant—as fleshless as a dried fish—who asked for leave of absence.

The deputy political instructor's first thought was that the lieutenant was joking, was pulling his leg, and he was on the point of throwing him out, when a note of terrible grief in the young man's appearance stopped him. He tried to draw out the lieutenant and at the end of the talk, he found himself heavy-hearted.

"We-e-ell," he said, breaking the long silence and puffing at his Ukrainian pipe. Then he repeated again frowning: "We-e-ell." The lieutenant was like many other platoon commanders he had known, with appropriate awards: two orders of the Red Star, one with part of the enamelling missing, and also the Military Service medal. Yet there was something in the lieutenant ... you could see he was a romantic, a dreamer. That type of man was given to sudden bursts of emotion. For instance this youthful knight of the woeful countenance was quite sure that one could love only once in life, that no other woman could compare with the one he had known, and furthermore, he was likely to go absent without leave in order to shed tears on the bosom of his beloved....

Yes, I can see he's quite capable of running away, devil take him! the D.P.I. told himself, pitying the lieutenant and feeling pleased at the same time that simple human emotions had not deserted the man; feeling pleased that the lieutenant had managed somehow to fall in love, that he was tortured by the feeling, pining for his beloved, thirsting for happiness. But if he ran away and was then packed off to a punishment squad....

The D.P.I. was deeply perturbed. He shifted about on his creaking stool, and stamped some strong tobacco into his pipe. He lit up, loosened the tobacco a bit, and uttered briefly, as a commander should: "Stop playing the fool and come to your senses! "

Sorrow burnt in the lieutenant's eyes. No words could bring him to his senses. Evidently he had decided firmly on something—exactly what, the D.P.I. did not know—and so he continued to talk, asking the lieutenant about his home and family, discussing the war and the Second Front, hoping to think up a way out while talking.

"Wait! " the D.P.I. even jumped up in his agitation, kicking the stool as if it were a football.

"You were born under a lucky star, Kostyaev! You don't know how lucky you are! My advice to you is don't try your luck at cards as you're so successful in love! ..."

He recalled that the political administration at the front was going to hold a seminar for junior political instructors. As many of the political instructors of the regiment had been killed during the offensive, he decided he would send Platoon Commander Kostyaev to it on his own responsibility and later, perhaps, would make him battalion political instructor—the man was young and well read, and in addition had seen plenty of fighting. "It'll be quite a way away but I expect you to be at the seminar on the dot! Will 24 hours be enough for you to spend there? "

"An hour would do." The lieutenant did not seem overjoyed. He had waited so long for this very moment, and something had died within him....

"Give me her address, I have to record it in the papers."

"But I don't know her address."

"You don't know? "

"I don't know her surname either." The lieutenant looked down and paused. "At times I think it was a dream.... And at times...."

"Well, you're a one, aren't you! " The D.P.I. looked at the lieutenant with renewed interest. "Never mind...." He made a helpless gesture. "But present yourself this evening to draw your rations, or you'll starve to death...."

What was he thinking about? What was he hoping for? What he had in mind? Was he thinking of how it would be when the two of them met?

He would come to the village, and sit down on the bench not far from her home, between two poplars looking like a couple of spindles. He remembered the bench and the poplars because it was not far from them that he had seen Lusya for the last time. He would remain sitting on the bench until she came out of her house. If she passed by without looking at him ... he would get up, go straight to the station and leave. Somehow he had persuaded himself into believing she would stop, would ask: "My goodness, Boris! You haven't run away from the front, have you? " And he would answer, just to scare her a bit: "Yes, I have! I've deserted for the sake of seeing you! "

And so there he sat, as he had planned, on the bench under the poplars covered with the first sticky whitish, tender leaves; he sat covered in dust from head to foot, waiting. Lusya appeared in the doorway, a shopping bag over her arm, and locked the door. He watched her intently, as she started on her way. What a miracle! She wore the same yellow dress, the same shoes. Only the shoes looked quite worn out, the toes were scuffed, and the dress had lost it black ribbons, the cuffs were badly worn and limp. She was thinner, with shadows beneath her eyes, her plait was arranged in a bun at the back of her head; her face looked older and sterner. She passed him by.

There was nothing for it but to go back to the station, to hurry back to his detachment, to go to the front and to die in battle.... But at that moment Lusya slowed down, and carefully, as if her neck were aching, turned her head, and exclaimed: "Boris?! "

She came up to him, touched him, ran her hand over his medal and orders, over the wound stripe, and stroked his cheek, feeling his stubbly beard.

"It's really you, Boris! "

With her shopping bag still over her arm, she slid down and lay at the feet of the lieutenant, pressing her face against them, frantically covering his well-worn, dusty boots with passionate kisses....

* * *

No, there was nothing like that nor could there have been. The infantry regiment had not been sent for reforming—it was reformed in action, and Boris, losing one after another of his soldiers before he ever got used to them, moved further and further, foot-slogging it with his platoon, and they were now in the Western Ukraine.

Shkalik was smitten with the night blindness that always afflicted him in spring, and was sent to a hospital, where he stayed on working as an orderly, which pleased the lieutenant greatly. But pretty soon Shkalik was back at the front, beaming because he was among his comrades again.

...Meanwhile the offensive continued, though it was already on the wane. The troops in the forward area were waging a battle of local importance, trying to improve their positions before digging in for a prolonged defence.

The headquarters of the regiment sent orders for the lieutenant's platoon to carry out a reconnaissance of a hamlet, if possible to take a rise on the right hand side of it, and to entrench themselves there. Mokhnakov spent a whole day in the battle outpost studying the terrain and all the possibilities through the binoculars, and at night he and his boys quietly wiped out the artillerymen and a German outpost. He managed to get into the hamlet with a group of automatic machine-gunners, setting up quite a racket there, letting rip with the guns, so that the nazis panicked and fled from both hamlet and hill.

The gunners settled in the deserted houses, which were connected by long trenches with the low hill, and were blissfully happy because there was no need for them to start digging. On top of the rise an observation post was left intact—even the stove was still burning merrily and the telephone had not been disconnected. "Hitler *Kaputt!*" the soldiers took turns to shout into the phone. From the other side the Germans answered *"Russische Schwein."* Snatching the receiver from one another, the triumphant gunners swore at the Germans, teased them and sang lewd songs.

The defeated enemy could not stand such polemics and disconnected the teleplone after promising the Russian Ivans *"Gross Kaputt."* In no time at all artillerymen turned up at the observation post the infantry had managed to win, and yanked the gleeful soldiers out of their cushy quarters. Swearing at the gunners, those gods of war who managed to turn up to take what wasn't theirs, the infantrymen went to the hamlet, and began cooking potatoes, recounting to one another how they had chatted to the Germans on the phone.

Mokhnakov and Karyshev were left at the observation post as liaison with the artillerymen. In the morning it was found that the entire slope of the hill, the depression beyond the hamlet's vegetable plots, and the vegetable plots themselves had been mined since winter—the Germans had been establishing another line of defence.

Shortly before midday a soldier was sighted out in the field, heading foolhardily across the depression, evidently trying to reach the rise and the hamlet in the shortest possible way.

"Who the devil can that be?" asked Karyshev, shielding his eyes with his hands from the sun.

Mokhnakov adjusted the telescope and looked through it: "It's a sapper," he announced with a grim smile, and before he could say anything else something banged like a door in an empty house, a grassy hummock leapt into the air and scattered, splashing out yellow smoke. "He-e-elp!" the words reached the men in the trenches, and Karyshev, straining his ears, beat himself in agitation on the thighs: "Christ, it's Pafnutiev!" and cursed: "What dragged you here, you old devil?"

"O-o-oh! A-a-ah! He-e-elp! He-e-elp!"

Karyshev stopped swearing, breathed heavily and began heaving himself out of the trench. Mokhnakov grabbed him by the belt: "What d'you think you're doing, you fool? Tired of living or what?"

Mokhnakov searched the entire hollow through the telescope. The terrain was covered with rotten leaves, on the hummocks lay strands of reed and hair grass and marram, through which the early, still whitish shoots of marsh marigold and needles of sedge were appearing. Among the hummocks, sending up sprays of water and mud, Pafnutiev was thrashing about, yelling and screaming, and above him a marsh snipe circled frantically, uttering shrill cries.

"You stay here!" Mokhnakov told Karyshev. He slithered down the slope, then got up, and, studying the ground attentively, checking every step he took, like a hunter approaching the mating place of woodcocks, he started down into the marshy depression. He was attacked by lapwings, which seemed to tease him, flitting past his face with mournful cries. "Go away, you fools! Off with you! " Mokhnakov wiped the sweat off his forehead and nose with his sleeve. "When it blows up where will you be? "

He managed somehow to reach Pafnutiev, and pulled him out of the mud. Pafnutiev's legs were torn open up to the loins by an anti-personnel mine. The grass around them had turned white from the explosion and smelt of rotten garlic. Mokhnakov suddenly recalled how his daughter—now quite and eligible girl—had after tasting a piece of salami for the first time kept telling everybody that garlic smelt of sausage. It was so rarely, and always unexpectedly, that Mokhnakov thought of his children, of his family. He now smiled at the precious recollection while Pafnutiev stopped shouting, scared at the sight of Mokhnakov's smile. "Cheer up," Mokhnakov muttered. "There, have a smoke! " He pushed a cigarette between Pafnutiev's lips, and patted his pockets, searching for matches—he must have lost the box somewhere. Pafnutiev feverishly reached for his breast pocket where his cherished cigarette lighter was:

"Take it as a memory."

"You and your memory."

The wounds required plenty of awkward bandaging. Mokhnakov pulled another packet from his pocket and tore it open with his teeth. Pafnutiev kept moaning and blaming himself.

"Oh, be quiet! You make my head swim! " Mokhnakov stopped him. "We have to help one another, nobody can survive in a war otherwise, so keep quiet...."

"Please get me out of here! I've a wife and children at home. You're a family man yourself.... My whole life.... I'll pray for you for the rest of my life...."

Meanwhile a stretcher was improvised in the trenches out of a couple of poles and a groundsheet. Before dispatching Pafnutiev from the trenches they poured a mouthful of vodka into his throat. Pafnutiev choked, opened with difficulty eyes that glinted feverishly and seemed to recognise

Boris, Karyshev, and Malyshev. "Forgive me, brothers! Goodbye! " Pafnutiev fell back on the stretcher and put his hand over his face. His Adam's apple, covered with grey stubble, worked up and down.

Karyshev and Malyshev lifted the stretcher. Boris watched until they reached the depression, while Mokhnakov grumbled away to himself as he tried to clean his tunic and trousers.

* * *

He was troublesome, that fireman Pafnutiev, he had a kink, as the two pals said, and they suffered for that man with his kink.

After carrying Pafnutiev to the field hospital—he was still alive—Karyshev and Malyshev were returning to the front and were already nearing the hamlet, tired after their effort, and not as watchful as they might have been. Suddenly, without an echo, a shot rang out. Karyshev took another step or two, still enjoying the blessed peace of rural eventide. Surely it couldn't have been a shot. It must have been a village herds-man cracking his long whip as he drove the cows back home from their first spring outing, their first taste of grass after a winter in the sheds. Karyshev's legs were buckling beneath him, but he could still see in his mind's eye the cottages, the poplars sharply silhouetted against the evening sky, and the pale greenish sunset—when his eyes caught sight of the front line, the belt of the trenches seemed to lash at his eyes, everything around him made a sharp turn and crashed on top of him—houses, trees, and sky....

"Brother! " shouted Malyshev in wild panic, trying to catch his falling comrade.

"Down! Down! " Mokhnakov kept shouting, running towards them along the trenches. Karyshev and Malyshev—experienced soldiers—dropped at once, flat amidst the hummocky grass, so that the sniper wouldn't finish them off.

The bullet had hit Karyshev beneath his right nipple, mangling a corner of his guard's badge. He was still alive when they carried him into a house in the hamlet, but he would not let them take him to hospital.

"I'm done for," he said with difficulty, gasping.

Malyshev tried to put something soft beneath Karyshev's head and back to make breathing easier; he kept wiping away the red froth that bubbled on Karyshev's lips, entreating him: "Won't you have a drink of water? Or is there something else you want? Tell us what you want. Just ask!" Malyshev's lips trembled, his face was grey, and his bald patch smeared with dirt. All at once he seemed to have shrunk, lost weight, and it was especially noticeable now that he was an elderly man. Boris waved his hand, gesturing to the soldiers to leave the house, and they went gloomily. Boris knelt before Karyshev, adjusted the straw around him, and remained as he was, not knowing what to say or do. A long thin sound filled the room, as persistent as a telephone buzzer. It was Malyshev trying vainly to suppress his sobbing.

Karyshev was dying. He shut his eyes—the sockets had become two round hollows—then opened them as if saying goodbye to the lieutenant. His gaze shifted to Malyshev. Boris realised he should leave the two friends alone, he straightened up and walked out on numb legs.

"My family—" Karyshev managed to whisper.

"Don't worry about them!... Be at peace about them in your final hour," Malyshev started keening in a sharp high voice like the true countryman he was. "Your family is my family.... How can I live now! What's there for me to live for."

Boris stepped into the darkness, groped about, and finding a pole or a pillar pressed his forehead against its firm cold side, repeating incessantly as if threatening someone: "That's how Russian people die! That's how they meet their end!"

It was quiet in the hamlet. Beyond it flares rose at intervals, their dead, melancholy light throwing into relief parts of orchards, little white houses hiding in them, and the sharp-topped poplars along the road, thrusting to the sky.

"He's dead."

Boris clasped Malyshev and not quite knowing what he was doing, began stroking Malyshev's cool bald head. Sniffing loudly, Malyshev told him what bosom friends he and Karyshev had been before the war, how they had got married on the same day, how they had joined the collective farm together. Whenever they had a drop too much Karyshev, wise man, would head straight for his home, without any noise, while he, Malyshev, fool that he was, would shout for the whole street to hear: "Open up the gates wide! ..."

In the night they buried Karyshev beneath the stars, quietly, without unnecessary fuss. They made a cross from a couple of poles, and the grave of this peasant from the Altai somehow fitted this abandoned West Ukrainian graveyard, with its assortment of crosses and tombstones carved with unintelligible inscriptions marking old graves here and there. Elder bushes grew around the graveyard and a low, prickly sloe hedge, already showing green, ran around it. A sinister bird rose startled from the single old tree which stood among the graves, and disappeared into the darkness.

Three crosses with horned helmets on top of them indicated fresh graves. As the party was returning to the hamlet Malyshev rushed over to these crosses made of poplar which was now throwing out new leaves, attacked them with a low growl, wrenched them out and threw them over the hedge. The rusty helmets followed the crosses, falling with loud clatter in the darkness.

Mokhnakov withdrew from people altogether, and crawled into his shell. Clusters of wrinkles ran from the corners of his eyes to behind his ears. His mouth became pinched, and the lips were chapped. He walked clumsily, as though he had frostbite. He slept little, ate little, did not drink at all, and smoked all the time. His military duty, however, he carried out with furious zest—he sought death.

But death kept away too.

He got some clean underwear and a knapsack. He put on the underwear, and hid the knapsack on the floor of the pillbox. There was something in it that felt like a round loaf of home-baked bread, but the men nosed out the truth: it was an antitank mine. What the sergeant wanted it for was anybody's guess.

After failing to recover immediately the rise taken from

right under their noses by our soldiers, the Germans sent their tanks into the attack. The Soviet artillery fired, damaging one tank, while the rest hurried on to the trenches, soon reaching the rise. The anti-tank gunners, after each onslaught on the fore-armour of the tanks, threw themselves into the foxholes, ploughing the muddy earth with their noses.

The tanks started "ironing" the trench. Sergeant-Major Mokhnakov kept his eyes glued to the telescope.

An old tank moving in a cloud of dust, its left, slightly loose track ringing metallically with every movement, its gun swivelling in motion, doggedly rolled onto the observation post. Fresh scratches shone in the fore-armour of the tank, the camouflage paint was peeling off like rags, like old skin being shed by a snake, and a fresh seam of electric welding ran along the belly from the fore hatch.

The tank had been fighting for a long time now, its seasoned driver manoeuvred smartly, bravely, hiding in the cloud of dust, taking care not to expose the flanks. One like that could do the damage of ten tanks! It must not be allowed past the trenches!

"The time's come, lad! " Swinging his sack over his shoulder, Mokhnakov pulled at the fat cigarette for the last time, stamped out the fag-end and jumped out of the trench. He allowed the tank to come so close that the driver swung back when through the open hatch he spotted the man materialising from the smoke and dust. On the other hand Mokhnakov instantly caught sight of the driver's burnt face, with its baby pink skin—the man had neither eyebrows nor lashes. He had been burnt more than once.

They looked at each other just for a moment but it was not difficult to guess from the deathly horror that showed in the pale eyes of the driver that he had understood: this Russian with the grim, set face was determined to die.

The tank jerked as the driver braked. But Mokhnakov had already managed to dive under the caterpillar track, which pressed his body into the previous year's dusty stubble. From the explosion of the anti-tank mine the old tank cracked open along the new seam and the tracks were hurled as far as the trenches.

At the spot where Sergeant-Major Mokhnakov had thrown himself under the tank a pit was left edged with scorched earth, the remaining stubble blackened. The sergeant-major's body, together with his war-ravaged heart, had been blown to smithereens and scattered all over the rise, the sunny side of which was already showing green.

In Mokhnakov's mapcase, left at the observation post, they found his medals pinned to a piece of cotton, and a note to the platoon commander. In it Mokhnakov asked him to take care of his wife and children. The address: the district centre of Motygino, Mylnaya Street....

But a few days later Boris himself was wounded in the right shoulder by a mortar splinter. He huddled for a whole day in a little dug-out, on half-rotted straw, nursing his arm, which was bandaged to his side; it seemed to have filled with blue dye and now shone as if smeared with gum. There was no one to take over from him—Mokhnakov had been killed, the other N.C.O.s had been lost during the spring offensive and Lantsov had been taken to the army newspaper. Of the old soldiers only Malyshev and Shkalik remained.

Tired and nervy after the battle, smeared from head to foot with the clay of the trenches, his soldiers who for the most part had come from hospital or were men gathered from Ukrainian villages, and kept going on whatever edibles came their way—for communications were cut by floods— went calmly on with their usual chores, now and then turning up at the commander's dug-out not so much for orders but to find out whether he needed anything.

Towards night the man on duty handed Boris a mess-tin, and left a rye cake he had made himself, wrapped up in a piece of cloth. Boris put his lips to the warm rim of the mess-tin, and in small hurried mouthfuls drank boiled water flavoured with old sugar beets, which did duty as tea. The cake was gritty—the soldiers had crushed the previous year's grain with their rifle butts and baked the cakes on sapper's spades held over the fire. It was as much as Boris could do to chew these pieces of mouldy grain stuck together, and he forced himself to eat it to the last crumb—the soldiers were sharing with him the last they had, and he respected their solicitude and care.

He drank what remained of the beet tea to relieve his burning throat, and curled up in his damp den. An industrious beetle awakened by the spring was digging the earth and the soil crumbled and poured onto Boris' face, some particles rolling into his ear.

Next morning the indestructible Filkin, his face adorned with a far from aristocratic beard, brought up reinforcements for the platoon—some fifteen soldiers born in 1925, and a junior lieutenant who had just finished military school.

Boris paid his farewells to the platoon, wished the new commander with his Komsomol badge long life and friendly relations with the soldiers; Battalion Commander Filkin embraced Boris and patted him on the back: "See you come back, Boris, I'll be waiting for you."

A horse and cart caught up with the lieutenant along the road. In it was Shkalik, who stood lapping vigorously with the reins. He had filled out during his time in hospital, and was pleased with everything, and especially with the cart, which the soldiers had managed to get by the simple expedient of pushing the driver off and throwing out the load of empty boxes. Then they had dispatched Shkalik to catch up with their wounded commander.

The lieutenant climbed into the cart with great pleasure and lay there with his face pressed against the straw, which smelt of mice. He was tossed from side to side when a wheel caught in a pothole, he was rolled about when the cart got into deep tank ruts, but even so he continued to doze, torpid from pain and fatigue.

Making encouraging noises and slapping the bow-legged horse on the flanks with the reins, Shkalik kept telling the tale of how clever they'd been about getting their hands on the horse and cart, of how the driver had at first reached for his rifle, but later on, when they had given him their rough cake and beet tea, and the battalion commander had treated him to a bit of good tobacco, he had bowed to the inevitable.

In the muddy hollow the cart got well and truly stuck. Boris tried to help Shkalik but their weak efforts proved ineffective. Calling out "Just a moment, Comrade Lieutenant," Shkalik energetically ran ahead of the horse, dragging it by the reins.

Pulling the dangerously creaking cart, the horse bypassed the swampy patch and charged into some bushes. Boris, his head lolling weakly, sat on the other side of the hollow, leaning against a willow trunk scarred with wheel marks. Suddenly there was a flash, a deafening roar, and billowing, acrid smoke. Coughing and choking, Boris dashed blindly down the slope. In front of him a wheel from the cart struck the earth and rolled away, crashing into a thicket; quivering bits of something soft rose above the thinning smoke and fell with a smack into the mud, and a strong smell of warm blood and explosives assailed his nostrils.

Shkalik had always been careless. But he, the platoon commander, who should have known better with his experience in the trenches, with his acute, now almost canine sense—what a fool he had proved to be, why had he relaxed his vigilance, why hadn't he sensed the danger? Here they were—right by him—the skull and cross-bones signs left by the sappers. What was the matter with him? Why was it that everything that had helped him hold onto life seemed to have gone numb within him?

"Poor luckless boy!" exclaimed, or perhaps thought, Boris, and rubbed his swollen, itching eyelids. Utterly at a loss, he stood for some time, looking around as if memorising this inconspicuous deserted place churned up by wheels, by bombs and shells, and he started off through the forest for the field hospital—stunned and deafened.

His wound ached terribly, his eyes smarted from the explosives, but there was no suffering in his heart. He was immune. He was immune to it all now, he'd seen so much. Only deep in his devastated self, in the near-void within him, something came to life, pushed against his breast, then collapsed, adding its mite of lead to the already entrenched, permanent pain. And still heavier became his heart.

There were crowds of wounded at the field hospital. Officers were attended to before soldiers, but Boris, who was accustomed to sharing the soldiers' lot, joined the general queue, letting those of the soldiers he thought worse off than himself go ahead of him.

Only a day later was he placed on the operating table.

The slow-moving, taciturn nurse did not bother to soak the bandages which by now had stuck together in rusty-coloured layers resembling three-ply, but tore them off; she mopped up the blood gushing from the wound with cotton wool and gave him a white pill. Soon Boris felt a cottony, clinging sleep steal over him.

A doctor, his sharp eyes glistening moistly and angrily behind his old-fashioned gilt-rimmed spectacles, awoke Boris when he banged him on the shoulder with his fist, asking where he felt the echo of the pain. "I don't know," said Boris in a limp, distant way, because the pain reverberated throughout his body. The doctor looked at his patient puzzled.

"Managed to get a drink or two already," he said and prodded the wound with a probe.

The blood came out faster, running in a stream that tickled Boris' back and stomach. He felt himself drifting away somewhere. They gave him an injection, rubbed his temples with ammonia-soaked cotton wool, and opened up his shoulder with a lancet, cutting it crosswise....

The senior nurse at the field hospital assured the lieutenant that in a week or two at the most he would be able to go back. This was unlikely—there was no such thing as a simple shoulder wound and with a wound like that one could not stir or make a single movement without aching all over. But Boris did not shout or swear, he did not demand to be evacuated to the rear, but, having become accustomed to his pain, he lay quietly in a tent, or in a field hospital lorry moving him from one location to another, gazing at the sky, wrapped in a permanent soothing peace, which seemed to swaddle him in a baby-like doze.

On a pleasant sunny day when the breeze brought the smell of snow from the forest and from the fields, where grey patches of snow still lay here and there—the smell of melting snow and the bitter honey aroma of the willow in bloom— Boris crawled out of his tent in his patched underwear, threw the much-darned blanket on the ground, and sank onto it. He sat leaning against the scaly trunk of a tree of a variety whose name he did not know, and he felt at peace with the world. Buzzing busily, their wings catching the sun, streams of bees flew past and settled on the flowering willow. The willow bushes hummed and swarmed with bees, they seemed to be smoking, and throwing out sparks.

Boris fell asleep to the bees' intoxicating hum, to the calls of little birds moving in the tree above his head, to the submachine gun-like rattle of a stork that was walking about the field, swaying drunkenly, every now and then stopping and standing on one foot, to all the peace-inducing sounds of spring so unlike riotous, springtime Siberia.

Although hearing every sound, feeling through the blanket the cold from the ground, which had thawed just on the surface, sensing the currents running through the earth, the stirring of the newly-born grass, Boris seemed to hear nothing, as if everything going on around him was being experienced not by him but by someone else.

Something touched his hand very gently, tickling it, and Boris opened his eyes with difficulty. A pretty butterfly was crawling along his wrist, with the serious air of a young doctor, as if probing with its antennae his soap-dried skin.

He watched the wary butterfly for a long time, so long that his eyes saw the black wing-like trimmings on the sleeves of the yellow dress, and the window-pane with its frosty tracery....

"Lu-sy-a!"

The butterfly fluttered off his wrist and settled on a bluish flower bud.

"Lu-sy-a!"

The butterfly clung to a naked stem like an emptied blood vessel, its wings pulsating, ready to take off.

"You haven't seen Lusya by any chance?"

Boris, smiling foolishly, gazed at a short-legged woman carrying a new zinc bucket over her arm.

"I'm asking you, have you seen our cook by any chance?"

He tried to make sense of what she was saying.

"What's the matter, have you lost your wits entirely? Don't you remember the cook who feeds you three times a day?"

Meanwhile the butterfly had flown away.

"I don't remember anything," said Boris with annoyance.

"I can quite believe it." The woman turned away, her short legs carrying her off towards the stream, and she called out even more loudly: "Lu-sy-a! Where the devil are you?"

"Where the devil are you, Lusya?" Boris dropped face down onto the blanket, which had a strong hospital smell. Lu-sy-a! Did you really exist, Lu-sy-a! ...

He sensed with his very breast the earth's hardly perceptible breathing, he felt that his pain, his feelings for the girl, his weak protest neither helped nor hindered the earth. It was busy with its eternal round. It was ready to give birth. And like every woman bearing a child, the earth was able to hear only what was going on within itself.

On his next round the chief doctor of the field hospital examined Boris, first his chest, then his shoulder-blades, knocked with his fist under Boris' right shoulder-blade, and seeing him flinch, asked sternly: "Painful?"

Boris admitted sheepishly: "It is."

The doctor regarded him with a touch of hostility through his glasses as he wound the blood-coloured veins of the stethoscope over his hand and said: "You've been quite a time with us. Quite a time...."

Boris caught the hostility in the doctor's voice and a badly concealed suspicion. He heard the servile giggling of the same short-legged nurse who had been searching for Lusya the cook.

"It's not a health resort, only a field hospital, after all! Every bed counts," came an energetic remark from the senior nurse, a woman with a face from an icon and eyes full of mercy, the same nurse who had so heedlessly given the lieutenant just a fortnight to be cured; but he had failed her and continued to occupy a bed in the hospital.

Crucified to his bed, the lieutenant smiled in embarrassment. So that's what it was! He was occupying somebody else's bed, once again undeservedly eating the bread intended for another man, breathing the air meant for someone else, living a life of idleness, when real men were fighting and dying for his sake....

Suppressing his rising fury, Boris said softly: "Then throw me out...."

The senior nurse, spoiled by flattery, power, and the attention of men, started. The doctor's gaze shifted in confusion. This no longer young and overworked doctor was somewhat frightened of the senior nurse for reasons known to the entire hospital staff. Such icon-faced women have often been known to rule over such tractable men. With her own advantage in mind she would separate him from his family, take him to a southern town where life was easier and where it was warm, and would drive him hard, the simpleton, for ten or twenty years more until he died from overwork.

"I don't want your hypocritical mercy!" Boris said clearly, looking straight into the nurse's haughty eyes, and added, choking with fury: "Get out! Or I'll tear off your bloody bandages...."

"You dare!" the senior nurse began.

"Get out! ..."

Looking pleadingly at the nurse, the doctor was retreating to the door, sweeping his helpers out of the ward.

"Now, now, don't take on so! Calm yourself...."

"Tie this hero to his bed! Give him an injection!" the senior nurse ordered in a loud voice, so that the wounded in other wards could hear.

Lord! And she's a woman, too! thought Boris, utterly drained, feeling his anger recede.

"Well, you've asked for what's coming to you!" growled one of the patients. "And through you we'll all suffer from this front-line hussy."

"Come on, you hero!"

The blanket was whipped off Boris, the duty nurse was aiming a full syringe at him and holding a piece of spirit-soaked cotton wool in the fingers of her left hand. The lieutenant bore the injection submissively.

"Don't tie me down. Please."

After tucking the blanket round him with a conspiratorial air, the duty nurse was heard to announce loudly in the next ward that she had seen to everything just as she was told. Adding that she quite approved of the measures because, given a chance, these wounded men could be quite a nuisance.

His mind sluggish and relaxed after the injection, Boris noted to himself once again: Yes ... she's a woman too....

He woke up quite weak and listless. Soft rain was falling, tapping at the tent like a chick pecking. He could hear the distant murmur of the forest, the whisper of the melting snow slithering down in the ravines, the call of the cuckoo....

Late at night, the doctor dropped into the tent. He had his grey topcoat on and his cap was pulled down over his forehead. His boots glistened and a few half-rotten leaves were stuck to the toes. For some reason, after his nervous outburst Boris' vision and perception were more acute.

"You're not asleep?" asked the doctor, and sat down at the edge of the lieutenant's bed, turning up the hem of his damp topcoat. He took off his glasses, cleaned them, and announced dryly: "I've decided to evacuate you. We made a mistake in the diagnosis. Your wound has taken a turn for the worse." After a long pause he said with a twist of his scar-marked lips: "Osteomyelitis cannot be cured in field conditions. As for mercy—you ought to know—there are always two sides to it!"

The doctor felt like talking, but Boris maintained a discouraging silence, waiting for him to go. The rain fell harder, tapping on the tent, with the same tone, the same note, making him drowsy.

"It'll spoil the road entirely," the doctor thought aloud, and got up bending his head because of the low ceiling. "Here's my advice to you: don't draw away from the people, otherwise loneliness will crush you. It's more horrible even than war...."

Out in the open air the doctor stood for a moment or two, then Boris heard the click of a torch, a sigh, and soft squelching footsteps which were soon swallowed up by the night.

Inside the tent it became quite cosy and peaceful. The rain and the breathing of the sleeping men made the feeling of peace tangible. Boris closed his eyes and lay quietly.

The thirst for life can create tremendous powers of endurance, a man can overcome a crippling wound, he can lift a weight far above his normal ability. But when there is no thirst for life a man is only a living sack of bones. Boris knew such cases from his front-line experience: even very strong men withdrew into themselves apparently without reason, like lizards hiding in the sand; they became lonely individuals among men, and were prone to proclaiming suddenly with a shattering assurance: "I'll be killed soon." Others even said when: "Today or tomorrow." And they never made mistakes. Almost never.

* * *

...In the hospital train Boris was given a middle, side berth facing the compartment of the nurse and the orderly, which had a patched bedsheet for a curtain. The nurse and the orderly were two very overworked girls, exhausted by the daily chores. They took temperatures morning and evening, dished out soup and porridge, cut up the bread rations, handed out bed pans, washed the wounded and cheered them up as much as they could. The orderly, whose name was Arina, a friendly, patient, good-humoured girl, tried to cheer Boris up, to draw him out, but his replies were so short, his apologetic smile was so forced, that Arina was driven to leaving him in peace and concentrating her attention on other men more ready for a chat.

When Boris was not dozing he would turn his head towards the window and see women ploughing the land with the help of bulls and cows, then sowing the fields the old way, taking handfuls of grain from a bast container hanging from the shoulder and casting it upon the ground with an almost musical sweeping gesture. He saw the skeletons of houses and their exposed chimneys amidst the ploughed fields and woods. Later the train ran past the villages of Central Russia with grey-roofed houses and low grey wattle fences or stone walls. Varicoloured fields of winter wheat surrounded the rickety cottages, coming close to their very walls. Here he saw a few tractors with sowers, and horses, their heads almost touching the furrows, dragging ploughs and harrows.

The eternal labour continued on the eternal, patient earth.

On the berth below Boris', a terribly thin, elderly man lay, criss-crossed with bandaging like a revolutionary sailor swathed in cartridge belts. He just about smoked Boris with his tobacco, coughing incessantly and blowing his nose with a trumpeting sound on the hem of his army issue shirt. Tired of lying on his stomach, the man asked to be moved on to his side. Arina shifted his bony frame. After cursing and groaning for a time, he looked out of the window and gasped: "Spring!... Christ, grass! Look at the earth, the earth! All steaming and smoking! Life's coming back! Would you believe it!... That bird, the lapwing. Gambolling about up there.... Oh ... the rook ... look at the rook! Bustling about, looking for worms in the furrows ... a serious bird.... It's got one, got one! That's the boy! Gobble it up, eat your fill! O-o-o-o-oh!"

The elderly man sobbed, his whole body shaking, and from that moment on, he behaved as if he were not quite right in the head. He ate his soup hurriedly, spilling it on the sheets and the pillow, drinking the last mouthful straight from the mess-tin. He would gulp down his porridge and bread in no time, and immediately turn to the window, laughing and commenting on everything he saw: "They're ploughing with cows here, too! No, Russia's not what she used to be! That lousy bastard Hitler, what he's done to us, sod him...."

"Look, dad! Hey, dad!" his neighbours appealed to him. "Remember the nurse and the orderly—remember they're women, after all."

"What've I done, sod it all? Don't tell me I swore...."

The other men laughed at this soldier. He took their jokes in good humour and went on expressing his delight in the same way, moving restlessly on his berth, smoking the crude tobacco and noticeably improving in health every day.

"I won't be any time now, girls. You wait and see!" he shouted through the window as if the women ploughing the fields could hear him. "As soon as they patch me up in the hospital, out in the fields I'll go and they won't see me for steam!" The word "field" he almost sang out, almost sobbed it. The man gave Boris his cheerful advice, too: "Keep your

pecker up, lad! You hold on to the grass, the spring grass.
It'll pull you out! You know the strength it has—it breaks
stone! And what's that now? What's that? With a beak like
a poker?"

"It's a judcock."

"What did they want to give the bird a silly name for? It's
a woodcock! A woodcock! And that's all! "

"Let it be a woodcock, if you like, only stop that jabber,
for God's sake! "

"Did I?... Not a peep out of me, not a word! The calf,
look at the calf! Look at it prancing about! You need a
heifer, that's what you need, curse you! ..."

They went on and on to the clatter of the wheels, the
chatter of the man. The blacked-out stations were left on the
other side of Moscow. Now the night was pierced here and
there with the lights of Russian villages; a sprinkling of station lights would rush towards them, bursting outside the
windows like the fire of ack-ack guns. The clicking of the
wheels resembled an exchange of rifle fire and the more
substantial noise of the wheels going over the points was like
bomb explosions.

The lieutenant had grown so used to the sound of the
wheels and all other sounds that the train seemed to him
noiseless, grown dumb. He seemed already to regard the
world like one outside it all. What's the meaning of it?
What's it all for? What is he, this village man rejoicing at his
own resurrection? What great happiness is there in store for
him? He'll be back to his eternal tilling of the soil, and one
day he'll drop dead on to that same soil. But perhaps this
very resurrection's happiness? Perhaps the path to it and the
hope of better things—that's what lends strength to men like
this one, to millions of men?

A fit of tearful sentimentality seized the lieutenant. He
pitied his wounded neighbours, the butterfly whose wind-
squashed body he could see on the window, he felt sorry for
a felled tree, the emaciated cows in the fields, the pale children he saw at the stations. He cried tearlessly when he
thought of the old man and his wife, the shepherd and the
shepherdess they had buried in the vegetable patch. He no

longer remembered their faces and thought they were like the faces of his mother and father, of all the people he had known.

Once Boris came to life when he heard the wheel-tapper beneath the window, swearing at everyone and everything not choosing his words, and in a real Siberian accent. In Boris' mind rose memories of the landing stage, with its smell of salt fish, the old dam with the birches growing on it, the churches with young bushes sprouting from their domes, and the flocks of swifts like so many crosses in the sky.

"Hey, friend!" Boris called out to the man in a hoarse whisper.

Arina, who had dozed off in her compartment sitting at the table, raised her head with difficulty, wiped her mouth on her scarf, went to Boris and lay her hand on his forehead.

The lieutenant's lips were bright red against the yellow face, like a dab of crimson on yellow cardboard; his eyes were bright and glowed with the final flame of life, his lips trembled—he could not get warm, though he had a high temperature.

"How I can help you I just don't know!" said Arina softly, then after a thought she came to life, ran to fetch a hot water-bottle and placed it against the soles of his feet.

"Sleep, my dear one. You must've been born unlucky. Something's gone wrong with you, hasn't it?" Arina patted the blanket, trying to lull him to sleep, as if he were a baby. But instead she fell asleep herself, her lips parted, her eyelids fluttering. This girl with a somewhat flattened nose, and straight, straw-coloured hair straggling from under the scarf wrapped round her head, radiated utter trustfulness.

She did not resemble Lusya in any way, this most ordinary of ordinary girls from Southern Russia, but she helped to revive the image of the woman whose face his memory no longer preserved—all he remembered of her features were her deep, improbably beautiful eyes. That woman—not fully understood, seen all too little—lived on in his memory as a sense of longing and the feeling was now burning, consuming his soul like some disease that coloured everything red and was unbearably hot.

Boris freed his hand from the blanket and touched Arina.
"I must be tired, falling asleep on my feet!" Arina started
up.

"You slept no more than a minute or two."

"M-m-m. Like one of God's own birds—the moment I stop
I'm asleep. And you—it seems you can speak after all?!
What's eating you, what grieves you?"

"I don't know, I don't know at all. It's here," he pointed
to his chest. "It hurts. It is as if everything here is one great
pain...." An attack of shallow coughing racked his body.

Arina gave him a drink of water from a mug. The coughing
subsided but his breathing came in spasms.

"Never mind, don't speak. Don't say a word," she said
drawing the blanket closer around him. "I don't like your
cough at all."

At a big smoky station, where the crew of the train
received food, fuel and other supplies, Boris came to once
more, when he heard music from a loud-speaker fixed on the
roof of the gloomy, soot-blackened station. His body tensed.
The sooty building, its walls peeling, the dirty, black railway
lines and the rooks in the black poplars, the carriages, and the
houses of an unfamiliar town scattered over the hilly
countryside, the people, with the dull eyes of hunger—everything began to assume a lilac tinge. It had begun to transform
the world, make it look young, renewed, when from a cloud
of smoke stepped a woman with a wooden suitcase—that very
woman, the only woman for him, whom he could recognise
now only with difficulty and only by her eyes, though he
used to think he could never fail to recognise her at once
among all the women in the world.

She was looking through the window of the hospital train,
and their eyes met. There was a flicker of recognition in her
face, she took a step nearer, but at once moved back and ran
her now indifferent gaze over other windows and other
trains.

A force which no longer belonged to him jerked him up.
Arina was asking him something at that very moment, shaking him as he strained towards the window of the carriage,
mumbling unintelligibly, and the effort brought on a fit of

coughing. He no longer heard the music—a cloud of lilac smoke billowed before him, and in its thickness the woman with the suitcase swam and swayed, sinking into oblivion.

A sudden coolness in the air brought him to himself. A spring thunderstorm was raging. Boris felt he could breathe easily in powerful gulps, as if the wind were blowing ashes from his chest, cleaning out everything, leaving behind emptiness and freedom. The spring storm raced after the train, the daggers of lightning sank into the roofs of the carriages and bubbles of rain washed the windows. Somewhere ahead of his carriage the engine gave a loud, boyish, devil-may-care hoot, and the rooks and the swifts in the gardens flickering past at every station opened their beaks in soundless calls.

Boris' heart, stimulated by the thunderstorm, was now subsiding with it, and with the receding, fading thunderclaps its beat became weaker and slower, weaker and slower. The train took off from the rails and was swinging towards the horizon, into the quiet, soft darkness beyond the end of the earth—it was sinking into oblivion, taking Boris with it.

Unwilling to stop, his heart thrust strongly once or twice at his exhausted, hollow chest, rolled out of it and disappeared into the bottomless pit outside the window of the carriage with a final murmur. Boris' body straightened out and was still. For some time yet under his half-closed eyelids the purple sweeping sunset burnt, but it quickly became a narrow, narrow crack, and imperceptibly turned cold and died in the lieutenant's glassy eyes.

In the morning, when Arina came as usual to wash Boris, she saw him lying, his lips wrinkled in a secret smile. Backing in terror, Arina shouted, dropped the can of water, and ran along the carriage.

The body was removed to a service carriage and placed in the unheated part. They covered him with a groundsheet, and he travelled that way across the steppe for a whole night amidst stacks of firewood, boxes, old stretchers and similar objects. As the train was going through the unforested regions of the Southern Urals someone pulled the jute out from the axle-box of that carriage to start a fire. The brakes became overheated, the axle got stuck, and the railway checker marked the carriage: "Out of Order." So it was left behind at a small station junction.

Arina was left with the carriage to arrange for the burial of the late lieutenant, and wait with the repaired carriage for the hospital train on its return journey.

The dead lieutenant proved to be just as awkward dead as alive, managing to die in a place where there was no grave-yard.

The station master declared that it didn't matter where the lieutenant was buried, it was all Russia. He made a coffin with boards from the roof of a shed, fashioned an obelisk out of a signal post, and the two men—the station master and the telephone operator—and Arina took the lieutenant in a luggage barrow out into the steppe, where they buried him.

When the burial was over the men took off their caps and observed a minute's silence over the grave of a front-line soldier. Arina—either as a sign of apology to the lieutenant or oppressed by the moment of grief and the meagre ceremony—shook her head sadly, saying: "Such a light wound and yet he died...."

They gathered up the spades and left.

Arina kept looking back as if still hoping for something, and wiped her eyes with an earth-covered hand.

"It could not have been such a light wound, my dear," said the station master, who looked strangely round-shouldered as if he had grown older. "But what can be done? Every one has his own death, as he has his own life."

The burial mound was soon covered with a sprinkling of grass, and one rainy morning the still fresh clods of earth were pierced by a tulip; a drop of moisture trembled at its beak for a time and then the tulip opened its pink mouth. The sinewy roots of steppe grasses and flowers burrowed deep into the earth, groping for the dead body, confidently surrounding it with their network, growing out of it and blooming and flowering above it.

* * *

And, after listening to the earth, now entirely covered with a down of feather grass, the seeds of other plants and the pungent-smelling wormwood, she confessed guiltily: "And I—I live, I live on. I eat and drink, I enjoy myself on high days and holidays."

The bowed grey head of the woman with the eternally sad eyes was covered with a dusting of seeds. The sun sank beyond the hump of the steppe, the sunset sky continued to blaze, and, listening to the steppe, she decided that he must have died in the evening. Death in the evening was sweet.

The sunset slowly paled. Its ebbing life slipped down the veins of the grasses into the earth. The steppe stirred and rustled with a dry, pure sound. Something furry, with shaggy paws, sped past, jumping up, then clinging to the ground, and jumping up again in the now hardly perceptible glow. It was a dry bush, uprooted by the wind that swept it on.

"O Lord above! " sighed the woman, and pressed her lips against what had once been a grave but had now become part of the great body of the earth. The bony thistle scratched like a timid mouse at the obelisk. Peace descended on the steppe.

"Sleep, and I'll be going. But I shall return. Soon. Very soon we'll be together forever...."

She walked, and her beautiful eyes saw not the night steppe, with its soothing rustle of grasses but a sea, a boundless sea in which the small obelisk was a lonely buoy rocking on the waves, and everything in this world was elusive, insubstantial.

While he or what had once been him remained in the silent earth, in the network of grass roots now dormant until next spring.

He remained alone—alone in the heart of Russia.

AFTERWORD

"How did you become a writer?"

I am often asked that question, just as all writers are. It is a question to which they can offer no very satisfactory answer, for the truth is that writers don't know the answer themselves.

It must be something one is born to. But even that I cannot state with any certainty, although I am willing to risk a glance over my shoulder at my own experience.

As a small boy I loved fairy-tales and the stories told by hunters and fishermen. And I also liked making up stories myself, inventing all kinds of yarns, for which I, of course, got into plenty of trouble. But that has always been the fate of the story-teller. All story-tellers at all times have been pushed around, abused, and persecuted, but people still don't seem to be able to get along without them.

And another thing. For as long as I can remember I have loved nature. I have loved the River Yenisei, the mountains towering over it, the sun and the flowers. Particularly the flowers. We have a lot of flowers in Siberia, but many of them possess no smell and, even when they do, the *starodub*, for instance, it is a dense, hidden, gloomy kind of fragrance, like the taiga itself. When you have smelled a Siberian flower you won't say to yourself, "Oh, how lovely!" Instead, you will probably grow silent and thoughtful, self-absorbed, and troubled by memories.

But there is more about this in the stories of childhood that appear in this volume. In the meantime I want to relate a little tale I heard once about why there are so many flowers in Siberia.

After the world had been created and people, animals, birds and trees were living in it, God set about his final task of sowing the earth with grass and flowers. And since the work of creation had taken long enough already, God decided to fly in an aeroplane instead of walk.

He began his working day at exactly eight in the morning like all other working folk, and he worked the whole day, casting handfuls of seed over the Russian land. At first he sowed his seed sparingly, without any hurry, but half the day went by and it was time for the creator to have his dinner, and still there seemed to be no end to Russia, and plenty of seed left in the sack.

So God began to hurry. Over the Urals he scattered the seed haphazardly and this region has remained patchy to this day. The Northern Urals, for example, have wonderful alpine meadows with a tremendous variety of flowers, but the southern end of the chain, particularly the Orenburg steppes, are rather bare and bloom briefly, only in spring. By the time he had crossed the Urals, our Lord began to feel rather weary. His stint was nearly over, but the vast expanses showed no sign of coming to an end, so he just let the seed trickle lazily through his fingers on to the birch groves and sparse stretches of woodland, and that is why western Siberia is mostly grass and wild strawberries.

The plane flew on and on, and still there was no end in sight, although evening had long since come and all working folk were resting after the day's toil. And this made the Lord quite angry and he cried out in a thunderous voice: "No one pays me any overtime! " And so saying, he tipped all the rest of the seed out of his sack over the Sayan Mountains, and the wind carried it right across Eastern Siberia and beyond Lake Baikal, all the way to the Far East.

I love that funny little tale, and I love my homeland, the rough, flower-rich land of Siberia. She taught me herself to marvel at her beauty, at her eternal kindness and infinite forbearance towards her ungrateful children.

Because I lost my mother early, I have always felt particularly drawn to my second and everlasting mother—the earth.

In 1938 I had a nasty accident and broke my right leg above the knee. In those days I was living in a children's home in Igarka. I was nearly fifteen, a cheerful and rather mischievous boy. It still causes me some remorse to think how bad I was at my lessons. But I loved reading, singing and skiing. For my performance of the song *The Engine Driver* at a local competition I was awarded a prize of a pair of Finnish skis. Fine, strong skis they were! They didn't break when I jumped with them from some fantastic height, but my leg did.

Since then I have never used a pair of skis for pleasure.

I was in hospital in plaster for four months and walked with a stiff knee for another year and a half.

My father and his second wife, my step-mother, who by that time were living at a logging camp, found me in hospital, insisted that without them I would break my head next, and took me off for the summer to the forest where my father was a foreman of a team of lumberjacks. He now had two more children from my step-mother and they led a hungry and not very united existence.

I had to do something for my living. But what?

Soon, however, they found me a job that I had always loved better than anything else in the world—fishing.

Three kilometres from the Yenisei, on Lake Makovskoye, my father built me a small raft out of well-seasoned logs, set up a little hearth on it with stones collected from the shore, and on this raft I lived and fished.

The soil round Igarka is permanently frozen and you cannot sleep on it without a thick layer of bedding, and in any case I would have been afraid to sleep alone on the shore of a lake in the taiga. But sleeping on a raft was quite a different matter.

I used to fish at sunset and sunrise with a rod and a spear. There was so much fish I had no difficulty in making a good haul. In the course of an evening I would catch nearly a sackful of perch and pike. I took my catch ashore, tipped it out of the sack on the yellowish frozen soil under a big cedar stump and it stayed fresh there until my father came to fetch it. When he collected the fish, he would leave me some bread and salt by the stump and hurry off to sell the fish to the passengers on the steamboats plying the Yenisei.

I would tie the raft to a pole in the middle of the lake, so that the breeze kept the mosquitos away, make up the fire and go to sleep on a bed of sedges with an old sheepskin to cover me. Out there I was neither afraid nor lonely, except for the first few nights, and soon I began to feel that I was part of the lake and all therein, that it had accepted me, and that our friendship was intimate and reciprocal.

It would not be long, only an hour or two, before the mists began to rise from the lake, briefly screening the sun as it rolled out from behind the stunted polar forests. The lake came to life.

The ducks were the first to appear round my raft. They dived under it, scavenging for crumbs, fish waste and anything else that might be going.

After them came the wild geese.

The noise they made, the fighting and scrambling! I soon got to know the characters of some of those ducks and geese. There were thieves and bullies and mild, hard-working types; there were coquettish young ladies, particularly among the red-headed widgeon. But on the whole they were a grand lot and I loved watching them. Sometimes they would make me laugh till my sides ached. But then I would remember that there was fishing to be done!

As soon as I made a cast the whole multicoloured crowd would go flapping and squawking.

Meanwhile the mists would dissolve and the lake would be bathed in sunshine. Dragonflies darted about over the grass and with a gentle whistling cry the swans would appear from behind a grassy spit of land. There were two of them in this part of the lake and they were hiding their already feathered young in the grass. They took no notice of me at all. Majestic and dignified, they glided out into the open water, chatting quietly to one another, and began to feed.

I would wedge my rod between the logs of the raft and watch the swans. Everything around me, the grass, the trees, the bushes, the lake itself, illuminated by the whiteness of these birds, at once seemed to acquire a new freshness and purity.

Sometimes I actually wept with the joy and delight that came over me at this sight. Never since then have I known such sweet and incomprehensible tears that made me shiver but melted my heart and made me want to love and be kind to everything in the whole wide world.

When my fishing days were over and I returned to the

children's home, I wanted to tell everyone about the lake and how I had lived there and what a wonderful time I had had

It was not long before I was given the opportunity.

In those days the town of Igarka was seized with the itch to write. And no wonder, for the whole country was talking and writing about it. News of this city that had boldly installed itself on the bank of the Yenisei, inside the Arctic circle, had spread round the globe. The townspeople were just as eager to talk about their town and their country as I was to tell about "my" lake.

All the schoolchildren of Igarka were writing stories and essays and publishing them in handwritten school magazines.

I wrote about a little boy who got lost in the taiga and found an unknown lake. My composition was called "Alive!". My teacher Ignaty Rozhdestvensky, now a well-known Siberian poet, said it was the best in the class and put it into the school's handwritten magazine.

Some years later I remembered my schoolboy composition and wrote a story for children called *Vasyutka's Lake*. It has been published and republished since then and although the story is not very skilfully written and I failed to describe "my" lake as I really wanted to, I am still fond of it.

But *Vasyutka's Lake* was not my first story. I had written another story before this and it appears in this volume under the title of *The Siberian*.

On leaving trade school, I started work near Krasnoyarsk as a train assembler. In the critical autumn of 1942 I volunteered for the front. I served in the ranks, was wounded, decorated and, finally, demobilised in 1945. My wife had also been a soldier and we went to live in her hometown in the Urals. It would take too long to tell how we lived in those postwar years in that smoky industrial town and it's not a very cheerful story either.

One day I happened to be present quite by chance at a meeting of a literary group attached to the local newspaper, where I heard someone read a story about the war. It had been written by a former frontline man who had become a journalist. What the story was about exactly I don't quite remember but I know that it made me furious. One might have thought the author had never been to war even in his dreams. There was a fighter pilot who shot down lots of enemy planes and even rammed one, then landed as if nothing had happened, received a medal and went home safe and sound. He was welcomed by his family and bride-to-be and the whole village as well, and what a welcome it was! If only one could re-live that story in reality. But the trouble was that you couldn't!

I had come out of the army with food tickets for a fortnight and nothing to wear but my summer uniform, shoes and a forage cap, and that was in the Urals in November. And my wife, too, had arrived with only her food tickets and two sets of underwear. We sold the second set at once to pay for our passport photos, then we set about making our life, studying, working, having children.

Anyway, after that meeting of the local literati I went straight to the sausage factory where I had a job as a night watchman and went on duty for the night in a little room with one solitary radiator, a bare electric light bulb hanging from the ceiling, a chair and the watchman's register on the table by the inkstand.

In that little room I had time to reflect on my life and mourn a little for my friends who had been killed. I could read all night if I liked. But that night I didn't want to read and yet I was restless. I couldn't get the foolish story I had just listened to out of my head. Why did anyone have to write so falsely about the war and the men who had fought in it?

The men I had known had not been like that.

Take Motya Savintsev, for instance. And at once I had a vision of Motya, alive, with his pock-marked face and fuzzily sprouting beard. A clumsy-looking chap, but very strong. When he was drunk he used to sing in a thin, high-pitched voice, and he was always saying I ought to marry his niece because he knew I had been brought up in a home and would have nowhere to go after the war.

One night he fell asleep over the telephone. It was a wet snowy night. I was on duty at the command post, and put a call through to him, then asked all the telephone operators to call him. On receiving no response from Motya, I went out of the dugout and followed the line to his battery, and there he was asleep with the receiver clipped to his ear, but the earpiece had turned outwards and he couldn't hear anything. I tapped him on the head with the receiver, whereupon he nearly jumped out of his skin and shouted, "Cuckoo speaking! " and I had to shove my cap in his mouth so that the battery commander wouldn't hear, or he would have got into trouble.

And one night I fell asleep myself and Motya came and woke me so that someone else wouldn't catch me sleeping at my post. While Motya was on his way to my post, a shell hit the hut where he had been on duty, and after that he decided that we were blood brothers.

Or there was the time when the unit was resting, and in the ignorance of youth I and a young friend of mine got ourselves taken to the guardhouse. Motya was sent to guard us and he was a bit drunk and declared tearfully that he would rather be under arrest himself because he could not stand guard over his frontline friends as if they were criminals, his conscience wouldn't allow it.

And on yet another occasion I ate some horseflesh that had not been properly cooked. No one else was affected, but I nearly vomited myself to death. Everyone was so used to seeing people killed by bullets and shell splinters that they took no notice of me at all. What of it if a man was sick once or twice! It was Motya who saved me. He found some milk somewhere and some poppy seed and boiled them up together, and his brew did the trick.

I will always remember the hill where I sent Motya myself, or rather, not quite myself; I received the order from the lieutenant and passed it on to Motya. He ran up that hill and mended the line and we brought him back dead. And after that it was a long time before I could stop calling the telephone operator at Nine Battery "Motya". Motya had nearly always been on duty at number nine, and we had all got used to his being there. He had thought of his call-sign "Cuckoo! " himself.

Now the cuckoo was silent. I still cannot forget how

Motya arrived in our unit, how he lived and fought and died. He died a fine death, in battle. And he met his death with the inborn composure of a man of the soil who knew how to live with a quiet dignity and die without hysterics or shouting of slogans.

I had known so many people like him. Would no one ever write about them? Perhaps they would, but not about the ones I had known.

So I wrote the words "Short Story" on the numbered page of that greasy, dog-eared log-book and below this inscribed the title that occurred to me then, *The Civvy*. Though I had known Motya at the war I could never think of Motya as anything but a civilian. He was so much a man of peace in every way.

That night I wrote thirty pages and it was morning before I noticed it. Of course, I was told off for spoiling the log-book, but I was so pleased with myself that the reprimand didn't worry me in the least.

I read my story to the literary group and they liked it. I realised later that it was not the way the story was written that they liked but the character of Motya himself, a living person with funny ways, not a bit like the fighter pilot who had been the subject of the last reading.

The story was serialised in the local newspaper *Chusovaya Worker*. The women in the sausage factory where I worked wanted to know how much I should get for it and declared that it would be a lot, because writers were never underpaid.

The paper was only a folded sheet in those days and the total fees payable to contributors amounted to seventy-five rubles (in old money) per issue. But I didn't know that and I was also hoping for a large sum with which I would buy myself a new hat and a suit because the army cap I had brought back from the war was worn out and I had no suit at all except my uniform.

My story did serve me well. It was adapted for the radio, then reprinted in the regional newspaper and the *Kama Almanac*, and I was offered a job on a newspaper.

And I did buy myself a new hat, but not a suit. Instead I bought a typewriter and set about producing a collection of short stories. This collection was published in Perm in 1953, a very thin and very weak volume. The opening story in it was *The Civvy*.

A few years ago I was rummaging in a drawer and came across my first version of the story written in the watchman's log. I read it through and decided that despite the lack of style Motya did come across as a living person, whereas in the subsequent versions most of the life had been taken out of him by my own corrections and the suggestions of various "experienced" people who had been over the story in their editor's clodhoppers that have a way of treading out all the most vital and spontaneous things in a story.

I decided to rewrite the whole thing. The new version was called simply *The Siberian*.

Later on, when I was studying at the Gorky Institute of Literature in Moscow, I told some of my friends the story of this story. They laughed, of course, and then one of them asked me if I had sent a copy of the story to Motya Savintsev's family. I admitted that it had never occurred to me. He was much surprised and reproached me for not doing so. Bereaved families attached such value to every line written about the dear ones they had lost, keep all their letters and so on, and here was a whole story which Savintsev's wife and children had probably never even heard of.

...Savintsev's family responded at once, his wife and the three children, all of them now grown-up. In the story there had been two boys and one girl, but in life it turned out to have been the other way round. Motya's son Alexander was a tractor-driver, as his father had been before going to war. His daughters were married.

I received letters both from Pelageya, his wife, and the children. Pelageya informed me that my story had been read aloud in the packed hall of the village club, and that "Every living soul there was drowned in tears when Matvei Savintsev got killed", and that the Young Pioneer organisation of Shumikha Village had been named after the village hero.

Another letter, from Matvei's second daughter, Valentina, living in Barnaul, arrived separately.

"Dear Victor Petrovich,

"This letter is from Valentina Savintseva, whom you have never met. You have done so much for us in writing a book about our father. It will be a great thing to remember him by. It is all we have, except for one old photograph. I don't remember him very well, but this is how we heard the news of his death. Someone said the war was over. Or perhaps it wasn't quite over and our troops were nearing Berlin. Mother, my sister and I were in the kitchen garden. We were so glad that father would be coming home that we jumped for joy. Mother had just been awarded the 'Valiant Labour' medal. And a few days later she was called to the village Soviet again. 'They must be going to give us something else,' she said. 'I've no time to spare as it is, and they keep calling me in.' We had been just about to go and fetch in the cow from the field. Mother had a rope with her, but we turned back and went to the Soviet.

"I can see that village Soviet now. It was all lopsided. There was a big porch in front, but without any floor. I don't know why. Instead there were two boards you had to walk across to enter.

"My sister and I stood on the steps and waited for Mother to come out. We thought she was going to get another medal and were arguing about who of us should wear it. And then Mother came out. As soon as she saw us she began to weep and cry out. She had a paper in her hands. We started crying too, although we didn't know why Mother was crying and for a long time she couldn't tell us.

"A lot of people gathered round and they all cried, and I went into the corridor and cried there.

"We managed to get along somehow. Many other fathers never returned. There was a crop failure and famine. We lived mostly on grass. Mother worked and Granny, Father's mother, looked after us at home. Granny gave us all she had and ate nothing herself. But when we sat down together to eat, when we had something to cook, my sister and I always waited for Mother and Granny to take the first spoonful before we began. Zoya and I had agreed upon that between ourselves. It may have been the lack of proper food that killed Granny because, when she was dying, she cried out, 'Throw that grass away. It's choking me! '

"We seem to have grown up almost without noticing it. I have a family of my own now, a husband, daughter and mother-in-law. My husband and I get on well together. We work in the same department on a building site and go to evening school. He's in the eighth form and I'm in the seventh.

"My sister Zoya is a milkmaid on a collective farm. Mother works on the farm, too, and Alexander is a tractor-driver.

"Forgive me, Victor Petrovich, for writing at such length. I don't even know why I have written you all this. Perhaps you won't be interested.

"I have been looking everywhere for a copy of *The Siberian* but couldn't find one. A woman promised to bring me a copy but she still hasn't done so. I should love to read it but I don't know where to obtain a copy. Mother has one but the whole village is reading it.

"Give my kind regards to your wife and children, if you have any. We are in lodgings at present but in a month's time we shall have a house of our own. We are building it now. Come and visit up for our house-warming."

I sent Valentina all the books I had written and I have reread her letter many a time in the past few years.

I have a file where I keep my readers' letters. Some of them are very sincere and deeply felt, but the one I value most is the letter from the daughter of my friend who was killed at the front. It has made my first story a hundred times dearer to me, imperfect though that story still is.

But what is perfection? Something of which every writer dreams. And I dream of it, too, although I know it is like the horizon, which always moves away as you approach it, and yet I still press on and with me unflaggingly goes the memory of my fallen comrades. Even in death they come to my support at difficult moments, help me in my work and watch me closely to see that I don't earn my daily bread too easily.